All
THAT
IT
TAKES

Books by Nicole Deese

All
THAT
IT
TAKES

NICOLE DEESE

BETHANYHOUSE

a division of Baker Publishing Group
Minneapolis, Minnesota

© 2022 by Nicole Deese

Published by Bethany House Publishers
11400 Hampshire Avenue South
Minneapolis, Minnesota 55438
www.bethanyhouse.com

Bethany House Publishers is a division of
Baker Publishing Group, Grand Rapids, Michigan

Printed in the United States of America

Library of Congress Cataloging-in-Publication Data
Names: Deese, Nicole, author.
Title: All that it takes / Nicole Deese.
Description: Minneapolis, Minnesota: Bethany House Publishers, a division of
   Baker Publishing Group, [2022]
Identifiers: LCCN 2021049537 | ISBN 9780764234972 (trade paper) | ISBN
   9780764239793 (casebound) | ISBN 9781493435951 (ebook)
Subjects: LCGFT: Novels.
Classification: LCC PS3604.E299 A76 2022 | DDC 813/.6—dc23/eng/20211015
LC record available at https://lccn.loc.gov/2021049537

Scripture in chapters 10 and 13 is from the New King James Version®. Copyright © 1982 by Thomas Nelson. Used by permission. All rights reserved.

Scripture in chapters 11 and 18 is from The Holy Bible, English Standard Version® (ESV®), copyright © 2001 by Crossway, a publishing ministry of Good News Publishers. Used by permission. All rights reserved. ESV Text Edition: 2016

Emojis are from the open-source library OpenMoji (https://openmoji.org/) under the Creative Commons license CC BY-SA 4.0 (https://creativecommons.org/licenses/by-sa/4.0/legalcode)

Cover design by Jennifer Parker

Represented by Kirkland Media Management

Baker Publishing Group publications use paper produced from sustainable forestry practices and post-consumer waste whenever possible.

22 23 24 25 26 27 28   7 6 5 4 3 2 1

For Connilyn

Thank you for the million *yesses* you've given me throughout
the years: the countless rapid-fire brainstorm texts, the mid-
deadline support interventions, the after-midnight theological
discussions, and the beautifully authentic heart-to-heart
chats about the things that matter most.
You, my friend, are irreplaceable.

I love you.

Even in literature and art, no man who bothers
about originality will ever be original:
whereas if you simply try to tell the truth
(without caring twopence how often it has been
told before) you will, nine times out of ten,
become original without ever having noticed it.

C. S. LEWIS, *MERE CHRISTIANITY*

• 1 •

Val

As the door to our new life swung open and my ten-year-old son rushed across the threshold to explore the second-story apartment, the *you-break-it, you-buy-it* policy flashed across my mind like a hazard warning. Because this wasn't just any rental property we were considering today. No, this one happened to be owned by my best friend's twin brother—a complication I hadn't anticipated when I'd agreed to take a job that would move us a thousand miles from the only place we'd ever called home.

"Hey, Tucker, slow down a bit, okay? This isn't our house," I called out as my son disappeared into one of the two bedrooms I could see from my stance near the front door.

Molly moved to stand beside me, studying my profile like a paid-by-the-hour detective as my gaze trailed over the sparsely furnished open-concept floor plan for the first time. I worked to keep my expression light, pleasant even. After all, it wasn't her fault that I still mourned the loss of the idyllic townhouse I'd researched online for hours before securing it with a deposit last month. Nor was it her fault that the same idyllic townhouse had been sold for cash only five days ago by the owners who'd emailed

7

me a simple *we're sorry for the inconvenience* along with a bank receipt of my returned deposit check.

"I know it's not totally comparable to the townhouse you loved on Garden Street, but I've always thought of this upstairs apartment as classically cute with a side of quirkiness. But there's no pressure to say yes. The decision is yours to make, Val." Molly spoke in the same cautiously bright tone she'd been using with me ever since the night I called her distressed over not being able to find another rental in my price range before our move date from Skagway, Alaska, to Spokane, Washington. But before I could even suggest a delay to our moving timeline, Molly had cut in with an invitation for us to stay with her and Silas, in their guest room, *"for however long it takes to find the perfect home for you and Tuck."* And though her offer was kind and generous, I could read the undercurrent of low-level panic between the words she wasn't giving voice to: *If you don't come now, you likely never will.*

And I wasn't sure she would have been wrong.

"I'd offer to show you around," she said, with a sweeping arm gesture, "but I'm guessing you'd rather take a self-guided tour?"

I smiled up at her. "You really don't mind if I wander on my own for a minute?"

"Not at all." She waved me on. "I know how you like time to think. Just pretend I'm not here, okay? Unless you have a question about something—then I'll gladly reappear." She perched on the arm of a long green sofa and slipped her phone out of her purse, likely scanning through a lengthy list of missed notifications. Of the many hats Molly wore, *property manager* wasn't a common one. But seeing as her brother, Miles, was currently out of the country on business, she'd taken on the temporary role as his stand-in landlord until his return. Whenever that was.

"Thanks. I won't take long."

As much as I enjoyed Molly's positivity and enthusiasm, I needed to think logically about this important next step without being influenced by her good intentions. Accepting the marketing position she'd offered me at her latest business-with-a-worthy-cause was one thing, but selecting my first home with Tucker was something else entirely. When I'd said yes to this job, I'd promised him somewhere special, somewhere worth the tearful good-bye to his grandparents and the subsequent long-distance relationships to come for us all. Somewhere worthy of uprooting our entire lives for. A familiar wave of nausea swelled inside me as the doubts crept in once again.

I pressed a tight fist to the tender joint in my left hip. My muscles were extra stiff from travel—and likely from a night spent wrestling through anxieties not even a promising salary could rectify completely. Because while my new job would provide enough financial freedom to secure a path independent of my parents and the souvenir shop they'd owned for decades, the workload itself wouldn't provide much in the way of a creative challenge. It was that compromise I'd weighed out for months before finally accepting Molly's offer.

I released a tension-filled breath and took in the freshly mopped faux-wood floors and the cozy kitchen nestled just beyond a wooden vintage dining table set for four. I peeked down the hallway and into each bedroom and bathroom, opening the closets and cupboards. The compact footprint of the apartment as a whole didn't bother me, considering our living quarters had been half this size in my parents' house.

Returning to the dining area, my gaze landed on the view beyond the sliding glass doors that led to a small deck: acres of springtime wildflowers, dewy green grass, and a coniferous forest surrounded by foothills. It certainly wasn't difficult to imagine my son smack-dab in the middle of it.

"It really is beautiful out here," I said, heading over to the large picture window that spanned nearly the entire length of the exterior wall of the living room. "Peaceful."

Molly stood from the sofa and made her way over to me. "Pretty sure I used those exact same adjectives on our drive out here."

"Did you?" I teased through a grin.

She nudged me. "You know I did. And you also know that Silas would be thrilled to teach Tucker more about the game of darts if you decide you'd rather pass on this and wait for something else to open up in your price range. You can stay with us for as long as you need."

But while dart games with Silas might be fun for a few evenings, I had nightmares of Tucker lassoing Molly's mosaic lampshade from Paris or bowling with the frosted glass orbs she kept in a decorative vase. The Whittaker household was not what one would call *kid friendly*. Plus, Silas and Molly hadn't even hit the three-month mark on their nuptials. The last thing any of us needed was an accidental privacy breach on the newlyweds. We would all benefit from my saying yes to a place sooner rather than later.

"I truly appreciate how accommodating you've been to us—"

"Are you kidding me? No." Molly's shoulder-length blond hair swished and curved around her neck as if she were filming a product review for dry shampoo. Yet her days as a high-profile beauty influencer had downshifted dramatically since partnering with Silas at his residential youth program last year. It was through their combined efforts at The Bridge Youth Home that the vision for Basics First, a one-for-one specialty online boutique store intended to benefit aged-out foster teens, was birthed. For every dollar spent at the boutique, one dollar would be donated toward supply backpacks for teens transitioning into independence. In time, Molly hoped the online platform I'd helped them create would branch into a brick-and-mortar store, but for now, our focus was on the grand opening next week. I'd been told the production warehouse was nearly up and ready.

"You're the one who's been incredibly accommodating, Val. I feel terrible about what happened with that townhouse you wanted, but I'm not going to pretend I'm anything but thrilled you said yes to the marketing position at Basics First." She beamed. "It will be just like old times, only better, because you'll be here in person with me instead of online."

That was the part of this move I'd been looking forward to the most—living and working in the same zip code as my best friend.

When Molly first hired me as her virtual assistant four years ago to help with her growing social media platforms, I had no idea how that one opportunity would branch into many, or how our friendship would blossom into what it was today.

"Hey, Mom, can I go outside? There's a barn across the street with some goats and a least one horse that I could see from the window in my bedroom. Oh, and there's a fire pit out back like the one Pops built last summer. Did you see it yet? This place is *awesome!*"

I angled to face him, his exuberant expression everything I'd banked my hope on these last few days. "Yes, you can go outside, but—" I held up a finger before he could rush for the door. Tucker only knew one speed: fast. "You stay on this side of the street, all right? I want to meet the neighbors before you start running all over the place."

"Okay, I will! See ya!" He flew out the front door at a cadence my legs could never duplicate and tromped down the outside stairwell, shaking the walls and rattling the windows. I made a mental note to talk to Tucker about neighborly conscientiousness. Up until now, we hadn't lived near anyone but family.

"So . . ." Molly waggled her eyebrows. "It sounds like Tuck's already picked out a bedroom for himself, and it also sounds like you're planning to meet the neighbors. Does that mean what I think it means?" Molly's voice buzzed with renewed energy as she ducked her head into my line of sight.

"I think it means there's a lot to like about this place." *But can I make it a home for us?*

She squealed and clasped her hands under her chin. "Oh, Val, I know this move is a huge change from where you came from, but I really think you'll be so happy here once you settle in." She looped an arm around my shoulders, our nearly five-inch height difference glaringly obvious as she pointed out the window toward Spokane. "There's tons of activities for Tuck to do in our little city and lots of good people for you both to meet." She pursed her lips momentarily, her sapphire eyes twinkling in a way my brown ones never could. "Plus, you have to admit, the timing of Miles's place coming open the day before you arrived feels more than coincidental. I could hardly believe it when he called yesterday to have me schedule the cleaners after his last tenant moved out. I mean, what are the chances? Not to mention the rent is a bit less than you were budgeting for. And of course, there's the added bonus that you already know your downstairs neighbor."

At the mention of Miles, an unexpected warmth coursed through me. Which I immediately doused with a cold splash of reality. Pastor Miles McKenzie was an adventurer by nature, a traveler of exotic places and an extroverted humanitarian who never seemed to sit still for longer than a minute. And while he'd been nothing but kind to Tucker and me during our brief encounters at the fundraising event we attended last fall and again during Molly and Silas's wedding this March, I was certain that other than his sister, the two of us had little in common.

I cleared my throat. "And Miles . . . he's good with this arrangement?"

"Absolutely. He's tired of renting this place out to fickle frat boys from the college. Trust me, you and Tucker will be dream tenants for him."

In the driveway below, Tucker waved to the horse across the street with one hand while clutching a fallen tree branch in the other. And something about the sight caused my chest to squeeze. *"Give that kid space to roam, Val. Heaven knows you never got much of that when you were growing up."* It was the first thing my dad had said when I'd told him about the job opportunity last fall, followed by, *"Tuck needs room to run and play and live like a little boy and not like a miniature employee of Gold Diggers Souvenirs. Don't worry about your mom, kiddo. She'll come around eventually. You're twenty-nine. You've more than earned the right to decide what's best for you and Tucker by now."*

I'd relied on my parents so heavily over the years, trusted their instincts as my own, and meshed all our future plans with theirs . . . until now. Until I realized that if I was ever going to fly from the nest, I would actually have to open my wings and take a leap. *Again.*

Before I could stop myself, I glanced to the nook in the living room wall to my left. An immediate visual surfaced in my mind, one of a small studio setup, complete with the gear I'd packed away in a thick plastic crate labeled *Fragile.* It wasn't a large enough space for professional use, of course, but it could work for something hobby-sized. Because that's all my filmmaking dreams would ever be for me now: a hobby. An activity to dabble in after my responsibilities with work and family were met.

My attention snapped back to Molly, who was still talking about the benefits of living in a larger community. How much had I missed?

". . . and Miles knows way more than I do about the area. Pretty sure he knows everyone who lives on this street, too. He'll be happy to introduce you to all the—"

"Molly—"

"—neighbors here as well as his friends at the church and—"

"Molly, no." I shook my head while confusion crimped her brow.

"No, what?"

I took a second to gather my thoughts, to find a way to explain what I had yet to voice. "If we take this apartment, it's important to me that Miles understands we don't want or expect any kind of special treatment from him while living here." I paused, careful in how I approached this next part of our conversation. "I'd never want to impose on his personal life or tangle the natural boundary lines between a tenant and a landlord. Despite the two of us having a connection to you, I'd like to think the rest of our lives could be kept separate."

Because the truth was, this was my chance to spread my wings. To figure things out on my own. To finally live life without a crutch. Not to create a new one.

Molly's nose twitched a second before her lips curved into a comical grin. "You do hear yourself, right?"

"Yeah, why?"

"Because first of all, my brother hasn't had a personal life to speak of since, well, I'm not even sure when." She laughed at that. "And second of all, the guy racks up more airline travel miles in a year than anybody else I know, so I really don't think a *boundary breach* will be much of an issue. That's why I'm the one here and he's the one south of the border, enjoying all the ridiculously hot spices he can get his grubby hands on."

For the first time since we landed in Washington, I felt my body relax and my lungs exhale a worry-free breath. Because this time, when I took in the apartment like a panoramic photograph, I did so without a shadow of hesitation. *I can make this place a home.* "We'll take it, Molly."

"Fantastic." The spark in her eternally optimistic expression caught fire as she slipped her phone out of her pocket. "When would you like Silas to organize the moving crew? It's amazing how motivating the promise of hot pizza can be to a bunch of older teens." Silas had kindly offered the services of the youth he worked with for our move-in day, and given the fact that my leg would balk at climbing up and down those stairs more than twice, I wouldn't turn him down. Plus, I'd had the pleasure of working with the majority of those kids on a video compilation I'd created last fall for The Bridge. It would be nice to see them again.

But before I could reply, Tucker bounded up the stairs and shot through the front door once again, this time carrying two fishing poles that didn't belong to us. "Look, Mom! Miles must like to fish, too! I found these in his shed. Maybe he'll take me to the river when he gets home, and we can be fishing buddies."

Molly bit back a laugh as my own mouth fell open to form a silent O. Apparently, my boundary conversation had been misdirected. Tucker was the one in need of a few pointers regarding appropriate neighborly conduct, and by the looks of it, I should probably get started on that sooner than later.

· 2 ·

Miles

If mission outreach locations could be chosen like a favorite sports team, Mexico would be my top pick. The food, the culture, the people, the pungency of their hottest chili peppers—I'd looked forward to this trip every spring since I was an intern pastor at Salt and Light Community Church in Washington State. And while there was no better welcome to receive on the planet than from my charismatic friends at *La Iglesia del Rey de la Gloria*, a lively church plant just twenty miles east of Puebla, the news I'd come to deliver in person had tainted every handclap and *aleluya*.

Much the way continued budget cuts had tainted the majority of my year as an outreach pastor.

I took a long swig from the warmed Coke bottle I'd set in the shade hours ago, then picked up the only good hammer I could find from the rusted toolbox in Pastor Romero's shed. I began the rhythmic process again, nailing down the wooden rails for the ramp I was building off his front porch steps. I only paused the swing of my hammer to wipe my brow or reach for another nail as I worked my way down. Dust coated my hair and caught in my throat, and yet I needed to swing this hammer almost as much as

Pastor Romero's daughter needed a suitable wheelchair ramp as she recovered from her bicycle accident.

The church here had an accessible ramp on the outside of the building, but the Romeros, like so many of the servant-hearted leaders I'd met around the world, chose not to redirect their resources into the repair needs of their own homes—not when the needs of their church members were so prevalent. It was a stark and unsettling contrast to the mentality of the church I served in back home. Or at least, the new mentality, anyway.

I rolled my head from side to side, feeling my shoulders stiffen at the thought of the exorbitant spending and expansion plans that had immediately followed Pastor Neil Archer's retirement announcement two years ago. After thirty-one years behind the pulpit of Salt and Light, Pastor Neil had passed the baton to his oldest son, Curtis.

"Pastor Miles?" An unfamiliar voice interrupted my next strike, causing my swing to falter and the hammer to come down within a centimeter of my left thumb.

Alejandro Romero. The eldest of the five Romero siblings. Startled by the sight of a maturity only time and distance could achieve, I shook my head in obvious disbelief, then pulled him in for a hug, clapping him hard on the back. "Ale! Hey, bud!" I hadn't seen him since my last visit, and since I'd arrived, he'd been helping out at his uncle's church for most of the month. I'd extended my trip with the hope I'd get to see him before it was time for me to leave.

I'd been around thousands of teenage boys over the years due to various ministries: summer camps, outreach trips, weekly discipleship groups. But Alejandro was as unique as his perspective on life. And there was no doubt I was a better man for having known him. "I was hoping I would get to see you."

"I wasn't able to leave *mi tío's* house until today, but yes, I hoped for that, too. I heard you are staying to work a few more days." His English was nearly flawless now, as it was with most schoolchildren in this part of Mexico. But what struck me most about him wasn't his eloquent way with words . . . but that Alejandro Romero no longer had the presence of a child. Had somebody told him? Did he know what I'd had to tell his parents over a steaming plate of chili relleno just three nights ago?

With a confidence I hadn't owned until my early twenties, fifteen-year-old Alejandro gestured to the stack of plywood next to the Romero's weathered front door. "You could use some help, yes?"

I laughed for what could have been the first time in days, maybe longer. "I certainly could. Here." I handed him my hammer and made a show of looking him up and down. "I see you've been eating your vegetables since the last time I was here."

He tipped his head, processing my American idiom, and then cracked an open grin in understanding before gesturing to me. "I'm trying to catch up to you." He measured the gap in the air between my six-foot-one height and his. "Almost there."

I laughed again at the five-inch gap he displayed with his fingers. "Yes, almost there."

From the corner of my eye, I assessed him from head to toe, noticing that Alejandro's faded athletic shoes had two large splits in the rubber soles. A familiar pain thrummed inside my chest at the sight. Even the lowest-standard thrift store in America would have tossed them from the donation box.

"Your parents said you've been helping at your uncle's church. How long of a walk is that?" Only Alejandro's father, Ricardo, owned a car in this family, and he needed it for daily errands and visitations. Or in today's case, for the gathering of construction materials.

"About two hours. Not bad." He shrugged. "The best part is I got to eat *mi tía's* tamales four nights last week. They are the best in all of Mexico," he said with a lowered voice. "Don't tell *mi mamá* I said so."

"Ah, so that's the secret to how you've grown so quickly, then?"

"*Sí.*" Alejandro smiled at me, then pointed to the skeleton of the ramp I'd been working on all morning. "Maria will be happy for this," he said. "The accident has made her . . ." He closed his mouth and searched for the word. "Depressed. She hasn't seen her friends much because it takes two men to lift her out of the chair and down the steps. Raphael works at the market most days, and *mi papá* is often at the church."

"I was sorry to hear about her accident," I said. "This should make things easier for her to leave the house without having to be lifted each time." Perhaps my visit here would be salvaged if I could leave them with one thing repaired, despite what I'd been asked to tear down. At the very least, perhaps my guilt would be eased.

I forced myself to switch mental gears and to concentrate on the task at hand with a boy I only got to see once a year. "What did you help with at your uncle's church this week?"

"I preached."

"Did you?" I asked as Alejandro moved to lift the sheet of ply-wood from the back of Pastor Romero's '91 Toyota pickup. To-gether, we slid it on the ramp between the two-by-four rails I'd built. We picked up our hammers, though the one I used now was more of a mallet, and tacked it in place. All the while, I watched Alejandro closely.

"It was my first time at his pulpit, but my uncle has been sick on and off for a month, and he asked for me to come. It was an honor. His church is getting very large now—twenty families."

Twenty families. I could only imagine Curtis Archer's response to dedicating funds to a ministry with only twenty families in light of all the cutbacks at my home church. Of course, he had no prob-lem funding a lobby coffee bar with paleo-approved, gluten-free baked goods each weekend. I tried and failed to douse the rising heat in my chest with the last drops of my flat Coke.

I set the empty bottle down in the dirt. "I'm sure each of those families were blessed by your faithfulness to serve them."

He dipped his head low. "*Gracias.*"

The contrast between the young boy I'd met on my first out-reach here, whose interests included playing soccer with neighbor kids and mimicking all I said and did, to this now almost-man with traces of facial hair, a stout physique, and a presence that spoke of wisdom beyond his years was astounding. His transformation was as startling as it was sobering. *What on earth do I have to show for my life over the same stretch of time?*

"What do you want to do after school?" I asked, setting the second sheet of plywood in place with his help.

There was a slight question in his eyes, as if he were trying and failing to translate my question. I rephrased. "What do you plan to do for work after you finish with your schooling?"

"I will be a pastor. Like mi papá. And like mi tío."

A sudden loss of air caused my lungs to restrict. There had been no missed translation at all. There simply hadn't been another answer. And by the determined expression on the boy's face, it wasn't because he didn't have other options he could pursue. No, Alejandro believed what I had believed at his age: that there was no greater purpose in life than serving in full-time ministry. It was in his DNA, the same as it was in mine.

The Romero family had dedicated their lives to serving others— to the feeding of hungry families, the care of orphans and widows, and to the faithful delivery of a hope-filled message given to the community they loved in both word and deed. Which was why this cutback was the most painful to deliver. And why I'd fought to deliver the news to them in person. Pastor Ricardo Romero and his wife, Elena, deserved to hear from a man they'd come to trust that the financial support they'd been receiving for close to seven years would be coming to an end. A man too sickened to reveal that the same funds once allocated to aid the lost and the vulnerable would soon be redirected.

To debt.

I'd prepared for despair, for shock, for every emotion that came when someone received upending news. But instead, Pastor Romero had reached for his wife's hand and said with a firm voice, *"God sees us. He has been faithful to His church here, and He will continue to be faithful. Now we watch. We wait. We pray."*

I cleared the well of emotion from my throat and looked across the completed porch ramp at his son. "You'll make a great pastor, Alejandro, like your father. He's trained you well in the ministry of caring for people. He's a good shepherd." In truth, outside of my own father, I only knew one other man with the kind of faith Pastor Romero lived out on a daily basis: my mentor back home, Reverend Carmichael.

As we cleaned up the remnants of wood and put away stray tools, I asked Alejandro a handful of questions, got him talking about the different events that happened in his week, about his friends, his school, his siblings. He told animated stories, and I chuckled several times at his descriptions. Yet all the while, I worked to shake the heaviness I'd hoped to escape while here. A heaviness that had pressed on my chest for months now.

"... your sister?"

Embarrassed that the noise inside my head had muted out Alejandro's voice, I stopped picking up the remaining construction debris and asked him kindly to repeat himself.

"Your funny twin sister. She is good? What does she do when you're not home?"

I smiled, not surprised at all that he'd remembered my many tales about Molly. She'd always been a point of humor in my conversations over the years, and the twin angle was a good way to open dialogue in new settings. "Yes, she is good. And she does just fine without me, I promise. She keeps herself plenty busy." I'd lost track of how many work-related responsibilities Molly oversaw now. Between her service projects and her new marriage, there was little time for us to play catch-up these days. Even before the wedding, our conversations had become as spotty as yesterday's international cell coverage. Despite the frustrating connection, I'd needed to ask her a favor. In my haste to fly down here, I'd forgotten to schedule the final walk-through so I could return my last tenant's deposit. It was due back to him by tomorrow.

No matter how many times I asked her to repeat herself, I only caught every few words of Molly's rushed reply before the call had dropped, but her tone had indicated she'd been both willing and eager to help me out.

Although I appreciated the passive income the rental apartment above my house provided, I wouldn't miss Zack or his country-music-blaring ways when I returned home. For the first time since I became a homeowner, I was looking forward to some peace and quiet. The stress in my head was loud enough these days on its own. I didn't need any extra complications to add to the mix.

"Molly actually got married in March," I said, continuing the conversation. "Her husband is Mexican."

Alejandro's eyes widened. "Really?"

I nodded. "He was adopted as a young boy and grew up in the States, but his birth mother was from Tijuana. He's been helping me with my Spanish."

Alejandro ticked up his eyebrow and twisted his mouth into a wry grin before rattling off a long sentence to me in Spanish. I picked up on a few words. "Uh . . . something about getting a Coke and going to the market."

"Yes! Good! You are *finally* getting better."

I threw a piece of chipped wood at his leg, and Alejandro leapt out of the way just in time with a hard laugh.

"Come on, let's go. It's hot."

As he started toward the edge of the road, I patted my pocket to make sure I had my wallet on me. I'd be treating us today. And the rest of the days I had left here. It was the least I could do.

Alejandro tipped his head to the side and squinted his eyes in my direction.

"What?" I asked.

"If you married my cousin Victoria, then your children will match your sister's."

I laughed openly at the offhanded remark, and together we strolled the dusty streets of a city so unlike my own, which was likely the most appealing quality about Acajete at the moment.

"You know, Victoria is only a few years younger than you. Nineteen."

I side-eyed him, working to school the humor in my voice. Nine years my junior was more than a few. "And does this cousin of yours happen to be the daughter of the same aunt who makes the best tamales in all of Mexico?"

He nodded vigorously, and once again, I laughed. "Now that is a tempting offer."

The sound of car horns and mariachi music blaring from rows of stores up ahead quieted our conversation momentarily, though Alejandro's glance had flicked my direction several times. "Your thoughts have not changed. You do not think you will marry? Perhaps you are like Apostle Paul, from the Bible. Married only to your ministry." It was clear he was referencing a conversation we'd had on the subject last spring after a sweaty game of street soccer. Both Ale's father and brother had been present, all curious in their questions and gracious with their insights on the subject, which was not always the case when it came to my choice of marital status. A single pastor who chose to remain single was rarely understood in today's world.

There had been one woman, however, who'd turned my head in this last year. But she'd been off limits for multiple reasons—not the least of which was her lack of interest in me.

"I never claim to know what the future holds." More so now than ever.

Alejandro gestured to a store on the left, and we waited several minutes to cross the busy street. After we jogged to the other side and navigated around a group of playing children, he caught my attention again. I expected another question about women or marriage or any number of things on a teenage boy's mind. But instead, with earnest eyes, he said, "I hope you will remember us after you leave. I hope you will remember our home, and La Iglesia del Rey de la Gloria. And me."

My throat pinched tight as the revelation to my earlier wondering became clear. His parents had told him the reason for my visit. And Alejandro was too perceptive not to deduce the ramifications of such a weighted decision: that without funds, without a continued financial partnership, these annual service trips would become increasingly more difficult to continue. "I could never forget you."

After a slow bob of his chin, he turned into the store to find his brother, leaving me to ponder a question I'd been asking myself since the moment I boarded the airplane that brought me here: What effectiveness did an outreach pastor have if he could no longer go to the places God had asked him to serve?

I wished these next few days could be prolonged to an indefinite period of time. The list of unknowns waiting for me at home surpassed the dread of anything I'd encountered on the mission field to date. The Romero family had been the final cut—the hardest one by a factor of ten.

Perhaps it was time for me to make some hard cuts of my own. The loyalty I felt toward Salt and Light, starting from the time I was a passionate teenager eager to serve, was nearly unrecognizable now. My twin sister was happily married. My ministries were nearly obsolete. And my dad hadn't stopped hounding me about taking a position with his church-planting organization abroad since the day I was ordained.

Maybe it was time I changed my standard reply from *I'm still needed in Washington* to something else entirely. Because the truth was, I wasn't sure where I was needed anymore.

The last time I'd had the opportunity to live overseas had been when I was seventeen years old, alongside my parents—but Molly had wanted nothing to do with that life. She'd threatened mutiny if our parents made us move again after we'd just enrolled in the high school near our grandmother's house in Spokane.

The fireworks inside our home that summer were explosive as my parents fought against the inevitable. But I knew my sister. And short of hog-tying her to an airplane, there would be no convincing her to go with them willingly. Even to me, it was clear that what Molly needed most was a permanent address.

My decision to stay back was a simple one really: Molly refused to leave Mimi behind, and I refused to leave Molly behind. And just

<del>23</del>

like that, the summer-long standoff in the McKenzie household ended as abruptly as it had begun. Our parents left for their first international assignment just four weeks later.

But unlike then, I wasn't seventeen anymore. And now there was nothing and no one to hold me back.

· 3 ·

Val

Taking a momentary break from unpacking, I paused to listen to the sounds of Tucker's imaginary play on a back deck that had only become *our* back deck a day ago. His rope dangled over the second-floor railing, the end attached to a swinging bucket filled with whatever randomness he'd managed to unpack in the thirty seconds he was inside his new room.

I reached for the next item packed away inside a heavy utility tote, enjoying the fresh spill of natural light that warmed the living room. The two-bedroom, one-bathroom layout was indeed a bit quirky, like Molly had said, with built-ins and extra closets that didn't seem to serve much of a purpose in their current state. But none of that mattered, because this place, this mini sanctuary nestled on a quiet street in the middle of farmland only twenty minutes from a bustling city . . . was all ours.

And that made it absolutely perfect for us.

Sitting back on my haunches, I rubbed at my left hip and stared out through the large picture window overlooking the south side of a mountain I hadn't yet learned the name of. To my parents and most other Alaskans, this mountain would have been deemed a hill, but even still, there was something comforting about its

25

presence all the same. Something solid and sturdy in the wake of change. Something secure that reminded me of a psalm I'd read recently from the Bible I purchased after flying out to help Molly and Silas at the fundraiser they hosted at The Bridge eight months ago. It was that weekend when Molly had first brought up the vision for Basics First. It was also when I'd started to understand that Molly's change in career direction was more than surface-deep.

I shifted my attention from the window to the next-to-last box and pulled out a framed picture of my parents I'd planned to put in Tucker's room. Of the many photos I'd taken, this was his favorite of Gram and Pops.

In many ways, this image of my parents was imperfect—off center, a bit overexposed, my mom midsentence into a story while my dad focused on a distance far beyond what my camera lens could capture. With his arm draped loosely around my mother's shoulders, the two stood in front of a home that also doubled as a profitable business four months out of the year. A pang of guilt thumped my chest at the strangeness of not being there for the upcoming tourist season. It would be the first one I'd ever missed—the first summer I wouldn't be the one replenishing shelves from the stockroom or closing out sales in the evening so my mom could chat with cruise goers after they made a mad dash to Main Street.

My mother had been born in Skagway, and my father hadn't returned to Colorado since the last summer he worked as a king crab fisherman in his early twenties. Their dreams and their livelihoods were as intertwined as their home had become with Gold Diggers Souvenirs.

A package deal I'd walked away from when I said yes to this move.

"Mom? Can I FaceTime with Gram and Pops?"

"Sure, I think my phone is on the table." As uncomfortable as things had become between me and my mother in these last few weeks over my decision to take the job, Tucker was her only grandchild. And I'd just moved him eleven hundred miles away. I couldn't blame her for being a bit clingier than usual.

"Gram . . . I can't see you. Your camera's not working right again."

Tuck dashed into the living room, holding the screen out for me to see a picture of the shag carpet in my parents' den/stockroom. And then my mother's wool-socked feet.

I took the phone from him briefly. "Hey, Mom, remember to hit the circle icon with the arrows on the bottom right. Otherwise Tucker can only see what you're looking at and not you."

"Valerie? Is everything okay? You didn't respond to my last text."

"Everything is fine," I said in the calm tone I'd adopted for all my interactions with her as of late.

"Did you connect with a massage therapist there yet? I emailed you a list of names in the area referred by Doctor Haskins—"

"I'm good, Mom. Everything is great." I glanced at my son and smiled. It didn't seem to matter that I was an adult with a career and a child; my disability would always take priority in my relationship with my mother. The specialists, surgeries, physical therapists, and custom orthopedic inserts promising to help my balance as I relearned to walk at the age of ten. For nearly two decades, the ramifications of a traumatic injury affecting the growth plate in my left hip, which shortened my gait, had been my mother's primary focus. And even now that I was twenty-nine years old, my mom seemed unable to separate the woman I'd become from the fragile child I'd once been. "Tuck is here waiting to show you around our new place."

An unnatural quiet filled the space between us. "Well, your father will want the full tour, too. You know how he hates to miss out."

Comments like that made me question if my mom viewed my dad the same way the rest of the world did. As the video cut from the floor to her nostrils and back to floor again, Tuck and I bit back a laugh. We were becoming well acquainted with this comedy routine. Right about now was usually the point in time when my mom would search the entire house trying to locate my father, hollering his name and turning on lights in darkened rooms to no avail. History would prove that he wouldn't be in any of the five places she first suspected, and then we'd wait as she tied her boots and trudged outside and down the walkway. This would eventually lead to her discovering him in his small workshop just twenty-five paces away, smoking his pipe while bribing the neighbor's dog with treats to stay on the bed of blankets at his feet. In truth, Ruby had as many owners and names as she had guesses on her breed. But no part-time owner fed as much bear or moose jerky to her as my father did. Her loyalty to him was secure.

Heavy Darth Vader breathing and shuffling sounds persisted as my mother opened the workshop door. "You out here, Dale? We have a call."

"That Val?" My father's voice brought an involuntary sigh of relief.

My dad's aging face came into view. Oh, how I wished he'd give up the pipe. I could practically smell the tobacco through the screen. "Hey, Dad."

Sure enough, he was sitting in his lone brown recliner in the center of his shop, dog bed at his feet, and no sound but the pop and crackle of his small wood-burning stove to entertain him. Just the way he liked it most. "Hey, kid."

"Dale, they're in their new place. Tuck wants to give us the grand tour, and I knew you wouldn't want to miss it." My mom was an expert at filling every millisecond of quiet with words, which was precisely why my dad had made his workshop into a silent retreat of sorts. It was also the only place my mother allowed him to smoke. "So either you set down the pipe while I'm out here, or you come inside the house like a warm-blooded human being and watch from inside."

The twinkle in my dad's eye as he looked at me through the screen caused my heart to swell. My father was likely the most patient man to have ever walked the earth. "I think my answer will depend on what kind of tip I'm required to give the guide after the end of such a tour. Not sure if I can afford him."

Tucker laughed and brought his face into the screen. "You have lots of cash, Pop. And I know where you keep—"

My dad's hard cough boomed through the speaker of the phone. "Man code, Tuck. Never break the man code."

Tucker zipped his lip, and my mom chided them both for being in a club she'd been left out of since the time Tuck was a toddler.

Phone in hand, Tuck skated away on his socks to begin the grand tour of our new residence, starting with his bedroom while I located the last utility box to unpack. It was a box that had required the strength of both Silas and several of the boys from his residential program to carry up the narrow flight of stairs last night. If not for their help, all our stuff would still be piled on the ground in front of Miles's front door. Not for the first time, I was glad my new landlord was still away doing whatever it was he was doing. I'd have hated to disturb him with all the ups and downs and general upheaval of moving.

I touched the latch on the side of the heaviest crate I'd paid to have shipped here, debating on whether to open it or not. The old camera and video equipment housed inside had taken me years to collect. Each piece represented my adoration for film, along with the countless evenings I'd spent studying editing techniques and scrolling for amateur filmmaker contests I'd never submit to. Well, with the exception of one.

My mind skipped back to the interview invitation I'd received just seven days ago while packing up my bedroom in Alaska. A familiar temptation washed over me to pull up the email and re-read the fine print again, to brainstorm any possible way I could make an unpaid film mentorship work while juggling a more-than-full-time position at Basics First and one incredibly active ten-year-old. But no matter how prestigious the directors involved with the Essence of Filmmakers Mentorship were, or how coveted the Volkin Award had become to the industry, I knew the answer. I'd known it even before I'd asked God to take away my desire for film and replace it with the honorable causes Molly was so passionate about.

I simply needed to let the opportunity go.

I managed to push the crate against the wall closest to my workspace, nearly tripping over Tucker's plastic lightsaber in the process. I'd have to ask him to help me move this one into a closet later, as his strength now surpassed mine. A somewhat pitiful, yet realistic, observation as I'd watched him carry up boxes and suitcases yesterday that I could hardly lift. My boy hadn't even hit puberty yet, and already he was as tall as my five-foot-one frame. Though we rarely discussed his birth father, Tucker's height was projected to be much closer to the other half of his DNA than to mine.

I'd just plopped into my desk chair to begin the slow process of hooking up my computer monitors—both fit securely into the built-in nook I'd chosen for my office on the far side of the living room—when Tucker slid into view, phone still in hand.

". . . and this is the kitchen." He pivoted. "Here's our stove and our fridge. Oh, and this is our pantry with no food." Tucker opened and closed the door, and I sighed at my mom's dramatic gasp.

"We're getting groceries tomorrow!" I called from the other room.

"But this is my favorite part," Tucker went on, completely oblivious to the grandma grenade he'd just tossed. "A spaceship closet!"

My ears perked at his wild imagination.

"Hold the camera up higher, Tuck. Is there a light in there?" my father asked.

"Yeah. I just . . ." The straining sounds of him up on his tiptoes and then eventually of him moving a chair to reach the pull cord made me smile. There were many physical traits Tucker and I didn't share—his lean, lanky height to my elfin shortness, his ice-blue eyes to my average brown ones, his wavy brown-blond locks to my straight, muted auburn hair I kept trimmed to just above my shoulders—but when it came to his resourcefulness, that one had definitely come from me. "Ta-da!"

"Interesting. That's an old intercom. There on the back wall. I haven't seen one like that in a long, long time."

"Yep, that's why it's perfect for my new spaceship."

"It's an elevator of some kind," my dad assessed resolutely.

An elevator? Is that what it is? I'd only briefly glanced inside that closet, observing the relic of a speaker with yellowing buttons and dials that didn't seem like they'd been used since the house was built. Then again, I hadn't paid much attention to it after Tucker had claimed it for his spaceship. We certainly didn't have an overflow of linens or towels, so I hadn't a single protest to his claim.

I moseyed into the kitchen, stretching out the stiffness in my hip as I walked.

"Oh, Tucky, please get out of there!" my mother shrilled. "That is not a safe area for you to play in—and don't you press any of those buttons!"

"The buttons don't even work, Gram. See?" Tucker said, pressing literally every button he could in the confined space.

Once again, my mother gasped as if she'd been the one falling down an abandoned elevator shaft.

"Okay, Tuck. I think we're good on the tour." I ushered him out of the dimly lit closet and reached for the string to turn off the light, bracing my hand against the wall as I did so. I could barely pinch the string between my forefinger and thumb.

"I'm super starving, Mom," Tuck whined as I closed the Door to Impending Death. "Can we order a pizza now?"

I nodded to him off screen and mouthed that we'd look for a place in just a minute.

"Val? Val? Can you come back to the screen, please?"

Reluctantly, I did as my mother asked, coming into view with a look I usually reserved for public outings. An expression my dad described as my *untouchable* look. "Can you explain why there is an elevator in your kitchen? Are you not on a ground floor? You know how tough stairs can be for you to navigate at times. Also, why haven't you purchased any food yet? Are you two tight on funds already?"

"Mom, we are *fine*. The elevator is a nonissue, it's not even connected." Or at least for the purposes of this conversation it wasn't—I'd have to look into that ASAP, though. "And yes, our apartment is on the second floor. Remember how I told you it's owned by Miles McKenzie—Molly's brother? He lives in the house below us. It's only one flight of stairs up. And just to be clear, I ordered our groceries online this afternoon. They'll get dropped off at our door first thing tomorrow morning."

Though her eyebrows were still rumpled, she gave a hesitant nod and then shivered.

"Bev, why don't you head inside and warm up. I'll be in as soon as I put the fire out."

My mother looked between my dad and me on the phone for a good five seconds before conceding to his request and calling out to Tuck on her way out that she loved him more than the summer sun.

The second she exited the shop, my father's gaze leveled on me, and I knew what was coming next. I held up my finger, asking him to wait so I could redirect Tucker elsewhere. I tasked my son with looking up the highest-rated local pizza joint in the area on his kid-filtered iPad. Within seconds, he was out of earshot.

"It's hard for your mom to let go, kiddo. Have patience with her. This learning curve's a tough one."

"She treats me like I'm an incompetent teenager." I regretted the choice of words instantly. Because I had been an incompetent teenager once. And my folks had been my only bailout plan. A cycle that had been on repeat since my premature birth, it would seem.

He sighed. "Your mother would rather climb a glacier barefooted than hear that either you or Tuck have lacked for anything."

"But that's the thing, Dad. It's only been a few days and already she's worried that I've forgotten to buy groceries? It's like she's hoping I'll fail and have to come back home." I huffed a sigh. "When will she trust me to make my own decisions—my own mistakes? I'm not nineteen anymore." I never had a reason to skirt the truth with my dad. He liked a straight shooter as much as I liked shooting the arrow straight.

"She's not hoping you'll fail, Val. She's just protective. And one day, you'll find that regardless of how old Tucker is, your desire to protect him will feel just as strong as it did when he was five." He winked and cleared his throat. "But I didn't keep you on the phone to talk about your mother. I want to know what you decided about that film program. The one that emailed you last week."

It took me several seconds to switch mental gears, and when I did, I shook my head. We'd already gone over this. "Dad, I told you, the mentorship is unpaid. And they didn't actually offer me anything yet, just a chance to secure my place in a round-robin-style interview. Right alongside a few dozen other film junkies who submitted."

"How many others?" he asked, though it wasn't because he didn't know the answer. He did.

"Dad—"

He stared me down until I answered.

"Twenty-five," I said.

"That's right. Out of how many applicants?"

I shrugged. "I'm not sure. A thousand, maybe?" But likely more. Truthfully, when I'd applied, I hadn't expected to make it into the top hundred, much less the top twenty-five. "But they only choose ten for the mentorship, I think."

"So why stop now? You've already passed nine hundred and seventy-five of those junkies—as you called them." His top lip curled north. "Who's to say you can't beat out a few more?" My father didn't understand much about the film world, but he was the only person outside of Molly's Hollywood contact who even knew I'd applied for the program through Volkin Film Academy at the first of the year.

"You'll regret dismissing that interview," he said.

"Maybe, but the timing isn't right." I rubbed my lips together, tried to smile. "Besides, by next week, I'll have plenty of work to keep me busy."

"You've had enough work to keep you busy since you were ten years old. Work has little to do with what's good for your soul."

My *soul*? Such an unfamiliar word choice for my father to use. Then again, few people understood my fascination with film the way my dad did. After all, he'd been the one to show me a video of a young man with cerebral palsy running across the finish line of a race unassisted. I'd cried for an hour in my bedroom after watching it, wishing I could be that brave and secure in my own body. Wishing I could drown out the voices of middle school bullies who'd chanted every slang word to describe someone who walked differently than them. Someone who would always register *less than* on the scale of what the world found acceptable.

"Well . . ." I cleared the tightness from my throat. "I should probably go figure out dinner for Tuck since he's *super starving*."

But instead of the chuckle I was hoping to get from my dad, he simply tapped down his pipe and said, "Striking gold takes as much risk as it does time, kiddo. Don't settle for pyrite."

A saying as familiar to me as the smell of his favorite brand of tobacco. I'd been taught how to pan for gold since before I could read, pointing out the differences that made up the most common of the iron sulfide compound as customers lined up in the Alaskan sunshine to try their luck. But luck didn't often come with a single pan of dusty rocks. Or even a hundred pans.

Just like life.

I said good-bye as Tucker flopped himself on the couch in the living room. "Found a great pizza place! They have super weird toppings, too—even fruit! But they have four hundred and eighty-three reviews with an average rating of four-point-eight stars."

Again, so my kid. My previous work with Molly had meant a lot of conversations pertaining to average ratings and reviews. "Sounds like a solid choice. What's the name?"

"Mad Hatter Pizza. I want the cheeseburger patty deluxe."

I raised my eyebrows, and Tucker chuckled.

"Can I order a large, Mom?"

"You are ten. You do not need a large pizza all to yourself." And he was smart enough to know I wouldn't touch a pizza with the name *cheeseburger* in the title. I tossed a pillow at his head, and he quickly reached for his lightsaber and batted it away before it could make contact.

"I'm practically eleven. And besides, Pop always says I'm a growing man."

Pop also used to say I was the size of a woodland fairy. But I certainly wasn't gauging my pizza order on that. "Let me look over the menu, and then I'll let you order for us both online."

Lying on his back across the entire sofa, Tuck picked up his lightsaber, the ominous pulse of Star Wars echoing through the room as he made invisible figure eights on the ceiling.

But instead of pulling up the menu, I pulled up a new text from Molly.

Molly

I need you to call me ASAP

Molly's texts were almost never one line. They were wordy and fluffy and usually interspersed with more emojis than letters.

"Tuck, go ahead and order me a small Hawaiian. I need to make a quick call to Molly in my bedroom."

"Does that mean I can order a large?"

"Only if you promise to eat the leftovers for your next two meals."

"Deal!" He sat up and hunched over the screen. Online ordering was a new life skill he'd learned since our move to the Pacific Northwest.

"Our address is written on a note on the fridge," I called out as I entered my bedroom. "And the blue credit card is in my wallet."

"Got it!"

Before I sat on my bedspread, I tapped on Molly's contact info. She picked up before it even had a chance to ring.

"Hey."

It was incredible how a single spoken syllable could relay so much about the direction of an entire conversation.

"Molly? What's wrong?"

"It's . . ." But the muffled sounds that came next shot terror through my limbs. And then it was Silas's voice I heard. From somewhere close in the background. "Sweetheart, maybe I should talk to her for you."

"No, no. I can do it." Another sequence of short sniffles followed by a weighty sigh. "I'm at the warehouse."

"Okay . . ." Odd, since Molly told me all the merchandise had already been sorted and readied for the official grand opening of Basics First next week. We'd scheduled our marketing plan to include several livestreams from the warehouse.

"The alarm company called me tonight, said there was something suspicious happening inside the building." The cadence of her voice was rushed. "But when they sent an officer to check it out, it wasn't a break-in. It was an electrical fire. The fire department came right away, but they say the entire warehouse is . . . flooded. All the equipment, the computers, the headsets, the donated supplies, the inventory stocked in the back room . . . *everything*." She was openly crying now, and I realized that my own throat felt tight with unshed tears. "They won't let me go inside."

"Oh, Molly, no. Tell me how I can help. We can head over now." I stood up from my unmade bed, realizing only then that I had no quick way to get to her. We didn't yet have a car of our own.

"No, don't. There's nothing more we can do here tonight. I just got off the phone with Mr. Richards." Al and Sophia Richards were the funding behind Basics First and Molly's celebrity collaborators in Hollywood. Big names with even bigger hearts wanting to help vulnerable young adults transition into adulthood. In nearly every way, they were the perfect visionary match to Silas and Molly and their efforts at The Bridge. Their partnership had formed easily, and within only a few months, the four had brainstormed the business model for Basics First.

"They're going to open an insurance claim first thing tomorrow morning," Molly said.

"Right." I nodded, though I had zero understanding of how such a process worked. "Please let me know what I can do to help—phone calls? Website updates? Whatever you need, okay? I'll stay close to the phone tonight if something comes to mind."

"Val." Only this time, when she said my name, her voice sounded different. Anxious. Fearful, even. "The fire chief said the damage was . . . extensive. He said it could be months and months before we're up and running."

My mind crawled to catch up to where she was headed. And then, like a sliding car approaching an intersection, it crashed headfirst into something solid. "The job." *My job.* The job I'd finally had the gumption to move eleven hundred miles for. The job that would finally get us ahead financially and allow me to save for a permanent home. The job that would finally take me from a dependent adult to a fully independent single mom.

"I obviously can't say for sure how long the opening will be delayed, but you know I'll do everything in my power to figure something out for you—between my tasks at The Bridge and The Heart of The Matter podcast, I can at least give you enough part-time assistant work to float you financially until we know more." But the thought of moving all this way to once again be Molly's part-time assistant was one I couldn't even process. "Let's regroup about this tomorrow afternoon, after we consult with the insurance adjuster. I just don't want you to panic."

She doesn't want me to panic? Was that even a possibility at this point? My mind was already spiraling down, down, down.

"I'll be fine," I lied. "You just focus on what you need to do at the warehouse, okay? Keep me posted."

"Thanks, Val. I will. Love you."

"I love you, too."

But as our call disconnected and I stared blindly at my bedroom door, it wasn't only the gut clench of fear I felt at my unknown employment status . . . not entirely, anyway. There was something else in the mix. A surfacing question that began a gentle knock against my rib cage, seeming to ask, *What if . . . ?*

· 4 ·

Miles

After a three-hour flight delay, two cramped middle seats in economy, and one layover without enough time to purchase anything more than prepackaged airport food, my mood had taken a nosedive.

Trip destinations changed often in my line of work, but my drive-home-from-the-airport routine had been the same for years: one large cheeseburger patty deluxe pizza to go—with extra jalapeños—and a check-in call with Rev to debrief whatever I didn't want to forget once the travel exhaustion cleared and real life set in again.

Only this time, I drove I-90 West in complete silence. I didn't stop at The Mad Hatter, even though my stomach revolted at my rebellion. And I also hadn't returned Rev's call. Even now, just five minutes out from my house, I couldn't force my finger to tap the voicemail notification he'd left as I'd boarded my second plane. My conscience pricked at the thought that he could have been calling for reasons outside of the norm. After all, he was in his late seventies. On the tail end of a deep breath, I scrolled through my new voicemail list, skipping the two from my sister, and tapped on his number. A half second later a low gravelly voice flooded my car speakers.

"Miles. Hey. You've been on my mind, son. I pray your time in Mexico was good for your soul, even if it was hard on your heart. Call me when you're able. Praying for you."

How was it possible that even when I was out of the country Rev still had more clarity on my life than I did? The answer was the same reason why I couldn't bring myself to hit the callback option. I was too tired to recount my conversations in Mexico. And I was too cowardly to tell him I'd updated my résumé and sent it off to my dad while I'd sat in the Denver airport.

Rev was a big subscriber of the restlessness-isn't-the-same-as-a-release mindset when it came to ministry. And seeing as he'd only recently retired from the church he'd pastored for forty-five years . . . I'd say he'd earned the right to that opinion.

But that didn't mean I wanted to hear it again tonight.

Tonight, all I wanted to do was sleep. For a day. For a week. For a month. And yet somehow I knew the exhaustion that thrummed through me now wasn't linked to insomnia or travel or any of the tense muscles spanning my legs and back after working in the sun for over a week.

No, this exhaustion was the kind that settled deep in my lungs, revealing itself with every breath I exhaled. And I despised it.

I'd call Rev tomorrow.

My headlights reflected off the black asphalt of my street, immediately pulling my mind back to the pit-filled, rocky streets I'd walked with Alejandro. How different his two-hour walk to his uncle's church would be on smooth pavement. But at least he wouldn't have to take that walk wearing split rubber soles anymore.

After he'd turned in last night, I'd snapped a picture of the shoe size stamped to the bottom of his worn soles. The minute I was back on the airport's Wi-Fi, I'd ordered two pairs of new sneakers. Now he'd have one pair to travel the distance between churches, and one to share with his younger brother, because knowing Alejandro, there wasn't a chance in this world that he'd be okay receiving such a gift, knowing his brother's shoes were in a similar condition. And yet, even imagining the smile that would light their faces upon such a delivery wasn't enough.

None of it had felt like enough.

As I rolled to a stop in my driveway, the dim amber light shining from the bathroom window in the upstairs apartment caught my eye against the midnight backdrop. Molly must have forgotten to turn it off after she did that final walk-through for me three days ago.

For all of one minute, I debated going up there to turn it off, but the pull of a hot shower before falling into a dreamless oblivion won without a fight. Dealing with it now versus dealing with it in the morning wouldn't make much of a difference.

I dropped my bag in a heap at the front door, turned on a single light in the musty hallway, and stripped off my clothes on the way to the bathroom. I needed a shower almost as much as I needed a full night's sleep. But as I turned the shower faucet on, the water responded with half the pressure. A rare issue, and one I only dealt with on occasion when a tenant was running multiple loads of laundry. Or, rarer still, if a tenant was taking a shower at the same time as me. But seeing as Zack moved out last week, I had no explanation for the pressure change tonight.

Too tired to care, I stepped into the weak stream . . . only to step out five seconds later, half-frozen.

No hot water.

Really, God? I pressed my forehead to the glass shower door. *Could you allow just one thing to go according to plan?*

I scrubbed a towel over my dripping hair and threw on a pair of jersey shorts, not bothering with shoes as I stepped toward the utility room at the rear of the house to check the ancient hot water heater. But as I did, I heard a distinct creak above me. I stopped. Waited. Shook my head to clear my ears, then continued on toward the water heater again.

As I crouched low to check the pilot light, there was no mistaking the sound of footsteps trailing overhead.

Somebody was up there. But who? Zack was long gone to Tennessee by now, but that didn't mean he hadn't shared his lock code with his school buddies—it certainly wouldn't be the first time. And that was only one of the many issues we'd had as landlord and tenant over the last year. In my brief and spotty phone call with Molly, I'd forgotten to ask her to reset the code on the keyless entry after the walk-through.

A forgotten bathroom light I could ignore. But one of Zack's friends living here like a squatter? Not a chance.

The low thrum of adrenaline pushed the heaviness of travel from my muscles momentarily as I grabbed my phone and crept out the back door to the side steps. The wood planks were cool against my bare feet, but if Bruce Willis could handle a dozen terrorists without the need for shoes on Christmas Eve in *Die Hard*, then I'd be fine handling an uninvited guest.

In my six years in this multiunit home, I'd never advertised vacancies to my apartment. It was rented by word of mouth only, and usually to a church member's connection—someone's college-age son, nephew, or grandson. A young man in need of a place to stay during the school year. And because I didn't live in a typical suburban neighborhood, the chance of somebody simply happening upon a vacant apartment at just the right time with a working door code was slim to none.

I turned my phone's flashlight on and lit up the top steps, since the floodlight on this outdoor staircase had been burned out for months. I made no effort to hide the loud creaking of the stairs as I climbed the short summit. After all, I wasn't the one trespassing on private property.

I also had less-than-zero desire to walk in on a scenario I couldn't unsee. A six-pack of beer and a sleeping bag on the floor I could handle. But my quota for breaking up secret rendezvous for underage, overly hormonal adolescents had been filled after years of leading youth summer camps and all-nighters in the church gymnasium. Co-ed sleepovers were never worth the stress. I didn't know how my brother-in-law managed an entire mansion of hormones at The Bridge.

I pressed the four-digit code on the numbered padlock and continued shining my flashlight through the darkened window as I did.

"Hello?" I pushed inside the apartment, ready to confront whichever of Zack's school buddies was in residence. I'd offer him the night to sober up, see him out the door tomorrow, and change the code the second he was gone.

Only my eyes never had a second to register much of anything except the disorienting flash of electric blue slicing through the darkness. The shrill of a female's scream mixed with the unmistakable galactic hum of a Star Wars lightsaber crackled my eardrums as something hollow whacked against my skull. I stumbled forward, tripped, and smacked the side of my face on something as solid as it was unforgiving.

Apparently, I was no Bruce Willis after all.

· 5 ·

Val

"Did you kill him, Mom?" Tucker's voice bounced off the midnight-dark walls as he stopped short of the stranger on his knees in our living room. The one clutching his face with a groan.

"Stay back, Tucker," I said, failing to catch my breath. "Turn on the lights and get my phone."

My sweaty grip on the dented lightsaber had faltered some when I'd fallen back against the dining room table. My swing hadn't exactly gone as planned. Nor had the intruder's fall as he'd hit the corner of my studio equipment crate.

I'd only had about a five-second warning, stepping out of the bathroom in fresh pjs and wet hair to search for the most weapon-like item I could access, grip, and wield over my shoulder before he'd broken into our apartment. Though I'd read accounts of mothers who'd lifted cars to save their children with superhero-like strength and adrenaline, I'd never experienced anything like it before . . . until tonight.

The overhead light illuminated the dazed man as he lifted his head, and I noticed a trickle of blood seeping through the gap in his fingers. Then our gazes collided for the first time. My body flashed hot then cold, then hot again. Suddenly I was the one wishing I'd been knocked to the ground by a child's toy.

No. *No, no, no.* Please tell me I hadn't just tried to behead my landlord.

"Val?" His voice was as disbelieving as the realization in my head. "What are you . . . *why* are you . . . ?" Hand still clutched over his left eye, he shook his head, revealing a sneak peek at the gash across his brow bone. "I don't know what's happening right now."

That made two of us.

"My mom just tried to kill you with my lightsaber. Look, she even dented it!"

We both looked up at Tuck, who had slipped the toy from my now-limp hand, examining it with awe in the light.

"Hey, Miles," Tuck said as if all were right in the world. "I was hoping you'd come home soon."

Miles lifted his non-bloody hand and offered a short, uncomprehending wave.

"I . . . I'm . . ." But I stopped whatever nonsensical explanation was about to escape my mouth and instead instructed Tucker to get a washcloth from the bathroom cupboard. He obeyed quickly.

Miles worked to place his foot on the floor in an effort to stand, but the movement tilted him slightly off balance to the right. I reached out for him without hesitation, gripping his muscular forearm, all too aware of the irony playing out between us as I, the woman with the balance issue, steadied a man twice my weight. But it was the least I could do after nearly giving him a concussion. Which I still wasn't certain he was in the clear of yet.

He waited a beat to catch his breath before attempting to stand again, this time with my help. My chin tipped north as my gaze tracked his full height before I pulled out one of the dining room chairs that had come with the apartment.

"You should probably sit down for a minute," I said.

With one palm still pressed to his bleeding brow, he took my suggestion without further commentary. Which was probably for the best, as I was still trying to wrap my mind around the fact that Miles was here. In my apartment. Shirtless and bleeding.

"Here, Mom. I got it wet and then squeezed it into the sink like you always do for me." Tucker handed me the wet rag, and I proceeded to give it to Miles. We were acquaintances, maybe even a half step above that, considering our mutual affection for his sister. Even still, we weren't familiar enough for me to play the part of nursemaid.

"Looks like there's a gash on your brow bone," I said, pointing at his face, as if the source of the sticky red moisture coating his left hand wasn't as obvious to him as it was to me. Gingerly, he pressed the compress to the wound. "It might take a few minutes for the blood to clot since it's a head wound. They usually bleed more than other places on the body, even with firm, direct pressure." And then, if that wasn't enough, I continued on like some sort of a representative for WebMD. "Which can make it difficult to get a read on how shallow or deep the cut is. If you need stitches—"

A hollow-sounding laugh broke my sad attempt to salvage his first impression of me as a responsible tenant.

"Believe me, stitches would be the cherry on top of this week." His warm hazel eyes flicked up to mine then, causing a different sort of weakness to soften my knees this time as he readjusted the compress. In only a few seconds, his paled cheeks returned to a sun-kissed tan that seemed to match the rest of his . . . exposed skin. I chided my wandering gaze and focused on his face just in time for Miles to ask, "Would you mind filling me in on some of the blanks I seemed to have missed while I was gone?"

"Sure, yes. Of course." I nodded, and my throat dried out in a way not even a gallon of water could have soothed. Pulling out a chair for myself, I sat opposite him at the table, fisting my hands tightly underneath it. "I'm guessing you didn't know we'd moved in yet?"

"I can promise you that if I did, I wouldn't have barged in like this at midnight."

"Right." My gaze drifted south once again to his tanned shoulders and chest before snapping over to the R2-D2 placemat Tucker was insistent he needed to complete his schoolwork. "I was under the assumption that you and Molly had already talked through all the details."

"*All the details* of what?"

"Renting your apartment to me." But there was no head nod to follow my statement, no sudden recognition that he'd forgotten this fact after what had appeared to be a long travel day for him. I tried again, "She said you two discussed the apartment when you called her a couple days ago."

As if trying to recall exactly what had been said on the phone call in question, he spoke slowly. "You're referring to the call about the final walk-through I asked her to do after Zack moved out?"

"Yes, which should have also been when she told you about a possible new tenant who'd just had a rental property fall through only days before your apartment came available . . . ?" There was unmistakable hope in my voice, but unfortunately, this was the part of their conversation I was foggy on. I hadn't pressed Molly for the exact verbiage between them. Obviously, that had been my first mistake.

Miles stared at me through one unblinking eye.

"No . . ." And then he paused and seemed to consider something. "But to be fair, our connection was in and out during that entire call before the coverage dropped completely. She did leave me a couple voicemails, but I haven't listened to them yet." He stretched his neck, closed his unaffected eye, and released a long exhale. "I'm sorry, I had no idea the apartment was occupied." He shifted the compress and opened his eyes, his gaze spearing into me the way it did each time we interacted. "Or that you'd even moved to the area."

Hot dread pooled in my stomach at the implications of such a terrible misunderstanding. I couldn't lose this apartment. And I couldn't go back to Alaska jobless, futureless. I knew that failed trek home all too well to do it again. Because if I did, that would be it. My life would be there indefinitely, co-parenting Tucker with my folks, and working in their store just like old times.

"Does that mean we can't stay here?" Tucker asked, alerting us both to his presence just a few steps away from the table.

"Buddy, why don't you head back to bed, okay? It's after midnight. We'll talk about this at breakfast tomorrow."

"But, Mom . . . I don't want to go back to Molly's house again. It's *sooooo* boring there."

"Tucker." My look was of the stern variety this time, and he clamped his mouth closed and trailed back to his room in slow motion.

"I'm terribly sorry, Miles. I never should have assumed you knew we'd moved in without talking to you myself, and of course, I'm mortified about . . ." I pointed to his head.

"It's not your fault. We were both just surprised to see each other, is all." He studied me and then pulled the washcloth away. "How does it look?"

I stood, assessing him as closely as I dared. "It clotted. The cut doesn't look too deep, but I can look for a butterfly bandage in one of my boxes if—"

"Nah, I'll be okay." He scooted the chair back and stood, our bodies too close for comfort. I took a step back. "Would it be all right with you if we continued this conversation tomorrow? It's been a really long day."

"Of course." For me as well. "You're positive you don't need a bandage?"

I watched for signs of dizziness or loss of balance as he neared the door. Tucker I could catch, but Miles? Not a chance.

For a full five seconds he didn't speak, but when he did, I couldn't help but hear something in his voice I'd never been privy to before. *Defeat.*

"I just need to sleep."

In every one of my previous encounters with Miles, he'd been easygoing and upbeat, ready to assist in any situation and take on any challenge that came his way . . . not that I expected him to be cheery with a possible concussion. But something was different about him tonight, *off* in a way I couldn't quite place. Something that caused me to want to ask if he was okay, in more ways than just a bleeding head wound.

But I didn't ask. Because I was me. And he was my best friend's brother. And there were already too many lines that had been crossed tonight. I didn't want to complicate anything more than I already had by showing up unexpected in his house and bashing him with a plastic sword.

"Okay, well, I'm sorry. Again. For the misunderstanding."

He pulled open the door, turned back to me. "If a strange man was coming up my sister's steps at midnight, I would hope she would have done the same thing." His eyes flicked to the lightsaber on the ground. "Only with a much more substantial weapon." His attention dipped briefly to the smile emoji pajamas I'd put on directly after my hot shower—a Mother's Day gift from Tucker that couldn't be more opposite of the gray jogger pants I'd normally be wearing at this hour. "Sleep well, Val."

"You too." And then he was gone, trudging down the stairs to his home located directly beneath where I stood.

Alone now, I rubbed at the throbbing pain in my mid-back, the place where I'd crashed against the hard edge of the dining room table. The tender beginnings of a bruise was already starting to form. Not a new experience for me by any means. I was well versed in the art of falling.

After checking in on Tucker's sleeping form, I meandered back to the living room, where I'd been crunching numbers on my budgeting spreadsheet before deciding on a shower to warm the chill in my bones at all the unknowns to come.

Ignoring the clock, I logged back in to my laptop, scrolling the sites I used to find odd jobs in the low season when the souvenir shop collected dust and debt during the long wait for summer. These sites were how I'd originally found Molly—on a group forum for paid-by-the-hour virtual work. She'd been in need of a part-time assistant, someone to help with creating content for a growing influencer channel. It was hard to believe how drastically those followers had multiplied over the years, soaring from a few thousand when I first began to millions. So many opportunities had opened up for her since those early days, and still more were on the horizon, even with tonight's setback at the warehouse. That was the thing about Molly; she wouldn't stay down for long.

I skimmed through multiple job postings—most people requesting virtual freelance work I could do half-asleep. Work that required knowledge but not talent. Time but not heart. Experience but not risk.

Not unlike the marketing position I'd taken at Basics First.

"Don't settle for pyrite." My dad's words boomeranged inside my brain again as I hovered my mouse over my inbox and then clicked through to the invitation from Essence of Filmmakers Mentorship once again.

> Congratulations, Valerie Locklier. You've made it into the third round of finalists for Essence of Filmmakers through Volkin Film Academy. You're now in our top 25!
>
> Please click the link to register* to be interviewed for your chance at a one-on-one mentorship that will take your film talent to the next level while you work toward entering a film competition with a grand prize of $50,000 and a personal film studio outfitted for you by our sponsors.**
>
> * Interview registration open until 12:00 PM EST, May 28.
>
> ** To see the full list of our sponsors click here.

The bolded date at the end of this week drew my eye down the page as I carefully read through the fine print at the bottom, comprehending for a second time that the mentorship would require a large amount of time and mental bandwidth I couldn't possibly provide while also working full-time for an employer. But . . . *what if?*

The question circled my heart again.

I clicked out of the email and back into the budget spreadsheet on my desktop, where I'd deleted the monthly paycheck I'd planned our current budget around. But what if I cut the car budget in half and moved some other figures around, making sure to include the rent price Molly had quoted me when she leased me her brother's apartment sans his consent? I thought back to the fiasco that had occurred only steps away from where I now worked at my desk. And then my thoughts wandered a bit further. Had Miles managed to find a bandage for his eyebrow? Had he been able to fall asleep easily like he hoped? And what mood would he be in tomorrow—irritated by the memory of the night before? Ugh. I pressed the heels of my hands into my eyes and took a moment to breathe. If Molly hadn't been dealing with her own crisis tonight, I would most definitely be requesting a thorough explanation of every word she'd spoken to her brother on that phone call.

After stretching my neck side to side, I got back to work. I needed to figure this out tonight so I could make a plan for tomorrow. And the tomorrows to come after that.

Using the arrow of my mouse, I highlighted the column of my current savings. As of tonight, we had just over sixty days of emergency expenses to cover rent, groceries, gas, utilities, Wi-Fi, and the garish price of private medical insurance for the two of us. After a few more calculations, I settled on the figure I'd need to bring in each month via freelance work if I was to move ahead with the interviews and, by some miracle, get selected by a coach for the duration of the twelve-week program.

The figure staring back at me was daunting, yes, but if I worked nights and most weekends on virtual contracts . . . I could manage it. Especially if my new landlord was willing to let us stay for the rate Molly quoted. I hoped to discuss the terms in full with him tomorrow, without the presence of a lightsaber.

I bit my bottom lip and registered for the video interview.

Maybe I could pan for gold one more time.

◇◇◇

"I think I might have heard his car. He could be home now!" Tucker popped up from the dining room table, which doubled as his homeschool desk. We'd moved during his last two weeks of school, so I was overseeing his final assignments for the year.

"He's not home yet," I said. I'd been watching for signs of the same thing, but for completely different reasons than Tucker.

"But I just want to check. I bet he knows the horse's name, Mom."

I shot a look over my shoulder and noted that my son's math book had been open to the same page for the past two hours. "Tucker, the horse's name won't change between now and whenever you decide to finish up the last of your schoolwork today. If you want to visit the horse across the street, then you need to get those last five problems done."

"I bet he likes apples. Did you know most horses *love* apples? I researched it." Tucker stared in the direction of the property adjacent to Miles's, wonder in his gaze. We'd seen the dilapidated barn when Molly had first taken us to check out the apartment, and Tucker had been begging to meet the horse ever since. "Do you think Miles knows the owner? Maybe they're looking for a rider?"

"Tucker." I sighed. "Please pay attention to your schoolwork."

Only, I hadn't been much better than my son when it came to focusing today. Between waiting for Molly to return my call after her update with the insurance adjuster and keeping busy with mundane tasks I could easily complete with a distracted mind, I'd been engaged in a mental game of worst-case scenarios since the moment I watched Miles pull out of the driveway nearly four hours ago.

Perhaps last night's attack hadn't been that big of a deal for him? Was it too much to hope that a good night's sleep might erase the memory of me treating him like an armed robber?

A text vibrated my wrist, appearing on my watch screen. *Molly.*

I scrolled and scrolled through her dramatic explanation.

Molly

Val! Oh. My. Gosh. Miles just called me . . . I'm dying. No, I might actually be dead. This text is being sent from The Great Beyond. I swear to you on our friendship that I thought Miles heard me tell him I'd found him a new renter before our call dropped. 🙏 And for the record,

I did leave him two voicemails regarding the terms you and I discussed. I'm soooooo sorry! ☹ It's hard not to think the world is ending at the moment, but I know it's not. I just got off a long call with Al and Sophia Richards and their insurance adjuster . . . it's not the best news for Basics First. Looks like I'm going to have to fly to Cali several times to work out financials and a new opening plan for fall. But for now, you just try to focus on these three things for today: 1. Miles is totally chill and everything will be fine. 2. You love me. 3. You know I have your back for life. I'll call you later to discuss job stuff and everything else. XOXO

I stared down at my wrist, taking a deep breath and trying hard not to hold a grudge against the woman who'd taken a chance on me when I'd needed a place to flex my creativity other than the window displays at my parents' souvenir shop. Molly had said yes to me when the world had often told me no.

Val

Curious . . . what exactly did your brother tell you about last night?

If there was even the slightest chance that Miles had kept the part about me assaulting him to himself . . . it might help me gauge how our next interaction would go. The more information his sister could give me, the better prepared I would be for round two.

I grimaced as Molly returned my text with a GIF of Anakin Skywalker using a blue-bladed Jedi weapon.

Fantastic. Just fantastic.

Molly

But on the bright side, it's safe to assume he won't be trudging up your steps at midnight again.

Also, he's planning to come talk everything over with you soon. Let me know how it goes! ♡♡♡ And again, I'm super sorry!

The blue Honda Civic pulling into the driveway stole my attention and, unfortunately, Tucker's as well. He leapt up from the dining room table and raced to slam the now completed math worksheet on my desk.

"Done!"

He practically flew across the living room to the door.

"Tucker, wait—"

"Gotta go, Mom. Miles is here!"

"Tucker Matthew, you stop this instant."

Tucker slammed to a halt, the door open wide to the outside world, awaiting his big escape to the farm across the road.

"You did not ask to be dismissed, and I have not checked over your work."

He threw his head back, groaned. "But, Mom, I've been waiting all day for Miles to get home, and I don't want him to leave again before I get to ask him!"

"Um . . ." A throat cleared. "Knock, knock." The distinctly male voice called up the outside staircase from a place beyond where I could see. Smart man. He was probably afraid of what I might whack him with today if he knocked on the actual front door. "Val? Is this a good time for us to talk for a minute?"

Tucker swiveled his bright blue eyes to me, and I inhaled a deep breath, mustering up every ounce of courage I possessed to plead our case. I gave a short nod, and Tucker waved him up.

"You can come up. My mom's not doing anything."

"Tucker," I hissed, shaking my head. The kid never failed to test my mortality.

"What?" Tuck asked, confusion crumpling his face. "You're not doing your video stuff. You always say that's the kind of work that takes the most brainpower."

Slowly, I breathed out my nose and stood just as Miles came into view of the doorway. Immediately, I could tell he was in far better spirits today. Everything about him looked fresher and lighter. And I was glad that at least one of us had been blessed with a good night's sleep.

"Your face looks way better than it did last night," Tucker said matter-of-factly.

"I appreciate that," Miles replied in the same manner. "Did I overhear you had something to ask me?"

"Oh, he doesn't need to ask you right now if you're busy," I cut in. "It can wait."

Depending on how our next conversation went, I would be having a serious refresher with my son about keeping appropriate boundaries with our neighbor if we were all going to make this arrangement work. It would be a learning curve my son knew little about, given he'd only shared living quarters with blood relatives.

"Now is a fine time." Miles leveled his gaze on my son. "What's up?"

"Do you know the horse's name who lives down the road? Also, do you know if he likes apples? Or if he needs a rider? Because I can ride him."

The tic in Miles's cheek caused a tiny ounce of the tension to release in my chest.

"Her name is Maple Syrup."

Tucker scrunched up his face. "The horse is a girl?"

"Yep. She's a pretty old one, too. But she's kind. Can't say if she's been under saddle or not, but I have seen Kadin give her apples. Carrots, too."

"Who's Kadin?"

"He's Millie's grandson. He lives there with her full-time." Again, Miles seemed to contemplate something. "Are you going into fifth or sixth grade next fall?"

"Fifth. But I'll be eleven in four and a half months."

"Not that you're counting down or anything." Miles laughed, and the sound was even more charming than I remembered. "Kadin just turned eleven in January. He's just one year ahead of you in school, and I'm sure he'll be happy to make a friend in the neighborhood. There aren't too many kids your age around here. He was actually out on his skateboard when I passed by a minute ago."

Tucker's eyes grew round as he turned back to me. "Mom, can I walk over there? Please? I finished my schoolwork."

"I don't know, Tuck. I'd like to meet him and his grandmother first." I hadn't had many opportunities to practice the whole *letting go* part of parenting. Despite the few times I'd left him with my folks to fly out here for either a Basics First meeting or for Molly's bridal shower a few weeks before her wedding, we'd rarely been separated from each other.

"Please, Mom? I'll use my *best* manners. Promise." Tucker's pleading hands matched the emoji Molly had sent only minutes ago.

"Ten minutes," I compromised. "And then you come back and check in with me, okay? I still need to grade your assignments."

"Yes, ma'am!"

In a flash, Tucker was out the door, and I was left with Miles and the butterfly bandage holding his eyebrow together. He looked like he'd been in a brawl at a seedy bar, instead of beat up by a woman who barely registered three digits on the scale after a night of pizza and ice cream.

"How's your eye—"

"I was hoping to—"

"You go first," he said, gesturing to me.

I shook my head. "No, this is your apartment. You go ahead, please." After all, much of what I wanted to discuss had to do with whatever arrangement Miles was open to.

He raked a hand through his latte-brown hair and exhaled a brief sigh. "I talked to my sister a bit earlier. Sounds like there was more than one unexpected event that occurred last night."

I nodded, unsure of the direction he would take this conversation but prepared for whatever trail he steered it down. "Yes, what happened at the warehouse is terrible."

"Yes." It was his turn to nod. "Almost as terrible as me barging in on you without checking my voicemails from Molly first. They would have explained the footsteps I heard after I got home from the airport." Again, he cleared his throat. "I promise I don't make a habit of dropping by a woman's home unannounced. Present conversation notwithstanding."

A shy smile crept over my lips. "And you should probably know that I don't make a habit of using my son's Star Wars paraphernalia for violence."

His expression matched my own, and it was nice to see Miles look a bit . . . well, more like himself today. "But how were you to know I wasn't part of the Dark Side?" He tapped his bandaged eyebrow. "It's practically good as new now."

I couldn't help but laugh at that. The bluish hue surrounding his eye told a different story.

A beat of awkward silence bounced between us, highlighting the unfinished business left to be discussed. After a deep breath of my own, I took the lead.

"I realize that me living here wasn't a part of your plan, Miles. So if you had something else—or someone else—lined up, then Tuck and I can figure out a different housing solution." A positive-sounding yet completely unrealistic statement, as I was well acquainted with the current housing situation in the area and with the fact that I no longer had a full-time job to reference on a rental application. "But if there's a chance that you are open to us renting from you, then please know I'm prepared to pay whatever your going rate is—whatever you collected from your last tenant. I'm also prepared to sign a rental agreement and pay the standard deposit fees." I swallowed as he angled his head to the side, watching me, as if he was trying to decode my words. As if there was some deeper interpretation he might miss if he didn't pay close attention. "Also, as far as Tucker goes, we've been discussing appropriate boundaries between neighbors. But I can assure you that we'll plan to keep to ourselves whenever you're home."

Miles slid his hands into the front pockets of his dark denim pants and continued his silent staring game. "What made you decide to move?"

"What?" Of all the responses I'd anticipated, that hadn't been one of them.

"What made you decide to take the job with Molly at Basics First? Last we spoke, you were leaning toward declining the position she offered. You said you couldn't imagine being away from Alaska during tourist season. Your folks still have that souvenir shop, right? I'm just curious what changed your mind." The casual way he asked made it feel like we were picking up a conversation we'd left off days ago. At the most, weeks.

But it had been months—*plural*—since I'd last seen or spoken to Miles. So how had he possibly remembered a ten-minute interaction while we'd waited outside Fir Crest Manor, ready to greet Molly when she arrived in the wedding limo with her parents? It had been nothing more than a polite conversation to fill the heavy silence between two almost-strangers who were each playing an important role for the bride, a woman they both loved dearly.

Miles had asked me a couple questions during our brief reprieve from the wedding party chaos, and I'd answered him honestly, perhaps more candidly than I should have. I'd told him that even after the trips I'd taken to the Basics First warehouse to stage pictures of the merchandise for the meetings with Molly and Silas and the founders, I'd been unsure.

I blinked up at him, searching for a truthful answer. "Tucker was ready for an adventure to the lower forty-eight."

"And you?" he pressed.

"Me?" My watch vibrated my wrist, my pulse apparently increasing enough to register a change to the heart rate monitor.

"Were you hoping a move would bring you some adventure, too?"

This was perhaps the thing I would struggle with most about Miles McKenzie. He was a question asker. The sort of person who not only listened and remembered everything he heard, but someone who could easily engage in conversation with literally anyone.

Someone eager to share stories and swap favors.

I knew his type well.

"I'm a single mom. I'm not looking to add any more adventure to my life."

· 6 ·

Miles

One thing that had struck me about *Video Val*—the name I'd called her before I realized Molly's long-distance, virtual assistant was an actual, real person—was that when she chose to speak, her words were both guarded and direct. For such a petite person, she carried a boldness not limited by her compact size . . . or by anything else, for that matter. She didn't cower, and she didn't often beat around the bush. Even still, I suspected there was an entire world of unshared thoughts being filtered inside her head at all times.

Val was mindful of her words, but she wasn't transparent—a distinction I made when I'd first met her last fall at the fundraising event my sister and Silas had organized for The Bridge. A fundraiser Val had played a significant role in as the event's official videographer. And it hadn't only been her talent that had intrigued me.

"Is there a date I can anticipate you'll make a decision by?" Once again, her deep brown eyes shone with a restraint that spiked my curiosity.

"A decision about . . . ?"

"About renting your apartment to us."

"Oh." Had she actually been worried I'd kick her out? "It's yours, Val. For however long you need it."

She blinked, her face unchanged. "Don't you want to discuss the lease terms? I was hoping we could negotiate at least six months to start, although if you'd be willing to go longer than that, I can estimate a move-out date for the contract—"

I waved off her concern. "I'm not worried about a contract. Why don't we just take each month as it comes. I'm guessing there's a lot up in the air right now considering what happened last night." I paused and then thought to clarify which of last night's happenings I was referring to. "At the warehouse." I scanned the room I hadn't yet seen with two functioning eyes and noted the flattened boxes leaning against the fridge. "Is there anything I can move for you? I'm happy to take the cardboard down to the recycling bin." I made a move toward them.

"That's actually one of Tucker's chores for later. He can do it."

I paused mid-step. "Okay, anything else I can do for you while I'm up here? I'm happy to help." I didn't see any other boxes to unpack or furniture to be moved. Whatever Val had brought with her from Alaska had been fairly minimal. With the exception of her elaborate desk setup, which held monitors and tech equipment I couldn't begin to identify, there was little else I didn't recognize in this space.

Other than the expression on Val's face, that was.

"Miles," she began with an exhale, and I wondered how many words per second were traveling through that mental filter of hers at this very moment. "I know I'm your sister's friend, but this rental arrangement won't work if . . ." She stopped, waited two seconds, and tried again. "What I mean to say is that I won't feel comfortable living here if we can't be straightforward with each other."

"That's fair." I had a deep appreciation for honesty. "Is there something you think I need to be straightforward about with you right now?"

"Not that I know of . . . no."

"Then, is there something you'd like to be straightforward about with me?"

Her chin rose an inch, which brought her full height to my shoulder. Maybe. "I need you to know that I don't expect or require any special treatment from you. I'd like to be treated the same way you'd treat any tenant."

I recalled my brain-numbing conversations with Zack and his gang of basement-dweller friends who spoke fluent gamer and consumed cheap pizza six nights a week. Val didn't even belong in the same stratosphere as those clowns.

"Sure, that sounds good," I managed.

"Thank you." She tilted her head, revealing the short ponytail resting at the base of her neck. Simple and understated, much like the gray zip-up hoodie and jeans she wore today. It's possible Val might be the polar opposite of my sister. I supposed somebody had to be the balance of Molly's overexaggerated, fussy outfits. I much preferred Val's uncomplicated style to all the texture and sparkle Molly wore. Not that I cared one way or another about fashion. No matter what my sister preached to her massive following, clothes only served one purpose in my mind, and it had nothing to do with *making a statement*. "I really appreciate you being so flexible with all this, especially considering the rental market being the way it is right now."

I had no idea what she was referencing. Of course, I'd been a bit out of touch with my own community as of late. Not surprising, as Pastor Curtis had me playing bad cop so he could drink his oat milk lattes in his father's old study while I shut down our ministry outreaches abroad.

"I'm glad the timing worked out," I said, pressing my palm to the doorjamb and twisting back. "But just so we're clear, that figure Molly quoted you for rent—it wasn't accurate."

Her face tensed momentarily. "Okay, I wondered if it was too low. How much will it be?" The careful way in which she asked was almost comical. But whatever hiccup was happening at Basics

First would certainly mess with Val's position. Or, at the least, delay it. And a delay would come with some financial fallout. I quoted Val my adjusted monthly rate.

Her jaw slacked. "But that's half of what Molly told me."

I shrugged. "It's what I charge."

She was already shaking her head. "That's not . . . that isn't nearly enough. Not for a place this clean, and with this kind of view and neighborhood and land."

I simply smiled. "Do you plan on having gaming parties with twenty smelly dudes when I'm out of town, or blaring Luke Bryan until two in the morning on weeknights?"

"Of course not."

"Then it looks like we're all squared away."

"Really, Miles." She shook her head. "I at least need to pay you a deposit. Tucker is . . . well, he's—"

"A preteen boy?"

"Yes."

"I interned with our middle school pastor for two years during seminary. I'm not worried about Tucker in the slightest. He's a good kid."

Her expression softened, and I was suddenly, keenly aware that Val would be the first female I'd ever rented my upstairs apartment to. Although something told me that if I mentioned that fact in this conversation, she'd find a way to tack on an extra fee to her rent payment.

Val gingerly touched the back of the office chair she stood next to, shifting her weight from one standing leg to the other, as if she needed a break. I could sense that she was attempting not to draw attention to herself, but I'd noticed, of course. The same way I'd noticed most things having to do with Val anytime I was around her. Once, after my sister's wedding rehearsal dinner, I'd asked Molly about the way Val favored her left side and the limp that seemed to grow more pronounced with fatigue, but Molly had shut the conversation down immediately, her protectiveness leaving a mark in my memory I wouldn't soon forget.

"Why does it matter? It's not like the way she walks changes anything about who she is. Just please don't bring it up to her, okay? She doesn't need to feel any more self-conscious than she already does. She hates crowds."

And though I'd kept my word to my sister during the wedding weekend, I had asked Val to dance at the reception the following night, a request she'd politely declined before excusing herself from the dance floor altogether to linger near the back of the ballroom for the duration of the evening.

I'd watched the way she'd observed people that night, how she seemed to track a room full of conversations, how she studied actions and reactions, comings and goings. She certainly didn't miss the details when it came to others, yet she was very selective in the details she gave away about herself.

"Hey, Mom?"

I turned at the sound of Tucker tromping up the stairs, trailed by Kadin.

"Hey, bro. How's it going?" I gave Kadin a fist bump as Val moved toward us, leaning ever so slightly against the wall. "You're getting good at that skateboard. You'll have to teach me some of your new tricks soon." I glanced back toward Val, but the instant she noticed me watching her, she dropped her eyes.

In typical Kadin form, he downplayed the attention, but not before his neck blotched with red. "Sure. Anytime." And then, as if he'd remembered something important, he looked up eagerly. "My grandma said I can go to Dude Camp. We just have to wait till next month to sign up."

It was easy to read between the lines of what he didn't say. Money was tight. I'd need to ask Gavin to check on the scholarship we had in place for tough family situations like Kadin's. "Awesome. Registration is open for you anytime." I smiled. "Did you know I'm the hike leader this year?"

"That's cool."

"What's Dude Camp?" Tucker asked, his face already radiating excitement.

"It's a three-day camp our church leads for boys in fifth and sixth grade. Hikes, games, campfires, cookouts."

"I want to do that! Mom, can I do it, too?"

"We'll talk about it, Tuck."

I didn't miss the way Val released a slow breath and touched her son's shoulder. She redirected her attention to Kadin. "Hi there, I'm Tucker's mom. It's nice to meet you, Kadin."

The stringy-haired kid with a splattering of freckles glanced at her for all of one second. "Hey."

"Miles said you're eleven?"

Again, Kadin nodded.

"Can I show him my room? He wants to see the Millennial Falcon that Pop gave me for Christmas."

"Sure," Val said hesitantly. "Just keep the door open, okay, bud?"

"Yep." Tucker was already ushering Kadin through the living room and into the hall that separated his room from his mom's.

When her gaze followed after them, I lowered my voice to half volume. "I've known Kadin since he moved in with his grandma four years ago. He's a shy kid, but he's respectful. Doesn't have a huge social life, but Millie does her best by him. She has some physical issues that can make certain tasks difficult for her at times." The instant I spoke the words aloud, I wished I could retract them. Of all the things I could have said, why had I gone with that?

Val hadn't missed my blunder, either. Her silence did nothing to cool the heat creeping up my neck. I cleared my throat. "I'd be happy to introduce you to her whenever you're up for it."

"Sure. Thanks," was all she offered in reply.

I drummed my fingers on the doorjamb and worked to reroute our conversation to a more comfortable landlord-tenant discussion. "You'll notice the bathroom door can stick at times. If that happens, just pull up on the knob to break the seal. And there's an old elevator in the kitchen; it's been broken for a decade, so my tenants usually just ignore it."

"And Tucker can't get it going again?"

"Not unless he's a secret mechanic. I looked into it once, but it takes some specialty parts to fix it since it's vintage."

She nodded, relief relaxing her features.

"Oh, and the hot water heater. We can't take showers together."

Once again, her eyes shot to mine, large and unblinking as my words caught up to my ears. *Idiot.* Was it too late to blame my stumbling speech on a slow-acting concussion? "Obviously, that came out wrong. *At the same time* is what I meant to say. That goes for running laundry and the like. But I'm usually gone from eight to at least six in the evening. Sometimes longer, depending on the day."

"We'll be sure to run our laundry when you're at work, then. And everything else that requires a significant amount of hot water."

"Okay, great." Yet I was all too aware that I'd never gone into this much detail with any of my past male renters. I stepped onto the landing outside the front door, staring down at the narrow steps that led to the driveway. "I'll be fixing the outdoor floodlight soon. It's been on my to-do list." *For more than a year.* I didn't share that slice of information.

"There's no rush. I don't have a vehicle yet, so we don't go out many places in the evenings."

Volunteered information. Noted. "You looking for a car?"

"I'm still researching."

"I'm not a car expert by any stretch of the imagination, but I have purchased quite a few used vehicles over the years. I have a couple trustworthy contacts in the area if you want to text me a list of what you're looking for. I can see what they might know."

I pulled out my phone to get her number, but instead of offering it to me, she simply said, "That's all right. I enjoy researching and hunting for good deals. But I do appreciate the offer."

It only took a few seconds of silence to realize Val was not planning on adding anything more to this exchange. So I gripped the railing that ran parallel to the outdoor stairway and made another mental note to check the stability of the structure when I changed out the floodlight.

Halfway down the stairs, I twisted back and said, "Welcome to the neighborhood, Val. I hope you find just the right amount of adventure here."

She smiled at that. "Thanks. I hope so, too."

· 7 ·

Val

I abhorred reality television. Which, I realized, could seem like a contradiction, given my obsession with documentaries and autobiographies. But reality TV wasn't actual reality. It was staged, dramatized, and overedited to bring viewers to producer-led conclusions—all while using cheap camera tricks paired with manipulative background music. And yet I would never throw shade at any of the participants of said shows again. Because right now, I was starring in my own hellacious version of one.

The red recording light at the bottom of the virtual conference room glared back at me as the clock ticked closer to yet another opportunity to engage in the worst of crimes: small talk. The round-robin-style video interviews for the Essence of Filmmakers Mentorship through Volkin Film Academy was a revolving door of meet and greets, stiff smiles, and fumbling self-promotion. But out of a pool of twenty-five candidates and ten coaches, I'd been selected for a one-on-one video interview session five times today. And none of them had gone especially well.

In the reminder email I received two days ago with the invitation link, passcodes, and limited bios on each Volkin-approved film coach, words like *chemistry*, *compatibility*, and *charisma* were used to describe the types of candidates who would land one of the coveted apprentice spots. *"Ten lucky finalists will be selected by ten talented industry professionals for their chance at an exclusive mentorship opportunity that will culminate in a nationally recognized documentary contest."*

Two of my fifteen-minute interviews had ended before the allotted time, while two others had shown initial sparks of interest followed by glazed-over expressions as my answers stalled out and stumbled over themselves. The fifth had told me up front that he was looking to recruit a fellow *gorehound*—a term I had to secretly Google on my phone under my desk. Turns out, he was a horror film enthusiast. Also turns out, he and I were not a match.

The timer at the bottom of my screen ticked on. For one hundred and eight minutes I'd sat in a live holding queue, waiting to see if my bio and video upload samples would be requested for another interview round. And though the virtual conference rooms only held the chosen candidate and requesting coach, I wasn't naive enough to believe there was anything *private* about these meetings. Just like a lemur trapped inside an observation habitat at the zoo, I knew every one of my answers was being evaluated, scrutinized, dissected.

And judged.

This whole process was way more nerve-racking than a timed test.

Give me an essay to write anytime. Or a ten-page paper, for that matter, on any number of subjects that I could research and put into my own words. But don't ask me to think on the spot. Don't ask me to provide meaningful answers that determine my future without adequate time to prepare.

I tried to work the moisture back into my too-dry throat without making it obvious. I'd spent the bulk of last night reading from multiple sources online about best practices for video interviews. There was a strong case made for not drinking or eating on camera, as both had been listed under the *sloppy* and *unprofessional* columns. And since I never knew the exact moment a new coach's face might appear in my queue, I continued my still-as-a-statue pose and waited for an alert *ping* in the remaining twelve minutes.

A name lit up at the bottom of my screen and my eyes widened to the point I wasn't sure I could normalize in time for a face to appear. Victor Volkin of the Volkin Film Academy had just requested an interview with me. Not only was he the creator of the mentorship program, but his collection of awards could rival some of the biggest names in Hollywood.

The *ping* reverberated through my speakers.

Mr. Volkin joined my virtual conference room.

"Greetings," said a man who could have doubled as the real-life Gaston from *Beauty and the Beast*, if Gaston were middle-aged and received the latest treatments in anti-aging technology. "I'm Victor Volkin. Please excuse the interruption, but I wanted to personally congratulate you on being this year's top recruit pick. Your résumé is quite profound, to say the least. The samples you provided have caused quite the stir among the coaches. It's rare for a . . ." He cleared his throat. "For someone of your youth to be drawn to the grittier, darker side of humanity. But that's precisely the kind of no-fluff courage we applaud around here. And by the sounds of it, you've already secured a placement with Mark Douglas. Rest assured, his coaching techniques are endorsed by the Volkin Film Academy." His dimples popped just above the scruff along his jawline. "This industry could use more daring, intelligent females like yourself, Ms. Adrian."

My cheeks went from oven-hot to broiling in under two seconds. "I'm sorry, but, um, I'm afraid there's been some kind of a . . . mix-up. I'm not Ms. Adrian."

His smile dipped, but there was no comment from him.

"My name is Val Locklier."

This last bit of information seemed to snap him into action, and he glanced down at his phone and then up at me again. He held a finger to the camera as if to say *wait for it*. And then he scrolled and read, read and scrolled some more.

Was he not familiar with our bios and headshots? Perhaps I'd been one of only a few female candidates and he'd simply clicked on my queue before double-checking my name. To say the film industry was male dominated was putting it mildly.

I rubbed my damp palms down the thighs of my denim pant legs under the desk, still waiting for Mr. Volkin to make eye contact with me once again.

"Locklier. Locklier. I don't see you on my list of candidates." Another slow and torturous scrolling period that ended as abruptly as it began. "Oh, yes. There you are. It would appear I clicked into the wrong queue." He set his phone down and glanced at his flashy watch before looking at me again. "I'm eight minutes ahead of schedule."

"Oh . . . okay." I had no idea what that meant for me or why he continued giving me that expectant stare as if I should know what to do next. Clearly, I'd missed this particular protocol in the preparation email sent out by his academy.

Five light-years of awkwardness spanned the silence.

"Why don't you—"

"Would you like me to—"

"Yes."

"What?" I asked in an octave unfamiliar to my own ears, unsure what he was agreeing to.

He waved me on with the enthusiasm of someone swatting away a gnat. "Go ahead. Pitch to me."

Go ahead. Pitch to me.

If there were two more atrocious phrases strung together in the English language, I wasn't familiar with them.

Without a lead to follow or any real understanding of what a director of his caliber might be looking for in a coachable contestant, I opened my mouth and tested fate for what would surely be the last time. Sweat prickled down my spine as I cleared my throat and worked to recall my monologue.

"My name is Val Locklier, and I've worked as a virtual marketing assistant in the beauty and fashion industry for three and a half years for an influencer with a multimillion following, on several popular platforms." So far so good. At least I had this part down. "I've created and edited raw video content and series pieces, as well as directed and produced a short campaign film for a nonprofit youth home last fall. To date, that video has been viewed more than four hundred thousand times and—"

He yawned. Victor Volkin actually yawned, and then he leaned back in his chair.

"Your longest cut?"

Longest cut . . . longest cut . . . *oh*! "The campaign video was cut to just under five minutes, as it was intended for cross-promotion on multiple platforms, but I've edited compilations upwards of twelve."

He pursed his lips, scrutinized me, and then said, "Twelve minutes."

It wasn't a question, and yet he let the words dangle like an invisible noose as he cocked his head to the side, his eyes dancing with a humor I didn't find the least bit amusing. "Twelve minutes of fashion vlogging does not constitute enough work experience in my book for a chance at fifty grand, a complete studio setup, and a plethora of future contacts seeking up-and-coming film entrepreneurs—much less my time." His Gaston-like smirk twisted at something inside me. "So what else is there? What am I missing? Because that can't be all of it." He turned his phone screen around to the camera to show me my name and the minimal amount of credentials underneath it. "There has to be something more to your résumé for you to have made it into the top twenty-five, Val Locklier." He eyed me, as if this was the time to unload the nonexistent film internships I'd held back or the extensive schooling or travel I'd done—something extravagant that might persuade him to overlook my lackluster bio.

But no words would form. Because I had nothing else of significance to offer him.

At my silence, he looked wickedly satisfied with himself, as if he'd discovered the one unflavored jellybean in a dish of colorful choices. "Documentaries, even docu-shorts, are often longer than twelve minutes. And all of them have multiple points of view, plot structure, and purpose."

Black globs swam in front of my vision as the cold claws of rejection gripped my throat.

He began to lace his fingers and then thought better of it, reaching for and twisting off the metal cap of a Pellegrino. "Since you seem to be content with wasting what will likely be your only chance with an expert who is willing to give you his undivided attention, I'll use the remainder of this time to educate you on how I've coached my directors to mentor their apprentices using the Volkin Methods." He took a drink of his sparkling water. "Firstly, I instruct them to seek out candidates who are willing to deliver unapologetic depth—the kind of scandal-driven, politically charged, irreverent messaging that spikes morbid curiosity *and* mass appeal. Our content speaks to the perils of the human condition. To that single last flicker of hope after a soul has been sucked dry and left to shrivel next to an empty bottle of tequila. We hold nothing back from our viewers." He narrowed his eyes. "The coaches I've trained throw their mentees into the deep end of the pool without a life preserver. It's the strategy that's made me not only the best educator in my field but a three-time Academy Award winner. For those candidates fortunate enough to be selected for this acclaimed one-on-one film mentorship, they should expect weekly critiques of their edited cuts, rigorous project deadlines, and a schedule dictated by their coach. Essentially, for the next twelve weeks, their life will not be their own." He paused as if to allow me a sliver of air to breathe, only I'd forgotten how to take in oxygen.

"I won't speak for all the coaches who participate in my program, but I don't see how a contestant who's spent three years playing dress-up on camera and filming reviews about mascara and lip gloss would be worth anyone's time to coach. My professional recommendation would be for you to take a film course from my online school, enroll in a summer internship, compile a new résumé with fresh samples, and then try this contest again in three to five years depending on your acquired experience. There are no shortcuts in this race."

But instead of ending the video call right then the way I anticipated him to, Victor Volkin suddenly swiped his phone off his desk and flicked through several screens, scanning and reading at a manic pace as if looking for something. After several seconds, he slammed his eyes closed and cursed. "Well, well. Mystery solved." His glare incinerated my insides. "You were endorsed by Al Richards?"

Static sizzled up my spine and snapped in my ears. It took a moment for the name to register. I'd only ever met Al Richards in person once, and our interaction had been brief, given he'd flown in to view the warehouse in Spokane with his wife. But before Molly could officially introduce us, Al Richards had complimented me on the campaign video I'd produced for The Bridge on such a short timeline. It was later that week that he'd emailed me the information about the film mentorship and encouraged me to apply with my work. I hadn't realized until this moment that he'd actually *endorsed* me for the program.

"Um . . . yes, sir."

Another hard huff of air. "And why exactly did you withhold that information when I asked you about your *other* qualifications?"

"I guess because I hadn't realized until now that—"

"Not only does Al Richards own a third of Hollywood, he owns the lease on my production studio." He swiped a hand down his face and tugged at his jaw, closing his eyes for several excruciating seconds. "One hour."

"Excuse me?"

"I'll leave your name and sample videos in the priority pool for one extra hour. If a coach happens to be interested in you, then you'll have an invitation link to an interview at two o'clock. You understand?"

I nodded as he edged closer to the camera, his voice a terse hiss. "But let me make one thing perfectly clear to you: Al

Richards's name might be stamped on your application, but it's *my name* on this mentorship program. I'm the one who's made the industry connections. I'm the one who's brought in the high-brow sponsorships. And I'm the one who has set the bar for this film competition time and time again." He stared me through. "Essence of Filmmakers is a competition built on *my* sweat and hard-earned experience—*not* on favoritism or charity cases." He cleared his throat and stretched his neck side to side. "Now, if you'll excuse me, I have a qualified candidate to welcome aboard."

Ms. Adrian, no doubt.

Throat on fire, I nodded once and forced out the words, "Thank you for your time and for—"

"If you receive an invitation link and choose not to show, I'll assume you've forfeited. But if a coach doesn't show, you can assume your application has been passed over for the final time." And if his expression was any indication, that was exactly what he hoped would happen.

He ended the call.

Dazed and left to stare at the mirrored image of myself alone, Victor Volkin's words rang in my ears again. *"Essence of Film-makers is a competition built on* my *sweat and hard-earned experience*—not *on favoritism or charity cases."*

And then another boomerang soundbite hit me, one from a past I'd tried so hard to bury in the graveyard of my regrets. One of a weak girl who'd been lured by the false promises of acceptance and approval only to be tossed back out to sea like a dead fish.

I'd never be that girl again.

On stiff legs, I pushed up from my chair and forced myself to walk, to move no matter how painful it was without first pausing to stretch my hip. Out of the corner of my eye lay the cardboard remains of what was left from the recycling pile Tucker was supposed to take out before he left for a service day at The Bridge with Molly and Silas. Through blurry vision, I slid the flattened boxes up the side of the fridge to get a better grip before tucking them under my right arm. I needed the fresh air and the distracting challenge of walking down the steps with cargo in tow.

One step onto the rain-dampened landing outside my front door and I was already breathing in short, hard pants. I stared at the gauntlet before me. This was a mental game as much as it was a physical one. There were twelve steps to the bottom. Twelve steps to prove to myself what could never be proven to someone like Victor Volkin: that a lifetime of determination and hard work couldn't be measured on a one-page bio or a seven-minute video interview. I steadied myself on the top stair and willed the muscle spasm in my left hip to relax. By step three, the boxes had started to slip from under my arm, but I pressed them tighter to my side. I wouldn't let them fall.

I have a wonderful son. I have a loyal best friend. I have two loving parents. I have a safe place to call home. I have work that can provide for us.

The mantra I rehearsed to myself whenever rejections rose to the surface was almost enough to block the image of Victor Volkin's smirk from my short-term memory . . . *almost.* Because somewhere in the back of my mind I teetered with the idea that he was right. That maybe my lack of experience would never allow me to find a legitimate place in this world. I had no formal training and no eye-catching talent to flaunt.

I was simply a woman with a well-connected best friend.

On step ten I'd decided I should forfeit. Why should I even bother to check for another interview link from a coach? One extra hour wouldn't make a difference to my bio. It wouldn't change the fact that I simply didn't have what it took to make it in this industry.

By step twelve, every piece of cardboard dropped to the muddy ground below in a loud, soggy heap, and I could only stare through blurry eyes at the mess I'd created.

"Val? Are you—?"

Miles jogged around the back side of the house, a bottle of Coke in hand, his eyes wide at the sight of the cardboard at the bottom of the steps. Alarm flashed across his face as he looked from the pile back to me. *Don't say it.* I pleaded with him silently as he appeared to be examining me for any sign that I, too, might have slipped.

Don't ask me if I'm okay. Or if I need help. Please don't ask me anything.

As if reading the words inside my head, he simply set his Coke down and bent to gather the dirty cardboard that was obviously not meant to be a welcome mat at the bottom of his stairs.

"I can do that," I said, taking the final step down into the shallow puddle, fighting for balance as I bent to retrieve the corner of one of the less submerged pieces. Only this time, Miles ignored my brush-off. In one large scoop, he lifted the awkward stack into his arms, opened the recycling bin with his elbow, and proceeded to slam dunk the cardboard inside.

I expected a lecture to follow—something about how I should really ask for help next time, but instead, Miles's lips tipped into a soft smile.

"Your timing couldn't be better," he said. "I just came outside to take a quick breather myself after the rain cleared up." He lifted his Coke bottle. "Can I get you one? I'd welcome the company."

The invitation was such a shocking interruption to my overprocessing mind that I actually nodded.

And I didn't even drink soda.

"Great. Head on back to my patio and I'll grab you one." Miles jogged around the corner to the back of his house, collected a second bottle, and met me in his backyard. The acres of grassland surrounding us had no boundary line or fence. And beyond the cinderblock fire pit located only a few yards away from his paved patio was all open land as far as my eye could see. Limitless and free. And something about the landscape of fir trees and rolling hills and patches of wildflowers . . . reminded me of the best parts of home.

I inhaled the fresh air, breathing the familiar comfort into my lungs.

"Feel free to take a seat if you'd like. I dried it off already with a towel." He pointed to his oval patio table, where exactly one chair sat. "I've been sitting and staring at my screen all morning. My brain could use the extra circulation."

I skimmed my fingers along the back of the chair with no intention of sitting. "Mine could, too, actually." *Understatement.* I tilted the open bottle into my mouth and sipped the fizzy carbonation until my tongue tingled from numbness. As I pulled the Coke away from my lips, our gazes met. "Thanks for this. I haven't had one of these in . . . I don't even know how long. But it's better than I remembered."

"And probably more addicting than you remember, too." His eyes crinkled, and I noticed there was almost no trace of the bruising around his brow now. "Mexican Coke is way better than what we have here in the States, though I won't try and claim it's any better for you." He shrugged. "It's a luxury import I try to keep on hand for the days I need it most. You're welcome to one anytime. They're in the fridge in my garage."

I pulled the bottle away to inspect it, only just now seeing the differences in the nostalgic curves of the glass neck and the few Spanish words printed on the label, and once again, his generosity stunned me.

I rubbed my lips together before asking, "And today is one of those days for you? A Mexican Coke day?"

"Definitely." He nodded with a grin. "Although it seems to have taken a recent turn for the better. Thanks to you."

I smiled politely. "I didn't even realize until now that you were working from home today." Honestly, when Molly picked Tucker up this morning at ten, I'd assumed Miles was long gone. He seemed to leave between seven thirty and eight each morning. I figured I'd just missed the sound of his car tires crunching over the gravel driveway because I'd been focused on getting ready for my interviews. My stomach cramped at the reminder.

"Yep, been here *all* day." He breathed out a long sigh, and for a brief moment, I saw the same flicker of doubt cross his features as the night he discovered me in his apartment. "I have a report due tomorrow morning for a staff meeting, and I knew I wouldn't be able to stay focused at the church office. Too much distraction there. I figured a change of scenery would help me think more clearly." His laugh was self-deprecating. "So far that hasn't been true. Turns out, staying home isn't quite as distraction-free as I thought. YouTube is a dangerous rabbit hole. Somehow one video click about corporate budgeting morphed into a video about a thirteen-year-old Norwegian boy who won an international singing competition, which then morphed into a collection of videos about goat farming in Guatemala."

I quickly covered my mouth to keep from spitting out my drink. Miles laughed, too.

"I can so relate," I said.

He tipped the neck of his bottle toward me and lifted an eyebrow as if in challenge. "I don't believe that for a minute."

I rumpled my face. "What? Why not?"

"Because the way Molly tells it, you're some kind of ultra-disciplined creative prodigy who works at superhuman speed."

His words were so ironic given my morning that I couldn't help but say, "Trust me, not everybody feels that way about my work."

"But I bet the people who matter most do." His face softened into an inquisitive expression I'd seen before. "I also bet you can accomplish double what I can in a workday at home—maybe even triple." He squinted up at the sun breaking free of a cloud. "Plus, you're doing all that *and* raising a great kid. In my opinion, that should add a lot more weight to your career accomplishments."

A rush of warmth swirled in tandem with the cool fizzy beverage in my belly. While I'd never claim to be any kind of prodigy, he wasn't wrong when it came to my dedication. For going on four years, I'd taught myself everything I could about video marketing and production for Molly's platforms. I'd sacrificed sleep and any kind of social life for the betterment of my family and, consequently, for the hope of a future career in the arts. Victor Volkin may not see my specific experience as valuable, but what

I'd learned in that time had shaped me into a better listener. A better visionary. A better creator. A better editor. And, I hoped, into a better mother and friend, too.

"I can give you an insider's tip if you'd like," I offered, surprising myself in the process. "To double your work time."

"If it involves not taking a break for a Mexican Coke, then . . ."

I laughed. "No. It involves a customizable app that will help your screen-time discipline. I've used it for years." I told him the name of it, and he quickly typed it into his phone. "It's essentially a timer that will block whatever your specific clickbait temptations are—Guatemalan goat farmers included."

"Hey, now, those goat farmers are quite the hot commodity." His humor-filled eyes cut to mine. "I actually did learn a few things while down the rabbit hole of my internet distraction time today—like, did you know there are actually some reputable goat adoption programs out there for impoverished villages in need of resources?" He paused a moment, then blinked and shook his head. "Well, anyway, at least a bit of my lost time went to educational purposes. Still, thank you for the insider's tip—there really is an app for everything, I guess."

"I suppose that's true." I studied his face for several seconds longer, wondering why he'd stopped his train of thought so abruptly. And then, in an act just as shockingly uncharacteristic as me drinking a Mexican Coke with my landlord in the middle of a workday, I raised my half-empty bottle to him. "Here's to Mexican Coke days and to finishing them out stronger than they began."

The intoxication of his grin spread throughout my entire body. He clinked his glass bottle to mine. "I'll drink to that."

∞

In the time it took me to hike up the stairs, set the empty Coke bottle down on my desk, and settle in at my laptop, something had shifted inside me. A new resolve to give this opportunity one last shot, not because Volkin's opinion of me mattered, but because, as Miles suggested, there were other opinions that *did* matter to me . . . including my own.

And I didn't get this far just to throw it all away by not showing up.

As the minute hands on my wall clock marched toward the next hour, I jotted down an idea I'd had for a pitch on the downfall of big-dollar tourism in small towns across America. I'd seen the impact in the economy firsthand and could speak intelligently on the subject if I did receive an invitation to pitch to a coach one more time.

An invitation link popped up in my email with two minutes to spare, and my eyes fluttered closed. I breathed out a prayer and clicked into the private queue, where a woman in her midsixties with pale skin, high cheekbones, and a trendy pixie cut filled my screen. The shocking ice-tone of her cropped hair accented a pair of teal-blue eyes that sparkled despite the digital barriers between us. Even still, I didn't recognize her. I was certain I hadn't read her bio or seen her picture among the other directors listed on the Volkin Film Academy website.

"Ah, you must be Valerie Locklier," the woman said with a dramatic flourish that hinted at an English accent. "I'm Gwendolyn Chilton. I'm the newest coach to participate in the program this year, though as you may notice, there is little else new about me. I just hope that once I earn my wings, they'll be custom fit for a fashionably late, trendsetting sixty-seven-year-old like myself."

Even without her sharp wit and inviting smile, this woman was already up a hundred points in my book just for getting my name correct on the first try. Her sophisticated accent was a win, too. "It's a pleasure to meet you, Ms. Chilton."

"Please, call me Gwen," she said. "Though I do keep hoping that one day I'll wake from a deep slumber to an announcement that I'm part of a royal lineage somewhere and I'm to be called Lady Gwen thereafter. I really should have fought harder for that role in *The Princess Diaries*."

It had been years since I'd seen that movie, but I could easily picture the casting. I felt my eyes widen. "You mean Julie Andrews's role?" Had she been in competition with *the* Julie Andrews? It certainly wouldn't be a hard stretch to see her as the queen mother in *The Princess Diaries*.

"No, no." She waved a hand. "For Anne Hathaway's character. Can't you see the striking resemblance?" She batted her eyelashes and then gave me a wink.

"Oh, of course." This time I couldn't help but laugh. "I don't know how you weren't their first choice."

"Well, I do, but that's an entirely different story for an entirely different day. So what about you, dear? Any secret identities you wish to take on?"

This was certainly not the interview I'd been expecting. "Me? No . . . but my son often wishes he was born into a professional rodeo family, though I don't think that has quite the same prestige as a royal family."

Gwen laughed easily, and for the second time during any of these interviews, I did, too. "I take it you're not a bull rider in your spare time?"

"No, ma'am. I'm definitely not."

She hiked a pristinely drawn eyebrow in my direction. "Perhaps a little rodeo could help broaden your creative horizons, hmm? One never knows what might spark a little inspiration."

If Gwen wanted to believe I could hold my own for eight seconds on a bucking bull, then I wouldn't challenge her. Though I couldn't imagine anybody challenging her on anything. "Maybe so."

Gwen picked up a coffee mug and sipped on it in a way that looked neither unprofessional or sloppy. Maybe she really was secret royalty. She peered at me for several long seconds, and I wondered if this was the moment she would bring up my lacking résumé. "I'd like to speak frankly with you, Valerie. May I do that?"

My insides collided. "Yes, certainly."

Over her coffee mug she lifted a notebook, glanced at whatever was written there, and placed it on a surface below the camera's eye. "I watched some clips from your earlier interviews today." She paused, and I was certain she could hear my internal groan. None of my interviews could be considered great, but the few minutes I'd had in a queue with Victor Volkin were straight up abysmal.

"I'm going to go out on a limb here and guess that you're not much for first interviews, correct?"

Heat flamed in my cheeks. "That's right, ma'am."

"Nor do you have much in the way of professional film experience." She lowered her glasses and once again directed her gaze down at the notebook off screen. "At least according to the professional side of the application."

I swallowed, preparing myself for the imminent end of this conversation. "That's also correct, ma'am."

"And your video content and editing time has primarily been limited to a single focus in the beauty influencer arena—though I did watch the examples you uploaded, and it's easy to see your raw talent. On a side note, that Molly gal is adorable. I learned a few techniques on tying scarfs, so thank you for sharing that particular upload." She grinned, and I mirrored the action though my insides had begun to congeal. She was right about Molly. She was a showstopper in every environment she was in, even this one. "But what really caught my interest was the video you produced for the vulnerable young adults at that residential home—well done. You had me misty-eyed thirty seconds in."

The compliment was so unexpected that I felt the prick of emotion in my own eyes. She was the first coach to mention my work in such a positive light. "I really appreciate you taking the time to view my work. Thank you."

"Of course. I'm a fan of doing my due diligence." She nodded and studied me. "Which is how I found out that you're completely self-taught. No internships or traditional training."

Despite the disappointment that ribboned through my chest at the thought of sealing my fate with this final admission, I pushed the words out. "Yes, ma'am. That's true."

With pursed lips she bobbed her chin up and down, considering me. "And that, Valerie Locklier, is precisely why I requested an interview with you today. That, and the fact that I respect Al Richards and his opinions in a way I respect very few in my profession. Plus, I see a bit of myself in you." She paused. "Did you realize that you are only one of three women to make it into the top twenty-five?" She waited for me to shake my head. "It's true. But what else is true is that I'm desperate to see a woman from a small town with a big dream sail past some of these hotshot, arrogant men and win this whole thing. You up for such a task?"

I fought the urge to triple blink or ask her to please repeat herself, as my ears had turned mute for several seconds. "I'm . . . um . . . what?"

"In my opinionated opinion—as my husband, Frank, likes to say about me—this industry doesn't need more Victor Volkin juniors running amuck in our arena, creating drama and mayhem for the sake of shock value. I believe what our world actually needs is *hope*. Originality? Sure. Artistry? Why not; life's too short without it. But where we often get it wrong is in the storytelling. Crafting a good *story* often takes as much willingness as it does vulnerability. That's an absolute must for me." She leaned in closer to the camera. "I am not a traditionalist when it comes to my craft or when it comes to coaching. My methods are unique from Volkin's, which is why I'm looking for a unique candidate."

A flashback to Volkin's approach to coaching recycled in my mind. The whole throwing his recruits into the deep end without a life preserver bit. Not to mention the requirement of handing over my entire schedule and personal time.

"May I ask about your methods?" I asked.

She smiled brightly. "You most definitely should ask about them, but I won't be able to provide specific answers until there's a signed agreement between us. What I can tell you at this point is that I am not in the business of producing filmmakers. I'm in the business of creating visual storytellers."

Visual storytellers. I'd seen that phrase bouncing around some of the film forums I followed, but somehow, when she said it, it sounded far more prestigious and enticing.

"If you'd like to take the next step with me, then I'd like to email a short list of prerequisites for you to send back, and schedule a call with you later this week."

I couldn't stop my eyes from rounding. "Absolutely, yes. I would love to—"

She held up a finger. "But I will need your answer to a very important question on that phone call first. And if you can answer it to my satisfaction, then I will tell you more about my methods. Sound fair?"

I could barely contain myself at the idea of not having to answer her on the spot. "Yes. Very much."

"Do you have something to write with?"

I didn't have a notebook handy, so I used one of Tucker's schoolwork papers and flipped it over. "Ready."

I scribbled down the question quickly, working to keep my excitement over the turn of events from combustion.

"Good luck, Val. I'll be in touch with you soon."

"Thank you—yes. Okay. Bye."

When she ended the call, I threw my hands over my face and squealed, stomping my feet on the floor like a child who'd just been thrown a surprise birthday party.

Immediately, I clicked out of the online conference site and looked up Gwen's IMDb. Turned out, Gwendolyn Chilton had spent a fair amount more time in front of the camera than behind it. I felt foolish for not having recognized her from her supporting roles in several box office hits in the late '80s to mid '90s. It was clear Lady Gwen—a name that had already taken root in my mind—had been a phenomenal actress before she'd ever tried her hand as a director in her late fifties. The woman was the owner of two Emmys. So why was she a brand-new coach in this competition? This certainly wasn't her first dive into the world of film.

I clicked on the link to a title that had been released just three years ago. She'd been both the talent and the director of a short

documentary called *Keeping My Womanhood Despite the Odds.*
It was a fifty-five-minute piece about holding on to femininity after
her double mastectomy. The film had been nominated for a Crit-
ics Choice Award, but it was the articles mentioned on a Google
search that caught my eye. Several articles, actually.

I skimmed through the headlines interspersed in a paragraph
about Gwen's fight against ageism in Hollywood:

"Ageism: Still Alive and Well in Hollywood"

"G. Chilton Leaves Set, Threatens to Sue Over Script Rewrite"

"The Fantasy of Staying Ageless in Hollywood"

"Does Hollywood Shun Actresses Over Fifty? Gwen Chilton
Certainly Thinks So . . ."

"Senior Stereotypes in Hollywood Are Harmful to Society"

I clicked on the last headline, as it was authored by Gwen
Chilton herself, holding my breath over her pointed commentary
regarding Hollywood's mistreatment of senior actresses. She documented several scripts for roles she'd taken on in her late fifties
and early sixties that either changed mid-production to a dialogue-
less presence or transformed her character into a self-deprecating,
dementia-heavy stereotype. Her fight for a level playing field when
it came to her male counterparts—who still played the romantic
lead well into their late sixties, while she and her female colleagues
were offered the crabby grandmother role—had garnered much
attention. Not all good, either.

According to the articles, Lady Gwen's less-than-soft-spoken
opinions had caused many directors in the industry to shun her
film projects and pitches at every turn.

I slumped back in my chair and replayed our entire conversation
for a second time. The meaning of her *Princess Diaries* joke was

now notably more profound than it had been fifteen minutes ago. Gwen was here, at Volkin Academy, in this Essence of Filmmakers program, not because she was bored and needing a retirement project. But because she needed to grow her reputation in the film industry once again. This time as a respectable director.

Perhaps Lady Gwen and I were more alike than I'd first realized. Gwen Chilton had known fame, red carpets, and success, but she also knew what it felt like to be an outcast. And I wanted to work with her more now than I could remember ever wanting anything.

Which was why I'd have to nail her test question.

I stared down at the words I'd scribbled on the back of Tucker's math worksheet and released a long exhale.

That wasn't going to be easy.

· 8 ·

Miles

There was no shortage of lunch invitations on a church campus our size, but not even Taco Tuesday with Gavin and his youth interns could entice me to leave today. Not after being stood up at this morning's all-staff meeting by the very man who'd required the report I'd spent weeks slaving over.

I smacked the rubber ball hard against the wall of the old church gymnasium, then shuffled right to slap it again on the bounce back. I hadn't missed a single return hit in the last thirty minutes, and my sweat-soaked back was proof. The inside of this hollow, outdated auditorium had seen more than its fair share of my sweaty T-shirts over the years, though. It had been a refuge to me since I was seventeen years old . . . and one of the last remaining spaces within Salt and Light that hadn't been the recipient of a Pastor Curtis update plan. But that was only because the "new and improved" gym was located on the far east side of the campus.

"Should have known I'd find you here."

Gavin's voice was as distinct as his trendy haircuts. He was five years my senior yet barely looked a day older than most of the high school students in his youth ministry. He also happened to be a good friend.

"Hey," I said, smacking the ball in his direction and making him hustle in his black jeans and logging boots that had yet to step foot on a wooded trail. The irony and subsequent harassment of his chosen attire had become a favorite pastime of mine since he joined the staff five years ago. "Hope you left your ax and chainsaw in the car. I hear security has tightened their protocol recently."

He dove to make the hit in time. "That may be, but I guarantee Nicky's wrath for leaving a chainsaw in the same vicinity as Zoey's car seat would surpass even the highest voltage Taser."

I laughed and returned the ball. I'd known Nicky since our church youth group days. After her first marriage to a cheating drifter dissolved shortly after her second daughter was born, she'd put herself through college and finished her nursing degree. Gavin had only been on staff with Salt and Light for a few months when he started making inquiries about the cute single nurse who volunteered during our church summer camps. The two were married by the following summer and had welcomed Zoey, surprise daughter number three, into their blended family in record time.

"You missed Taco Tuesday," Gavin huffed out the last words as he strained to catch the ball in both hands and tucked it under his arm. He rotated to face me.

I wiped my damp forehead with my shirt sleeve and headed to grab a clean towel from my sports bag. "Wasn't that hungry."

"Is that even possible? My girls still joke about the time you packed away an entire calzone by yourself." He dropped the ball to the floor and passed it foot to foot, as if his leather boots didn't weigh as much as each one of his legs. Gavin was built like a sports car. Solid, flashy, and compact. His stature and stride made him a far better soccer player than a wall baller.

"It would have been a crime to waste that much mozzarella and Italian sausage. Somebody had to eat it."

"So you're not hung up about this morning, then," Gavin asked without actually asking. "Because I'm sure PC has a legit excuse for why he couldn't be there."

Only the youth and select staff members referred to Pastor Curtis as *PC*—not surprisingly, I wasn't part of that exclusive fan club. Nor did I have any desire to be.

"Oh, I'm sure he does," I said in a tone that declared the opposite.

While I couldn't remember Curtis missing a single staff meeting since he stepped into his father's shoes as lead pastor, there was a first time for everything. And today, that first time looked like Curtis skipping out on a grueling financial report he'd asked me to deliver. The same report that justified every dollar my department had spent on the outreaches and teams I'd led abroad, as well as the missionary families and organizations we'd helped support since I became the official outreach pastor just over five years ago.

"That report, though . . ." Gavin whistled low. "It was impressive, bro. I overheard a couple of our elders say the same. You should feel good about what you accomplished, regardless of who wasn't there to hear it. Though I'm sure PC will hear all about it. You presented a great case for the ministries you've helped establish and gain independence." His shook his head, chuckled. "Maybe even too good a case."

"Meaning what?"

He shrugged and kicked the ball up to his hands, spinning it on his pointer finger before passing it off seamlessly to his opposite hand. "Just that you've met more goals in full-time ministry than most pastors I know, and you're not even thirty yet. You're like some kind of Energizer Bunny—always *going, going, going.*"

"Yeah, well, I'm afraid I won't be *going* anywhere for a while." Not if I stuck around here, anyway. "Curtis grounded my entire department, remember?"

Gavin's expression dipped from confident to chagrined in a matter of seconds. "Yeah, I know. That's tough." He stopped the spinning ball and raked his free hand through his forest of spiked hair. "It will be weird—you sticking closer to the office for a while. Don't get me wrong, I believe in PC's vision about focusing our resources on our local community while we're in this economic downturn, but I haven't known you to stay put for longer than a month or so at a time."

"Yeah," was all I could say in response as I tugged off my shirt and slipped on a fresh one. Because he wasn't wrong. I'd never imagined staying put for longer than a month—not when there was a world of needs waiting to be met, to be reached, to be served. My travel schedule had been a perfectly timed rotation of comings and goings for the last several years. A mix of new and old. Of service projects in Haiti with a team of parents and teens, followed by care package deliveries to faithful families in places lacking in basic supplies. If I wasn't planning a trip, I was likely getting ready to leave for one or just getting back from one. But the idea of "sticking closer to home for a while" because of some kind of local vision strategy pushed by Curtis didn't sit right with me. Few things did these days.

I'd written something similar to my father just last night, hoping to get a read on the emails I'd sent him last weekend. Email exchanges had been our default method of communication for the last decade, given the constant time change between us. He and my mom were currently on their way to visit several new pastors in Mumbai, following a trip to Hong Kong to do the same. It explained his delay in getting back to me after I'd sent him my résumé. Even still, it was easy to sense his excitement about the possibility of us working toward a common vision, together. For a common purpose. At the same mission organization.

Though my father was encouraging about the change I was contemplating overall, he gave no absolutes on timeline, only rough estimates. *"Some positions can be filled within weeks once they open. Others can take months or even up to a year. There are too many variables to speculate, but having a family connection already in the field should certainly help. You'll want to start acquiring letters of recommendation from the various ministries you've worked in now. That can also help cut down on training time—another plus."*

In our final back-and-forth exchange sometime around midnight my time last night, he did ask me to be open to broadening my vi-sion from Mexico to include all of Central America. *"Expanding the region can get you on the ground with us sooner, son. Give me the word, and I'll adjust your application."*

I hadn't answered him back yet. Mostly, because I didn't have an answer to give him yet.

A gnawing guilt ate away at my conscience, and I knew why. I hadn't told Rev about any of this yet—nothing about my home-coming since visiting the Romeros in Acajete, and certainly not about the pending decision to leave my home church and go to work for my father. And seeing as I'd met with my mentor—or at the very least, spoken to him—nearly every week since my parents first went overseas when I was a teenager, this wasn't the norm for us. And his voicemails and text messages revealed he knew it as much as I did. But something was still holding me back. Something I wasn't quite ready—or willing—to pinpoint.

"At least things around here are finally beginning to stabilize," Gavin said with something like relief. My brain took a hard right, then slammed to a stop.

This was where Gavin and I differed the most. Not on issues of theology or doctrine or even on the ways we chose to burn off steam in a gym. But when my world had been rocked by the take-over of a man I'd disliked since adolescence, Gavin's world had remained stable. Unaffected. If anything, the youth department had only benefited from Curtis's recklessness.

The flashier the upgrade to lights, sound systems, and lobby furnishings, the more interested the youth in our community be-came. And more youth meant more parents. And more parents meant more committed revenue.

"Not sure everybody sees it that way," I said, knowing he was looking at one of them.

"Maybe not. But it's how I'm choosing to see it. If I don't believe God's church can heal from the wounds inflicted on it by flawed human beings, then what place do I have preaching to a bunch of kids who want to believe in something bigger than themselves?"

I couldn't disagree with him. And even if I could, I wouldn't. Gavin was as loyal as he was peaceable. The same way I knew he would never willingly wrong me, I also knew he would never cross the line when it came to pushing back against Curtis. There was so much more at stake for him. So much more for him to lose. He had a wife and three daughters to support on his salary, plus hundreds of students in a ministry looking to him as their leader. Truth was, the only person who would be affected by my decision to leave Salt and Light and Pastor Curtis J. Archer would be me and me alone.

Gavin cleared his throat, breaking the last of my unwanted introspection for the day and pointing to the exit doors. A reasonable lunch break had ended a while ago. "Anyway . . . you're still up for helping with Dude Camp this summer, right?"

The question jolted a new and welcome train of thought as I remembered Kadin and Tucker standing next to me in Val's apartment last week. "I wouldn't miss it." Dude Camp was the highlight of my summer, and no matter what happened with my dad and his church-planting organization, I'd make it a top priority. I wished I could have done something similar with my own father at that age. It was an honor to act as a stand-in dad for a group of boys who wished for the same.

We pushed out the door and toward the stairs, leading to the offices. "Where are you at on registrations and scholarships?" I asked.

"Hovering about the eighty-five percent mark, I think. Why?"

"I have a couple boys in my neighborhood who are interested."

"That's great," Gavin said, using the voice every dynamic youth pastor on earth possessed.

"Yeah, I think it would be good for both of them. You remember Kadin? The kid raised by his grandma in the big farmhouse on my street?"

He pondered my question for a second, but I could tell the instant he placed him. Gavin had a photographic memory when it came to the students he served. It's what made him one of the best in his field. Even now, with close to six hundred kids in his ministry, if Gavin had a face-to-face interaction with a student, he rarely forgot them. "Yeah, I do. Red hair, kind of scrawny. Likes skateboards, right? He needs a scholarship?"

I nodded, my thoughts moving on to Tucker and his overzealous excitement at the mention of Dude Camp . . . before I recalled Val's hesitant face. Had money been the reason behind her reluctance? Or had it been something else? "I'm not sure yet about the other kid, though. I'm just getting to know him. His name is Tucker. His mom is a good friend of Molly's. They're renting the apartment from me."

Gavin's expression morphed into something far more expressive than I'd been anticipating. "You're renting to a single mom?"

I shrugged as if Val and Tucker had been one in a sea of many mother-son duos I'd rented to. "Yeah. Her rental fell through right before she moved to town. The timing worked out for us both."

My mind found its way back to Val, the way it did every time I took a break from financial reports or mission application preferences. I thought about the timing of hearing her on the stairs yesterday just as I'd stepped onto my patio, of the way ice had shot through my veins at the sound of loose cardboard hitting the ground, of the way her eyes had silently pleaded with mine to let the incident go without a word. And then, I recalled a new sequence, pausing on the way her petite mouth had curved into a shy smile as she toasted our Mexican Coke day.

Gavin studied me a second more. "Hmm."

"What?"

His face was coy, yet his tone was anything but. "Nothing. Nothing at all. But I do know a thing or two about single moms, you know, if you ever need any advice."

I chose not to touch that particular bait. While many in my professional circles understood my convictions on staying single for the sake of my ministry, Gavin had never been fully on board. After all, he hadn't met Nicky until he was thirty-one.

"So should I get that scholarship form from Erika, then?"

And just like that, his amusement sobered. "Erika was let go." He shook his head, likely recalling how he'd been the one to give her a job straight out of high school as the youth administrative assistant. "Sorry, I didn't realize you hadn't heard. But yeah, it happened while you were in Mexico. Her position had already gone down to part time so . . ." The dangling end of that sentence didn't need to be finished.

"Where did all her responsibilities with student ministries go?"

"They were consolidated," he said plainly. "But I'll make sure you get the form."

Consolidated. More lingo that had come after the transition in power. "Fine. Thanks."

"Just let me know if you need me to sign off on anything. I'm glad Kadin's coming back—and bringing a friend with him." Gavin turned toward his office, taking note of his smartwatch. "I've gotta head out early today. Zoey has an end-of-the-year preschool sing-along with her class. I'm picking up the big girls from school on my way over. They didn't want to miss it." He laughed. "There's nothing sweeter than a bunch of four-year-olds singing off-key and out of sync." He unlocked his door and pointed at me. "Let's do coffee soon to discuss Dude Camp deets. I'll buy."

"Sounds good."

He had almost disappeared behind his door when I said, "Gavin?"

"Yeah?"

"Give Zoey a congratulatory high five for me."

He smiled. "Will do."

∞∞∞

My first stop on the way home was to the hardware store for some anti-slip grip strips. I planned to tack them on this evening before I fixed that burned-out floodlight. Not surprisingly, Tucker was waiting in the driveway ready to greet me before I even placed my car in park.

"Hey, dude." I reached into my back seat for the hardware bags.

Tucker held his hand out to take one from me. "Guess what?"

"What?" I asked, already smiling at the excitement in his voice. The kid was like a constant confetti cannon. Maybe I should bring him with me to the church office sometime. Everyone I knew could use a little Tucker-sized enthusiasm in their life.

"We *almost* bought a car today."

"Oh, really?" I asked, feeling a niggle of something I couldn't quite identify. Though Val had assured me she was fine car hunting on her own, I'd reached out to my used car contact in the area for a list of current inventory, which I'd been planning to casually forward on to her tonight. Via email. Since I still didn't have her phone number. Sure, I could just ask Molly for it, but experience had taught me that the less Molly was involved in my living arrangement with Val, the better. "Was something wrong with it?"

"Mom said it smelled too much like cigarette smoke. She hates that smell, even though I told her Pop's shop smells a bit like that, too. But she says it's a different smell." Tucker shrugged. "So, we didn't buy it. But Mom did buy us ice cream cones, so I'm fine if it takes a while longer."

"Because you'll get more ice cream cones that way?"

Tucker nodded, unabashedly. "Yep."

I chuckled and headed to the staircase. Tucker followed. We only had an hour or so of daylight left, so despite my rumbling stomach, I needed to work on the stairway first before I went in search of sustenance.

But by the time I reached the bottom step, the smell of fresh garlic and sautéed onion taunted me through the open windows of Val's apartment. Whatever she was cooking up there would far surpass whatever I'd find in my desolate pantry.

"So besides almost getting a car today, what else have you been up to?" I asked Tucker after I retrieved my toolbox from the small shed at the side of the house.

Tucker skipped over my question with one of his own. "Are you going to build something, Miles? Need help?"

"Not building anything, but I could use your help. Want to separate these traction strips for me?"

"Sure, I can do that. I helped my pop a lot in Alaska. He let me use his tools, too. Even his special ones." Tucker plopped the hardware bags on the ground and rummaged through them to collect the tack strips. "And today Kadin and I were farmhands for Grandma Millie. My mom met her this morning, and she says I can go over there after dinner once I'm done with my chores. We just have to play outside."

I smiled. "I'm glad you and Kadin are getting along so well."

"I've never had a neighbor my age before."

It took some work to control my expression. "No?"

He shook his head. "Nope. Only old people lived near us in Alaska. And Ruby."

"And Ruby is . . ."

"A dog. But not *our* dog. She's more like a shared dog. Everybody knows she likes my pop best, though. He feeds her bear jerky in his shop. But I'm not supposed to tell the other neighbors that."

"Right." I laughed. This kid was something else.

"I wouldn't trade Ruby for Maple Syrup, though. Even if she is mostly blind."

At this admission, my laugh deepened. Gosh, after a day trapped at the office, Tucker was the best remedy.

Val cracked open the door at the top of the stairs, releasing even more of that delicious aroma into the atmosphere. "Everything okay out here? Tuck, are you giving Miles space like we talked about?"

But before I could answer that he was more than okay, my stomach growled with a ferocity that sent Tucker howling.

"Whoa!" He pointed at my abdomen. "Was that your stomach?"

"Sure was. Whatever your mom's making up there smells amazing." I glanced up at Val with a smile before addressing Tucker once more. "You're lucky to have such a good cook for a mom."

"She's a super good cook! My pop says she's better than my gram, but I'm not supposed to say that where she can ever hear it."

An ongoing theme with him it would seem.

I held the first step strip in my closed fist instead of prepping to adhere it.

"What are you two up to down there?" Val asked with a crinkled brow. She stepped onto the edge of the landing and my pulse spiked. Though Val was a grown woman who had likely navigated hundreds of staircases without issue, I couldn't stop seeing that cardboard heap at the bottom of the stairs, grateful it hadn't been Val. Still, if there was anything I could do to prevent a misstep, I'd do it without hesitation.

I glanced at Tuck, wondering if I, too, should have done like his pop and asked him not to reveal all the details of our work efforts today.

Tucker held up the strips. "We're putting these things on the stairs."

Too late.

I definitely wasn't a believer in asking a kid to hold an adult's secret, but with Tucker, a case could be made for the contrary.

Before he could say more, I cut in. "I've actually been meaning to replace the old traction strips for a while now. Figured if I was changing out the floodlight, I might as well replace the grip strips, too. The extra traction will be good for the winter months."

But since it was only the start of June and snow wouldn't be back until late November, my lame explanation fooled nobody. Val was too smart not to connect the dots.

She was quiet for the better part of a minute as I imagined her filtering out a dozen possible replies, most of which would include calling me out for doing exactly what she'd asked me not to do: give her special treatment.

But then she surprised me and said, "If you don't already have other plans tonight, you're welcome to join us for dinner, Miles. It will be ready in about fifteen minutes."

I lifted my gaze to the top stair, scanning her old-school style black-and-white Vans, purposely frayed jeans, and black T-shirt with the words *Be a Gold Digger* printed in yellow across the front with a small white logo for her parents' souvenir shop stamped underneath.

I smiled at the clever pun, ninety-nine percent certain she was the designer behind it. "Then you can bet we'll be finished in fourteen."

9

Val

I'd had a few out-of-body experiences in my life—though most of them had been in the context of a crisis. Still, the fact that I'd just invited Miles to dinner was nearly as surreal as the fact that I was no closer to solving Gwen's question than I was when she asked it. And the truth was that without Miles's Mexican-Coke-on-the-patio chat yesterday, I likely wouldn't have gone back for that last interview at all. It was only right that I offer him a hot dinner, especially after I'd heard the rumble of his stomach from twelve stairs up.

Twelve stairs that now boasted sandpapered steps for reasons I could easily guess, given the initial look of panic on his face yesterday when he saw the cardboard on the ground. He wasn't wrong to add the grip strips. He was a landlord and I was a liability. I wouldn't fault him for taking precautions.

I stirred the cream-based Alfredo sauce I'd made from scratch and checked on the garlic bread broiling in the oven. Contrary to what my dad insisted, I held no culinary superpowers. I wasn't a highly skilled chef by any stretch of the imagination; I simply enjoyed the preparations of a home-cooked meal. And for whatever reason, something about the process of seasoning and tasting, stirring and sautéing, forced a part of my brain to function that was otherwise dormant. And I needed all my cylinders firing if I was going to come up with a semi-intelligent answer for Lady Gwen's story riddle.

What's a storyline that has never been told?

I glanced at the question I'd rewritten on a three-by-five card an hour earlier in black Sharpie, as if I could somehow trick my mind into seeing it with virgin eyes. Despite hours spent Googling uncommon tropes, story premises, and skimming blogs written by best-selling authors, I'd so far found nothing that felt like an answer Lady Gwen would accept.

In our brief time together, I knew she wasn't the kind of person who'd want a quote from a story craft textbook. She wanted original. Fresh. Real. And yet . . . I had no idea how to give her that.

Tucker pushed the door open wide and waved our landlord inside as if this was all routine—the two of us sitting down for a home-cooked dinner with a man who wasn't related to us.

Miles chuckled but remained a step outside the door, his head peeking around the doorjamb as he eyed the wooden spoon in my hand. "Is it safe? I know better than to pass this threshold without asking permission first while you're holding a potential weapon."

"It's safe," I assured him, smiling as tiny pricks of heat warmed my cheeks. "This spoon will only be used for cooking tonight. Promise."

"I might need to get that in writing." He lifted his palms as he entered and turned his wrists midair. "Mind if I wash up in the bathroom and then help set the table? Or whatever else needs to be done before that goodness you're cooking over there is plated."

"Actually, everything is pretty much ready. Tucker can set the table."

"I think it's only fair that I repay Tucker for his help downstairs by doing at least one of his chores."

"You want to do my chores?" Tuck asked in awe as he raced to wash his own hands in the kitchen sink.

"Why not? You helped me outside with some tough man labor, didn't you?"

Tuck nodded as Miles made his way to the restroom in the hall. Once again, I was struck by Miles's ability to engage in several levels of conversation at once as if there was nothing to it at all. As if there was nothing that caused him to feel how I felt ninety percent of the time around people I hadn't known my entire life: awkward.

"My chore list is on the fridge!" Tucker called through the apartment as if it were the ten-thousand-square-foot manor Molly and Silas ran their youth program from and not our one-thousand-square-foot apartment.

"Tucker," I said in a low voice only he could hear. "Miles is just being polite. You can do your own chores, including setting the table."

"Yes, ma'am."

"What's a storyline that has never been told?"

I whipped around, nearly knocking into Miles, who was now staring over the top of my head at the note tacked to my fridge.

"I'm guessing that's not Tucker's chore list," he added.

Tucker, who was gathering utensils on the opposite side of the kitchen, snorted with laughter. "Nope, that's not my chores, that's my mom's test. She's having an important call with a famous film lady who makes movies. But not any movies I've seen. I already asked."

I closed my eyes, regretting not asking Tucker to keep that tidbit of information to himself.

"A film director? Wow," Miles said, his eyes dipping to mine.

"Mom makes documentaries sometimes when she's not doing her other jobs."

"No," I corrected, tapping the spoon to the side of the stainless steel pot and turning the burner off, though the burner in my cheeks remained on high. "I don't actually make documentaries, it's just a hobby I—"

"I remember the video you created for The Bridge last fall. It was excellent. I think I must have shared it from all of Salt and Light's social media platforms. Have you made others?"

"Nothing professionally, no. I just—"

"Mom's getting a job that doesn't pay money. It just pays experience. Unless she wins the big contest, and then she'll get *lots and lots* of money. I really hope she does, too, because she promised to take me to a rodeo. Have you ever been to a real rodeo, Miles?"

Appearing whiplashed by my son's incessant need to overshare our personal business, Miles looked between us. "Uh, no, Tuck," he said slowly. "I don't think I have been to a real rodeo before. But I also haven't been invited to dinner by a host with such a fascinating career opportunity."

"Oh, it's really not. I'm not even sure what will come of it yet." I shook my head and shot a side-eye at one blissfully unaware Tucker, who was now gathering placemats from the lone shelf in the not-an-active-elevator closet. "It's just a film mentorship that culminates with a film project." I paused from lifting the pot off the burner and looked at him. "But you shouldn't be concerned; I have plenty of other paying jobs to cover rent."

As I poured the cream sauce over the drained pasta noodles, the oven timer beeped.

"I'm not concerned in the slightest, Val." He winked as he slid a potholder onto his hand, and something inside me seemed to combust as he did. "Can I take something out of here for you?"

"That's our bread."

"Perfect." He opened the door, and a waft of buttery garlic filled the kitchen as he reached inside for the baking sheet. "So you were saying something more about the mentorship? Also, does the film project happen to be code for film *contest*?"

I couldn't help but smile at his none-too-sly tactics. I hadn't planned on saying anything more about the mentorship or the contest, and yet he was studying me as if we were several layers deep into a conversational lasagna. I focused on my pasta, finding it less invasive to share these details if I wasn't making direct eye contact with him. "It's more of an intensive creative program for novice filmmakers hoping to advance to something more . . . professional." I mixed the pasta in with the sauce, feeling the weight of his gaze on my profile. "It's through Volkin Film Academy in Hollywood, which is why the interest is higher than for other programs and why the prize package is larger than other film contests out there. But the real draw for me is the opportunity to be coached one-on-one by a professional within the industry. That kind of experience is . . . almost unheard of."

It was only because of Miles's lack of response that I shot a quick glance in his direction. He stared unabashedly. "Sorry." He shook his head. "That's just . . . that sounds really impressive. To be selected and coached one-on-one, you must have beat out quite a few candidates. Hundreds? Thousands?"

"Thousands!" Tucker all but shouted. "Pops told me this morning that Mom beat out thousands and that I should be super proud of her."

The tips of my ears were now completely aflame as Miles continued to stare. "I think your pop's right, Tuck."

I cleared my throat. "I still have one last hurdle to go before anything's official."

He pointed at the question on the fridge. "Does it involve that?"

"Yes."

"Is it supposed to be a riddle?"

I laughed. "I think so, actually."

I went to lift the pasta bowl, but Miles's hands were there first. "I got it. I'm guessing you'd like this on the table?"

"Yes, thank you."

As I placed the bread in a serving bowl, I mentioned that I also had a small chopped salad in the fridge.

Miles didn't wait for an implicit ask, he simply opened the fridge, took out the salad bowl, and set it next to the pasta as Tucker finished filling the glasses with ice water. We moved to sit at the table together, and Miles pulled out my chair before taking a seat of his own beside me. He reached for the bread bowl and passed it to me. But Tucker had already bowed his head and clasped his hands.

"Oh, sorry." Miles set the bowl down. "Go ahead."

Miles met my eyes, and I smiled as Tucker prayed for our dinner and, naturally, for me to win the film competition so that we could go to a real rodeo someday.

"Thank you for the prayer, Tucker," Miles said as he finished.

Tucker took a slice of bread and chomped on it without bothering to add anything else to his plate. "We never used to pray," he announced to our dinner guest, who happened to also be a pastor. My skin flashed seven shades of pink. "But now we do, because Mom says it's good to talk to God, especially when He gives us good things. Like pasta."

Miles nodded at him without missing a beat. "Your mom's a very wise lady." He grinned at me. "And a fabulous chef, too. This dinner smells divine. Any other secret hobbies you'd like to share?" He filled his plate with pasta, salad, and bread, and made no effort to conceal his approval over every bite.

"No," I said, lifting my fork and twirling my pasta round and round. "I'm afraid not."

Miles looked unconvinced as he chewed and swallowed. He took a sip of his water and then asked, "Any promising leads on a car yet?"

I shot Tucker a suspicious glance. Had he told Miles about our failed attempt at car-buying today? I would need to start specifying shareable and non-shareable information.

"Not many, no. It appears the inventory is low for quality cars in our price range."

"May I ask what price range you're looking in?" At my hesitation, he added, "I think I mentioned that I have a good friend who's a car dealer and often gets incredible deals at auctions. I've owned several of his finds and have even dabbled in some car flipping from time to time on my own. He's reliable, and he can work with almost any price range."

Once again, Miles had attempted to smooth over my worries

in a matter of seconds. Though I'd had every intention of finding a car on my own, he appeared eager to assist. And for the life of me, I couldn't understand why. I played the scenario all the way out in my mind—what was the harm of involving him? Even if I gave him our information, it wouldn't automatically mean he would find something for us. And if he did, it wouldn't mean anything more than if I'd gone directly to a dealer. *This is Miles*, I coached myself. *Molly's brother. You can trust him.*

"All right," I said, "but it's okay if nothing turns up. I know what I'm asking for is hard to find in our budget." Without smelling like the bottom of an ashtray, that was.

I rattled off the details, and he simply slipped out his phone and shot off a text to his friend, clarifying a few specifications with me and asking for my phone number, which he added to his contacts. "I bet old Bill can find us something. He's good people."

Us. The word stood out as I tore off the corner of my bread.

"Can't tell you how many times his expertise has kept me out of trouble."

Miles didn't seem like the kind of guy who ever got into trouble. He was thoughtful, kind, respectful, and dedicated to a profession of helping others. Certainly not a classic recipe for disaster.

After a few moments of contemplative chewing, Miles took a drink of water and then enthusiastically exclaimed, "This might be the best home-cooked meal I've eaten in years. And I recently ate some highly reputable pork tamales in Mexico."

"You've been to Mexico?" Tucker's eyes grew wide. "Do you speak Spanish?"

"*Un poquito.*" Miles drew his pointer finger and thumb together. "Just a little bit."

"When is your next trip?" I asked before taking a bite of my salad.

Miles's expression slacked slightly. "I actually won't be heading out anywhere for a while."

A myriad of curious questions ribboned through my mind—had

his role at the church changed? Was there some sort of personal reason behind such a statement?

Miles set his napkin down and studied my face. "So what do you think the answer is?"

I blinked. "The answer?"

"To your riddle." He pointed behind me at the fridge.

"Oh." I shook my head, switching mental gears completely and debating on how best to respond. "Honestly, I'm not sure. I've come at it from every angle I know of. I've looked at individual premises and tropes, and I've also tried to combine concepts and then dissect them again. But instinctively, nothing feels quite right yet."

"What do you know about the person asking the question?"

I thought for a moment. "Her name is Gwen Chilton. She's been in the film industry for decades—television, movies, screenplay writing. She moved in the direction of independent films and documentaries a handful of years ago. Gwen definitely has her own methods and way of thinking."

"So when she talks to you, do you get the feeling she's more interested in testing what you know or learning about the way you think?"

Another intelligent question. "Definitely the latter."

"Mom, can I have two more bites of pasta and be done? I promised Kadin I'd help him feed the animals after dinner." I checked Tucker's mostly finished dinner and nodded, all while Miles loaded another round of food on his plate, only he didn't touch any of it right away. His gaze came back to me first.

"I have this older friend who loves to ask questions. And he's good at it—I suppose with his age and experience, he should be. But almost always, when he asks me a question, he doesn't want me to just show up at the destination with the right answer. He wants to listen to me jog a few laps around the track first, take a few detours, and then trace back my steps for him."

I took a sip of water, pondering that. "So maybe her question is more abstract than literal."

He shrugged. "Maybe."

Though I wanted my mind to race forward again toward the resolution of an answer, I forced myself to slow down. To take apart the question little by little.

"Your pasta's getting cold." Miles pointed at my plate with the prongs of his fork.

"It's okay," I said, my mind still stuck on the problem at hand. "I make this dish a lot."

"Then I hope I'm lucky enough to receive an invite the next time it's on the menu, because this is last-meal good, Val." His attentive gaze caused a forbidden flutter to swirl inside me. "Also," he announced with a smile, "I say we break this riddle down step by step. We'll tackle it together."

I shook my head. "I'm sure you have better things to do with your evening."

"I promise you," he said, eyes still intent on mine, "this is by far the best use of my time all day."

The high-pitched scrape of Tucker's chair against the flooring snapped my attention away from the handsome man at my table. Before my son excused himself, he patted Miles on the arm and made sure to let him know that dinner cleanup was also one of his chores.

With a gleam in his eye, Miles considered this new information. "I think dish duty is a fair trade, especially since I wasn't much help with setting the table."

"Miles, you do not have to do the—"

"I made a deal with Tucker," he said without missing a beat. "And I intend to keep my word, unless there's a reason I shouldn't?"

Slowly, I gave in and shook my head.

Tucker smiled and kissed me on the check. "Bye, Mom."

I pulled him back to look him in the eyes. "I want you home before dark, okay?"

"Got it." He planted another kiss on my opposite cheek. "See ya."

And just like that, he was out the door and headed down the steps.

Miles turned back to me. "He's a great kid."

Warmth blossomed in my chest. "He is."

"Now." Miles looked back at me. "Where were we?"

I took a deep breath. "A storyline that has never been told," I said slowly. "If it's not about genre or plot or hook or trope . . . then I need to zoom out further."

Miles nodded, eating once again with no sign of stopping.

"Which means I need to focus less on the story itself and maybe more on the telling of it."

"Good." He pointed to me with his fork. "Explore that idea. How *are* stories told?"

I pressed my lips together, thinking. "There are numerous story mediums in our world—oral, written, those portrayed through the arts like theater, paint, and film. But so many of those stories are just different combinations of the same key ideas that have been regrouped and retold for thousands of years. Basic plot lines with a unique twist. A classic storyline with some original flare. I mean, look at the holiday romance movies that come out every fall. You can pretty much guess what's going to happen in every scene, yet if there's a new title and a new cast of actors, we turn them on."

"Speak for yourself. I'll live contentedly for the rest of my days knowing that Silas will be the one subjected to Molly's holiday movie obsession from now on." Miles leaned back in his chair and glanced up at the ceiling. "So if stories are just combinations of different plot points—then what's the key difference in them all?"

I tapped my leg with my fingers, running piano scales on my kneecaps though I'd never played an instrument a day in my life. My eyes snapped back to his. "The storyteller."

His face opened, his green eyes dancing with a delight I was certain my own face expressed.

The words came slowly but steadily as the thought worked itself out in my head. "Every story is original not because of the plot . . . but because each storyteller behind the pen or camera or canvas has an original perspective."

"Sounds like you cracked it, Sherlock."

A bit stunned, I blinked up at him. "Do you think that could be it—where Gwen wanted me to get to?"

"I think it'd better be it, because that's too good an answer to waste."

At his generous assessment, my shoulders began to relax.

"Your call is Friday?"

"Yes," I answered. "In the evening."

"Well, here's hoping for a round of celebration ice cream. I owe you."

"I think I'm the one who owes you," I confessed. "I'm not sure I would have gotten to that conclusion without your prompts."

"Does that mean I'm Watson in this whole scenario?"

I laughed. "Sure."

Miles's kind eyes swept my face as I made a move to finally take a bite of my pasta.

He stuck out his hand. "Don't do it." He pushed his chair out from the table and stood up. "Let me warm that up for you."

"I eat cold food often. I'm a mom, remember? I don't mind it."

He continued to hold out his hand as if any future argument would be promptly dismissed. "If there's one appliance I know how to work, it's the microwave. Don't rob me of my only talent in the kitchen."

His eyes pleaded with me to release my hold on the plate. "If you insist."

He gave a slight bow. "I most definitely do."

◇◇◇

After eating my warmed helping of pasta and failing to dissuade Miles from loading the dishwasher and wiping down the table and countertops, he walked over to my workstation, hands tucked inside his pockets, and scanned the monitor, laptop, hard drive, and other organized tech paraphernalia. "You know, when I first saw this setup, I wondered if you secretly worked for NASA. But now it all makes sense. You're not a secret spacecraft engineer, you're a secret filmmaker." He rotated to shoot a glance at me over his right shoulder while I propped myself on the arm of the sofa, facing the large picture window where I could just make out Tucker and Kadin sitting on the fence in the last winks of daylight. "Did Molly ever tell you my nickname for you?"

My attention turned from the two boys back to Miles. I couldn't possibly have heard him correctly. "What?"

"Video Val."

"Video Val?" I repeated, likely sounding as stupefied as I felt.

He nodded once. "When Molly first told me she hired you as her virtual assistant to help with her channels, I wasn't sure you were actually real."

"Real as in . . . *human*?"

He laughed sheepishly, causing the corners of his eyes to crinkle all the more. "I almost had her convinced you were some sort of AI. I kept the joke up for a long time, but it became increasingly more difficult to sway her when she started referring to you as her best friend." He gave me a lopsided grin. "But I'll confess that before she met Silas and the residents at The Bridge, there was a small part of me that worried she might have invented you."

"Well, to your credit, it was probably strange to hear your sister talk about some random woman in Alaska she'd only ever seen through a screen."

"Right. And I'm sure you've noticed that Molly sometimes has a tendency to . . . exaggerate details."

"Really? I hadn't noticed that, no," I teased back.

His gaze stilled on me then, and something I couldn't identify stilled inside me right along with it. "Although this time, I think her description of you has been pretty much spot on from the beginning."

"Because I'm not actually a robot trying to take over the world?"

"That could be part of it." He rotated to face me fully, offering me a lopsided smile before clearing his throat. "I, uh, I never got a chance to tell you this at the wedding. But thank you for being such a loyal friend to her, especially through all the challenges she dealt with last year. It's not difficult to see why she fought so hard to get you here."

My throat tightened at his unexpected compliment. And yet . . . I couldn't help but feel the weight of his words press against my conscience. "Her friendship has meant a lot to me, too." I hadn't quite figured out how to tell Molly about the opportunity with Essence of Filmmakers. There was little I kept from her, and yet the balance between friend and employee was always an interesting one to navigate.

He raked a hand through his hair and tipped his head toward my desk. "I should probably give you back your evening. I'm sure you have plenty of top secret filmmaker things to get to on this computer." He winked. "Thanks again for dinner. I'll let you know what I hear from Bill, the car guy."

"Oh, sure. Thanks," I said, with the strangest desire to ask him to stay longer, or perhaps to give him a reason to want to stay longer. Why hadn't I made dessert? Or at least bought a carton of ice cream?

On his way to the door, he stopped at my bookshelf and tapped on the spine of a book I'd been slowly trekking my way through for weeks now.

"*The Four Branches of Systematic Theology*," Miles said with a hint of something I couldn't discern. He twisted to look at me. "You reading this?"

"I'm only about halfway through it. It's not exactly a light read."

Miles laughed openly. "That has to be the understatement of the year. I read this in seminary. It was brutal."

Heat crept up my neck at the thought of Miles asking me my take on any one of the heady contemplations in that text. Truth was, I'd purchased the book out of curiosity more than anything. After watching Molly's transformation last fall, I wanted to have a better grasp on the faith she'd grown up with. And though I'd been watching Pastor Curtis preach online each Sunday at Salt and Light for the last seven months, I wanted to know more. So when I'd researched several theological websites on doctrines and foundational truths and this book had been mentioned as an "exhaustive approach to explaining the fundamentals of the Christian faith," I'd purchased it.

So far, though, it had just been pretty exhausting. Period.

He pursed his lips together for a moment before speaking. "I know I've already established that I can't cook and that any Watson-like abilities I may have exhibited here tonight are limited at best, but I do have quite a few books on apologetics. You're welcome to any of them."

"I really appreciate that. Thank you."

With a single bob of his head, he reached for the doorknob. "I'll be praying for your talk with Gwen."

And though I'd heard that phrase spoken flippantly dozens of times in my life, when Miles told me he'd be praying for me . . . I believed it.

· 10 ·

Miles

It was rare for me to spend much time inside the church office, as the dust on my desk and bookshelves would attest. But even after my cubicle was promoted to a window office with an actual door shortly before the turnover in leadership, I hadn't frequented this space much at all. I preferred to be out with people, living life and doing ministry together as a partnership.

Only two and a half hours had passed since I'd arrived this morning, and already I felt like a squirrel in a cage. The desk work I usually slated for slower Thursday afternoons was finished by ten, as were the phone calls I usually saved for when I was commuting.

All with the exception of one call—Rev. I still hadn't called him back. And he'd left me two more voicemails.

I knew I needed to fill him in on what had been going on since Mexico . . . and yet, if I filled him in, I'd have to put into words the reality of my current situation: My role here had changed, and I wasn't sure when or *if* it would ever change back.

Or even if I wanted it to, given the circumstances.

I dragged my finger along the spines of my books, searching for a title that had come to mind late last night as I tossed in bed, replaying my conversation with Val. A smile tugged at my mouth at the mental image of her casually leafing through the pages of a hardback book that had nearly cost me my degree. Of all the books in the world to glean insight from, she'd chosen one on systematic theology. I shook my head, half chuckling to myself, half groaning. By Molly's account, Val's faith journey had gained significant traction over the course of the last eight months, but she still preferred to check things out from a manageable distance. A consistent quality I'd come to expect from my upstairs neighbor.

The harsh double-tone alert from the speaker of my desk phone paused my bookshelf perusal.

"Pastor Miles? Sorry to interrupt. Do you have a moment?"

"Yes, that's okay. Hello, Sue."

"Hello. Pastor Curtis has requested a meeting with you in his office this morning. And from what I can see, your schedule is . . . fairly open today. Can I book you for an eleven o'clock with him?"

My jaw clamped down hard as I glanced up at the clock. Fifteen minutes. "Sure, that works. Thank you."

"My pleasure." The speaker clicked off.

So Curtis hadn't canned Susan yet. *Good.* She'd been his father's secretary, as well as one of the original church planters for Salt and Light nearly thirty years ago.

I crouched lower to the ground, continuing my search for the title. Had I loaned it to Gavin? But just as I was about to stand, I saw the worn red spine I'd been hunting for. I slid the book under the flap of my satchel and then stopped to say a prayer for Val. For her interview, for her nerves, and ultimately, for the faith journey she'd embarked on.

Two steps out of my office door, I felt the distinct pull to go back inside and pray for my eleven o'clock meeting with Curtis.

I should have listened.

◇◇◇

"Miles," Pastor Curtis said in a tone reminiscent of our youth. Only those days were a long, long time ago. "It's great to see you."

He stuck out his hand as I walked into the office and glanced at the man seated to his right. A man Gavin referred to as Curtis's personal IRS agent. Leonard had been hired in from the outside as some sort of leadership coach. I wasn't sure of the exact title he held, but he was rarely seen anywhere in the building without Curtis. And that only added to the inner-office chatter pertaining to what his actual role was within Salt and Light, though many believed he was the number cruncher behind the majority of our budget cuts this last year. In the simplest of terms, Leonard was our bailout plan.

"Pastor. Leonard." I shook each of their hands and took a seat in one of the new white modern chairs in his office.

Curtis sat and relaxed in his chair behind his desk. He had on his usual dark muscle T-shirt and high-end denim, a brand I'd never heard of much less knew where to buy. Though the man had fathered three children by his thirtieth birthday, there wasn't a trace of the "dad bod" that men in our circles joked about. I supposed the post-workout protein drink on his desk made sure of that. "I trust your trip south of the border went well? Refreshing, I hope. I'd love to take Brenna to Cabo someday, but that's a bit complicated with the kids." He smiled. "Trying to plan a week away anywhere without children requires almost more preparation than it's worth."

"I wouldn't really know." About any of the subjects he spoke about. Marriage, children, Cabo. The closest town we'd served as a church was nowhere close to that oceanfront resort city. But instead of saying any of that, I took a lesson from Val and filtered, filtered, filtered. "But Mexico is a unique place with special people."

"Yes, and we're thrilled Salt and Light could play such a positive role there for as long as we have," Curtis said, leaning forward on his forearms. "We've appreciated your dedication to so many families and ministries abroad, Miles. The Ramirez family included." He flashed his post-Invisalign smile at me. "By the sounds of it, the debrief report you gave the staff yesterday was quite impressive. I'm sorry to have missed it."

"It's Romero," I corrected.

"I'm sorry?"

"The *Romero* family is who we've supported as a church in Mexico."

"Oh, right, yes. Sorry." At least he had the decency to look slightly embarrassed at his slipup before he turned to reach for a printed document attached to the clipboard Leonard was never seen without. "We actually received quite an affirming email from one of the family members you visited. I thought you might like to hear it. It's from one of their older sons, I believe."

"Alejandro," Leonard supplied.

Something about hearing Alejandro's name spoken so flippantly between these two men caused my core body temperature to rise several degrees. It was one thing to talk about missions as a whole, as a broad category within the confines of a church business meeting. But there was nothing about Alejandro or the Romero family that was generic to me. They weren't names plucked from a church website directory. They were my friends.

Pastor Curtis slipped that dentist billboard smile back on. Rarely did he ever let it fall, at least not in public. But I'd known Curtis J. Archer before he possessed even an ounce of desire to follow in his father's footsteps, much less in Christ's. Years before he'd become a husband to Brenna Lawson and a dad of three. My memory of him as a punk kid bent on pushing the limits without having to pay the price for his many indiscretions was still quite fresh in my mind. Even a decade later.

"'Dear Pastor Curtis Archer,'" he read. "'I pray God, our loving and gracious heavenly Father, blesses you and your church for many generations to come. Our church, La Iglesia del Rey de la Gloria, has been greatly blessed by your faithfulness and by the faithfulness of your fellow servants.

"'Thank you for sending Pastor Miles to us. He has helped my family and our church family for many years. We know God will continue to use him to further the mission of the Gospel and to plant new seeds in new places.

"'All praise be to God. Your humble brother in Christ, Alejandro Romero.'"

Pastor Curtis lowered the email. He watched me as if waiting for my response. But while my lungs remained constricted to the point of pain, there wasn't a chance I would show any amount of vulnerability in this office. I had nothing more to say on this subject. My voice on the importance of missions abroad had been heard and subsequently rejected in meetings just like this time and time again.

But perhaps Alejandro's voice had made a case for himself.

Somewhere around the half-minute mark, the silent game ended and Pastor Curtis spoke. "If only every ministry could be resolved in such a profound and redeeming way. You're welcome to keep this." Paper in hand, he reached across the desk for me to take it. "I hope you see this email the way I do—as a testimony to your faithfulness, Miles. Every minister I know could use these types of hopeful reminders that God is always working out a plan before us and behind us. His faithfulness is evident in your ministry and in your life."

I stared down at Alejandro's words, hearing his voice in my head, seeing that contagious grin in my mind. I wondered whose laptop he'd used to write this. His father's? His uncle's?

I glanced up in time to see a silent exchange of power between the two men sitting across from me.

Leonard was up next.

"As you may have heard, we've been consolidating some positions and responsibilities within the staff as a part of the Equipped for Stewardship plan we began last September. Salt and Light is continuing to do our part to reduce our bottom line and operate out of a place of contentment and gratitude as we seek discernment for God's greater good." His pause caused every hair on the back of my neck to rise. "Due to the recent changes within your position as Salt and Light's outreach pastor, we've concluded that your current ministry load is no longer—"

I didn't wait for him to finish. I turned to Pastor Curtis. "If I'm being laid off, then please tell me outright. I don't need a speech." I'd given my life to this church, to the ministries it had represented locally and abroad, since I was seventeen. I'd grown up here—both physically and spiritually—but I wouldn't be placated. If they were cutting me loose the way they'd done to so many others, then they'd better have the decency to tell it to me straight.

Curtis raised his hand as if that gesture alone could calm me. "You don't need to worry, Miles. We have no plans to let you go. We see you as a valuable team player for the Salt and Light family. Rest assured that every staff member has either had, or will have, a meeting just like this one to assess their current role for both effectiveness and efficiency during our financial restructure. I assure you, your job is not in jeopardy. We're simply asking everyone to make allowances for change as we navigate this new season together." He smiled wider, then nodded to Leonard. "Please continue."

Leonard looked down at the clipboard for what I could only assume was a prompt for the next portion of his statement. He repeated his last line again. "Due to the recent cutbacks and changes in your position as Salt and Light's outreach pastor, we've concluded that your current ministry load is no longer serving you or our team most effectively. After assessing the new flexibility within your schedule, Pastor Curtis, as well as our vision team, has allocated a new ministry to you that we feel will better serve the needs of our local community and church staff during this time. We ask that you be open-minded to these changes and address any concerns in a scheduled follow-up meeting so we can better serve you." Leonard lifted his chin, his expression neutral. "Do you have any questions before we unpack the responsibilities of your new outreach?"

My new outreach.

My gaze cut between them both.

"Yes." I directed my response to my pastor. "I do have questions." Many, in fact.

Pastor Curtis's upbeat expression faltered. "Please, feel free, Miles."

"Is there a reason I wasn't included in a vision-casting meeting regarding a department I've spearheaded for the past five years?"

Leonard opened his mouth to speak, but Curtis signaled otherwise. "Logistics. We met while you were out of the country."

"And if I had been in town, I would have received an invite to join this assessment of my *flexible time*?"

"Not necessarily. Our vision team has worked tirelessly and prayerfully to be as—"

But I didn't wait for him to finish. The blood I'd kept cool for more than a year, as I'd watched the slow demise of our financial accountability and the steady rise of our overall debt as a church, had now grown thick with heat.

I addressed Leonard first. "I don't want to rush the punch line here, but it sounds like after I was told to suspend the majority of our support of ministries abroad—ministries and families we've been in a relationship with for decades, I might add—that now I've come home to a demotion."

Curtis leaned forward, folding his hands. "We don't prefer the term *demotion*, Miles. Your monthly salary will stay the same, but some of your duties, like those of most of our staff, have shifted. I realize that several of the cutbacks we've faced as a church this year have been directly linked to our outgoing support for external service projects, but let me assure you that the outreach department is far from the only department that's been restructured. Every budget change we've made has involved prayer, sacrifice, time, and a significant amount of strategy. The down economy has made things difficult for our church as a whole, but we're determined to find our footing again and come out stronger in record time."

The down economy. Three words that rattled inside my head. The blame had to go somewhere, and *poor financial decisions* certainly didn't preach as well to a congregation as *the down economy* did. My jaw ached as I forced myself to envision the calm and mild manner of Rev and the clearheadedness of my father. Neither of them would let their personal frustrations get in the way of what really mattered. The church. The people. The ministry. But those lines were becoming more and more blurred for me.

"My hope is that you'll find these new opportunities to be surprisingly rewarding if you're willing to give them a chance," Curtis said. "Sometimes change is what we need, even if it's not what we planned for."

Leonard didn't miss a beat. He was ready, guns loaded and safeties off. "Your current position with Salt and Light has transitioned into an outreach position for Riverside Family Resource Center. Your official title will be resident support pastor. You can expect to receive an email with your complete job description and responsibilities within the hour."

"Riverside Family?" I repeated for no other reason than to confirm I hadn't suddenly lost my sense of hearing. "As in, I'll no longer be on staff here—at the church?"

"You'll still be on the payroll as an employee for Salt and Light, but you'll no longer be considered an active staff member at this campus," Leonard said. "If possible, we'd like to see you transition from this office to the Riverside facility by early next week."

Now this was a plot twist I hadn't seen coming.

Pastor Curtis leaned forward to address me again. "I believe your unique skill set and experiences, as well as your knowledge of how to assist people and families in need, will be a blessing to that facility the same way it has been to the families you've served here and abroad. Your experiences have equipped you as a leader, and I hope as a visionary, as well. That's what the center needs most—a renewed vision, a relevant purpose within our community again." He paused, his expression shifting to something momentarily indecipherable. "Whatever you need to make a successful transition there, please don't hesitate to ask. Riverside Family has been an asset in our community for many years, and I'd like to ensure it stays that way."

I slumped back in my chair, trying to recall the last time I'd even stepped foot into that building. It had been at least three years. Before Otto died. And before Pastor Archer Sr. had handed his life's ministry off to his son.

Long ago, Pastor Archer and Otto Matteus's unique partnership had been revered by our community. Otto focused on meeting the physical needs of families in our community, while Pastor Archer provided faithful spiritual leadership and direction. Today, though, Riverside Family Resource Center was little more than a hodgepodge of stale vision. After Otto passed and Pastor Archer retired, the center was grandfathered in as one of Salt and Light's *external* ministries. I'd assumed Riverside had already been placed on the chopping block, since the services they offered there were a depletion of budget, time, and resources—not a gain. Due to some of the more sensitive ministries run out of that facility, Salt and Light had assigned several intern pastors there over the years.

I guess I was now the replacement of an intern.

Yet somehow I wasn't being demoted.

Pastor Curtis stood and reached out his hand to me for a second time. And like a spineless fool, I took it. "I'll be praying for you, Miles."

I wasn't even ten steps outside of his office when I reached for my phone and banged out a follow-up email to my father. Brief and to the point.

> Expand the region on my application to include all of Central America. I'll be ready to act when the time is right.
>
> Miles

And then after five minutes of deep breathing and a stroll through the parking lot, I fired off another text. This time to Rev.

> Miles
> You around?

> Rev
> At the dock. Pick up two huckleberry milkshakes. Bring a jacket.

> Miles
> 5:15?

Rev

Does a retired man care about time? See you then, son.

○○○

Before he retired, there were only two activities Rev could be found doing on a weekday afternoon: studying his Bible or some other theological text for cross-referencing, or eating one of the many low-fat baked goods his wife, Cynthia, made him daily.

In retirement, he simply combined actions one and two but had traded his location from a church office to the small fishing dock just two miles west of their home. Rain or shine, he set up camp several hours a day to watch the river. To fish. To pray.

This time of year the trail down to the dock was wet and marshy, the wind cool even through my light jacket. Yet the backdrop of the sun on the water always made up for the sodden ground. As did the assuring presence of Rev. Of the many shifting variables in my life, Rev had never been one of them.

"Here you go, chief." I handed him the requested milkshake and took a seat in the open chair he always set up beside him. He was known to say, *"Never know who might need to stop by for a sit-down."*

I'd always thought Rev's smile was the most identifiable characteristic about him. Sure, he was linebacker large, and his skin was three times darker than my deepest shade of tan, but to know Rev meant to know joy in a way I could only attribute to him.

"Mmm. Cynthia's coconut-oil, monk-fruit oat muffins are good, but . . ." He shook his head, gripping the milkshake with mitt-sized hands and taking a second long pull on the straw. "There are just some things that can't be substituted this side of heaven."

I laughed and followed suit with my own shake, my gaze locked on the reflection of the lowering sun as it shifted in the river's slow-moving current. In another month, when the dam opened, the sound of the river would compete with our conversation. "Agreed."

"So, tell me, Miles, what's *not* wrong with your life?"

His signature question of the last decade was more than just an opener I'd come to expect, but a five-minute exercise in gratitude. A warm-up stretch before whatever mental lap he was about to send me on.

Without much thought, I rattled off my usual stream of answers first, those he often referred to as the surface grabs: my faith, my family, our health, my relationships, my education, my access to clean water, food, and shelter. And after those, I had to reach a bit deeper. Sometimes that reach came easily as I named specific blessings that resonated with my day or week.

But today, I stalled out somewhere around the fifty-second mark.

Rev arched a thick eyebrow in my direction as my mind detoured around anything having to do with my job or the church or with ministry in general. I sighed so long it triggered a yawn, and then both his eyebrows rose.

"Sounds like it must have been a day," he said.

"Try a year."

He chuckled good-naturedly and tapped his watch. "You still got some time left on the clock."

I rallied again and dug deeper, picturing a friendly face I hadn't expected to surface during this routine exercise. And then a second face in her wake. "My new upstairs neighbor, Val, and her son, Tucker, a home-cooked dinner invitation, and a good conversation that got my mind off my own issues for longer than an hour." A convicting insight.

"Good," he said, his attention focused on the eddy a few feet from where we sat. "I didn't realize you'd rented your apartment out again."

I laughed. "Neither had I, actually. It happened while I was in Mexico." He turned his head in my direction, and I simply said, "Molly."

"Ah." He chuckled. "No further explanation needed."

If Rev knew how that first encounter with Val had unfolded, I'd never hear the end of it. "Yeah, it was a surprise, but a good one." Better than good, really. Val and Tucker had only been in the apartment for a short time, and yet I liked coming home knowing they were there. I liked that Tucker waited for my car to arrive each evening. I liked that Val had smiled at me of her own volition multiple times now. And what a stunning smile she had, too. "You may have met her, actually—my new tenant. Val Locklier. She was Molly's maid of honor."

I realized, suddenly, how important it was to me that Rev might recall something about her. That he might have noticed her in some way despite Val's affinity for slipping under the radar, a skill set of hers I'd noticed on more than one occasion.

"Oh, yes. I think I did meet her at the wedding." Rev nodded confidently. "She brought Cynthia some water from the kitchen during the reception."

I frowned, certain he couldn't have the right person in mind. Val hadn't been anywhere near the kitchen during the reception. She'd been confined to the same wedding-party-only banquet table at the front of the room just like I had been. She'd sat only three seats away from my assigned place setting. I didn't say as much, but Rev could read my nonverbal cues as well as I could read his.

"It was her. Val." He confirmed again. "Cynthia had a tickle in her throat during the father-daughter dance. Our water pitcher on the table was empty, and she couldn't stop coughing. I'd gone off to find a server when Val tapped her on the shoulder and offered her a new bottle of water. I made a point to ask her name and thank her again before we left." He smiled. "A young woman small in stature yet strong in spirit."

A fitting definition of Val to be sure. And the timing of their interaction made sense, as she'd vacated the dance floor with the determination of Cinderella at the stroke of midnight.

Rev stretched his long legs out and leaned back against the canvas of his chair. "Did you have your debrief on Mexico today—on the Romero family?" His question forced my mind to take a hard left down an alley I'd been trying to avoid until I vacated the church parking lot.

"No, that was yesterday. Today was a different meeting altogether." I leaned forward to set my milkshake on the shaggy wooden boards below my chair and rubbed my palms together. "I was demoted."

The announcement was obviously not what Rev had been expecting. "In what way?"

A pitiful attempt at a laugh escaped me. "Every way: my title, my job description, my actual duties, my work location. All of it. Oh, but not my pay. Yet." The *yet* may not have been noted by Leonard, but it was there in the subtext, I was certain. "I'm no longer the outreach pastor at Salt and Light. It appears my entire department has been *restructured*." The word was almost as unsettling as my demotion. "I'm now the resident support pastor at Riverside Family Resource Center."

"You forget the church I pastored was fairly simple, Miles. We didn't have a coffee shop or even a dedicated preschool ministry. We had adult church and nursery." He chuckled. "So you'll have to forgive me if I don't know what a resident support pastor is."

"Honestly, your guess is about as good as mine." The description I'd been emailed this afternoon regarding my new role was vague at best. "I'm not even sure what's gone on at that center since Otto died. The only real instruction I received was to bring some renewed vision to the place." That was pastor speak for *be prepared to pick through the ashes of a three-year dumpster fire*. I kicked at a pebble balancing between the two slabs of wood underfoot. It made a tiny ripple as it hit the water. "I don't know, I think all of this is the sign I've been waiting for."

"And what sign is that?"

"To move on. To leave all the church politics here behind and take a new position within my dad's organization." I shook my head, my frustration fueled by a rising hurt I'd yet to give voice to. "I've poured years of my life into the missions program at Salt and Light, built it from the ground up . . . and to what end? To watch it all crumble under a poor leader with poor money management and poor accountability?" I stared out at the swirling rapids and waited a beat before I could say the last of it. "I sent my résumé off to my dad last week. I'm hoping to apply for the first open position in Central America."

For nearly a minute, Rev remained quiet. The same way he always did when I brought my father into our conversations. Even now, as I approached my twenty-ninth birthday, he was careful not to contradict my father's guidance. He'd always worked to keep the lines between us clear. After all, Rev had been my father's pastor once, long ago. His hands had baptized my dad in the Spokane River, the same way they'd once baptized me and my sister. Which was why it had come as no surprise when my father had asked Rev to watch over us after he and my mom moved overseas a decade ago.

"And what was your father's reply?"

My dad's response had come just as I was leaving the office today. "He encouraged me to be patient for the right position and to gather up the necessary documentation here in the meantime—letters of recommendation, service project reports, financial support pledges, etc." I tried to work out some of the discouragement from my tone. "He also said the estimated wait time for the type of position I'd be in line for can be upwards of eighteen months." Rev's continued contemplation had me building up a ready defense. "But you and I both know that to start over fresh at another church and rebuild anything similar to what I was able to do under Pastor Archer Sr. would take a minimum of three to five years. And that's only *if* I can find a church willing to look at missions the same way he did. So even if I did have to wait the full eighteen months, it would still be shorter than starting over completely." The only question now was what to do in the meantime. I was half tempted to cash in my savings and arrive unannounced to serve with the Romeros until I got my official assignment from my father.

Rev's nod was slow, but not in an affirming way.

"What?" I twisted my head to look at him straight on. "I want to hear what you're thinking."

"I'm not sure you do."

But in that instant, I was ready for it, for the pushback I'd been both avoiding and anticipating from him on this subject for quite some time now. "This isn't some knee-jerk reaction, Rev. It's been two hard years since Pastor Archer retired, and I've stayed through it all. Curtis's bad leadership decisions are what caused the massive department changes, budget cuts, layoffs, renovations, updates, and low staff morale." I shook my head in disgust. "My demotion today is my release."

"Is it?" he asked. "Has God told you He's released you from the ministry He gave you here? Because so far, all I've heard is what Miles has to say on the subject, not what God is saying to you about it."

"I don't have a ministry here anymore—that's what I've been telling you. It makes no sense to stick around when there's nothing left to stick around for."

"Isn't Riverside Family a ministry, son? Do you not think God can use you wherever He deems fit—at least while you wait and pray about your next steps?" Rev asked without waiting for my response. "You might not be able to make sense of God's plan or timing, but I can promise you that He isn't confused. Your growing frustrations about Salt and Light don't change the bigger picture." His gaze locked onto mine. "In the midst of trials, it's tempting to confuse *release* with *relief*. But make no mistake, they are not interchangeable. One is long-lasting, the other fleeting." He clasped his hands together. "I know which one I'd prefer. Do you?"

I huffed a breath as the familiar restlessness returned—that gut clench I'd been trying to escape for months now only to fail at every attempt. I hadn't heard God speak to me about anything of significance in a long time. Certainly not in regards to my future. "I can't seem to figure out what He's been saying to me."

"Elijah wasn't sure either when he stood at the mouth of that cave. He wanted all the drama and the signs, only that's not actually what he needed." And then in his deepest, most persuasive preacher voice, Rev declared, "'And behold, the Lord passed by, and a great and strong wind tore into the mountains and broke the rocks in pieces before the Lord, but the Lord was not in the wind; and after the wind an earthquake, but the Lord was not in the earthquake; and after the earthquake a fire, but the Lord was not in the fire; and after the fire . . . a still small voice.'"

I'd read that passage in 1 Kings a dozen times, written essays on it, even taught at a conference in Orlando last summer about the emotional highs and lows we often faced as church leaders, but when Rev quoted Scripture, it came alive in a way I couldn't hope to replicate, causing every hair on the back of my neck to stand at attention.

I stared deep down into the river once more, dusk covering us both in shadow while the sound of the current continued on despite the lack of visual.

"That still small voice will speak when you're ready to listen. Your job is to slow down long enough to hear it."

· II ·

Val

I'd never been to a funeral, but I imagined that if I had, it would feel similar to entering a warehouse where the death of something good—something honorable and worthy—had passed away unexpectedly only a week before its test flight into the world. Strangers all around us spoke in hushed tones, wore somber faces, and donned specialty attire as they assessed the damage of all that had been lost. Molly and I were counted among the authorized personnel taking note of any dry, undamaged merchandise to be counted among the salvageable inventory.

While wearing our safety goggles and hard hats, we sorted through the wrung-out remains inside the skeleton of a business that had yet to expand its wings. Molly had reached for my hand as we'd crossed the threshold into the tomb-like space, and I knew the gesture had less to do with the multiple tripping hazards I'd spotted upon first glance and more to do with the grief she'd been internalizing for days. On the car ride over, she'd been all bubbly questions and talking points with Tucker before we'd dropped him off with Silas for a day of projects at the ever-expanding campus of The Bridge.

But instead of opening up to me once we had a moment of privacy, Molly did what she did best—she talked about any and everything with the exception of one thing: her grief over Basics

First. Then again, I was the last person on earth who could pass judgment for deflecting difficult emotions.

There were few people who knew just how much time and energy Molly had put into taking Basics First from the visionary stage into a reality. And perhaps that was the most enviable quality about my best friend: Molly's heart and passions had become fully aligned into one singular, focused mission—a concept I could only appreciate from a distance, as I was forever playing catch-up in a race I wasn't quite sure was mine to run.

As carefully as possible, I traversed across the concrete floor to where Molly had paused her incessant trash cleanup to stand in front of the inspirational quote wall she'd chosen with her awaiting employees in mind. Myself included. The thought caused something in the pit of my stomach to squirm. I still hadn't told her yet. Not about the possibility of the film mentorship. Not about Lady Gwen. Not about a realization that was dawning brighter with each passing day.

"Hey," I said gently. "So I found this empty bucket to make it easier to sort the . . ." I worked to rephrase my wording. The idea of calling any of the damaged inventory *trash* didn't seem kosher, given the circumstances. Not when Molly had spent so much care in handpicking the items that Basics First was meant to sell in their online boutique store. It was more than just merchandise; each sale meant the donation of a backpack of supplies given to aged-out foster kids ready for independence.

I gazed down at the plastic bucket swinging at my side and finished my sentence. "To keep whatever valuables we find in the stockroom."

I approached her from behind, reading several of the wall quotes she faced.

Stay Humble. Work Hard. Be Kind.

The COMEBACK is always stronger than the setback.

Let all that you do be done in love. —1 Corinthians 16:14

"Molly? Are you doing okay?"

But somehow in the time it took Molly to form an answer, the toe of my left foot snagged on a piece of slick debris, throwing off my gait. And without a solid structure to right myself with, the balance battle was lost before it began.

Instinctively, I released my grip on the bucket I'd been hauling to brace for impact. I landed hard on my backside, skidding across the sleek concrete into a starfish-like position as the hollow clatter and subsequent recoil of the bucket rang out like a round of gunfire, never ending in its quest to capture the attention of every living thing within earshot.

Including the half-dozen suit-wearing professionals.

"Oh no! *Val*!" Molly's near wail only added fuel to the fire as alarmed expressions morphed into urgent questions like *Does she need help?* and *Is the girl injured?* and *How did she fall?*

My mortification sank to a new low, but I managed to shake my head emphatically, pushing myself upright without so much as a grimace. "No, no. I'm all right. Really. Just tripped and lost my footing." If embarrassment could leave a permanent stain on one's skin, mine had surely been marked for life.

"What about your hip?" Molly asked in a worried tone, eyeing my left side warily as she extended her hand to me. "Is it . . . I mean, do you think you could have injured it worse?"

When I'd first explained the elephant in the room to Molly after meeting her in person last fall, the conversation had gone exactly how I'd anticipated. Molly had been a flurry of curious questions, sympathetic head nods, and fervent speeches about how I should feel empowered as a woman with a minor disability to be living in this age and time. All of this was a precursor to a tight hug and a teary benediction: *"The way you walk doesn't change anything about who you are, Val. I hardly even notice your limp. It doesn't change how I see you."* And while I knew she meant well—that her words had been spoken out of love and concern—my limp *did* affect how I interacted with the world. I couldn't turn it off any more than I could command myself to grow three inches taller.

But despite spending a lifetime practicing the art of living unseen by the outside world, I grew weary of trying to hide from the ones closest to me. I didn't want to play both offense and defense when it came to the people I loved.

And yet, I hadn't a clue how to change that.

"No," I said in answer. "My hip will be fine." I focused on standing without a repeat incident and calculated the fastest route to the stockroom. Whatever injuries I did or did not have, I certainly wouldn't be doing any assessments under the scrutiny of strangers.

My elbow throbbed as I reached for the metal handle of the discarded bucket, but Molly got to it first. She threaded her arm through mine, and I was grateful to be putting an end to the spectacle I'd caused without further delay.

With my cheeks still aflame, I walked in tandem with Molly toward the back room, only to be stopped by a man wearing a neon safety vest with a distinctly Christopher Walken vibe of sharp cheekbones and sunken gray eyes about him. "You took a pretty hard tumble over there, sweetheart. Hope you're okay?"

"Yes, sir. I'm fine."

He pointed to my left leg. "I noticed the way you were favoring your left side when you first came in, *before* you slipped inside the warehouse." He gave a half turn, as if to make a show of the eyes and ears privy to our conversation. The witnesses. "It's my top priority as the chief safety inspector on site to ensure that every aspect of this project follows protocol, including our authorized visitors." He took a card out of his front vest pocket, handed it to me, and then eyed the name sticker I wore on the front of my blouse. "I trust you signed a safety waiver as you entered, Val?"

"Yes, sir," I said flatly. "I did."

"Good, good. That's what I like to hear." His gaze wandered to Molly, his perusal of her as slow as it was obvious. His smile revealed several discolored teeth. "I'd be happy to sit with your friend in the lobby while you finish up your business here, miss?"

Molly opened her mouth to respond, but for once, I beat her to the punch. This wasn't the first time a person in authority had played the safety liability card on me, although it was hardly the most common interaction I dealt with in public. No, that interaction belonged to the well-meaning stranger who went out of his way to try and *fix me* with a quick prognosis or therapy treatment recommendation. Even my own mother was guilty of that—sending me articles about the wonders of acupuncture or cupping or her newest fascination: float therapy. But short of explaining my entire medical history to a stranger, I'd learned long ago that there was no abbreviated version that would cut down unsolicited advice quite as well as saying *thank you*.

But to Ed the Safety Regulator, I simply said, "I'll be fine, thank you anyway."

"Ma'am," he said, tipping his gaze down to me, "are you sure this is the best environment for someone with your . . . condition? I'd hate for something more serious to happen that might put you or our job here further at risk."

"She said she'll be fine," Molly said in a voice I'd only heard her use when speaking of her ex-talent manager.

Amused, the inspector glanced back to Molly. "Can I trust you to stick close by, then, for the duration of her visit?"

Molly clenched her fists at her sides, her indignation heating the space between us with each passing second, yet it was obvious she was completely out of her depth on how to handle such a patronizing remark. Unfortunately, I was not.

"You can't seriously be—"

"We'll stick together," I said, cutting her off. My neck was hot, as droplets of sweat gathered under my arms at his condescending gaze. I knew that look well. Once upon a time, it had been worn by a man who once claimed to adore me. "Thanks for your concern."

"No problem, sweetheart. Keep my card handy. Let's hope you don't need it." With a wink, he turned away, adding yet another tally mark to my being treated like a helpless invalid in need of a capable adult.

I shoved his card and his ignorance deep into my front pocket while Molly's grip on my arm tightened as we negotiated the warehouse floor together. Her lips were smashed into a thin line, which told me to prepare for a heated follow-up as soon as we found a private moment alone. Only, when she opened the door into the dark stockroom and flipped on the light, every ounce of rigidity in her body fell slack. And in an instant, the humiliation that had lit a match within me just moments before now cooled into the icy chill of heartbreak as I watched an array of emotion flash across Molly's face.

This tiny room that had once been stocked to the brim with glittered candles, lamps and vases, pillows and throw blankets, wall art and picture frames . . . was now a prison to broken dreams. All her organized overflow boxes, once labeled and numbered, had slid off their shelves sometime during the sprinkler onslaught and now lay warped with the aftermath of water damage.

Molly's hand flew to her mouth, and for the first time since her phone call to me the night of the fire, Molly released a sob so shattering it could have sliced through bone.

"This is . . . it's too much, Val," she whispered. "The damage. It's everywhere, in everything. None of this is salvageable."

I wrapped my arms around her middle, tightening my hold as if she were Tucker after one of his breakdowns over not having a real dad, and not my best friend who stood nearly six inches taller than me. Yet no matter our differing heights, her need for comfort and reassurance was the same.

"It's not too much," I soothed. "You can do this, and you will. One step at a time." Words that came easier to speak than to live by. "I know the cleanup seems overwhelming right now, but every day you show up, every day you put in the work . . . will be one day closer to your grand opening goal, and one day closer to supplying backpacks to those teens in need."

"I just hate this feeling so much—this helplessness." She scrubbed at her eyes without a single smudge to her mascara. "I think that's the worst part of this, you know? That feeling of wanting something so badly and the fear that it might not happen because it's simply out of my control."

Yes, I did know—quite well, actually.

I said nothing for several seconds until Molly's gaze shifted from the open box of warped paper journals at our feet back to mine. I might not ever know what she saw in my face in that moment, but I knew what I saw in hers: the commitment to fight for something bigger than herself. A resolve to risk, to try again, to push back against the helplessness and pick up every shard of the broken remains.

To take every damaged piece and mold it into something purposeful.

Something good.

Something right.

Something worthy of being seen.

I knew all of this because I felt it, too.

Only *this* battle, the one Molly was armoring up for now . . . it wasn't meant to be my battle. Molly would always have my loyalty and love, my friendship, my deepest support for her causes, but whether the film mentorship with Lady Gwen panned out or not, I owed Molly the truth. No matter the cost.

Because perhaps the first real step in being seen by those you loved was lowering your guard enough to risk being honest.

◇◇◇

On our way back to the car, the insurance adjuster and contractor caught up to Molly, confirming a timeline neither of us was surprised by after seeing the extent of the damage for ourselves: five to six months until the warehouse would be ready for business again. I waited to see if Molly would slip back into the somber shell she'd worn on the drive over, but it appeared that whatever revelation had happened inside that storeroom wasn't temporary. For either of us.

As Molly merged onto the freeway, I cleared my throat and prayed the timing of this conversation wouldn't feel like a kick-her-when-she's-down gut punch. "Molly, I was hoping we could talk for a few minutes. About something important."

"I was just thinking the same thing, actually." She glanced my way with tender eyes. "But first, I really need to apologize. I intended to say something to you as soon as we got a minute alone, but once we walked into the stockroom, well, my emotions got the better of me. I'm sorry."

My mind crawled backward, realizing with sudden clarity that our subject matters for this conversation had not been taken from the same page.

"There is nothing that happened today you need to apologize for." If anything, I'd be the one apologizing to her in a few minutes.

"That man." Molly shook her head, breathed out hard. "The safety inspector guy." She gritted her teeth, her jaw flexing under the strain of it. "I should have put him in his place when I had the chance."

"No," I said resolutely. "You handled it just as you should have."

She glanced at me. "What? No way. He was completely in the wrong for how he spoke to you, and he deserves to be reprimanded."

When I didn't respond immediately, she looked at me again. "Why aren't you saying anything? Do you not agree with me? Val, he assumed that you couldn't—"

"I know what he assumed. And I can't control every assumption or opinion about why I walk the way I do." Which was why I often limited the potential of opinions I had to be around. "He was only trying to do his job."

Molly's lips smacked open as she looked from me to the open freeway ahead. "Are you actually *defending* him?"

"No, I'm trying to explain him to you—his type, anyway." I'd known plenty of *Ed*s over the years.

"Val, he asked me if I needed him to sit with you—like I was your babysitter or something!"

I grimaced at that. If I could count the times people handled me with childlike terminology due to my stature alone, I'd have long ago run out of fingers and toes.

"See? And *that* reaction right there is why I should have said something—as your friend. He insulted you, *belittled* you. I'm going to report him."

I sighed. "Molly. You have a lot going on in your world right now—way too much to be worrying about an ignorant inspector and his poor vocabulary choices. This is not your battle to fight."

"But is it yours?" she asked once, followed by a much quieter, gentler version. "Is this the battle you fight often? Because I guess that's what I realized in that moment—why I froze instead of fighting back right away—is that I've never had to deal with something like that before. Not in that way. Rude people online? Absolutely. Trolls on my channels? For sure. But know-it-all Eds who presume they can just boss you around like you don't have a voice or choice of your own?" She shook her head insistently and then pressed her back against the driver's seat, her expression haunted. "Have I . . . have I ever done that to you, Val? Have I ever been a Safety Vest Ed to you?"

I laughed in a way only Molly could make me laugh. "No. I can assure you that you've never been a Safety Vest Ed to me. But if you had, I would have told you to pluck that one wiry gray hair sticking straight out of your right eyebrow."

"Oh my gosh, I totally saw that, too! It was like an antenna searching for a transmitter signal or something. I will never understand why some people refuse to pluck what really should be plucked." She changed lanes and tilted her head in my direction again. "But please, if I ever say or do anything insulting or idiotic out of my own ignorance, tell me. Promise me you'll tell me."

"I will, I promise." I gave her a reassuring smile, and then took a deep breath, getting ready to take a leap where I'd only envisioned taking a first step. "You've always been so generous to me—as an employer and as a friend."

"Wait—if you're about to tell me you've decided to move back to Alaska then I should probably pull over. I promise I won't interrupt you again, but if that's the conversation we're about to have, then I'll need to prepare myself for it. Silas will not take it well if I tell him I was blubbering on the freeway going seventy miles an hour."

"I'm not moving back to Alaska."

"Okay." She breathed out, the tension in her shoulders visibly relaxing. "Okay."

"But I do think it's time for me to step out on my own. Apart from your business endeavors and projects." I took a short breath. "You deserve to partner with someone who is as passionate and excited about the strides you're making inside the foster care community as for the work itself. And I'm realizing only now that . . . I don't think I'm that person. I've tried to be, even thought that once I was on the ground here and removed all other options for myself, I could grow to be. For you. But when everything happened that night at the warehouse, I don't know . . . I began to wonder if maybe my leaving Alaska had less to do with your job offer and more to do with the freedom I needed to find here. The freedom to pursue some of my own passions."

"Wow, that's . . . I wasn't expecting that." Molly's contemplative demeanor was difficult to assess from my place in the passenger seat. She took the exit off the interstate, slowing the car to a mere thirty-five miles an hour as we weaved through neighborhoods intermixed with fields of soon-to-be-harvested wheat. "I was just telling Silas the other night how worried I was that I might have damaged our friendship by begging you to come out here. Nothing I set up for you has gone according to plan." She paused. "But maybe that's because God's plan for you is better than my plan for you?"

I smiled. "Could be." I was still new to understanding how God's plans worked, but the idea didn't sound wrong to me. In fact, it was the best explanation I had for all that had happened since my arrival, as well.

She signaled a right onto Miles's street. "Do you have another job lined up? And what specific passions are you wanting to pursue?"

"You're not upset?" I asked, trying to gauge her response.

"Upset? My best friend just moved to my city from Alaska and is living with my brother and—"

"Um, let's rephrase that last part, shall we?"

"Ha, right." She laughed as we approached the house. "My best friend *is renting an apartment from my brother*, which means I get to see you both more often. So in short: absolutely not."

Standing at the end of Grandma Millie's driveway, Kadin waved at us as we drove past. We both waved back.

"Val, I want you to be happy. Like the mysteriously ridiculous kind of happy someone as gracious and patient and kind as you deserves. So, if that means you work for someone else at some other company, then you'll have my wholehearted support. Because that's what you've always given to me."

Before I could formulate a worthy reply and fill her in on my hopeful next steps, the phone on my lap began to vibrate with the alert of a video call.

Lady Gwen Chilton.

What? Why is she calling me now? By the clock on Molly's dash, we still had four hours before our scheduled call later this evening. My heartbeat started into a rhythm twice its usual cadence.

Molly pulled her blue Mini Cooper into Miles's driveway, stopping just short of Miles, who was currently washing a car. He waved at us, though I didn't have enough brain function to reciprocate. That, and my hand was currently occupied in a white-knuckled grip on my phone.

Molly propped her door open. "Are you coming, or—" She glanced down at my vibrating phone, Lady Gwen's name displayed there in giant print across the screen. "Who's . . . Lady Gwen?"

I shook my head. There wasn't time. "I can explain later. I just . . . I really should take this call. It's important." Panic warred against the logical part of my brain that told me there was absolutely no way I'd make it across the driveway and up the stairs to my apartment in time to answer it. But this certainly wasn't how I'd planned on taking this call.

"Sure, sure. Take it from my car if you want. I'll go chat with my brother." Molly reached into the back seat to grab the bakery box she'd taken from the warehouse before slipping out of the car.

At the last possible second, I swiped right on Gwen's name.

"Good afternoon, Mrs. Chilton." I tried to work the wonkiness out of my smile, though I was all too aware of the animated scene playing out through the windshield with the McKenzie twins. Miles snatching the bakery box, Molly swatting him on the shoulder and pointing to the wet, shiny car. I forced my eyes back to Gwen's smiling face.

"Oh, good, I was hoping you'd answer." She held up a coraltipped finger. "And before you start to question my memory, I do realize I called hours before our scheduled time. But one thing you should know about me right up front: I abhor schedules. Almost as much as I abhor rules. That said"—her bright coral sunhat flopped into the frame, and she flicked it out of the way—"I am quite a fan of spontaneity, especially when it leads to either beauty or fun." She tilted her face to the camera. "Are you wondering which reason led me to call you early?"

I nodded, working to follow her complex conversation trail.

"Both." Her exclamation was giddy. "My son invited us out on his new sailboat tonight for a sunset dinner. And life is too short to miss a sunset dinner on the ocean, wouldn't you agree?"

"Absolutely," I said, though I'd never been on a sailboat. A fishing boat in the middle of the Pacific, yes. But fishing boats in Alaska weren't a leisurely boating experience. I spent more than half the time retching over the bow while my dad told me the nausea would pass soon enough. It didn't.

I glanced up in time to see Miles point to my phone and give me a thumbs-up. Molly must have mentioned who I was speaking to. I focused my eyes on Gwen once again. "Sounds like a great evening."

"I certainly hope your evening plans entail something equally as fun up there in Washington—though I much prefer the weather down here in SoCal to yours."

Laughable, really, as my plans tonight would certainly consist of several hours of freelance work to pad my draining savings account. "I'm sure I would, too, but at least it's a good twenty degrees warmer in Spokane than where I grew up in Skagway."

She gave an exaggerated shiver. "You must be full of some amazing stories from living up there in the tundra!"

Gwen would be quite disappointed by the stories I had to tell. It was the stories of others I aimed to share with the world, not any of my own. "Alaskans are pretty acclimated to the winters up north."

She shook her head again, more adamantly this time. "I'm solar powered, which is why I must always live in the warmer regions. But I applaud your bravery!" Her eyes sparkled that brilliant Caribbean blue. "So I looked over all your prerequisites and appreciated your examples of edit cuts and shot knowledge—all easily passable. Your technical skill test gets an A from me." I hadn't been too concerned about that part of the process, but relief coursed through me just the same. "But now I'm wondering about your thoughts on the question I gave you: What's a storyline that's never been told, Valerie?"

When Gwen said my full name, much the way she said anything, it sounded distinguished and sophisticated and made me want to sit up as straight as possible and tuck in my chin. Involuntarily, my attention cut to Miles, who was now leaning against the wet car in his driveway as he waited with his sister, and his gaze locked with mine. For half a second, my mind blanked out.

But then, like the flick of a switch, his assuring smile brought it all back to me.

Careful to keep my vocabulary professional, I took Gwen on the same journey I'd taken with my landlord over home-cooked chicken Alfredo, arriving at the destination with confidence: "Every story is original not because of the plot, but because each storyteller behind the pen or the camera or the canvas has an original perspective." At my proclamation, Gwen's face lit up with the same triumphant expression Miles had worn.

She backed away from the camera enough to show me her clapping hands. And not the sarcastic golf clap so many used to undermine their inferiors. But full-out applause. "Bravo! Bravo! With a mind like that, you are well on your way to becoming a champion in this arena, my dear." I couldn't help but beam at her high praise. "Which means, of course, that you have another question to answer for me today."

I nodded, anticipation fueling me as her smile widened.

"Valerie Locklier, would you consider being my protégé during the duration of the Essence of Filmmakers Mentorship?" She held up her hand. "Before you answer, you must know that the tasks ahead will require an earnest investment of your time, heart, creativity, bravery, and introspection of which you likely haven't experienced before. I'm not a dictator or a babysitter. When I give, I expect to be given back to equally—a joint effort built on mutual trust and dedication." She stared at me in a way that felt like a commissioning. "So I'll ask you again. Would you like to partner with me in the great quest of visual storytelling, Valerie?"

Partner. Her word choice stood out to me, as it was the same word Molly had used to describe our recent business ventures, and yet this context felt entirely different now. This wasn't me riding on the coattails of someone else's talent; this was me having to prove my own.

And suddenly, I was up for the challenge.

"I'd love nothing more."

"Then cheers to us, darling." She raised a glass of what looked to be lemonade. "I'll email you a list of assignments, as well as the dreaded schedule Volkin has us on." Her practiced eye roll was an obvious tell that she was someone with superior front-of-the-camera experience. "Okay, then, Lady Gwen is signing off for the night. But I'll be checking in on your progress at the start of next week."

Tears glossed my eyes as I smiled back at her with something akin to joy. Maybe this was the seedling to that mysteriously ridiculous kind of happiness Molly described to me earlier.

"Enjoy your dinner sail," I said. "And thank you."

For so much more than I could ever name.

· 12 ·

Miles

My sister had been labeled the "animated twin" since before we could talk. Animated, of course, was the tactful way of saying Molly's melodrama scored off the charts. Her ability to capture the attention of anyone within a thousand-foot radius was the stuff family legends were made of—which was why her career choice had come as no surprise to me. Nor had her success with it. She could turn the head of the perpetually distracted and reel them in as if she held the answer to their every need.

But not even Molly's latest update regarding the current state of the warehouse and her change of plans to shift the grand opening to fall could have pulled my attention away from Val. I leaned my back against the damp Subaru Outback I'd just finished rinsing, only half-tuned to Molly's verbal processing about the insurance adjuster's feedback, when Val cracked open the passenger's-side door. I pushed away from the car, the surprise I'd planned falling second to whatever had just happened on that phone call. The instant Molly had mentioned Gwen's name, the shift in my own nerves had been obvious.

"How'd it go?" I asked Val before Molly even had the chance

to turn around. "Were we right? Was that the answer she was looking for?"

Although the hint of pink on Val's cheeks seemed a good sign, the smile she was trying—and failing—to bite back sealed the deal.

"Right about what?" Molly asked, looking between us. "What am I missing here? What just happened?"

Val slowed her steps, addressing me first. "Gwen was impressed with the answer we came up with, yes."

And before I could pre-think the action, I strode toward her and gave her a high five, which, considering our height difference, was more of a low five. But a full three seconds after I smacked her palm with mine, I realized that any kind of fiving gesture when it came to an intriguing woman in my peer group was one-hundred-percent lame.

And if I wasn't totally convinced, the did-I-really-just-witness-that look on Molly's face confirmed it. She continued to eye us both in a way I didn't appreciate. "Can somebody please fill me in on what we're celebrating here?"

"Yes, sorry, Molly. I was hoping to get to this part of the conversation before we arrived back home—"

"But Safety Vest Ed butted in once again." The tone in which my sister spoke had me turning back to her.

"Wait—who is Safety Vest Ed?" I asked.

"A safety inspector at the warehouse," Val said, at the exact same time Molly said, "Also known as a discriminatory bully with a power complex."

"Molly, please," Val said with a resignation that piqued my curiosity even further.

Molly opened her mouth, but I beat her to it, my mind sand-wiched between the words *discriminatory bully* and *power complex*. I pointed to Molly. "Stop. Go back." Because if either of those descriptions was an accurate representation of their time at the warehouse, then I would most definitely have other words to say to my sister when this little huddle in my driveway concluded. Because normal people would have thought to *lead* with this type of information at the start of a conversation, not proceed to eat a stale donut and spend the next fifteen minutes discussing the tolls of water damage in a cement building.

I bit back my irritation with my sister and addressed Val directly. "Did something happen at the warehouse?" The mere thought of someone intentionally hurting her made my chest simmer.

Val shot Molly a look I couldn't decipher. But there was no denying now that something *had*, in fact, happened. Something involving Val. Something that made me want to know every last detail and make it right.

"It's been handled," Molly said in a too-flat tone that neither convinced or dissuaded me. "As much as some guy doing his job in the poorest way possible can be handled."

Val scrunched her brow at Molly's unblinking gaze, and I had the distinct impression I was witnessing a standoff with stakes unknown. Usually, in a staredown, my money would be placed on my sister. I once saw her take Silas down in a completely nonverbal battle of wills that left me twisting off the top to my Coke and settling in to watch the show for nearly twenty minutes on their sofa. But in only a few seconds, it was abundantly clear that Val could more than hold her own. It was also clear that she wanted off this subject ASAP.

I cleared my throat, having every intention to circle back to this conversation when the timing was right.

"Good," I said in a measured tone, tugging the damp towel off my shoulder. "I'm glad whatever it was is resolved."

Val offered me a grateful look as Molly released a tension-filled breath and did her best to redirect.

"So . . . ?" Molly smiled at Val. "Tell me your good news! And how this mysterious Lady Gwen plays a part in it."

I took a few steps back and began to busy myself with the car in the driveway—the one nobody seemed to take much note of, though it was literally parked six feet from where they stood. I supposed an unusual car in my driveway wasn't anything too out of the norm for my sister, though. Molly had seen a rotation of cars at my house over the years—always used, always hard-to-beat deals I paid cash for and could eventually turn into a small profit given the right opportunity and timing. My friend Bill had taught me a few tricks over the years. Outside of the passive income I made from renting the apartment, private car dealing had become somewhat of a hobby. One I might pick up again soon for my sanity's sake, seeing as my first day at Riverside Family Resource Center was a week from Monday.

Though I was obviously still in earshot, I busied myself as Val broke the news about her film mentorship to Molly and explained the implications of her future availability and workload. If my sister was shocked by her friend's sudden change of plans, she didn't show it. Instead, she congratulated Val the way I knew Val had congratulated Molly dozens of times over. And the selfless response made me proud to be her brother.

Molly pulled Val into a hug and then proceeded to do the same to me. "Silas says hello, by the way. And he also says you promised him another dart match."

I laughed. "I'm pretty sure Silas could throw a perfect game while blindfolded and hog-tied. He really needs to find better competition than me."

"Don't I know it. He *is* pretty ridiculous," Molly said in that lovesick voice she used whenever she spoke about her husband.

Hoping to starve the last of Molly's conversational needs and send her happily on her way, I chose not to encourage any more driveway small talk. It wasn't that I didn't enjoy my sister's pop-in visits, I just had a different agenda in mind for this afternoon.

"You know," Molly said with that same enlightened expression she'd worn earlier as she'd looked from me to Val, "we should all get together soon for dinner—the four of us. We haven't done that since before the wedding." She looked between us while backtracking to her car. But neither Val or I responded to her targeted invitation. My sister was a lot of things, but subtle wasn't one of them. "We could go to the new Indian place Silas and I love over in Coeur d'Alene. My bet is that Miles will eat his weight in garlic naan before we even receive our entrees." She opened the driver's-side door to a car built for a toy doll. "Let me know when you two are free, and we'll set a date. It will be our treat."

"Well, in that case," I said, deflecting from Val's silence. Molly wasn't the only McKenzie twin who could read a room, or in this case, a driveway. "I can't speak for Val, but I'm always up for an all-you-can-eat situation on my sister's dime."

"Exactly." She laughed and waved good-bye to us both before she sped down my driveway. "We'll get it on the calendar. Soon."

Before Val could turn toward the house, I pushed off the car I'd spent the last hour detailing. "How do you feel about the color silver?"

She twisted back and shielded the sun from her eyes. "Um . . . it's nice?"

"Good. I was hoping you'd say that. Color wasn't on your must-have list, so I hoped silver wouldn't be a deal breaker for you." I jogged around the side of the Subaru, taking the keys from my pocket. "If you like how she drives, I'm pretty sure you'll love the price tag, too. After licensing fees and taxes, you'll be about a thousand dollars in the black from the budget you gave me."

Val blinked, glancing from me to the Subaru. "Wait, that car is . . . that car is for me? How did you get it?"

"Bill called me from an estate auction yesterday afternoon, and I told him what you were looking for. He didn't have a chance to detail it, so he gave me an even better deal than usual if I did it myself. He did inspect it for any mechanical issues first, though. It's yours to test drive this weekend if you want to." Suddenly struck by the thought that I hadn't seen a certain shoulder-height kid running around, I asked, "Hey, where's Tuck?"

Val continued staring at the car, her response almost robotic. "At The Bridge. With Silas."

"Ah. Well, maybe we should pick him up from there?" Apparently, I'd just made myself a part of the test-driving package. "Unless you have other Friday-night plans, of course."

"I don't." She shook her head slowly, her gaze coming back to me. "Have other plans, I mean, outside of some freelance work I need to do tonight. But I think Silas and his brother were planning to take Tucker to the batting cages around five, and it's only . . ." She glanced at her fancy watch. "Two thirty."

"Would you be up for seeing some sights around town? I'm a pretty good tour guide." I leaned against the car, crossed my arms. "Plus, I still owe you a celebratory treat."

Val's eyes widened. "Um, you just found me a car. And cleaned and washed it for me. All debts are mine at this point."

"I didn't get to the entire interior yet, but it was in fairly good shape, other than the grandmotherly perfume smell. But I can tackle that after you decide on it." According to Tucker, Val was firmly opposed to cigarette smoke, but hopefully floral wouldn't bother her too much. "So, what do you say to a drive?" I said, realizing then just how badly I needed to get away. Though my workday had been cut shorter than usual today, the week had felt Groundhog Day long.

"I think that would be . . . nice."

"Yeah?"

She nodded, her smile blossoming in full, and pointed to her upstairs apartment. "I just need to pop inside for a few first. Gwen's sending over the list of official assignments and due dates, and I'd like to read them over. If there's anything on there like her riddle, I should probably take some time to mull them all over."

"Congratulations, again," I said. "And I apologize for outing your mentorship to Molly before you had a chance to."

"No, that's really okay. I'd actually been in the process of telling her when Gwen called."

"Ah, well good." I tugged at my damp shirt. "Is thirty minutes long enough? I could use a shower and a fresh change of clothes. I can wait, though, if you were hoping to . . ." If there was a non-creepy way of asking a woman if she was planning on taking a hot shower in the apartment you owned, then I was not privy to such insight. "That is, if you'll be needing hot water for anything, I can just . . . wait."

"It's all yours," she said with a laugh, before walking toward the stairs. "Prioritizing your hot water is the least I can do."

But her retreat sparked my memory. "Oh—wait! I have something for you, I just remembered." I jogged to my car parked along the street and pulled out the book I'd found in my office yesterday.

"You have something else for me?" I didn't miss the touch of exasperation in her tone as I ran back and placed the book in her hand.

"Miles, you've done too much for me already—"

"It's only a book. I think you'll find it a much more interesting read than that textbook you've been working through. And it happens to be one of my favorites."

"*Mere Christianity* by C. S. Lewis." She glanced up at me. "I read the Chronicles of Narnia series to Tuck last winter."

"A classic for sure."

A faint frown line creased between her brows as she stared down at the hardback in her hands, brushing her thumb over the embossed title in a way only those who understood the treasure of a book would do. "I'm just . . . I'm not sure I should take this."

Perhaps I'd misinterpreted our conversation in front of her bookshelf the other night. "I promise you, there's no pressure attached to this gift—none whatsoever. It's yours to do with what you like."

"It's not that. It's just, you've already given me more than I can repay." She tried to hand the book back to me. "I'm happy to purchase my own copy."

I stuffed my hands into my pockets and slowly backed away. "Gifts are not for repayment."

"Miles, really, I don't want to be a—"

"Just promise me we can have one conversation about the brilliance that is Mr. Lewis if you read it. That will be payback enough."

She lowered the book and tapped it against her leg. "I'll see you in thirty minutes. Enjoy your hot water."

· 13 ·

Val

Miles was waiting for me at the car when I made the trek from the stairs to the end of the driveway. Walking any distance in front of an audience came with a layer of challenges. In public, I braced for one of two reactions from strangers: the classic double take, or the puzzled expression followed by a slow perusal as I passed. But when it came to acquaintances and friends, the reaction to my shortened step was usually just the opposite, as if averting their gaze from my disability would somehow be more polite. Yet their discomfort spoke louder than their good intentions ever could.

And then there was Miles, who stared at me head-on, the corner of his mouth lifted to one side as he held up a crudely drawn map that appeared to have been penned with black Sharpie on the back of a pizza box lid. "Hey there. I mapped out a few places for us to check out. I didn't want you to miss anything."

As I neared him, there was no stopping my eyes from widening at the eleven stars he'd drawn along the curving lines of a road. He'd even gone so far as to detail a key in the bottom right corner. While Miles and Molly definitely had their own set of unique character traits, their desire to stuff as much activity into a single block of time was apparently a shared gene.

"Wow . . . that's quite an impressive tour you put together," I said, testing the upbeat Gwen-like tone I was trying on for size. I hadn't been on a Tucker-free, work-free excursion in months. Who knew? Perhaps adopting a bit of Gwen's carefree Friday-night attitude would bring some fresh ideas for the out-of-the-box assignments she'd sent over.

As if to prove I was willing to give this new adventure as a visual storyteller my best shot, I'd searched for the most colorful piece of clothing I owned in my minimal, mostly monochromatic closet. The winner: a white vintage Polaroid tee with a band of pink, orange, yellow, and blue stretched across my chest. Nothing like living on the wild side. My sixty-seven-year-old mentor was on a sailboat on the Pacific Ocean . . . and I was wearing a color spectrum sample as a T-shirt. I'd also taken the time to braid my hair and tie a gray hoodie around my waist. Didn't want to get too crazy and leave the house without one. "Do you think we'll have time for all those stops before we pick up Tucker?"

Miles looked up from the map as if only just now considering the time restraints. "I think so, but I'm good to play it by ear. Anything you'd like to add? Happy to make any adjustments."

I nearly laughed. "No, I think you've thought of it all."

"Hope so." He took the keys out of his pocket and set them in my palm. "You drive, and I'll navigate."

"You sure?" It was probably a ridiculous comparison to make, but the men I knew back home didn't give up their keys unless they were inebriated or maimed. And even then it was a toss-up.

He laughed. "Of course I'm sure. It's your car—or, at least, I think you're going to decide it's yours by the end of day. Some of the older roads downtown are a bit narrow, and the signage isn't great, but I have every confidence in you."

An odd floaty sensation pushed its way up through my core. I'd been half anticipating Miles to ask if the stiffness in my hip inhibited my ability to drive, or if I needed any kind of special assistance—it didn't and I didn't. But it wouldn't be the first time such an assumption had been made. But the truth was, driving

NICOLE DEESE

was actually one of the rare experiences I had that didn't remind me of my differences. And I loved every second of it.

"Thanks," I said, reveling in the weight of the keys in my open palm. "Now, would you kindly point out which part of the car is the steering wheel?"

I waited just a beat to see if my corny joke would hit its mark as Miles barked out a laugh that reverberated in the open air. Cheeks tinged with warmth, I smiled and made my way to the driver's door, popping it open and lowering myself onto the seat with ease.

"You know, for that, I should make you show me your Alaska driver's license." Miles dropped into his seat beside me, his knees smashing up against the dash while my feet remained yards away from the pedals. We reached for the height adjusters simultaneously and locked our seats into our respective settings.

"As you wish." Gwen's boldness must have rubbed off on me, because instead of shying away, I pulled my license out from the small card holder attached to my phone. I rarely carried a purse. Too cumbersome.

Miles held my license up, examining the state seal in the sunlight as I laughed. "Five foot one, huh? And I have to say, I've always been a personal fan of Hope. A solid middle-name choice if I do say so myself."

I swiped it from his hand. "Um, I thought you were just supposed to be validating that it's a real license."

"Consider yourself validated."

With a single turn of my wrist, I started the car. The quiet purr of the engine wove through me—a call to freedom if ever there was one. I bit my bottom lip, trying to keep my elation confined to the inside.

"Told you," Miles said with pride. "She's a keeper."

He wasn't wrong. I would have paid more for her—crushed rose petal scent and all. I shifted my attention back to my co-captain's pizza box map. "Where are we headed to first?"

"Bing Crosby's house."

"As in . . . Bing Crosby, Bing Crosby?" I'd probably watched

White Christmas with my mother more times than Tucker had seen *Paw Patrol* as a toddler.

"The one and only. He grew up in Spokane. The Crosby house sits on the Gonzaga campus. It's actually a museum now. We can also drive by the Bing Crosby Theater, too. It's only about five miles away or so, downtown. I'll explain the four quadrants of the city to you as we go. But first, you'll want to get on I-90 westbound. I'll point out the turns from there so you can enjoy the way she drives."

"Perfect." The easiest assignment I'd been given all day.

○○○

One Big Ben clock tower look-alike, two Bing Crosby destinations, and three signature Spokane sightseeing drive-bys later, my stomach was rumbling for something other than the half-eaten crumb donut I'd accidentally left the remainder of inside Molly's car.

"Ever tried pho?" Miles asked.

"Who?"

Miles laughed. "It's Vietnamese. It's spelled p-h-o, but it's pronounced *fuh*. Essentially, it's giant heaps of rice noodles in a bowl of killer broth. It's not exactly picnic food, but it's still cool enough outside that we could try our luck at a spot up the hill. We still have . . ." Miles looked at his analog watch. "A little over an hour and a half before we need to pick up Tuck. I can call in our orders, and then we can look over what's left to do on our list."

I'd never eaten Vietnamese food, but the idea of trying something Miles so obviously enjoyed was an easy yes for me.

"What's your heat level?" he asked, making the call on his phone. "On a one to five scale."

"Maybe a one and a half?"

"Come on, live a little. The spices are the *best* part. Trust me."

"Fine. I'll take a three, then."

Naturally, Miles ordered a five for himself.

Our food was ready and waiting when I pulled up to the restaurant, and in only a matter of minutes, Miles was navigating us up a hill to an overlook surrounded by pine and fir trees. I couldn't quite make out the view from where we'd parked, but with how curvy the road had been on the way up, my guess was that it had to be something pretty spectacular for Miles to have starred it on his pizza box map. So far, everything he'd shown me today had been worthwhile.

But maybe that had more to do with the company I was with than the destinations we explored. Miles was easy to be with. There was no pretense or awkwardness with him. He simply said what he meant—a quality I appreciated even if I didn't always reciprocate in kind.

By some sort of rare magic, the only wooden picnic table in the clearing was empty, though there were plenty of cars parked along the sides of the street.

"This spot is also a trailhead," Miles pointed out. "It's about a six-mile loop."

"Have you hiked it before?" I asked, absently wondering how many miles I could make it before my hip locked up on me completely. Probably less than one.

"Many times." He regarded me as he reached inside the car for our to-go bags. "It reminds me quite a bit of the trail we'll be hiking for Dude Camp later this summer. I'm hoping Tucker will be able to join us for that. He seems to love the outdoors."

"He does for sure," I agreed, careful not to overcommit. I certainly couldn't tell Miles about the tight budget we were on, as he seemed to have a knack for producing free or severely underpriced goods for our benefit all too often. Nor could I share my reservation about the rate at which Tucker seemed to be attaching to our downstairs neighbor. I needed to keep a better grip on that, make sure my son had a healthy understanding of what Miles was . . . as well as what he wasn't. Those lines were easy to blur for a ten-year-old. Just like they were easy to blur for a twenty-nine-year-old.

We strolled together at a speed that was likely half of Miles's usual cadence, but he stayed close until we reached the table, where he set down our dinner. Only I couldn't help but continue on a few steps more to where the golden glow beckoned. My breath hitched at the sight of a city spotlighted for all to see under the intensity of the sun's rays. There were so many textures and shapes to absorb—trees, water, fields. High-rises, bridges, and several ornate cathedrals. All of it strikingly familiar.

I lifted my hand, connecting the dots in the air with my pointer finger. "There's the Monroe Bridge, and the clock tower, and the university." Each and every place Miles had starred for us on his map was here for our viewing pleasure like the miniature town sets my mom put out each Christmas. "I can see the whole city from up here."

My city, I thought, the words unlocking a newfound freedom inside me as my gaze swept from right to left. One day, this view would be as familiar to me as it was to Miles. A revelation that caused a flurry of hope to fill my lungs.

Beside me, Miles tucked his hands into his pant pockets, his voice low as he spoke, "I needed this tonight."

"Thanks for suggesting a tour," I said, blinking away the sun spots in my vision.

"Thanks for agreeing to drive."

The shaded June breeze caused a scattering of goosebumps to rise on my exposed arms, and I shivered. Unknotting the gray hoodie from around my waist, I said a silent good-bye to the Gwen-inspired splash of color on my T-shirt and zipped the hoodie to my chin.

Miles eyed me, smiled. "Come on, let's get you warmed up."

After we made our way back to the table, Miles sat beside me on the bench so we could both face the view ahead. I could only imagine the sunset to come. When Miles placed the steaming bowl in front of me, I was grateful for the warmth curling around my face. I unwrapped the plastic soup spoon while Miles grabbed a set of chopsticks.

"There's another pair if you want them," Miles offered. "Also, there's no shame in picking up the bowl and drinking the broth. Bottom line—there's no wrong way to eat pho, except to not eat it at all."

"Good to know."

While Miles heaped several mouthfuls of noodles into his mouth, I tentatively sipped on a spoonful of broth, my tongue instantly tingling with a level of spice it had never been privy to before.

"So?" he asked. "What do you think of that level-three heat scale?"

Eyes wide, I held up a finger, trying not to cough out my answer.

"It's . . . good," I managed. Honestly, though, the flavor *was* good. *Really good.* Far better than what I'd been prepared for, even if my eyes were starting to tear up. I reached for a napkin. "Although the fact that you ordered a level five for yourself is . . ." I shook my head. "Concerning."

He laughed again. "Believe me, this is mild compared to some of the peppers I've eaten." His amused smile widened as he used his chopsticks to push a water bottle in my direction. "At least you're not cold anymore."

"True." I removed the cap and took a long, satisfying drink.

"So I've been wanting to ask you something."

I braced for him to bring up the situation at the warehouse today with Safety Vest Ed, but instead, he surprised me with, "Why documentaries?"

My shoulders relaxed. "My dad got me hooked on them as a kid."

"Like a father-daughter bonding kind of thing?" he asked before taking another bite of pho.

"Um, not exactly. More like a father-daughter pep talk type of thing."

It wasn't like me to reveal something so personal in such a casual way, but then again, there was a part of me that felt as if I'd known Miles for as long as I'd known Molly. I supposed that, in a way, Miles had become an extension of my friendship with his sister, someone hovering in the background of so many of our heart-to-heart conversations over the years. He'd unknowingly added depth to her childhood stories and life experiences long before I met him in person, and it was easy to imagine that Molly must have felt something similar when she met Tucker face-to-face for the first time, too.

Miles's curious gaze encouraged me to continue.

"I went through some difficult years. Well, probably more like a difficult decade."

Miles lowered his chopsticks, his attention now rapt.

"I was in a pretty bad skiing accident when I was ten." I took a deep breath, exhaled. "It was our big fifth-grade field trip right before Christmas break, and my mom was adamant that she didn't want me to go. But in the end, my dad had convinced her that nothing could go wrong on the bunny slopes." I smiled weakly. "Only, I didn't stick to the green run like I was supposed to. I followed one of my friends to the blue run—the intermediate slope—when our parent chaperone was looking after the other kids in our group. Halfway down, I was hit from behind by a skier who lost control. He was four times my size, and honestly, my memory is kind of a black hole after that. I was life-flighted to the nearest hospital with a shattered pelvis and femur."

Miles shook his head. "You must have been in the hospital for a long time."

"Weeks. But that doesn't count all the surgeries that came after, or the physical therapy. At one point, the surgeon told my parents I might not ever walk again because of where the break on my growth plate was located." I swallowed, my hand absently pressing against my left hip.

"I guess you showed them," Miles said in a way that caused warmth to course through my chest.

"I guess I did," I smiled back. "Although, learning to walk again wasn't my only challenge. When the arthritis set in, and my limp became more predominant, my teen years became especially difficult." I rubbed my lips together, remembering the depth of my depression. The days, weeks, months when I refused to leave the house. The worried, whispered conversations I'd overheard between my folks late into the evening. The way I felt like a prisoner in my own body.

"My dad isn't a big conversationalist, but he found a way to reach me that was all his own—through documentaries and videos about people who were thriving in life with all different types of physical limitations." I stirred my noodles, the spices mixing into a funnel in the middle. "There was something transformative about seeing a young girl struggling to put on her school backpack or walk across a room holding a glass of water, determined not to spill it . . . those were the videos that inspired me most. And I suppose in my own way, I'd like to inspire others through the same kind of medium. What Gwen calls visual storytelling."

That was the nice answer, the one packaged in a pretty inspirational bow that could likely win an essay on the subject if needed. But it wasn't the only answer to why documentaries mattered to me. It was simply the only one I could bring myself to speak out loud, even to someone as genuine as Miles McKenzie.

"I have no doubt you will." He rotated his water bottle and looked over at me again. "Is that the subject you want to make your documentary about? People who have . . . people who are differently abled?"

I smiled, appreciating his use of the most current terminology. "No. There's quite a lot out there on the subject already. I don't think I'd have a new angle to share." Plus, I had no interest in choosing a film project inspired by myself. Subject matters I researched and cared about, sure. But the idea of being my own muse for a film project was a nonstarter. "To be honest, I'm still in the brainstorming stage when it comes to project ideas. There's a lot of criteria to consider." Like having to find five separate individuals with unique story angles, all connected to a common theme.

"That's what you were waiting on Gwen to send you earlier—the rules of the mentorship."

"Yes, and her mentor assignments. Once I get to the actual storyboard stage, my project idea will have to be approved by her and the program director." The mere thought of having anything to do with Victor Volkin again made my stomach roil. "All of it will feel a lot more real when the gear package comes."

"Oh yeah? Does everyone in the competition receive one?"

"All ten of us, yes. Like everything else, there are a few stipulations with it. But ultimately, as long as we use it to shoot our submitted documentary at the end of the mentorship period, the gear is ours to keep." I couldn't dim my rising joy at the thought of holding that camera in my hands for the first time. "It will be the nicest setup I've ever had." *Times five.* "The real timeline for choosing my project will begin once the camera arrives."

"So what's your top idea so far?"

I wrapped my cold fingers around the still-hot bowl of pho. "Well, I know quite a bit about small-town tourism, but that would require a trip back to Alaska for interviews. . . ." I allowed the sentence to die a slow death.

"I take it that's not an option."

I stared at him a moment, putting words to thoughts I'd never before shared. "My parents would welcome me home at any time. They're good people—great people, even. But sometimes, even with the people we love most, space is required for growth. And I think we've all reached the point where space is needed, though my mother would likely never admit that. If she had her way, I'd stay locked in their storehouse with Tucker forever." My laugh was weak, and yet my words rang with the kind of pained truth that sent an ache through my chest. She called Tucker nearly every day, and though I always made a point to say hello and fill her in on some small detail I knew she'd appreciate, her disappointment over my decision to leave was still as evident as the day we boarded that airplane. "My parents need to find their own rhythm as much as I need to find mine with Tucker. It's been a long time since . . ." I stopped myself from continuing down that mental path. There were too many land mines attached to the one other time I hadn't lived at home with my parents. "Since I was free to make my own mistakes."

Miles's nod was both slow and reflective, and for once, I didn't let the observation slip away. "What are you thinking?"

"That our childhoods were pretty different," he said without hesitation.

I knew a bit about Miles's upbringing—at least, I knew what Molly had shared with me. "It must have been hard on you when your parents left. You and Molly were both so young."

He gave a halfhearted shrug. "Seventeen isn't so young."

"It's only six and a half years older than Tucker." My son's age was an ever-present measuring stick to most things having to do with time.

The wince Miles released confirmed he hadn't quite worked out the same math. "Well, yikes, I guess when you put it that way . . ."

And yet what other way was there to put it? The numbers didn't lie. The way Molly told it, Miles had volunteered to stay back from whatever mission they were leaving on in order to watch over her. I supposed it explained some of the reason he chose the career path he did—he had one foot in both worlds.

Miles drank the rest of his level-five fire broth as if it were apple juice, then started to launch into another round of questions for me, only this time I was ready for him.

"Nope." I shook my head. "You're not doing that again."

"Doing what? I'm just asking questions."

"That's right. But you've asked *me* ninety-nine percent of the questions today."

"So you're saying it's your turn now?" he chuckled as I nodded. "Okay, fine, what do you want to know?"

I racked my brain for something good.

"That pensive stare of yours is making me feel like I need to get a giant swinging spotlight for you to point at my face," he joked.

"I'm just thinking."

"You do that often."

But there had been one question I'd been mulling over since the night we'd solved Lady Gwen's riddle together. "Why is it you won't be traveling as much now?"

By the way Miles's face went from jovial to stoic in two seconds flat, I certainly hadn't lobbed an easy one at him. Perhaps I should have started with *"What's the spiciest pepper you've ever eaten?"* But I'd never been great at small talk.

"That's a touchy topic at the moment," he said on the tail end of a long sigh.

"My limp was a pretty touchy topic, too. Just sayin'." Apparently, my inside voice had broken loose. *What was in that broth?*

As if that was all it took for him to lower his guard enough to trust me, he responded with, "I've recently been reassigned."

"Reassigned? As in you're no longer working at the church?"

His eyes shifted left to right as if he'd missed something. "Have you been there—to Salt and Light?"

"Only online." My preferred method of churching was definitely via the Sunday-morning livestream, but I'd seen Miles on camera plenty of times. Whether he was giving an announcement or leading prayer or assisting somewhere in the background, it was rare I didn't see him at some point during the service. "It seems like a good place."

"I grew up there," he said, staring off toward the cityscape, a sad sort of whimsy to his voice. "I swear I've spent more hours inside that building than anywhere else in the world." His laugh was light, but something about it made my chest constrict. "We visited off and on when I was a kid. Our grandma lived in the area, and my dad had a mentor from his Bible college days nearby that he stayed in contact with pretty regularly—he's actually my mentor now." He paused, though I could tell his thoughts had not. "No matter where we lived in the country when I was a boy, Salt and Light was always a home base of sorts, even more so after my parents left. I can't imagine what my teen years would have been like without it, but honestly, it's hard to imagine what my adult life will look like without it, either."

"Where are you going?"

"To a place called Riverside Family Resource Center." He pointed down at the valley now awash under a kaleidoscope sky, waiting for my gaze to follow his finger. "It's just on the other side of the bridge and a few blocks over." The flatness in his voice held little back. Unlike me, Miles wasn't skilled in hiding his true feelings.

"You're not looking forward to that change."

This pause was longer, as if he was having to dig deeper for the answer. "Honestly? No. But even though the location may not be my first choice, my calling to care for people should be the same wherever I go."

"That sounds like a healthy perspective."

"Don't be fooled. That perspective is currently on loan to me, courtesy of Rev Carmichael." He chuckled self-deprecatingly and ran a hand through his hair. "But as you can probably tell, I'm not quite there yet."

"It's hard to leave the only place we've called home—no matter if it's a tourist shop in small-town Alaska or a megachurch in eastern Washington."

He tipped his eyes to mine again. "Has it been hard for you—moving here?"

"Yes," I admitted for the first time. "Change of any kind goes against my nature. But I've had to remind myself that every day I stay here, every new challenge I take on, every new memory I get to create with Tucker . . . is the making of a new history. One that is ours together. Don't get me wrong, I still love the security that comes with the familiar. But I'm slowly starting to realize just how limiting it can be to only know one kind of existence."

Something grabbed in my stomach at the collision of our gazes.

"Now that perspective sounds like the real deal. Yours must not be on loan."

I bumped his knee with mine. "I have every confidence that wherever you go, your calling to care for people will be obvious." It certainly was to me. "Most people can tell the difference between someone who genuinely cares for them and someone who is motivated by . . . other things. Other agendas." Unfortunately, I hadn't always fallen into the category I deemed as *most people*. I'd made some big mistakes that had come with even bigger consequences by not discerning motives correctly.

"I appreciate that, Val. Thank you." He gave a hearty sigh and stared out once again at the setting sun. "The hardest part will be staying grounded in one place."

I could only imagine how difficult that would be for him. "Are there at least options for you to travel again at some point?"

"There are some options on the horizon." He twisted his neck to look back at me, swallowed. "But all would involve a different level of sacrifice."

I'd only recently begun exploring the depths of God as a relational being last fall, but I had no doubt that what Miles was entrusting to me was rare, given his line of work.

"How will you know which sacrifice is the right one?"

The corner of his mouth lifted into a wry grin. "Please let the record show that you've been way harder on me than I was to you during this special edition of Q&A with Val and Miles."

I laughed but secretly reveled in the combination of our names.

"Rev tells me I need to practice being still." He glanced at me. "The whole 'be still, and know that I am God' kind of quiet doesn't come naturally to me."

"Perhaps that's because you're constantly in motion."

Miles reached for his phone and tapped the black screen until it lit up. "Have you been talking to Rev? Is this where he pops out from behind the trees and stages an intervention?"

I laughed, and once again, I saw the familiar resemblance of my best friend in him. "I think I must have the opposite issue. I get stuck in my head a lot—too much."

"You don't say?" he teased, nudging my arm.

I nudged back. "Really, though, I overanalyze everything a thousand times before I make a decision. It's a miracle I pursued the mentorship after only rethinking it for a few hours."

"Rethinking it?"

"When I agreed to take the job with Molly, my plan was to put money away and try my best to create a life for Tucker and me outside of the provision of my folks."

"Wait—and what about the film stuff? What was your plan with that?"

"I didn't have a plan for that. I knew I couldn't handle a full-time job with Molly, a film mentorship, and raising a son on my own at the same time. I figured it would be a hobby, and that maybe with time, the desire to do something more with it would just kind of . . ."

"Die," he concluded for me.

I sighed. "It was the responsible choice—it probably still *is* the responsible choice. Yet here I am, a single mom without a secure job, who took on a nonpaying mentorship that's going to require more time than I've ever put into anything."

"God's given you these unique talents so they can be used. I'm glad you're not keeping them hidden."

"You sound like a pastor."

"I hope I sound like a friend."

"You do," I replied softly. Only Miles didn't just *sound* like a friend—he was a friend. That truth wrapped around me like a welcome embrace.

"Val . . ." His expression grew serious as he searched my face. "What Molly said earlier today in the driveway, about a bully at the warehouse . . ."

I shook my head. "I'm okay, Miles. The guy was ignorant and condescending, but I'm okay. Really. I've let it go." I touched his arm. "You should, too."

He placed his hand atop mine, and something electric surged through me as he said, "You make that sound easy."

I slipped my hand from grasp and smiled up at him. "Nothing is easy without practice."

After a slow nod, in which Miles seemed to be contemplating something far deeper than this conversation, he reached for his pizza box map and slid it across the table toward me. "We still have time to see a few more things on the map before we pick up Tucker if we leave now."

But instead of jumping up and racing away, I continued to stare out at the horizon, hoping to remind him of our earlier conversation. The one about stillness. "Or maybe we could just sit here awhile longer. The sky is spectacular tonight."

From the corner of my eye, I watched his mouth curve into a grin. "It is indeed."

· 14 ·

Miles

It was strange how much power *context* had over perspective. A little over a week ago, I'd been a passenger in Val's new-to-her car, driving down this very street to point out a hundred-year-old landmark that upon its completion in 1911 was the longest concrete arch-bridge in the world. Today, I was more focused on the trash overflow on the walkways of Riverside Family Resource Center so as not to even recognize the five-o'clock shadow the Monroe Street Bridge had cast on the parking lot.

Then again, it was difficult to see anything over the economy-size box I'd been given to pack my desk in. Turned out, I had more things stored at the church office than I realized.

As news trickled down that I'd be overseeing the old family center, a few coworkers had banded together to throw me a not-quite-good-bye party, creating a cake tower out of the morning meeting donuts and taking a few awkward photos I was sure would never be posted to the website. Twelve years as a member of this congregation—five as the outreach pastor—had come to a full stop in a single afternoon. 7.2 miles had never felt so far to drive.

I positioned the tall box of books, notepads, pens, and gag gifts from Gavin and the youth interns higher and hit the buzzer on the outside of the door. No response. I hit it again, hearing the sound reverberate on the other side of the glass in a dimly lit lobby. Again I was met with silence. It was only ten till five on a Monday night; shouldn't this place be hopping with classes and support groups?

On the tail end of a hard sigh, I hefted the box to my left arm and dug for the key I'd been handed like a bronze medal. Upon entering, there was more than just the lack of light. There was also the lack of any kind of welcome desk. The last time I'd been here, there'd been a receptionist table with sign-in sheets and peppy music playing in the background. I flicked on the light leading to another dark hallway, noticing a billboard with an invitation to a Ladies Valentine's Tea Party. Though it was June now, I was impressed to see that at least someone had taken the initiative to host such an event at this facility. Until I read that it was dated for Valentine's Day of last year.

What a disgrace. I hadn't known Otto Matteus all that well, but what I did know was that next to Jesus and his wife, this family center had been the love of his life—his legacy, even.

I nearly tripped over an extension cord that seemed to run the length of the hallway leading to . . . I had no idea where. As I headed toward where I vaguely recalled an office being stationed, a thunderous pounding like a stampede of angered elephants cut through the soundless tomb of a building. The box slipped to my mid-thighs.

The drumming continued. Every three or four seconds. Two hard beats at a time, followed by brain-numbing silence. If this was the Rapture, then I'd missed a few key steps. Unless Christ had swapped the trumpets out for a full marching band.

I abandoned the box to investigate.

After hooking a right at the lobby and passing three large classrooms toward the auditorium, I reached the source of the noise. I pushed the swinging doors open, unprepared for the sight of twenty or so senior citizens sitting in front of stationary exercise balls, drumsticks in hand. The instructor at the front of the room commanded her own sticks up and down at the appropriate times to match the too-quiet music playing from her phone's speaker.

As if on instinct, the woman in her late forties twisted around. It took nearly five seconds for me to place the familiar yet out-of-context face staring back at me. Trisha Woodward, a longtime member of Salt and Light, and the only part-time employee at Riverside . . . though I hadn't a clue what all she did here. Unless I was looking at it right now.

"Miles?" She shook her head and then said my name again with more enthusiasm before halting her class by pausing the music. "Pastor Miles! You're here!" She smacked her hands together. "Oh, I was so delighted when I heard you were the pastor selected for Riverside! It was actually pretty crazy, because I literally told Ray just the night before the announcement that I thought you'd be the perfect fit for this job! I'm thrilled to see you here."

"Hi, uh . . . Trisha—and thanks. I didn't realize you'd—"

Trisha embraced me with fervor, then increased her volume to an ear-crackling decibel to address the group. "Class, this is Pastor Miles McKenzie. He's our new support pastor at Riverside."

Trisha and I had never been the hugging type of acquaintances. Not when she visited the church office for the annual Riverside Family overview report or any of the times she'd helped out at youth functions for her teenagers. But apparently Riverside didn't much care about the social norms of our past lives. This was a vortex all its own.

A wave of drumsticks arched through the open room. It was smaller than the church gymnasium I was used to, but it was definitely a multipurpose facility. At least that was promising.

"Hi there," I said, pulling on my invisible pastor hat. "It's good to see you all. What a creative way to . . . exercise."

Dozens of smiles met my sentiment and Trisha whispered, "This is our cherished senior club. Most of them have been participating in classes here at Riverside since well before Otto got sick. They take the shuttle from the retirement community down on Brook Street. One of our members saw this style of aerobics on a YouTube video. And I have to say, it's pretty fun, although I do worry I'll be the one in need of hearing aids if I keep instructing."

"Ah." I tipped my chin toward her, keeping my voice low enough not to trigger any actual hearing aids in the room. "Can you tell me where I might find a list of all the current classes and groups that meet here?"

She turned back to her students. "MaryBeth, would you mind conducting class for a moment, please? Feel free to start the music from my phone. Passcode's the same as always."

A lady in an athletic jumpsuit with graying black hair rose from her place in the front and resumed the beat.

Trisha pointed to the doors and led me to the hallway, her smile as kind as it had always been, and I found myself thankful not only for a familiar face but for a friendly one.

"I wasn't sure you'd still be working here," I said honestly. The information I'd had to go on was as sparse as the majority of these classrooms.

"Yes, Pastor Curtis has been so gracious to me. Even through all of the transitions—and there have been many, as I'm sure you know—he's fought hard for me to keep my twenty hours a week here at the center."

I willed the surprise out of my expression. He'd fought for Trisha to keep her part-time salary here while workloads at the church office were doubling? Surely she had to be confused.

"Do you mostly teach evening classes, then?" I wouldn't think that beating exercise balls with wooden sticks paid especially well or filled more than a few hours a week, but what did I know? I was now the sole caretaker of a midtown relic.

"Oh no. I mostly come and go to open the building and help people get signed up for events and such. It's been kind of sporadic since the last intern left three months ago. Not a whole lot of routine to keep." She paused. "I can't tell you what a relief it is to see you here, though. This place needs someone with your compassionate heart and leadership skills. Not much around here looks like it did before Otto passed, but there's still a handful of volunteers who've stuck through all the temporary transitions. I was so relieved when Pastor Curtis told me he was going to place a staff member here permanently. We can be doing so much more for our community, and the families and individuals who come now need much more consistency. Honestly, so do the volunteers."

I wanted to question her more about what Curtis Archer had told her about his plans of finding a more permanent replacement at the center, but I pushed my thirst for information to the side and tried to focus on the tasks ahead of me. I didn't know how long I'd be here, but I certainly intended to leave this place in better shape than I'd found it in. Plus, having a reference outside of the Salt and Light campus might prove helpful for my future steps. "So how can I find out who these volunteers are and what areas they oversee? I'd like to meet with them and see how I can encourage them in their current roles." Identifying my seasoned leaders was step one. Delegating those leaders into categories like outside maintenance, welcome station, and perhaps keeping an updated events calendar on the bulletin board wall would be step two. I didn't want to count the steps beyond those.

"It should be on the website, but . . ." The hesitancy of the statement piqued my curiosity.

"But it hasn't been updated?"

"Not for about two years."

A lucky guess. Working to keep my next sentence light, I asked, "And what about using Kevin from S&L? Technically, Riverside should have access to all the same resources as the church staff does, which should include our communications team."

She shook her head. "I've sent in at least three requests this year, but I know we aren't the priority around there. I mean, our center can't possibly compare to the needs of a ten-thousand-member congregation. It makes sense that they're having a hard time getting to us."

Only, it shouldn't have to make sense. Sadly, I had little doubt Trisha's suspicions were true. Those IT guys at S&L were swamped as it was, even without all the changes as of late.

"Would you happen to know where the username and pass-words are kept, by chance?" Because without a proper website, this place didn't have a chance at becoming a recognized ministry inside the community. Immediately, the pretty face of an incredibly talented woman who just happened to sleep one story above me surfaced in my mind.

"I think I do know where those are kept, yes." She pointed down the hall. "Have you been inside your new office yet?"

"I haven't actually. I was on my way there when I heard the, uh . . . pleasant sound of drumming."

Her laugh tittered down the hallway as she waved me on. "It's actually on the other side of the building. This side of the hallway leads to the multimedia room we were just in. That's where most of the support groups meet during the week and where we've done after-school care for single-parent families in the past." She pointed to the opposite hall that branched off the lobby. "This side of the building ends at the women's clinic. There's a locked door that adjoins a small conference room that connects to your office. For privacy. Back in the day, that room was used multiple times a week to counsel and pray with expecting mothers. But Nurse Charlotte only commutes to volunteer at the clinic on Mondays and Tuesdays now that things are . . . slower."

A fact I'd be checking up on ASAP. It was my understanding that the women's clinic—aka the crisis pregnancy center when I was growing up—was for women in need of medical attention and counseling by an experienced professional. And in my mind, that was one of the most critical resources Riverside Family Resource Center had to offer the community.

When we reached the office door, she pulled on the keychain around her neck and slipped the key inside the lock. I wondered who else had a key to the head office. She seemed to hear my unspoken question. "The interns used this office from time to time to make phone calls or work on their laptops for school or just hide away from their growing responsibilities at the center." Her eyes rounded, and she shook her head quickly. "Sorry, that was rude, forgive me. I'm sure the interns from the seminary meant well, it's just, if you don't have a heart for people who need a little extra in life, it really shows, you know?"

The target of her words landed square on the left side of my chest. I did know. I often vetted the volunteers who served on the missions teams I led abroad based on that same philosophy. If you couldn't see people—*really see them*—through their brokenness, their hardships, their unexpected circumstances, then you had no place serving in ministry.

I scanned the hallway just outside Otto's office, seeing his portrait on the wall with his life and death dates engraved underneath it. But something about entering this space made me a bit twitchy. Anxious. What would Otto think about me taking his place? For however temporary it was? I turned my focus back on Trisha, clearing my throat and my head in the process. "How long have you worked here at the center?"

Trisha's smile held a nostalgic gleam. "Oh, I was coming here long before Otto hired me on as admin. I joined The Well—that's our women's group—back in '03. Jackson was just a few months old, and I was lonely—desperate, even—to meet other women, some who understood what it was like to raise a baby on their own. I attended the support meetings consistently for three years before I met Ray at a summer kickoff event. He was the guy sitting in the dunk tank while the kids threw baseballs at the bull's-eye." She laughed and then sobered quickly. "Honestly, I don't know where I'd be today without Riverside, and without the services it's provided for me and my children over the years." Her eyes shone with moisture she tried to blink away. "I know a building can't be responsible for saving a soul, but in my hardest season of life, the people here reached out to me and showed me the truest nature of Jesus. And because of that, this place will forever be linked to my salvation story."

The conviction in her voice roused a feeling inside me that had long been dormant. A displacement I'd wrestled with long before I ever stepped foot into this building or took my last mission trip abroad with Salt and Light. Perhaps before I even studied to become a pastor.

"Anyway." Trisha swiped a finger under her eyes. "I believe the passwords you'll need for the website are in the top desk drawer there. Feel free to ask me whatever questions you might have. I don't know everything, but I'll be happy to assist with whatever you need during the transition."

I ignored the stab of guilt that followed her offer, seeing as one day, I would be yet another leader transitioning out of Riverside, looking to go elsewhere. But that day wasn't today. And it likely wasn't even a year from today, given the last email exchange with my father. What was it Val had said about every day being a new chance to help create a new history? Well, perhaps that applied here, as well. Riverside needed a chance at making some new history.

"Thanks, Trisha. I really appreciate your help today."

As she went back to her class, I collected the box I'd dropped in the middle of the hallway and set it on the floor in the corner of the office. Though my understanding of all my new role would entail was still sketchy at best, I did know one thing: Trisha Woodward was the true face of Riverside Family. If she'd take it, I'd make her the head of the welcome desk and all administration work. Effective immediately. As far as I was concerned, Riverside wasn't to blame for falling into disarray after the death of their faithful leader or the subsequent transition of responsibility to Salt and Light.

That blame fell on Pastor Curtis Archer.

Taking the binder—yes, an actual three-ring binder full of usernames and passwords and other vital information—with me, I took a thorough walk-through of the center. I opened every door, closet, and cupboard, jotting down notes of things to ask or verify in the coming week. Thankfully, the majority of the facility appeared to be in good working order. Nothing a big volunteer workday couldn't solve—step three of infinity.

Perhaps the most surprising observation was that most of the building didn't seem to get a lot of use during the week at all. I supposed in some ways, that revelation was worse than discovering unexpected disrepair. A facility that had open doors and rooms to share but had no visibility or connection to reach the very people who needed it most was clearly a wasted resource. So why hadn't Curtis shut it down the second he started making budget cuts?

It was a question I pondered until the last exercise drummer had loaded into the community shuttle. With more mixed feelings than I came in with, I locked up the doors and headed to my car. My list of upcoming projects multiplied with every step.

∞∞∞

Sometime after the eleven o'clock hour, long after Tucker had told me all about his day with Kadin and long after I'd devoured the reheated plate of chili verde enchiladas Val had offered me for dinner, I fiddled with the archaic website for Riverside Family Resource Center. Half the site had refused to load, while the other half was filled with a timeline of outdated events or pictures and articles dated before Otto's death three years ago.

And still, somehow, I'd managed to make it look worse.

The creak of footsteps above my head and the tug of a rolling chair I'd come to connect with Val's late-night hours was the only prompt I needed to send her a message. Desperate times and all that. I typed into the message box at the bottom of my laptop screen and clicked *send*.

Miles

Let's say you know a guy who likes to think he's techy when he's really not. And let's say that same guy thought he could update a very archaic website. And then let's say he somehow made it look worse. How much do you think that guy should expect to pay to have it completely redesigned?

Val

Does this non-techy guy happen to live close by?

Miles

I believe he lives very close by, yes.

Val

What's the hosting site?

Miles

Uh?

Val

Can you send me the link?

Miles

Warning: you may need to avert your eyes. It's bad.

Running a hand down my face, I sent her the link and waited an excruciating five minutes before she messaged back.

Val

I don't think this can be saved.

Something about her honest assessment made me laugh—hard.

Val

I just heard you laugh.

I laughed again, conscious this time of the way the sound traveled. I stared directly above me at the ceiling, imagining her sitting in front of her giant NASA monitor, her hair pulled back and away from the delicate features of her face. I remember Molly complaining about how more women should wear their hair down, that it's a better look for ninety percent of face shapes or whatever the statistic she rattled off was. But I'd seen Val with her hair down and with her hair pulled back, and maybe she just happened to fall into the ten percent category, but I didn't think she had a better or a worse way to wear it. I thought back to the way the breeze had blown the end of her braid over her shoulder while we ate pho at the trailhead and while we shared the most real conversation I'd had with anyone in . . . a long time. Her face hadn't lacked for anything that day.

Miles
It's super weird you can hear me.

Val
Totally weird.

Miles
So . . . is there any possibility you might be willing to discuss pricing options on how to make this site less of a hodgepodge of 90s clip art and more of a professional site that actual humans might be interested in?

Three seconds later, I heard Val laugh and immediately wished I could hear it again.

Miles
Heard that.

Val
If only I knew Morse code.

The slide tap, tap slide of her foot directly above me had me smiling. Val was far cheekier than she first let on, a fact I'd become more aware of since our sightseeing drive.

Miles
Pretty sure millennials replaced Morse code with texting. (Yet another strike against us.)

Val
True. Yet I must agree with some of those strikes . . . I miss straws.

I stretched my legs out on the couch, pulling my laptop from the coffee table to my thighs.

Miles
Don't judge, but I keep a stash in my car and in my kitchen. You're welcome to them anytime.

Val

That might be the best perk as your tenant so far. You really must advertise such a rare feature.

Miles

I'm not sure I should be flattered or crushed that you find my secret straw stash my best tenant perk when I gave you an 11-point sightseeing tour of our grand city last weekend. Is there a grading system attached to these perks?

Val

Mexican Coke Talks- 7.7, Decoding Gwen's Riddles- 8.9, Used Car Dealing- 9.3, Sightseeing and Pho- 9.5, Secret Straw Stash- 10.0

Better?

Miles

Much. Thank you for the insider's guide. I'll be sure to leave you a referral review.

Val

Oh! I nearly forgot about book referrals. Also a 10.0.

Miles

Wait—is that your way of telling me you finished *Mere Christianity?*

Val

Last night. Well, technically early this morning. So good. As your sister used to say for her best beauty products—"This earned a solid five lip smacks."

I busted out another round of laugher, imagining C. S. Lewis trying to interpret my sister's rating system of his spiritual prowess and at Val's quick-typing wit on a keyboard. So this was what really went on inside her head. . . .

Miles

I'm glad you liked it. Maybe we can discuss our favorite quotes along with your pricing for a new website soon? 🙏 Please don't turn me down, I'm desperate.

I had no idea if the center budget could afford Val's level of expertise or artistic excellence. I'd seen her talent at work for years on my sister's channels. She was hardly an amateur. And there was also absolutely no way I'd allow her to work for free, not when I knew part of the reason she was up working this late was to make ends meet. Tucker continued to be the easiest nut to crack when it came to getting the real insider's information.

Val

Why don't I work on setting up the framework for the site and you can send me information as you get it? I can come to the center and take pictures once I get my new camera. I'm talking through the contract regarding my gear with Gwen tomorrow. Should get it next week sometime.

Miles

That sounds quite prestigious.

Val

Technically, the contracts are issued from Victor Volkin's Film Academy. But don't let that fool you. Lady Gwen has high standards, too.

Miles

Why do I need her to be British?

Once again, I heard her delight upstairs and couldn't keep the smile from my face.

She sent a link and a picture then—Gwen's entire IMDb page complete with a gallery of pictures. I skimmed through the dates, the facts, the award nominations and accomplishments, and then read the information on her childhood.

Miles

Ha! I knew it! She looks like she could be a part of the royal family. Quite distinguished.

Val

Thus why I call her Lady Gwen. She said it on our first call as a joke, but the more I get to know her, the more fitting it is.

I clicked on a few articles with Gwen's name—most having something to do with age discrimination in Hollywood. I skimmed through each one, becoming more and more impressed with Val's Lady Gwen as I read on. I hadn't given much thought before now to the issues she raised, but her arguments were sound, the examples she cited as disturbing as they were unacceptable.

Miles

I'm glad you're working with her.

Val

Me too.

I yawned and glanced at the time on the bottom of the screen. After midnight. Sometimes I despised being an adult. What I wouldn't have given for another hour on messenger with Val Locklier and her winsome wit.

Miles

Okay, Night Owl, I have to be up early to go over some financials regarding the center. I'll start sending you all the updated information I can get for the website from Trisha over the next few days or so.

Val

Sounds good.

Miles

Don't stay up too late. 😊

Val

Shall I tally points for the Overprotective Landlord perk?

Miles

When can I cash these points in for friend points?

Val

Hmm . . . 😔 Consider them cashed.

Miles

Good. Now I'll sleep much better tonight.

· 15 ·

Val

I'd tracked the package from Los Angeles to Spokane for the last two days, receiving text updates at every post office check-in. I couldn't remember the last time I'd anticipated something as much as I had this gear. But here it was now. In my living room. Addressed to me. The Sony Alpha A7 III Mirrorless Digital Camera with 28-70mm lens and accessory kit bundle. The same bundle sent to every mentee selected for the Essence of Filmmakers Mentorship Program.

Tucker leaned over my shoulder as I knifed the box open. "Can I keep the poppers? Kadin and I can run them over with his skateboard."

I laughed. "Sure." Of course my son would be the most interested in the only obnoxious component of this entire package. He reached inside and pulled out the layers of bubble wrap and then sat back on his heels, waiting for me to pull out the camera. I pursed my lips together, my insides resembling the sporadic pops of excitement Tucker was about to partake in.

As my hands wrapped around the camera's sleek, cool body, my breath pinched tight inside my chest as if a single exhale might break the magic of the moment. It wasn't the first professional gear

I'd owned, but it was certainly the savviest. My iPhone's technology and video capabilities had long ago surpassed my previous gear. But this camera wasn't meant for hobbyists. This camera and the filters, tripod, and all five of the perfectly fitted lenses were for serious filmmakers. As was the custom rolling gear bag.

From my place on the floor, I took several minutes to examine every button and special feature in the ray of dazzling sunlight streaming through my living room window. I'd read and watched every piece of information I could find about its lightweight design and intelligent functionality. I took special note of first-time user tips, cautions, and highlights.

Now I just needed to figure out what on earth I was going to shoot with it.

The deadline for my approved project idea and storyboards was quickly approaching, and after today's call with Gwen, it appeared I was no closer to a breakthrough. I'd submitted three new pitch ideas via storyboards for her approval in the last two weeks, and she hadn't seemed excited about a single one of them. Certainly not excited enough to pass them along for Mr. Volkin's input. Perhaps I should be grateful for her vetting system, though I couldn't understand it. My ideas had been relevant, researched, relatable, and all revolved around multiple points of view. The 4 Rs of Volkin's Film Academy, which had carried over to the Essence of Filmmakers.

I'd said as much, too, as I'd worked hard on those storyboards, staying up long after I'd finished my freelance work.

Gwen had leveled her eyes on me. "The main problem, Val, is your ideas are all topics. Not stories. If there's no conflict, there's no story. If there's no tension, there's no story. If there's no real heart connection to your interviewees' main struggles and journeys . . . then there's no story." At what must have looked like a shadow of defeat on my face, she asked a quiet yet prodding question. "Have you ever spent time thinking through your own story, Val? I'm a firm believer that you can't tell someone else's story until you have a solid understanding of your own."

My story? I didn't have a story. Not one worth retelling, anyway. Gwen, though, now *she* had a story—multiple stories it seemed. She'd traveled, she'd adventured, she'd made a mark in Hollywood as an actress only to then battle cancer, undergo a double mastectomy, and have the determination and guts to push back against the industry norms. Not for her own sake. But for women everywhere. Gwen's story provoked change.

Something scratched at the corner of my subconscious, something dark and baiting, but like so many times before, I closed the door on its attempts for attention.

Tuck pecked me on the cheek, pulling me out of my introspection with a loud lip-smack. "Can I go over there now, Mom? Grandma Millie said that Kadin and I can give Maple Syrup a bath today as long as it's okay with you. It's going to be warm enough. She already checked the forecast."

Shaking away the last of the shadowy residue from my thoughts, I nodded. "Yes, you can tell her it's fine with me. Just be careful crossing the street. And please remember to thank her for the peanut butter cookies yesterday, too. I'll come take a few pictures of you all in a bit. You can send them to Pop and Gram tonight."

"Yep. I will. See ya, Mom." He leapt off the floor in a maneuver that would likely kill me, and I thought, not for the first time, just how good it was for Tucker to be here. How good it was for me, too.

My phone vibrated on the floor, knocking into my kneecap. And I knew even without looking at the screen whose name I'd see staring back at me.

Miles

So? Did the long-awaited package come?

I snapped a picture of the contents of said package and sent it off to him as if it was the most natural thing in the world to do. As if his anticipation for such a delivery had been as high as my own. What a crazy thought . . . and yet, Miles was the first to celebrate even the smallest of victories in my life. Over the last two weeks, our communication had increased exponentially. Our late-night messaging hours had transitioned into all-the-time hours. Just like the occasional dinner at our house had become a standing invitation he never refused.

Tucker loved this new aspect of our evenings—always entertaining Miles with whatever stories he'd saved up in his day. Often, Miles had stories of his own to share. The two were equally matched in the art of entertainment. Extrovert vs. Extrovert. I was happy to sit back and watch the show.

Last Friday, Miles had surprised us with a chicken pot pie one of the seniors at the center had made him, and as we ate it together, talking about our favorite childhood comfort foods, he'd said he would start bringing dinner home after work at least once a week. I wasn't sure what had stunned me more—the gesture itself, or the fact that Tucker and I had become included in his definition of *home*.

Miles

> That looks fantastic! Is it too soon to ask if you want to come to the center and take some pics for the website today?

I stretched my left leg out on the floor, flexing my foot and biting the smile from my lower lip.

Val

> Was already planning on it. I'm about to go take some test shots of the boys in just a minute. They're giving Maple Syrup a bath.

Miles

> Ha! Have fun with that. Tucker will be soaked by the end, trust me. You'll want to bring him a change of dry clothes.

His constant consideration of my son sent a dangerous appreciation through my core, a sensation I had begun to associate with everything Miles. Like the steady rise and fall of a chest, my awareness of his generosity, of his kindness, of his mindfulness when it came to anticipating the needs of others had become as ceaseless and involuntary as my own breathing. A disorienting revelation.

Val
Thanks for the heads-up.

Miles
See ya soon. Come hungry. I'll buy us pizza.

◇◇◇

For the first time since we moved into the apartment, I allowed Tucker to stay with Grandma Millie and Kadin while I left the house. They weren't quite finished with bath time on the farm, and Millie had just baked a fresh batch of chocolate chip scones for after they dried Maple Syrup—and themselves. Millie was a sturdy woman in her midseventies. She'd been a cattle farmer for the better part of her youth, inheriting this big farmhouse and ranch over thirty years ago from her parents. Her husband had passed away from lung cancer several years back, leaving her to tend to the chores of the land and house on her own. She had some issues with her eyesight, but the diagnosis didn't seem to hold her back, except in the way of driving. She'd had to surrender her license last year, yet even that didn't seem to dampen her spirits much as she beamed at her grandson, explaining that he was the best thing to ever happen to her and her old house. "*This old farmhouse needed some new life—and Kadin gave it just that. Energy and vibrancy galore!*"

I hadn't asked her more than a single question as I took footage of the boys laughing and soaking each other with the hose while they attempted to wash a nearly catatonic mare. But Millie had talked and talked nonetheless, sharing details of her past I couldn't imagine telling a close friend, much less a new neighbor. But even after I said my good-byes and loaded my gear into the car to head to the center, my thoughts continually wandered back to her. Who did she have to talk to in her day-to-day life? Other neighbors, maybe? Was she involved in a church? I'd ask Miles. If anyone knew, it would be him.

Miles must have been waiting for me when I pulled up at Riverside because he was outside before I'd even parked. He came around to my door, his cargo shorts and olive green T-shirt breaking the staunch mold I'd once reserved for "pastor" in my mind. If somebody told me that this man was actually the actor playing the body double for the real-life Pastor Miles, I would have believed them.

He draped a muscular forearm over the top of my door. "Nice looking ride you got there," he said as soon as I stepped out of the car, dipping his head to check the back seat. "No Tucker?"

"He's still with Kadin and Maple Syrup. You were right, I'm pretty sure the boys got more of a bath than that horse."

"Yeah, all effective bathing of farm animals comes to a halt when that hose comes out."

"Sounds like you know from experience."

"You know what they say. What happens on the farm . . ." He winked and pointed to the rear of my Subaru. "Your new gear in the back?" He opened the hatchback without waiting for my answer.

"Actually, I'd like to unload it myself—I still need to practice getting a feel for the weight of it."

When I first saw the option for a rolling gear bag in the bundles for us to select from, I'd all but gasped. Truth was, an over-the-shoulder bag would have been nearly impossible for me to carry, the shifting weight too difficult to maneuver safely.

"Wow." He tugged the bag to the edge of the trunk to examine it. "This thing looks snazzy."

I laughed at his word choice. "I'm pretty smitten."

"At least allow me to set it on the ground for you, Val." At my eyebrow raise, he held up his palms. "Blame it on my dad if you must, but I can't be the guy who stands by and watches a lady lift a heavy bag out of her car without at least offering to assist."

A lady. Not a lady with limitations. Or a lady whose body had been traumatically injured early on in her life. Just a lady.

I shook my head. "Thanks, but your muscles won't always be here to help." Instantly, my neck flared hot. Had that really just come out of my mouth?

Hiding my face from him, I reached into the car and tugged the heavy bag to the edge of the bumper. After setting my stance shoulder-width apart, I prepared to swing it to the ground. But before it could make a less-than-gentle landing on the asphalt, Miles shot out a hand to break the momentum. He guided it to the ground next to my Converse-clad feet.

"Thanks." I sighed. "Obviously, I'm gonna need some practice on the dismount."

"Anytime."

At his thoughtful response, I couldn't help but go back to what he'd said about his father. "You were lucky to have a dad who taught you such things. I wish Tucker could have had—" Shocked at the words that nearly tumbled out of my mouth, I redirected quickly, yet not seamlessly. "I'm thankful his pop has been able to teach him so much over the years."

The curious expression Miles wore begged a question I wasn't ready to answer—now or possibly ever.

Pressing the quick-release button on the handle, I locked it into position for my height. "We should probably get started with the pictures. The lighting will be perfect soon."

Thankfully, my new gear bag rolled and steered far better than it had unloaded. The glide of the wheels had next to zero drag, providing me extra confidence in my steps as we approached the entrance doors. Miles held them open so I could cross the threshold into the lobby.

"Welcome to Riverside Family Resource Center, Valerie Hope Locklier." He pointed to an empty desk at the right side of the lobby. "This is where Trisha Woodward, my part-time administrative director, works every Monday, Wednesday, and Friday, from nine to four. And in the near future, if you arrive on one of those days, she might ask you to sign in on this invisible clipboard right here. Or to leave your contact information over here"—he pointed to nothing on the tabletop—"on our yet-to-be-designed contact form."

"Ah, well, it sounds like she'll be a lovely asset to your team here. As will your sign-in system."

"Yes, our staff of two and a half won't be lacking for work anytime soon." He dropped his game show antics momentarily. "All joking aside, Trisha and her husband, Ray, have been regulars around here for many years. They've been a big help already."

It shouldn't have pleased me to hear that his new assistant was married, but it did, nonetheless. I glanced around the lobby at the incredibly reflective floor, the strong aroma of pine and citrus mingling in the air and taking me back to the days I was in charge of mopping the back room at my parents' shop. "Have you been . . . cleaning?"

He blanched slightly. "The place needed a good spit shine. I wanted you to see it at its best. For pictures."

He'd cleaned for me?

"So I take it there's not a custodian on staff?" It was hard to believe a facility like this could operate without a maintenance crew to help keep it clean. The building was the size of my old elementary school—not huge by any stretch of the imagination, but definitely not a *Little House on the Prairie* schoolhouse, either. It looked to be one story and shaped like a T, the hallways jutting off the main lobby like left and right arms.

"We have one deep cleaning a week—on Saturday evenings. That's the half part of our two-and-a-half staff members."

"Ah," I laughed. "Got it."

I glanced back to the empty parking lot and then down the dimly lit hallway. "Have you been here by yourself all day?"

"Not all day. Nurse Charlotte was here earlier. She helps with the moms' group on Monday evenings and also volunteers two afternoons a week in the clinic."

"There's a clinic here?" I glanced around, wondering how I'd missed that detail on my way in. "Where?" But perhaps a better question was *why?*

"It has its own private parking lot and entrance around back." He pointed to the right of the lobby, to an area I couldn't see from where I was standing. "This long hallway dead-ends at an exit door that leads directly into the lot."

I shook my head, still not understanding its purpose. "But what is it for?"

"Oh, it's a women's care clinic," he said casually. "Formally known as a crisis pregnancy center, but I've been told we don't use that terminology anymore—it's not relational enough." He shrugged, smiled, and went on as if completely unaware that his words had sliced through the padlock of a door I'd bolted long ago. Only now, I could see my feet walking across a white linoleum floor while the pungent notes of bleach and a cinnamon-scented holiday candle soured my stomach. I blinked up at him, the image fading as quickly as it appeared.

". . . did a lot of counseling back in those early days. It's why his office is attached to a private conference room that joins the clinic. Nurse Charlotte has a rotation schedule she keeps within about a seventy-mile radius of here."

Feeling a slight itch in the back of my throat, I worked to find my footing in this conversation again, using my camera as the prop I needed. "What all would you like me to take pictures of this evening? Anything particularly interesting happening around here tonight?"

"Funny you should ask. According to the class list located on our unreliable website, there could either be a girls' intro to dance class starting tonight in our multipurpose room or a teen boys' Star Wars trivia team meeting in there at seven."

His deadpan explanation caused a laugh to burst from my throat as the image of a lost ballerina pirouetting her way into a trivia competition with a dozen Jedi Knights was something I'd love to capture on film.

"Now you know a tenth of why I'm struggling to come up with a renewed vision for this place—it's a hodgepodge of ideas."

"A functional website should help." At least, I hoped it would for his sake. The stories Miles told about what had and hadn't gone on here since the director passed away had been borderline depressing.

"Which is exactly why I'm prepared to make you an offer you can't refuse in exchange for your brilliance."

"You know, it's quite possible that one of your Jedi Knights has a website hustle on the side. Not to stereotype us or anything, but we nerds usually tend to stick to nerdy hobbies and career paths. We aren't too difficult to spot in a crowd."

He lowered his hazel eyes to mine. "One with your creative eye and talent is, though. I don't want another dime-a-dozen website for this place, and with how busy the tech team is at S&L, they won't get to it for months longer. I want to hire the best, and that's you."

His words lingered in the space between us.

"Well, then," I began, hoping my tone registered steadier than I felt, "I'd better get to work on the exterior shots." I looked down the hallway. "Good lighting waits for no man—or woman. Do you have a place for me to unpack my gear?"

"Sure do. Right this way."

To my surprise, Miles's office didn't resemble him in any way. It was musty and dark, with the finishes of a man more than twice his age. Likely the same man with the kind brown eyes and flat white hair staring out from the framed picture in the hallway. The only wall hanging inside this room was of an eagle in flight, surrounded by mountains and a Scripture verse about renewing strength and soaring wings.

Though Miles had only been here for a short while, I wondered what his long-term plans would be for such a space. The office had decent functionality, yet the natural light was blocked by what had to be the drabbest curtains ever made. Heavy and thick, they could have been used in Alaska during our long summer days. My gaze slid to the cumbersome box filled with random office supplies on the floor that was perhaps the biggest eyesore in the room.

"What?" he asked, crossing his arms and leaning against the

opposite wall while I unzipped my bag. I slipped the camera out of the mold and reached for the appropriate lens to use outside. "What are you thinking? You made a face."

I rolled my eyes. "You and your sister are obsessed with my supposed *weird faces.*"

"I never said it was a weird face. You just have this one very distinctive Val look you get when you're thinking hard about something."

"Hmm." I draped the camera strap over my neck. "Do I?"

"Come on, Val." He drew the words out in such a teasing tone that if I hadn't known him, I would have thought he was flirting with me.

Wait—*was* he flirting? Did pastors flirt?

"You're deflecting," he continued. "You wanted us to shoot straight with each other. That was your deal, wasn't it? So? Go ahead. Shoot."

Once again, a disorienting sensation took over my body. I had said that to him—hadn't I? Yet whenever Miles repeated my words back to me, they sounded far more loaded than I'd originally intended.

He moved to sit atop his desk near me, watching my hands fit the lens. "My thought was just that this office feels a bit too . . . stuffy. It's not what I'd expect for a guy like you."

He chuckled. "You do realize I've only been on site here for just over a week, right?"

I opened my mouth to respond, but he cut me off.

"And what do you mean by *a guy like me?*"

There was nothing modest or veiled about Miles's stare now.

"Just that you're, you know . . ." Attractive. Energetic. Masculine. Extroverted. Social. Charming. Effusive. Witty. Compassionate. "Young."

Young? That was the adjective I was going with?

"Wow. Thank you so much for your insight."

I tilted my head, careful to keep the humor from my voice. "I actually do have some insight for you, if you want it. Might really help with your whole lack-of-a-clear-vision thing."

The sarcasm in his eyes shifted to intrigue. "Really? What?"

I crossed the room and pulled open the curtains. Light illuminated the space in an instant as dust particles swirled. "Voilà!"

Miles fought to keep a straight face. He lost. "You know, I might need to petition the elders to up our employees to three and a half. I'm pretty sure your clever ingenuity has been the missing link around this place."

"I'm not sure you can afford me," I teased.

"Me either, since every time I ask you for a quote on your website pricing you reroute the conversation."

I shrugged and moved toward my rolling bag once more, then noticed something green peeking out from the eyesore box by his office door. "Uh . . . Miles? Is there a reason you have a potted plant living inside your office supply box?"

"I don't own any plants."

I looked again. Sure enough, it was there, lying on its side, smashed between a Dwight Schrute bobblehead and what looked like a pen holder made of Legos. "Actually, you do. I can see it."

He crossed to where I stood in two strides and peered into the box. Without taking any special care not to disrupt the pebbles and dirt, he yanked it out. "You mean this? Yeah, it's not real. One of my coworkers at S&L gave it to me at my not-quite-good-bye party."

I confiscated it from him and worked to resituate the gravel and soil before holding it up between us. "Miles, meet your first succulent. You might think she's too perfect to be real, but I assure you, she is not fake. And if you take care of her basic needs, she could very well outlive your future children."

"*Her* basic needs?" he all but choked out. "Is she a plant or a mail-order bride?"

I went on. "She's pretty low maintenance, actually. Just be sure to give her plenty of sunlight, a couple tablespoons of water every few weeks, and definitely don't toss her into a box with staplers and other sharp objects and leave her for dead."

"Uh, it might be a good idea to stop referring to it as a *she* for that last one."

I smiled. "My mom refers to her succulents as her *pretty ladies*. She has about thirty of them inside the house and even more in her greenhouse."

"Excuse me?" He narrowed his eyes. "Go back. Did you just say your mom calls them '*pretty ladies*'?"

Oh, he didn't even know the half of it. "Yep, she also says her pretty ladies prefer being sung to over being talked to, and that they have their own song preferences. They aren't fans of Aerosmith."

"Valerie Locklier," he said in a mock-stern voice that had me grinning. "You are making this up."

"I promise you, I'm not. You can call Tucker right now and ask him about his gram's houseplant routine. He'll vouch for every word I just said." I placed the potted plant back into his hands. "Maybe you should choose a song for yours—for bonding purposes after such a rough start."

"Or perhaps I should give *this* pretty lady to another pretty lady who is much better at nurturing living things than I am." He pushed the succulent in my direction and stepped closer as a swooping sensation overwhelmed me at his compliment.

"But she can keep you company on your assistant's days off," I tried again, my voice faltering.

"I much prefer my present company."

And something about the way he said it, about the way his eyes skimmed my face and his strong fingers overlapped mine in a suspended handoff made my lungs feel tight with anticipation. Somewhere in the back of my mind, a voice told me to take a step back, to keep within the unspoken boundaries of friendship. But then again, I hadn't been the one to step in closer. He had.

"Do you ever . . ." He started, stopped, then started again. "Do you ever think about that night at the wedd—"

"Pastor Miles? Pastor Miles?" A singsong voice called from the other side of the door. Followed by a knock. Two. "Are you in the office? This is MaryBeth, the one who gave you the chicken pot pie. I tried to call, but nobody answered so I figured I'd just drop by. My grandson needs to enroll for Jedi Knights trivia. Is it too late to sign him up?"

Miles cleared his throat, his eyes still firmly on mine. "Hello, MaryBeth. Yes, I'll be right out. Can I meet you in the lobby? I can get you a form from the admin office."

"Sure thing, dear."

Before I could combust into flames at nearly being caught *making eyes* at the pastor, Miles touched the sides of my arms, which paused the tornado swirling inside me, and said in a voice only I could hear, "I'll catch up with you later, okay? After you're finished outside?"

I nodded, my voice lost to whatever world I'd just woken up from.

"Okay." He hesitated at the door, looking almost as confused by the last few minutes as I felt. He pressed his lips together and then said, "I'm glad you're here."

Only I wasn't sure exactly what he meant by that. Here, as in Spokane? Or here, as in on this Earth? Or perhaps here, as in inside this office, where we'd just shared a lingering look over a houseplant that caused me to wonder what might have happened if MaryBeth hadn't knocked.

The instant his door clicked shut behind him, I fell back against the desk and waited for my heart to resume to a normal human rhythm.

It never did.

· 16 ·

Val

I waited several minutes after Miles vacated his office to slip into the hallway and out the nearest exit. Yet even as I stepped into the fresh, early-evening air, I could still feel the way Miles's gaze had settled over my skin, as if we were two people engaged in more than the beginnings of friendship. Then again, I didn't exactly have the greatest track record when it came to understanding the mind or motives of the opposite sex. Maybe Miles hadn't felt anything at all.

After several cleansing breaths, I rotated to face the building, trying to get my bearings. Only when I did, I realized my internal compass was all discombobulated. I was nowhere near the front entrance doors. I was . . . somewhere else entirely.

The sign to my left read *Riverside Women's Care Clinic*.

I took a step back, as if an extra few feet could protect me from the onslaught of memories I'd managed to keep locked away for eleven years. *Eleven years.* Memories shouldn't be allowed to haunt a person longer than a decade—it should be a rule. After all, I wasn't even the same woman I'd been back then.

I tried the handle of the door I'd just exited. Locked.

Okay, fine then. I'd just take my time walking around the building and take some shots of the exterior as planned and be back to the lobby in a matter of minutes. *Simple enough.* There was no need to think beyond that.

With each step I took, I searched the area around me for hidden texture and pretty plays of light through the surrounding trees and foliage. I looked for uniqueness in color and for anything that breathed of mystery or intrigue. And then I brought the camera to my eye and snapped picture after picture after picture. With each one, I felt my muscles stretch and relax as if claiming a new truth with each captured image: *This is who you are now.*

Lost in a world all my own, I'd moseyed along the short side of the T-shaped building, only a few yards away from the entrance of the front parking lot, when I noticed an old blue Camry to my far left. It was so shrouded by the tree line that I would have dismissed it as abandoned if not for the fogged windows and the slight movement on the driver's side.

On instinct, I lifted my camera to my eye and twisted the lens to zoom in through the windshield to find a woman hunched over a steering wheel. Long dark waves of hair fell like a curtain on either side of her face, masking her features entirely. But there was no mistaking the shake of her shoulders. Though I couldn't hear her sobs from this far away, somehow I could feel them.

As if pulled by an invisible rope, I moved toward her, every alarm bell ringing in my head at what might come after I got her attention. But before I could decide on a window tap or a simple wave she might catch in her peripheral, she flung her head back against the driver's seat, twisted the key in the ignition, and stomped on the accelerator, peeling out of the parking space.

Only I was directly in her way.

"Stop!" I screamed and shot my hands in front of me. The screech and smoke of her brakes threatened a bone-crushing impact as I pictured myself being thrown from the hood of her car and abandoned on the asphalt, immobilized and shattered for a second time.

But like a movie stunt gone wrong, her bumper hadn't blown

through my kneecaps, and there was not a single piece of windshield to pluck from my scalp.

Her car hadn't even grazed me.

With maybe a fingernail's worth of distance between me and her plastic license plate cover, the woman's bloodshot gaze collided with mine for the first time. It was then I realized my initial assessment of her had been off. This woman barely looked to be a day out of high school.

The girl practically toppled out of the car, one hand gripping her doorframe, the other shaking as it extended toward me. The hem of her T-shirt lifted just enough to expose the swollen belly that had been hidden behind her steering wheel. *Pregnant*. The revelation shocked my entire nervous system into overdrive.

"Oh my gosh . . . I could have killed you!" Her hysteria was swallowed in a half sob. "I . . . I'm sorry! I swear, I didn't even see you there!"

"Do you need help?"

She swiped at her eyes. "No, I shouldn't have come here."

And then just as quickly as she was out of her car, she was back in again, slamming the door and cranking her steering wheel until the axles screeched in an effort to maneuver around me. Only I couldn't let her leave. I just . . . couldn't.

With every bit of strength I could muster, I scurried to stand directly in front of her car again, forcing her to slam on her brakes for a second time.

She raised her hands in a *what-are-you-doing?* gesture and cracked her window.

My heart beat so wildly against my ribs it was an effort to stay standing. "You can talk to me." Because I knew the face of this girl. I knew the look of desperation she wore now. And I also knew that desperate people did desperate things when they were hurting. "I know you don't know me. But I've been scared before, too." I shook my head. "And maybe . . . maybe if we can talk for even a few minutes, you might feel differently than you do right now."

Tears tracked her cheeks, running in long streams curving at the base of her rounded jaw. She'd heard me, I knew she heard me, but she did nothing. Gave me absolutely no response. Silently, I pled with the God who knew her name—the same God C. S. Lewis wrote about and Miles and Molly McKenzie spoke about.

The same God I'd only had a true relationship with for going on nine months and still wasn't sure where I ranked in priority to ask Him for a divine intervention. Yet it didn't stop me from trying.

Her fingers flexed on the steering wheel, and I was certain she was just one smash of the accelerator away from leaving me in her exhaust and never coming back. And everything about that outcome felt like the worst possible thing that could happen.

And right there, in the middle of the empty parking lot, she turned off her car.

From somewhere behind me, I heard the distinct close of a door and my name being called. My half rotation was brief, just long enough to convey that I couldn't risk dividing my attention. Not even for Miles.

With one hand on the door handle, the girl used the other to wipe away the hair matted to her teary cheeks. And then the door opened, and she stepped out.

"Are you the nurse?" she asked.

"No, but I know how to find one for you." I desperately hoped that was true.

Suspicion crossed her features. "The clinic is closed. The flyer at the gas station said it would be open till six, but nobody was here."

So she had come here to get help.

"It's quiet inside the center. I could find you something cold to drink, if you want to come inside for a few minutes." It was about all I could realistically offer her at the moment: a listening ear in a quiet space.

I prayed it would be enough.

"Do you work here?" she asked, her long dark hair falling in a tangled cascade down her back, revealing puffy eyes and a deep olive complexion.

Again, I shook my head. "No, I'm a friend of . . . I'm just a friend. My name is Val."

"I'm Carlee."

I had no real read on her expression, but when she finally exhaled a deep breath and touched her slightly rounded abdomen, she seemed to have made a decision to trust me. At least for now.

"It's nice to meet you, Carlee."

As her other hand dropped from the door handle and she shifted away from the car, my gaze snagged on a pile of blankets just beyond her steering wheel. And then to the black duffle bag on her passenger seat. The moment her eyes connected with mine, her voice broke to a strained whisper. "I had nowhere else to go."

"Then I'm glad you came here."

She moved toward me, halting her steps briefly as her gaze tracked something over my shoulder. No, not something. Someone.

Slowly, carefully, Miles walked toward us, his eyes alight with apprehension and something else I didn't have time to discern.

"It's okay," I assured Carlee. "This is Pastor Miles. He works here. He's safe."

I had no idea why those last two words had come out of my mouth, but as soon as I spoke them, I knew they were true. Miles *was* safe. And if she could learn to trust me, then she could come to trust him, too. There was no way around his involvement now. He would need to be a part of any plan to help her from this point forward.

Carlee gave a single nod of approval, and when my eyes connected with Miles, I stretched out my arm, inviting him to an inner circle I never dreamed I'd share with anyone ever again.

· 17 ·

Miles

If panic had a pulse, then mine had found a new max sometime between the squeal of car tires and a distinctly female scream.

I'd just finished walking MaryBeth through the archaic class sign-up sheet to enroll her grandson in Jedi Knights trivia when I heard it. A scream much like one I'd heard before, only not like this. This wasn't the sound that came from being startled or surprised. This was the sound of terror.

Like a slow-mo video I couldn't speed up with a single swipe of my finger, I sprinted toward the glass exit door at the end of the hallway, watching an irrational girl throw open the door to her vehicle, threaten Val, and then try to flee the scene.

But then Val had jumped in front of her car.

I blasted through the back door, a mix of hot adrenaline and icy fear racing through me as I called her name, only to halt as she shot me a look that froze me in my tracks. The fear reflected in her eyes was a different shade than mine. It wasn't bathed in self-preservation but in something else entirely. Something I recognized even from several empty parking spots away.

Val twisted around again to focus on the girl who'd nearly killed her seconds before, and all I could do was hope I'd interpreted Val's expression correctly: *Wait*.

I remained where I was for several minutes, watching them intently, their voices carried off by a breeze that didn't quite reach my ears. And then at a pace far too slow for my liking, I moved toward them.

It was then I saw. Then I understood.

This young woman wasn't a strung-out addict in need of quick cash.

She was pregnant.

Val's gaze steadied on mine, and I'd never wanted to be a mind reader more in my life—both to send and receive messages. Because there were definitely a few messages I'd like to send Val right about now.

"Pastor Miles, this is Carlee," Val said, her voice far more solid than I anticipated after whatever had gone down in the parking lot. "She'd like to meet with our nurse."

Our nurse. I didn't miss the pronoun. Or the indication that our nurse was still present at the center.

My pastor hat was more difficult to slide on than usual, but I supposed almost witnessing a hit-and-run would do that to a guy. "Sure, absolutely. I'm happy to let our nurse know you're here." I just hoped Charlotte wasn't halfway across Washington State by now, heading to her next clinic on rotation.

My gaze touched Val's again, and I was exceedingly aware of every breath I took and every word I spoke. I didn't know where the conversational land mines were buried, but I prayed I would avoid them. "I'll just open the door to the clinic for you both. There's a comfortable waiting room inside." I stared at Val, hoping to communicate what I couldn't say out loud. "It might be more private in there if . . ." *if you think she's safe to be alone with?* "If you'd like a few minutes to talk."

Though the only way I'd leave Val alone with this unpredictable stranger was if somebody knocked me unconscious and dragged me away.

"That would be nice, thank you, Pastor Miles."

I wasn't sure if Val had ever addressed me this way before today, but I was sure I didn't care for it. I didn't want to be Val's pastor. I wanted to be . . .

I closed the thought down before it could travel any further. This was not the time.

Val leaned close to Carlee, speaking to her again in hushed tones I was certain not even a canine could hear. I'd never understand how women could communicate in that low of volume and still seem to comprehend every syllable being spoken.

They followed after me as I unlocked the clinic door with the master key. Unsure of what state I'd find the place in, I could only hope Nurse Charlotte was a tidier houseguest than some of the volunteers who "managed their classrooms" in the main facility during the janitorial hiatus.

I quickly sent an abbreviated 9-1-1 text off to our nurse. If she was anywhere close, I was certain she'd respond. I was even more certain she'd come.

Walking through the two-room clinic, I flipped on the lights, taking note of the privacy door Trisha had told me about that led directly into my office. Carlee's baggy black shirt almost could have concealed her pregnancy when she stood still. But when she walked, there was no denying it. While she was a long ways off from the overly exaggerated waddle of women on sitcoms, there was a discomfort to the way she carried herself. I wondered just how far along she was. Overseeing a women's care clinic would surely test my ignorance in all areas of pregnancy and childbirth.

Ask me to build a shelter using random materials and minimal tools in a third-world country? I was your guy. Ask me to explain the developmental stages of a life in utero after conception? Definitely wasn't your guy.

Carlee situated herself in one of the blue vinyl chairs in the waiting room, her phone in her palm, her heels bouncing on the ground with a nervous energy I could feel even from the next room over.

The phone in my own hand lit up.

Nurse Charlotte

I'm only ten minutes away at my daughter's house. Coming now. Can you keep her there?

Me? Probably not. But I had every confidence that Val could do just that.

Miles

We'll do our best.

I glanced behind me to relay the information to Val, only she wasn't there. My gaze tracked back, realizing only then that Val hadn't followed us into the waiting room. She was still standing at the clinic's open door, her fingers gripped on the wooden frame, her right foot over the threshold.

"Val?" I kept my voice light as I approached. "You all right?"

But the answer to that question was as obvious as her unfocused gaze. Despite the fact that I was close enough to touch her, Val wasn't actually here with me. Her mind was elsewhere.

Gingerly, I placed my hand over hers, the cold tremble of her fingers the only response to my presence. I brushed my thumb across the back of her wrist, waiting until she blinked up at me and took a breath.

"I'm okay. I just needed . . . a minute," she said on a shallow exhale. "Where's Carlee?"

"Sitting in the waiting room. The nurse should be here in a few minutes."

And just like that, she'd snapped on a hat of her own, her eyes alight and attentive. "I need you to find her a water bottle and a snack. I don't know when she last ate, but she'll need something soon, regardless."

"Sure," I said, though I had no idea where I'd find either request. And I certainly wasn't about to stray too far. "I can look around."

"Thank you." She slipped her hand from mine and started for the small waiting area, but I recaptured it again, squeezing it twice in a wordless reassurance I hoped she understood.

202

Sticking to my task of searching out a suitable snack and drink for Carlee, I struck gold in a mini fridge Nurse Charlotte kept in the corner of the waiting room. There were apple juices, water bottles, yogurts, and several individual bags of trail mix. There was also a Ziploc bag of Twix candy bars in the corner. I left that one alone. I may not know much about women, but I knew enough not to mess with their chocolate stashes.

Before handing over the offerings I'd pillaged, I double-checked the expiration date on them all and then excused myself to my office, leaving the door propped with an old textbook from Otto's shelf. It was perhaps the best use for *The Four Branches of Systematic Theology* I'd found so far.

· 18 ·

Val

No one would have suspected that Nurse Charlotte hadn't planned on coming back to the clinic this evening. Her movements weren't rushed or agitated when she'd come through the door and apologized for running a bit behind schedule. There was no clipboard shoved at Carlee within the first three seconds of their introduction, and no list of intimidating medical jargon and procedures for her to wade through. There was just a kind middle-aged woman with brown skin and a bright smile to match her sunflower scrubs.

After shaking both our hands, she reached into the mini fridge and took out a full-sized Twix bar and offered it to Carlee. "I always reward the bravery of a young mother with a Twix. Because their bravery is not only for one, but for two."

Carlee took it, fingering the foiled package. "Thanks."

"You're very welcome," Nurse Charlotte said, giving me a wink before gingerly sitting knee to knee with Carlee on the oak coffee table in the waiting room. "Now, Carlee, I'd like to take you back to the exam room with me, but first I'm going to need a bit of medical information from you and a couple of samples if you're willing to provide them. Does that sound good to you so far?"

"Will I have to put on a gown?" Carlee asked.

"Not if you don't want to."

Carlee seemed to contemplate this as her hand moved from her belly to the chair arm. "Will I . . . will I have to see it—on the monitor, I mean?"

"That's completely up to you. I'd certainly like to have a thorough look at your baby, though, if you're okay with that," Nurse Charlotte answered sweetly. "But my ultrasound machine is also in the exam room."

Carlee glanced at me. She hadn't cried in the waiting room, and she'd been slow to share much about the broken home she'd run from, but there were pieces I could fit together on my own. "Are you going to come in with me?"

My heart raged hard against my rib cage at her question, but with as much of a reason as I had to say no . . . the wariness in Carlee's eyes was an even bigger reason to say yes.

"If you'd like me to, I will," I told her.

Carlee gave a shrug at my response.

Nurse Charlotte extended her hands to touch both of our knees as if the two of us were now a package deal like the Twix bar Carlee clung to. "I'm so glad you brought a good support system with you today. You might be surprised at how many young ladies change their minds in the parking lot before they ever step foot in the clinic."

Carlee and I shared a covert look before I said, "I'll wait out here while you go over your medical history, and Nurse Charlotte can let me know if you'd like me to come back once you're situated, okay?"

"Okay," she said, with a note of distrust.

The nurse assisted her to her feet, and I couldn't help but notice Carlee's height and curves. She dwarfed me by at least six inches, and the clothes she wore now did little to hide her shapely figure. Both the sweatpants and oversized T-shirt looked to have been purchased from the men's department. Or perhaps they were from a boyfriend's closet?

Nurse Charlotte escorted Carlee into the exam room, explaining each step of the process in a calm and professional manner while I took a deep breath and planted my elbows on my knees, my camera swinging between my folded hands. I wrapped my fingers around the smooth angles of the camera again, facing the lens at the ground so I could stare into the playback viewer.

I scrolled through the action shots of Tucker and Kadin. And then the shots of Grandma Millie's farmhouse, where I'd played with settings and filters. I'd snapped several pictures of her as she'd walked me along the fence, sharing memories of her childhood. I continued clicking the right arrow through my shots in the parking lot after I'd exited Miles's office, the ones I'd taken outside the clinic—the bricks and rock surrounding the walkway, the rhododendron bushes, a close-up of a ladybug perched on a waxy green leaf, the fence behind a private lot of the family center . . . and then Carlee, sobbing over her steering wheel just seconds before our worlds collided.

The emotion packed within the tiny two-by-three-inch screen seemed to reach between my ribs and clutch my heart, leaving me gasping for air. Because suddenly, the faceless form hunched in the driver's seat wasn't so faceless anymore.

She was me.

I'd felt that kind of desperation once, too. Pregnant, with few options and no hope. A girl who, only a few months prior, had been uncharacteristically giddy over a handsome deckhand asking for her number while closing up her parents' shop the summer she turned eighteen.

It had been easier than I'd expected to sneak out those first few times to meet him at the tavern down the road. And no matter how long he was at sea—days or weeks at a time—he always came back, always showed up at our spot on the corner of Kodiak and Fourth. *For me.* No boys my own age had ever shown that much interest, but Jesse had doted on me, offering compliments like candy and adult drinks like glasses of ice water.

His adventures at sea had been as captivating as his Texan accent, an opening to a new world with possibilities I'd never before considered. I didn't have to be myself with him, not when I could be the bolder, flirtier, funnier, sexier version of a girl who'd been so lonely for so very, very long.

Jesse made me feel beautiful, desired, wanted . . . *accepted*. The gap between flirtation and infatuation was bridged in less time than it took to bait a hook and reel in a catch.

With promises to stay in touch, we'd said our good-byes at the end of the fishing season . . . only I discovered a parting gift six weeks later. It was only then, after those two blue lines surfaced, that I was finally brave enough to act on my heartache. Because I finally had all the proof I needed: I belonged with Jesse.

My parents would never understand. My mother would never have let me go. Not after all the lies I'd told. Not after all the fights we'd had. And especially not after all the words said about greenhorns who only wanted to turn a quick profit and warm a few beds.

But the instant I'd knocked on that apartment door in Austin, I knew I'd made a grave mistake.

"Val?"

At the sound of Nurse Charlotte's voice, my neck jerked up, the camera in my hands swinging hard into my chest.

"Carlee's ready, if you'd like to come in and sit with her."

I pressed the heels of my hands into the chair's arms and pushed to standing. Twice I reached out to steady myself on the way to the dimly lit exam room, where tranquil, spa-like music played and where the walls were decorated with peaceful quotes and pictures. My mind rolled back again to the forbidden memory box I'd stored far from reach eleven years ago.

After Jesse's female roommate had opened the door that fateful day—as seemingly confused by my presence as I was by hers—I'd opted to roll my suitcase to the bottom of the cement stairs and wait for him to come home from work. Surely, he'd sort everything out. But his homecoming hadn't been the grand reunion I'd dreamed of. There was little recognizable about the fisherman who'd once sat with me on the pier, painting pictures with his words of expansive Texas skies and the kind of sticky heat that could stretch to Thanksgiving.

"You really made a mess of things—showing up here like this," he'd said by way of greeting, a cigarette hanging out the side of his mouth. "I don't need to give Chrissy one more reason to throw me out before I hit the road again this fall." He tossed the cigarette to the ground and snuffed it out with the heel of his work boot. The pungent smell of crude oil wafted from his work uniform, causing my sensitive stomach to roil.

Throw him out? "You mean . . . this isn't even your apartment?" It hadn't been difficult to find his address online, not after all the information we'd exchanged over the summer. *How had I convinced myself he'd be happy to see me?*

The charming accent that had once sent tingles to my toes when he spoke was nowhere to be found now. Instead, it was the chill in his eyes that caused me to shiver. "I never stay in the same place too long." The implication that he also didn't stay with the same woman for too long wasn't lost on me. "Look, I don't know what provoked you to get on a plane and fly to Texas, but if you were hoping to rekindle something, I'm not the kind of guy who drags around an anchor." He scanned me up and down. "Not even one as cute and lightweight as you."

The goosebumps on my arms spread rapidly over my body. "But I . . . I . . ."

He jutted his neck out, eyes wide, making a show of his impatience. But I didn't have words for this. None of this was how I'd rehearsed it in my head. "You what, darlin'? Were you hoping our little fling could last a bit longer? Well, while that's flattering and all, it's—"

"I'm pregnant."

It was his turn to be struck frozen without answers. To stare without blinking as if he couldn't quite comprehend my meaning.

"I found out last week, and I tried to call you, but—"

"Lower your voice," he hissed, glancing up the stairs. "It's not mine. I used protection."

"But I've never been with . . ." I shook my head, crossed my arms over my chest, feeling anything but protected now. "You were my first." *My only.*

"How am I supposed to believe that?" His eyes narrowed into slits. "There were a lot of lonely greenhorns on the loose over the summer. It could be anyone's."

As if he'd shoved me, I reached out for my suitcase to steady myself.

"Wouldn't make a difference even if it was mine, though. I have no interest in being a dad."

"Jesse, you down there?" Chrissy's voice reverberated in the cement tomb of a stairwell, and he immediately hooked one hand around my elbow and one around the handle of my suitcase, moving us at a speed that had me stumbling into the parking lot.

"Get in," he said, pointing to an old red truck and tossing my bag into the back.

Like a fool, I obeyed, too scared to do anything else.

We drove in silence for close to twenty minutes, the overpowering smell of cigarette smoke causing me to roll my window down only a few seconds in. My teeth chattered so hard that the very idea of being sick seemed impossible. Then again, this *entire situation* seemed impossible.

When we stopped in a parking lot with only a few cars, he opened up his wallet and tossed two fifty-dollar bills at me. "This is all I have left until payday. Take it. I don't know how much these things cost, but as far as I'm concerned, my part is done, you understand? I don't want anything more to do with this. Or with you."

On legs that no longer felt attached to my body, I'd exited that truck, and Jesse's life, forever.

"Feel free to take a seat next to Carlee, Val." Nurse Charlotte's voice sliced through my memories as she gestured to the stool at Carlee's shoulder, the one with a perfect view of the ultrasound monitor and the wall quote directly above it:

For you formed my inward parts; you knitted me together in my mother's womb. I praise you, for I am fearfully and wonderfully made.

Psalm 139:13–14

I'd read that passage in Psalms before. It was one of the Bible verses I'd seen printed on journals and made into sharable memes on social media. But I'd never read it in this context. I'd never read it while the skilled hand of a nurse moved a device over the belly of a pregnant teen to reveal the feet, legs, arms, torso, head, and beating heart of an unborn child.

Carlee's eyes remained focused elsewhere as the lively image of a baby danced on screen.

I reached for her hand, but she didn't squeeze back.

"That sound is your baby's heartbeat, Carlee. You can hear it's nice and strong."

The nurse turned up the volume on her machine, and the steady beat filled the room.

"That's really fast," Carlee said, her brow pinched as her gaze tracked from the wall to the screen, where the nurse was pointing at the tiny flicker on the monitor.

"It's a hundred and forty-two beats a minute. Right on track."

Nurse Charlotte's wand roved to several places on Carlee's belly, capturing images from different angles and taking measurements that caused the baby to kick and roll, as if it was annoyed by the unexpected invasion.

"My goodness, your baby is having quite the dance party in there. Can you feel that?"

"A little," Carlee said, her eyes catching on the monitor once again, this time for a few seconds longer. She laid her head back on the pillow, her lips pressed together and her breathing shallow, and I wondered what was going on in her mind.

"My daughter always said it felt like her baby was trying to play tag with the transducer during her ultrasounds." Nurse Charlotte glanced over at me momentarily. "Do you have any children, Val?"

A swell of emotion rose in my throat at the thought of Tucker. "I do. I have a son." A beautiful, healthy boy I couldn't imagine my life without. "He's ten, almost eleven."

"So this is a familiar sight to you, then," she added conversationally, continuing to measure and capture images.

Familiar? No. Little about this experience today had felt familiar.

"A bit," I said, my voice thick with remembrance.

"You can't tell someone else's story until you have an understanding of your own."

Gwen's words from earlier sideswiped me as Carlee remained as stiff as a mannequin on the exam table. I was almost relieved when Nurse Charlotte set the instrument down and offered Carlee a handful of paper towels to clean the gel off her abdomen. As soon as she wiped it clean, she pulled her shirt down over her torso once again.

"So it looks like your baby is measuring right at twenty-two weeks. Is that about how far along you were thinking you were?" Charlotte asked her.

"Somewhere around there, I guess."

"These calculations do have some wiggle room, but based on the last period date you remembered, I'd say just over five months is pretty accurate. You and your baby appear to be very healthy."

Carlee bit the corner of her lip. "When is full term again?"

"Technically, full term is considered thirty-seven weeks, when your baby's lungs are fully developed."

Carlee's slow nod indicated that she was doing some math calculations of her own.

"Would you like to know the gender?"

Carlee took a breath and then shook her head no.

"That's fine, but if you change your mind, you can ask me, okay? I'll note it in your chart. I'll also give you some of these pictures, if you'd like them."

Carlee seemed to consider this question for a moment longer, her eyes sliding right and then left. "Sure, I guess so."

Nurse Charlotte's smile was the knowing kind as she rolled her stool closer to where her patient sat. "Carlee, I know you're young, and I know you're confused and overwhelmed, but I've counseled girls even younger than you many times. None of the options we discussed earlier have to be decided today. And none of them have to be decided alone." She paused. "I have a special bag I'd like to give you before you leave here. It's full of prenatal vitamins and samples, along with some reading material for extra resources concerning you and your baby." She waited until Carlee met her eyes. "But your mental and emotional health are even more important to me than you getting the correct amount of daily folic acid, which is why I've given you some important contact numbers in your folder. My cell number is in there for you, too. And you have permission to call me anytime—even if it's three in the morning. You matter to me, and like I told you before, you and your baby matter to God."

Carlee swallowed, her voice coming out shaky and thick. "I'm not ready to be a mom."

"That's okay." Nurse Charlotte touched her knee. "Whether or not you decide to raise your child yourself is a decision you have plenty of time to weigh out in the coming weeks and months. And I'm committed to helping you do that if you'll let me."

As I watched Carlee rub at her temples, something inside my chest began to crack open.

"I'd like to invite you to a support group I help lead here for young mothers on Monday evenings called The Well. I'd love to encourage you both to attend." Nurse Charlotte glanced over at me before focusing again on Carlee's tense features. "I think you would benefit greatly from the support, Carlee. No matter what decision you make." Once again Carlee gave little indication of what she was thinking, but Nurse Charlotte wasn't through yet. "There's one more thing I'd like to discuss before you leave here."

Carlee lifted her eyes.

"Do you have someplace safe to stay tonight?"

The girl tugged at the hem of her shirt, twisting the fabric around her fingers as her lips trembled and parted.

"Yes," I answered, before she could utter a word. "She does. She can stay with me."

◯◯◯

As Nurse Charlotte and Carlee wrapped things up in the exam room, I tapped lightly on Miles's connecting office door. Before I'd even finished knocking, he was there, pulling it open, his nervous energy seeping into the narrow space between us. I dropped my hand to my side as we each took the other in.

"Hi," he said first. His hair stuck straight up as if he'd been fisting it only seconds before. "How is she?"

"Everything looks good with the baby, and Carlee seems to be doing okay."

"And you?" The concern in his voice continued to widen the fissure in my chest. "How are you?"

I glanced behind me, not wanting to be overheard. "Do you mind if I come in for a minute?"

"Sorry, of course." He took a step back for me to pass inside and then closed the door behind me, though I could feel the scrutiny of his gaze as I maneuvered around his cumbersome box of office supplies. "Sit, stand, whatever you'd like."

My hip was not up to the task of standing for much longer, so I took a seat in one of the chairs and stared at the succulent in the corner of his giant desk. Miles sat in the chair beside me.

"I might need your help with something," I said.

"You have it."

His willingness was one of the things I'd come to admire most about him. Miles rarely thought too long about anything without taking action. "Would you be able to pick up a small list of things from the store on your way home tonight? Mostly groceries, but there might be a few other items as well. I can pay you back, of course."

It was obviously not the question he'd been expecting, but he didn't miss a beat. "Sure, yes. Whatever you need."

ALL THAT IT TAKES

"There's something else, too."

He said nothing as his eyes scanned mine as if trying to get a read on me.

"If Grandma Millie isn't able to keep Tucker overnight tonight, would you be willing to let him sleep at your place?"

Surprise caught his face. "Are you going somewhere?"

"No, I invited Carlee to stay with me."

There was a brief pause, as if he had to replay my sentence for a second time before he could respond, but when he did, he led with an exhale. "I understand that you want to help her, Val. I do, too. But there are protocols for this type of—"

"It's not safe where she's been." I thought back to the car, to the bedding stuffed in the back seat, to her saying she'd found the flyer about the women's center in a gas station bathroom down the street from here.

"And it's also not safe for her to stay with you. You don't know her."

"Which is why I'm asking if Tucker can spend a couple nights at your house until I can help secure something more long-term for her."

"And what about you? While Tucker's safe and sound on my sofa, what will you be doing?"

"I'll be fine. She's not dangerous, Miles."

He stood then and raked his hands through his hair, gripping the back of his head and taking a step toward his open window. "Forgive me if I can't agree with your assessment, but I'm still trying to erase the image of her nearly flattening you in the parking lot with her car. Which . . ." He twisted toward me again. And though he kept his volume low, his voice simmered with passion. "That's the part I'm struggling with the most at the moment: you putting your life at risk when you couldn't possibly have known what she was about to do."

"I didn't risk my life—"

"You stepped in front of her car. I *saw* you. I watched you throw yourself in front of a moving vehicle and then try to rationalize with a young woman who could have been strung out on drugs or carrying a weapon for all you knew."

He saw me? I didn't know whether to feel touched by his concern or frustrated by it. I didn't need him to protect me, and I wasn't looking for a replacement parent. I'd been coddled enough for one lifetime already.

With more effort than I wished it would have taken, I pushed up to standing. "I didn't come in here to ask your permission, Miles. I've already invited her to stay with me for the night. You're certainly not obligated to do anything more than what you've done here today—which I'm grateful for—but I can handle the rest on my own. I just thought you'd want to know."

"I care about what happens to you." His earnest declaration made every cell in my body hum. "I don't want you to get hurt."

"I won't get hurt."

His face said he wasn't so sure. "Listen, I have contacts I can call on Carlee's behalf. There's a reputable shelter not too far from here that is far better equipped to deal with her situation—"

"I will *not* take her to a shelter."

"Why not?" he pushed back. "Don't you think she needs someone better qualified to—"

"Because I didn't need a shelter when I was in her situation. I needed a home. I needed a person who would sit with me and cry with me and tell me that even though nothing else in my entire life seemed to make any sense, that I wasn't alone. Carlee doesn't need to be sent away, she needs to be pulled close."

My bold words skimmed the surface of an even bolder truth, one I hadn't ever wanted to speak aloud. One I wished I could cut from my story even more than the scar tissue I wished I could cut from my hip.

But this wasn't about me—*this* was about Carlee.

For nearly ten seconds Miles and I remained at an impasse, but I knew no amount of time would cause me to cave. This was too important. Carlee was too important.

Finally, Miles spoke. "Tucker is welcome to stay with me for however long you need him to."

"Thank you." My exhale was the start of a release I knew couldn't be stopped once it began. I swallowed, fighting to hold myself together for just a few more hours. I could think about it all later, cry later, deal with the resurrected pain later. "Can I still send you a list?"

"Please do," he said gently.

"I appreciate it." I turned to go and placed my hand on the doorknob, ready to exit.

"Val? I do want to help."

Before I could respond, his chest was at my back and his hands were on my shoulders and his warmth was everywhere all at once, a silent comfort I hadn't even known I'd needed.

For just one second, I allowed my eyelids to close, allowed my mind to imagine what it might feel like to lean against someone so solid and strong and to pretend that what was growing between us was more than a casual friendship rooted in platonic touches and transactional conversations.

And for just that one moment, I gave myself permission to believe that someone like me could ever truly be wanted by someone like him.

But my emotions were far too tired to be trusted, so I twisted the doorknob and fought against the tight rasp in my throat. "I'll see you back at the house."

· 19 ·

Miles

I couldn't remember the last time I'd shopped for a woman. Molly had certainly never needed—or wanted—me to shop for her. And the handful of times I'd been put in charge of gathering supplies for outreach trips or church-wide events, the items were usually purchased in bulk from online retailers. So I was at a loss for how to handle an entire aisle of magical potions that claimed to hold the solution to every hair or skin issue known to humankind. Especially seeing as the personal care products I owned were modeled after the Trinity: three-in-one combinations that saved me time, money, and sanity.

I studied the alien list of items Val had sent to my phone, reading through the checklist of needs again. Of all the nights for Molly to ignore her phone. But then I remembered: Molly and Silas were on a plane to California tonight—something about a meeting with the co-founders to rework the financials for Basics First.

I went to Plan B and FaceTimed Gavin.

Seeing as Gavin had a wife and three daughters, he was an easy choice. If anyone could shed some light on the differences between clarifying and volumizing, it would be him.

"Hey," Gavin answered, and I immediately recognized the

background. He was in his garage. Sitting in a camping chair, an old cooler for his footrest. It was the best he could do for a man cave, living in the suburbs. His words, not mine. "You stood me up today."

"Stood you up for what?" I asked, lifting a bottle of *cream rinse* conditioner from the shelf and wondering what the difference was between that and a *thickening* conditioner. How was it possible for there to be so many bottles using the same key words that did completely different things?

"Our Dude Camp meeting. You're not bailing on me, right? I'm still counting on you to lead the hikes and—" Gavin stopped short and leaned closer into the screen. "Where are you right now?"

"The store."

"Yeah, I can see that. But why is there a row of pink hair scrunchies behind you?"

I turned to look over my shoulder. "What is a hair scrunchie?"

Gavin laughed. "Seriously, bro, what are you doing?"

I reached for a new bottle on the shelf, holding two in my free hand and reading their labels. "Tell me this: Is there a difference between a leave-in conditioner spray and a deep conditioning treatment? And is there a reason someone would ever need to use both?"

Without missing a beat, Gavin said, "Depends on the person. One is to comb out tangles, and the other one is to repair hair damage. I'd be willing to bet that Nicky and our girls have owned ninety percent of that aisle."

"Which is exactly why you're coming with me for the rest of this stuff." I tossed both bottles into the cart and rolled on.

He laughed again, obviously finding far more amusement in this shopping trip than I was. "Seriously, dude. What is this about?" His eyebrows shot toward his spiked hair. "There wouldn't happen to be a *woman* behind this shopping trip, would there?"

The way he said *woman* seemed to indicate that I'd only just recently noticed the fairer sex. Not true in the slightest. It had been a long time since I'd dated, yes, but I'd made peace with the idea of remaining single years ago. I'd been content to run at a different pace than some of my married friends and colleagues, although many of my reasons had started to dwindle in recent weeks. Even more so in recent hours. I could hardly wrap my thoughts around the events of today, much less my words. All I knew was that Val was . . . Val was something special. *Someone* special. And sometime between almost witnessing her death and watching her comfort a hurting stranger, my interest in her had multiplied by a factor of a thousand. "There is, yes, but it's not like that."

"Who is she?" Gavin's face lit up the way it did whenever he teased one of his guy interns for crushing on a girl. "Wait, are you shopping for your upstairs roommate? The single mom?"

I was surprised he hadn't remembered her name—

"It's Val, right? That's her name, the bridesmaid from Molly's wedding."

Bingo. "Maid of honor."

"I've never understood the difference."

I swung the camera to the wall of fruity soap concoctions. "Well, I don't understand the difference between what a bodywash, shower gel, or whatever this sea-salt scrub thing is. So I think we're even there." I tossed another three bottles of unknowns into my cart and hoped one of them would fit Val's request.

Gavin mockingly swiped under his eyes as if he were a proud mother. "Running a shopping errand for a woman. This is truly a big day in your life, Miles. You're practically on your way to a proposal."

I pushed the overfilled cart to the end of the hair products aisle and took one last turn toward the ladies clothing section, letting the phone ride on a box of cereal as I searched out the signage that led to my last category.

"Wait, why are you in MATERNITY?" Gavin's voice crackled through the speaker, and I reached for the volume control, tapping it down as my fellow shoppers turned their heads to stare at me. "Please. Explain. Now."

"It's not for Val. It's for a friend of hers—a teen mom, actually. She came in to the clinic at Riverside today."

A slow dawning. "Ah, that's tough, man."

"Yeah." Although thinking through the ways Val had sat with her, talked with her, cared for her . . . had certainly made it far less so for Carlee. But the comparison Val had made to her own experience—that had nearly gutted me. It wasn't the first time I'd wondered about the identity of Tucker's biological father.

"What all does she need—the girl?" Gavin asked.

I swiped away from his screen to read aloud the remaining items Val had indicated Carlee would need. "'Maternity lounge pants, size medium. Black maternity leggings, size medium, two pairs. Maternity tank tops, medium. Note: Neutral colors are best, no patterns.'" I tapped on the video screen again to see Gavin inside his house, strolling down his hallway.

"Hey, Nicky, do you still have that big tub of maternity clothes your sister gave you when you were pregnant with Zoey?"

Nicky's answer was muffled, but her confusion was evident as they discussed the tub in question. After a brief back-and-forth period, Gavin finally handed the phone off to his wife. I smiled as her familiar face appeared on my screen.

"Hey, Miles."

"Hey, Nick."

"I can put together a whole care package for this girl in about fifteen minutes if you're willing to stop by? Do you know her size?"

"Uh . . . medium?" A lucky guess.

She laughed. "Okay, well, just head over when you're done there. Between what my name-brand-only sister gave me during my last pregnancy and a few staple items I saved, I'm sure I can put together a good mix of supplies for her."

I imagined Val being on the receiving end of such a care package when she had needed it most. "You're the best, Nicky. Thanks."

"Yeah, yeah." She winked. "Honestly, though, if she needs something else, please don't hesitate to call. Actually, can we plan to talk next week, regardless? When Gavin said you'd gone to Riverside, I wondered about that clinic. I might like to get involved. With the girls all in school now, I have some time to don my scrubs again."

I swallowed the swell of pride rising in my throat. "I'm sure Charlotte would love to put you on the rotation at the clinic."

"Great. I'll be in touch soon."

As I ended the call, standing smack-dab between a row of nursing bras and strange-looking pillows curved like a C, I couldn't help but shake my head and laugh. I might not be on the mission field working in a war-torn country, but I had certainly crash-landed into unfamiliar territory as of late.

And strangely enough, I wasn't in a rush to leave it.

∞

Tucker ran to greet me as I heaved several bags up the stairs. Hefting the behemoth care package Nicky gave me would take some doing. It was times like these a functioning elevator would come in handy.

"Are there more bags to carry, Miles?"

"Oh yes," I said. "Quite a few actually. Is your mom upstairs?"

"Yep! She has a new friend staying over, so she's letting me sleep at Kadin's tonight!"

"You're a lucky kid."

He buzzed past me on the staircase to collect more grocery bags from the back seat. "Whoa . . . what is that thing?"

I didn't even need to twist my head to see what he referred to. "It's a care package."

"For my mom?"

In a way, I supposed it was. "Sort of, yes."

"How are you gonna get it upstairs?"

"Very carefully," I called down as I approached the top step.

"Ha! That's what my mom always says, too!"

I chuckled and tapped the door with the toe of my shoe. Val answered quickly, and her look of surprise at the arsenal of bag handles threaded through my arms was meme-worthy.

"Is all that from my list?" she asked.

"Um, not exactly." I set the load down on the counter and table, glancing around for Carlee. Val must have noticed.

"She's taking a nap in my room. I could tell she was exhausted after making a couple of phone calls once we got here. It sounds like she left her mom and stepdad's house in Boise last week." Val let the statement settle between us. If Carlee had left their house a week ago, did that mean she'd been sleeping in her car ever since? "She mentioned her aunt who works as a flight attendant—seems like she's pretty close with her, though she's not always available given the nature of her job. I asked if I might talk with her at some point."

"You're hoping her aunt might provide you with more information? Was Carlee open to that?"

"I think she will be with a bit more time. I plan to talk with her more tonight after dinner. I'll circle back to her aunt again." Val released a quiet sigh. "Carlee has a lot to process right now. I'm trying to give her extra grace."

As was I. "Okay," I said carefully, though I had a thousand follow-up questions, given the weariness I could see in Val's eyes.

"She's exhausted, though. I'm glad she's able to rest. I'll wake her for dinner, but I'm sure she'll sleep hard tonight after such a trying day."

"I'm sure you're right."

Val unpacked several grocery sacks, stopping at the bag of beauty care products. She picked up the two bottles of conditioner and looked up at me. "Did I accidentally put two conditioners on the list?"

"Uh, about that. You're gonna find a few extras of pretty much every item you asked for."

"Why?" The word was a laugh more than a question, which caused me to laugh, too.

"Because I'm not a woman. Let's just leave it at that."

Her hushed laughter could be a sleep soundtrack. Some people liked ocean sounds or nature sounds to fall asleep to. But I was pretty sure I'd choose Val's laugh over them all. Especially this one, when she was trying her best *not* to give in.

"Also, you should probably know, I totally forgot to call in a pizza order for us."

"That's okay," she said. "I can whip something up with these groceries."

Only I'd noticed the way she'd favored her left side as she'd put said groceries away. "Actually, why don't I do it? You can tend to Carlee when she wakes up, and I'll cook . . . something."

Again, her eyes grew wide. "You'll cook?"

I nodded. "I can't promise it will be amazing, but if we lower the standard to edible, I think I can pass."

She held my gaze. I was certain she was about to insist she be the one to cook in her own kitchen, when she said, "Carlee doesn't like onions. I asked her about any food allergies and aversions earlier."

Of course she had. Val was nurturing like that. "Got it. No onions." Before she could change her mind, I whipped out my phone and Googled *dinner recipes for dummies*. "You don't need to worry about a thing. I'm on it. Will Tucker be staying here for dinner or going to Millie's?"

"Grandma Millie's," Tucker answered, pushing through the front door. "But I need to get my bag and my pillow, Mom."

"No, first you need to give me a hug." Val went to him, wrapping her arms around his slender frame and kissing his temple in a way that caused me to stare at the two of them, this packaged pair who'd invited me into their world. "No electronics past nine."

"I know, Mom. Grandma Millie said that's her rule, too."

She squeezed him tighter. "And no movies we haven't already watched together. If you have a question, you ask Millie if you can use her phone and call me, okay? And make sure you use your manners—say please and thank-you, even if you don't like something she makes for dinner."

Tucker tilted his chin to stare into her eyes, even though there was hardly a difference between them in height. "Got it."

She kissed the tip of his nose and then pulled him close again. "I love you, Tuck. Never forget that."

"I won't. But does this mean you'll say yes to Dude Camp? The permission slip is still on the coffee table for you."

"I won't be able to look at it tonight, but we can talk about it later."

He sighed. "Okay."

After Val retrieved Tucker's bag and pillow and gave him some final instructions, I watched her close the door and go to the window, no doubt to ensure he crossed the road without issue.

"You're a fantastic mother."

Slowly, she rotated to face me, her petite silhouette haloed by more than the golden hue of a waning sun—but by a strength that far exceeded her stature. "I do the best I can."

"It shows." And I knew in that moment, something else was beginning to show, as well. Something all new, and yet completely bewildering.

After a long wordless stretch, I gestured to the sofa behind her and cleared my throat. "You should take a break while I make dinner. I've got this."

And with little more than a nod, she did exactly that, grabbing her laptop on the way to the sofa while I pretended to know what I was doing in the kitchen. But the truth was, cooking was hardly the most critical thing I was trying to figure out tonight.

· 20 ·

Val

With the number of times Miles had insisted I keep my expectations low when it came to his skills in the kitchen, his grilled cheese sandwiches— which contained more butter than my mother's Thanksgiving mashed potatoes—were a welcome reprieve to the strained quiet in my apartment. And yet somehow, Miles had managed to inch the conversation along, doing exactly what Miles did best in a crowd of unfamiliar and potentially uncomfortable company. He treated everyone like a lifelong friend.

Carlee had remained guarded about her home life—her mother and stepdad number three in particular. But through Miles's ease of communication, she'd shared other details as the night went on, like how she'd couch surfed several days last week before spending the last two nights in her car. When I asked what she was driving so far north of Boise for, she simply said, "I grew up near here until I was twelve. I always wanted to come back. So I did."

"And is this also where your Aunt Lizzy lives when she's not on an airplane?" Miles asked, but Carlee shook her head.

"No, she has a place with her boyfriend in San Francisco. He works at a big science lab. Tests health foods and protein shakes and stuff."

"Ah, I bet that's an interesting job," Miles commented in reply.
Again, Carlee shrugged. "Sure, I guess so."

When she'd yawned, I asked if I could help her go through the
tote Miles's friend Nicky had given her, but Carlee had mumbled
that she was too tired tonight. It was easy to assume Carlee was
uncomfortable with the idea of unsolicited help. Yet another thing
the two of us had in common.

But after Miles had gone downstairs for the night, and after
Carlee had taken her shower and readied herself for bed, her long
hair smelling of peach-scented conditioner, she paused in the doorway of my bedroom and said, "I don't understand why you would
do this for me when you don't even know me. It doesn't make any
sense. But . . . thanks."

It makes more sense than you know, I thought. "I'm just glad
I can help."

I still had more questions about Carlee's future than I had
answers, but for now I would focus my prayers and efforts on
helping her find a suitable place to live and a job with people
who would be supportive of her situation. I wondered if the
group Nurse Charlotte co-led—The Well—would have any helpful resources.

Though I had contract work to tend to tonight, as well as a
film project idea to generate, I couldn't stomach the idea of any
woman with an unplanned pregnancy not being able to access the
resources at the women's clinic at Riverside—particularly a nurse
like Charlotte—simply because of a poorly maintained online
profile. I couldn't stop thinking about the flyer Carlee had found
in a gas station near the clinic. How long had that flyer been there?
Whatever the answer, it certainly hadn't been coincidental. I may
not know a lot about God's mysterious ways, but I did know that.
After all, I'd been the recipient of a similar kind of intervention
once.

Laying my other work aside for now, I reacquainted myself
with the Riverside website, pleased with the new template and
main design I'd created fairly easily. But tonight I'd added stock

photos as temporary placeholders, along with bolded headers for the resources and classes the center provided for families of all shapes and sizes. I wasn't finished yet, as I'd still have to go back to Riverside for some promo video footage and pictures, but I made sure to highlight the Women's Care tab on the main page and provide a quick-access button to hours, location, and emergency contact numbers for crisis counseling. As I typed the contact information, my pulse thudded hard in my throat. The same undeniable sensation I'd attempted to shove away earlier.

Pushing away from my desk, I attempted to stretch my back and hip before walking to the sink for a glass of water, encouraging my mind to search for a different kind of familiar to land on. A safer kind of familiar.

As I turned on the tap and filled my glass, I pictured my childhood home in Alaska, imagining what my folks were doing after closing time on a Tuesday night. Watching an episode of their favorite crime show, or perhaps playing a game of gin rummy with Sue and Jerry next door.

Last time we'd spoken, I'd filled my dad in on the film mentorship details and made a point to ask my mom for her cowboy cookie recipe, telling her I wanted to bake something to share with Grandma Millie for a change. But this new family equation I was testing out still felt top heavy with dynamics I didn't know how to balance from a thousand miles away.

The ding of my messaging window redirected my attention.

Miles

I'm pretty sure I saw you flick on a light a moment ago . . . you still awake?

Val

Should I be scared that you're watching for signs of life so closely?

Miles

Probably. Is Carlee asleep?

Val

> I think so. Pretty sure I heard her going through that tub of clothes from your friend's wife a while ago, though. Thank you again for hefting that all the way up the stairs for her.

Miles

> I'll be sure to thank Gavin and Nicky for you. I was just the messenger.

Though he was certainly much, much more than that.

Miles

> Next question: on a scale of one to ten, how likely are you to come out and sit by the fire with me in the next five minutes?

I rose up on my tiptoes to peer out the kitchen window at the back of the house. Sure enough, billows of orange-tinted smoke met my curious gaze. Only Miles would start a spontaneous bonfire in his backyard at ten thirty on a Tuesday.

Val

> Um . . . I'd like to say a 9.5, but unfortunately, I'm not exactly dressed for a campfire. I'm in my pjs and all my sweatshirts are hung in the bedroom where my guest is sleeping.

Miles

> If I promise to give you first pick of my best sweatshirts, would that push you to a 10?

Though there were at least a hundred responsible reasons I should say no to his invitation—starting with finishing the Riverside website and ending somewhere between not wanting to add further complications to our already complicated living arrangement . . . my heart overrode my head as I typed my reply.

Val

> Be down in 5.

True to his word, Miles held up three hooded sweatshirts as I rounded the outside stairs onto his back patio. Every one of them looked as if they would swallow me whole. The first was solid black, the second was plum colored with a gorgeously designed Salt and Light logo on the back, and the last was a faded gray hoodie with a retro Mexican flag stretched over the chest. I chose that one. It seemed the most like Miles.

"Good choice. That one happens to be my favorite," he said, handing it off to me. "Although I'm pretty sure four of you could fit into this thing."

He wasn't wrong. Not only did the hem fall to my knees, but the sleeves hung so far past my wrists that I struggled to push them up. He laughed at my attempts and stepped forward to help roll them up, like I was a third grader and not a woman inching her way toward thirty. *Awesome.*

"I got this sweatshirt two trips ago. It was an impulse buy from the Mexico City airport. I figured I'd been there enough times to justify at least one tourist item." He finished rolling the sleeve on my right arm and then moved to my left, taking a step back when he was done to assess his handiwork. I held out my arms and gave a wobbly twirl. "I'll admit, though, it looks far better on you than it ever has on me."

I eyed him suspiciously, my cheeks heating at the thought of how ridiculous I must look in my pink-and-gray plaid sleep shorts and XL hoodie. "I highly doubt that."

His smile pulled to one side. "You shouldn't."

And once again, that sizzle from earlier today—the one that sparked and snapped as he told me he cared about what happened to me—was back, coursing through me with a ferocity I couldn't deny. But as quickly as it came, I reminded myself of the type of guy Miles was: a friend to *literally* everyone he met. I was no different. And wasn't that exactly what I'd wanted from him? What I'd asked of him, even? To be seen and treated the same way as he treated everybody else? Mission accomplished.

He cleared his throat and gestured to the fire pit surrounded by cinder blocks a few yards out from his paved patio. "I only have one outdoor chair, so I did my best to improvise. Nothing screams *bachelor pad* like having to use a chair from the dining room set your parents gave you before they moved overseas at a campfire."

I laughed as we trekked across the lawn, realizing only then that the scars on my left leg were fully exposed. If Miles had noticed, he hadn't made it obvious.

Naturally, when we arrived at the fire he offered me the better of the two seats, and something about the coziness of his sweatshirt and the flames engulfing the firewood and warming my bare legs had me completely spellbound. For several minutes neither of us spoke, and I appreciated the contemplative quiet almost as much as I appreciated the myriad of colors on display before us.

"Your decision on Carlee today . . . it was the right one. I know you don't need my validation, but I wanted to say so just the same. She's obviously been through a lot. I only wish she had better support earlier on in life."

"I'm sure she wishes that, too."

"What do you think she'll decide? About the baby? Do you think she'll choose to be a single parent and raise a child at her age?"

"I really don't know. Even if she was handed the best support system in the world, that decision . . . it feels impossible when you're the one having to make it."

I could feel the way his interest deepened at my response. "And yet you made it."

Everything in me wanted to let the conversation die there, to stay quiet the way I usually did when the subject of unplanned pregnancies or single mothers or any of the equally sensitive and related topics were discussed. Because raising a child on my own did not make me an expert in the arena of single parenting. Just like having a lifelong limp didn't make me an expert on articulating the thoughts and feelings of every woman with a physical limitation. I was only one person. One voice in a crowd of many.

But the way Miles was looking at me now didn't feel like he was hoping I would speak for the majority.

The drumbeat in my chest thudded again, the pounding so hard and intense I had no choice but to give it my full attention.

I coached myself through my next several breaths . . . and then opened a box I'd kept sealed for more than a decade. "My decision to raise Tucker as a single mom came after a long list of other hard choices." I stared into the open flames, weighing the cost of the story I was about to share. "When I told you my dad was the one who got me interested in documentaries, that was true, he was. But while the documentaries we watched together about people overcoming great obstacles were inspiring . . . none of those were the documentary that . . ." The image of Carlee up on that exam table this afternoon materialized in my mind, bolstering my courage to continue. "That saved my life."

And ultimately, the life of my baby, too.

Though the fire still roared, I was far more in tune with Miles's steady breaths than I was the crackle of wood. And whether it was the fact that he was a pastor or that he was my best friend's brother or that he was a person who made me feel like I was someone worth knowing . . . I suddenly *wanted* to be known by him.

I told him about Jesse. I told him how we'd met as I was cleaning up the gold panning supplies in front of my parents' shop. I told him about the late nights at the tavern and the naivety of a girl who wanted to be her own woman despite the consequences. I told him about the lies and the arguments with my folks, about their concern that I was getting too attached to a greenhorn who would be headed home at the end of the fishing season. I told him about the two blue lines and about booking a flight to Texas on a new credit card in my name. And then I told him about Jesse wanting nothing to do with me or my baby and how he threw a hundred dollars at me before kicking me out of his truck.

But as I turned to the next page of the story in my mind, the one I was reliving one painful memory at a time, my bravery faltered, and I skipped over the next chapter completely, scrambling for a transition that would bring me to the next sequence of events.

I didn't dare risk a glance at Miles; instead, I coached myself to finish strong.

"I found myself alone in downtown Austin, during one of the coldest winters on record, rolling my suitcase through unfamiliar streets, headed nowhere. I was so lost, in every possible way. All I wanted was for things to go back to normal again." I clasped my hands, rubbing my thumbs together. "Only I knew there wasn't a normal for me to return to. It was too far away. Too far gone. I'd messed everything up by believing in a person who never had any intention of staying with me." Emotion caught in my throat, and I took a second to steady my breathing.

The wafts of smoke stung my eyes and burned my throat. "I walked and walked and walked that December night, but I had no plan of what I should do or where I should go. My hip cramped so badly that I had to stop several times so that I wouldn't trip and fall. I'd never felt more alone in my life.

"By the time I ended up at the river, I was shivering so hard from the cold I could barely stay standing. It was then I convinced myself that there was nothing left for me. No reason to keep trying to find acceptance when I'd just given myself even more of a reason to be judged." I studied the flames, feeling the heat of Miles's gaze even more than the heat from the fire. "The current wasn't fast, but I've never been a strong swimmer. I figured if I could just jump in . . . it would all be over soon enough. I grew up in Alaska. I knew all about the risks of hypothermia and how fast it can set in once your core temperature starts to drop. I knew exactly how my body would shut down, which organs would give up first. The fight would be over before it even began." Tears slipped down my cheeks, drying from the heat of the flames before they reached my jaw.

I turned my face to his, a question on my lips that I'd never before voiced to another living soul. "Do you believe God can speak through an advertisement?"

"I believe God can speak through anything He wants to," he answered, his voice little more than a rasp.

And something about his response, about the radical mercy of a God who had seen me at my lowest and reached His hand out despite it . . . broke the remaining seal on my lips. "I had just pulled out my phone to send a final text to my parents, apologizing to them for being such a screw-up, but when I lifted my eyes from the screen, I saw a billboard directly overhead, above the bridge I'd passed under. I hadn't noticed it the entire time I'd been walking along the riverbank. But it was there, painted solid black with bright white letters. It read: *Pregnant? Alone? Call us. There's hope for you.*"

Miles's mouth gaped, his own eyes glassy and reflective in the firelight.

"But instead of calling the eight-hundred number, I searched the website listed instead. There was a short three-minute video on the main page. It wasn't professional or even that great of quality. But the young woman they featured was a girl just like me, crying in an old wooden rocking chair. She had my same fears and my same regrets and my same questions about the future. The frame cut away to an older woman then, who was rocking her grandchild in that same old wooden chair. And the words on the screen said, '*Even though you can't see the future . . . God can.*' By the end of it, I was crying so hard I could barely dial the phone number on the screen. Her name was Pauline, the woman who answered. We talked for almost an hour, and she convinced me to call home, to call my parents. I was on a plane back to Alaska the very next morning."

Miles blew out a hard breath and scrubbed a hand down his face.

"I know," I said, trying to release him from the pressure of a response. Because chances were high that wherever he thought this conversation would lead tonight, it wasn't to where I'd taken it. "I know that was a lot. Please don't feel like you have to say anything."

"No, that's not . . ." He huffed out a hard breath. "It's not that I don't have anything to say to you. It's that I have too much." The sudden thickness in his voice made it difficult for me to breathe. "But if I could only say one thing in response, I'd want to thank the eighteen-year-old Val who chose not to jump that night. Because even then, God knew how much I'd need to know her one day."

Before I could stop it, a sob broke from my chest, and then Miles was there, pulling me out of my seat and wrapping his arms around me in a hug so tight I wasn't sure if my feet were still on the ground. He held me, my head pressed to his mid-chest, as if this was the most natural posture for us both.

"Thank you for trusting me," he said, his quiet voice rumbling against my ear. "I won't pretend to know what it cost you to share that with me, but I hope you know that even before you told me, I already believed you were exceptionally brave."

His words clung to my heart. "I've never told anybody that much before. Not even your sister."

His breathing slowed as his palm moved across my upper back. "In my line of work, I've been fortunate to hear some pretty miraculous stories, but there have only been a handful that have made me want to weep like a child. God's given you a powerful testimony, Val. A powerful tool."

Every muscle in my body tensed at his words, and he drew back far enough to search my face. "But it's your story to share, when and how you want to. I just hope I won't be the last person who hears it."

I blew out a shaky breath, forcing the pulse thrumming in my veins to quiet and still. "Thank you. You've been so . . ." I searched for an adequate expression of all Miles had come to mean to me and my son over the last month, only to come up short. "I don't think I can ever repay the generosity you've shown me and Tucker."

When he didn't respond, I tilted my chin to see past the night's shadows where a visible struggle blanketed his features. "I don't want to be paid back, Val."

The unspoken *"Then what do you want?"* lingered in the space between us, yet my mouth refused to release the words. This wasn't a territory I knew well, or at all, really. And out of the two of us,

I was the one who shouldn't be trusted to interpret relational dynamics.

"When I heard you scream today . . . when I saw you step in front of that car . . ." He squeezed his eyes closed, as if replaying the moment again even now. "I've never been so terrified in my life." Each word he spoke dug deeper than the one before it. "And I don't ever want to feel that way again." He swallowed and brushed his fingers along my cheekbone, past my ear, along my jaw. "You asked me to shoot straight with you. And I told you I would. I told you I wouldn't treat you any differently just because you were Molly's friend. But I'm finding that to be impossible because *you are different*. And you've made me think differently— *feel* differently than I ever thought I would feel." He stopped, took a breath, restarted. "I realize my timing is probably all wrong, but I don't want to wait on a second chance that may or may not come. Especially not after I thought I could have lost you today."

His gaze seemed to reach for me then, and for the first time, I allowed mine to reach back in full.

"I care about you, Val. As more than my tenant. As more than my sister's friend. As more than any kind of friend, if I'm being honest. But if you tell me you don't feel the same way, then we can let this conversation die with the fire, and you can trust that I'll respect your space and boundaries from this point on."

If his gaze hadn't been filled with such raw intensity, I might have been tempted to search for a loophole inside his words, some reason why he couldn't possibly mean what I hoped he meant. But the conviction in his voice had unsteadied me. And my thoughts spun in tandem with my firing pulse. "I don't want space from you." In truth, I wanted whatever was the opposite of space from Miles. "I care about you, too."

For all of a minute, we simply stared at each other, allowing this new revelation to settle in and make room for whatever unknown territory would come next.

"I don't have a plan," he admitted with so much earnest sincerity it almost hurt. "At least, not one that goes much past this moment right here, but I know I don't want to push you. I know I don't want to rush you into anything you're not ready for."

Though I was nodding, my focus had long ago shifted to his mouth, to a pull so impossibly difficult to break now that the words had been spoken. Because all along, in every glance I'd dismissed, and every conversation I'd discounted, there had been something of substance growing between us.

He touched a fingertip to my creased forehead, just between my brows. "What I wouldn't give to read the thoughts behind this expression."

"Maybe you should try reading them again," I said, a hint of invitation to my voice as I tipped my gaze to meet his.

With his arms still looped around my back, he cinched us tight, until our faces were as close as a shared prayer. And this time, when he searched my eyes, I knew he couldn't possibly misinterpret the truth staring back at him. Because I'd given him something I'd given no one else: the most fragile piece of my heart, the unedited version of Val Locklier.

When his lips first grazed mine with a dizzyingly soft invitation, it wasn't my insecurities that answered, but the revived dreams of a woman who'd shut the door on possibility long ago. There was no hesitation now, no mixed feelings of doubt or confusion. My response was clear, open. His fingers pushed into my hair, his hands braced at the back of my neck as if no single kiss could ever be enough. I couldn't imagine it would.

The need for more was neither pushed or expected, yet it was there between us just the same, like an equally sought-after exploration of hands and mouths and breaths all intertwined into one persuasive rush that left us dazed and unsteady. In moments, our kiss slipped back into a slower rhythm once again. To the tender newness of the present. And the hopeful promise of a future unplanned.

It was Miles who pulled back first, Miles who broke from my mouth to kiss my cheek and then my temple, where his lips lingered. He swayed me gently as he murmured, "I much prefer this outcome to what happened at Molly's reception."

His words were so unexpected that I pulled back just enough to give him an I-have-no-idea-what-you're-talking-about look. "What outcome?"

"When I asked you to dance and you said—"

"I don't dance." I remembered the moment well. "Because I don't."

"Only I distinctly remember seeing you swaying to the music in the back of the hall. Alone," he said playfully.

"And *alone* is the key word in that sentence," I teased back. "I don't do dance floors. Besides, there was an entire room full of pretty, single women who wanted to dance with you that night."

"I only had eyes for one pretty, single woman, and she seemed to prefer the back of a reception hall to my company."

"That's not—" I shook my head, my words lost momentarily at such an astonishing comment. "I don't do dance floors with crowds of strangers, Miles. I don't like to be stared at."

"And yet I've done little else but stare at you since the day we met."

He was staring even now as the smoke from the fire swirled around us.

"Well, you're . . . different."

"How so?" He pressed a kiss to the tip of my nose.

And this time, I didn't need to overthink or sort through a dozen possible adjectives to describe what I meant. I simply said, "Because you're comfortable."

And even under the shadow of night, I saw the way his eyes lit up. "I think that might be the best thing you've ever said to me."

He pulled me close again, rotating me so that my back was against his chest, where I could easily rest my head and where his arms could hold me tight. Together, we searched the starry night sky above in a contented silence that filled me with the kind of joy only C. S. Lewis could bring to life on the page.

"Miles?" I asked on a yawn.

"Hmm?"

"I'm thinking about Tucker." I wasn't quite sure how to end that statement, because this was a first. There had never been a man in our lives, not in this type of capacity anyway. Whatever steps came next were uncharted territory. "I think it's best we don't . . . I think it's best we try and leave things the way they've been around him." Although I didn't have to say that Tucker was among the more curious variety of kids. Miles had seen that trait firsthand.

"I'll follow your lead when it comes to Tuck, Val. Whatever you think is best for him, we'll do."

"I appreciate that." And then another thought. "But since we're on the topic, there's another relative we should probably consider . . . one of yours."

"One of . . ." He threw his head back with a groan and searched the sky. "Molly is going to be absolutely insufferable when she finds out."

"I wish I could disagree." I bit my bottom lip to hold back a laugh. "But it sounds like she'll be pretty busy flying back and forth to California this month for Basics First, so that could possibly buy us a little extra time."

He side-eyed me before taking my hand and leading me back to the stairs and up to my front door. "Let's hope you're right."

· 21 ·

Miles

A few years ago, I'd stupidly agreed to a round of "Truth or Dare" at a senior boys' overnighter. Gavin had been short a male chaperone; I had been short a decent excuse. So when the question "When and where was the last time you kissed a girl?" was asked, I was faced with a conundrum of epic proportions. I'd just witnessed these guys dare a kid to lick the arm of the hairiest player in the group, and another one to hand over his phone for a full minute while his team sent random texts to the victim's contact list.

So, I'd chosen truth. "Twenty-three," I'd said. "After a day hike at Tubb's Hill."

The group had erupted with the kind of laughter that transformed a face into resembling a squish ball. *"But that was like . . . three years ago!"* one particularly obnoxious mathematician had calculated. But he hadn't been wrong. At the time, it had been three years since I'd kissed a girl. But it had also been roughly the same amount of time since I'd made peace with staying single for the sake of my ministry. A decision I hadn't anticipated would change given my vocational choices and on-the-go schedule. After all, if God wanted my single status to change, then He'd have to make it clear by putting someone directly in my path.

And He had.

He'd dropped her directly into my house.

And either my recall of twenty-three-year-old Miles was faulty, or the kiss I'd waited another five years for was simply beyond comparison. Because kissing Val had been worth every second of the wait.

"Pastor Miles?" Trisha's voice pulled me out of my daydream, back to the digital volunteer roster for Riverside. She'd been updating it, since there were people listed who'd moved out of state in 2017.

"Yes, sorry." I scrubbed a hand down my face. *Time to refocus.* I scanned the bottom of the Excel spreadsheet. *Wow. Seventy-two. More than I thought.* "What do you think about making an RSVP column for the upcoming work party? I was planning to make some calls later today."

Her eyebrows rose a full inch. "You were? I figured you'd want me to do that."

"Nah, I think a personal introduction can make an ask for help feel more like an invitation rather than a drain on someone's time."

Obviously, this was not the answer she'd been expecting. She smiled brightly. "Okay, yes, that makes sense, but I'm certainly not opposed to helping. Volunteer calls usually fall under the admin umbrella."

I moved toward the printer. "I'm sure there will be plenty more phone calls to make in the coming weeks and months. Oh, and speaking of calls, did you get my email about Gavin's wife, Nicky? She's going to start shadowing Nurse Charlotte in the clinic starting on Tuesday. That's where I'll be working through the volunteer list today, actually—in the clinic. That waiting room could use some touch-up paint. I found the color in the janitor's closet this morning and ordered a fresh can. Also, we should probably order more snacks and drinks for in there, too."

Again, her eyes rounded.

"What?" I looked down at my shirt. Had I splattered salsa there earlier?

"It's just . . ." She tilted her head to the side. "You seem extra happy this week. Energetic."

I felt extra happy and energetic this week. And like maybe staying at Riverside wasn't the worst assignment I could have been given. Not if it kept me close to Val and Tucker. I thought back through my texts with her earlier this morning and smiled.

"What can I say? Life is good." I swiped the freshly printed spreadsheet off her printer and headed for the lobby. "Let's connect again in a few hours."

"All right," she said with a laugh. "I guess I'll prep some of the classrooms, then."

"Perfect." I popped my earbuds in and headed down the long hallway to the clinic. It was time to give this place the kind of attention it deserved.

◯◯◯

Somewhere around volunteer call number forty—after leaving approximately thirty-three voicemails while simultaneously doing touch-up paint work in the clinic—Val texted.

Only there were no words in her text. Just a link.

I pulled out my right earbud and set the paintbrush back into the tray.

A website for Riverside Family Resource Center surfaced on my phone screen. Clear. Bright. Streamlined. And most important, from this decade. I scrolled through each tab, noting the extra care she'd taken on the women's care clinic and contact information.

Val

> Obviously, I still need to update pictures and add some videos to highlight a few of the classes, but what do you think of the concept overall? Are there any edits you'd like me to make?

> Also, I printed off some photo/video waivers I can bring Monday night when I take Carlee to group. I altered a few details for the purpose of the center, but it's probably a good idea to

have people sign one before their faces go on
the site.

Miles

I really like you.

A full minute went by before Val sent a reply.

Val

🙂

Miles

The website looks fantastic. For the 483,798
time, please invoice me your hours, and I'll send
what you've done so far on to Trisha. How's
your other job? The one that pays in experience
only?

Val

Slow going. Tucker is currently trying to teach
Carlee all the card tricks he knows, which means
every ten minutes he calls me in to pick a card,
any card.

Miles

😂

And how's Carlee?

Val

She seems . . . okay? Hard to know. Woke up
pretty morose this morning. But she gave me
her aunt's number. I already left her a voicemail.
Oh, and guess what?

Miles

You're having a hard time concentrating at work
because you keep thinking about kissing your
neighbor by the fire?

Just me, then?

Val

🙂 No, it's not just you.

Grandma Millie stopped by earlier with a quiche, and she met Carlee. She mentioned having a spare room she'd rent to her with an attached bath. We're going to walk through it later today and discuss logistics. I've been praying for a good option for her. It could take a few days to get it all cleaned out and ready first, though.

I studied the word *days*. As in plural. I'd known there wasn't any possible way Val would stick to hosting Carlee for just one night.

Miles

I'll be happy to help Millie move furniture whenever she's ready. Hey, are you good if Tucker comes over for some guy time tonight? I have a project I was going to ask him to help me with.

Another long pause.

Val

Is this an attempt to score more landlord points? Because you are maxed out for the month.

Miles

And then what? I drop to zero again? I think we need to better define this point system.

Val

Tuck will enjoy that. Thank you.

Miles

Tell him I'll be home with pizza around six.

Val

Will do.

Miles?

Miles

Yeah?

Val

I really like you, too.

∞

Tucker kicked back on my sofa and tossed my old Koosh ball up in the air, catching it with ease on the way down, barely missing his empty paper plate where his pizza had been wolfed down. "Do you think you could talk to my mom about something for me?"

I rumpled my brow, afraid to say yes to all the possibilities a question like that might imply. "Uh . . . is there a reason you don't want to talk to her yourself, bud?"

He sat up straight, the Koosh ball dropping to his lap. "I *have* talked to her myself—like a million times! But she just keeps saying the same thing." Tucker tick-tocked his head to each side and raised the pitch of his voice. "*'We'll discuss it later, Tuck.'* But when my mom says *later*, it usually means we'll discuss it never."

Ah, so this was about Dude Camp. I'd been wondering what the holdup was. I'd heard Val use that line with him multiple times now. If it was finances, I wished she'd just submit her hours already so she could get paid for the work she'd done for Riverside.

"Do you think there's a reason she would say no to you going?"

He threw up his hands, his preteen body a limp noodle on my sofa. "There shouldn't be. Kadin gets to go, and he doesn't have a real dad, either."

The statement momentarily knocked the wind out of me. "Are you concerned about that?"

He shrugged, but his face remained scrunched in a pout.

"There will be a lot of boys going without fathers for a variety of reasons," I tried to assure him.

He lifted his gaze to mine. "Did your dad take you to Dude Camp?"

I worked the moisture back into my mouth. "My dad didn't take me to Dude Camp, no. We didn't have that when I was a boy." But even if we had, I knew my answer would be the same. My dad had been busy leading other types of excursions for the sake of his ministry. It had been Rev who took me on fishing trips and bought me my first set of hiking boots for my eighteenth birthday.

"But you'd take me, right?" he asked. "And we'd stick together."

"Of course."

He nodded, his entire countenance lifting. "Will you tell that to my mom? I think she's just worried about me or something."

I pushed aside the scraps of the cheeseburger patty deluxe pizza we'd devoured soon after he'd come down. "I'll talk with her."

He beamed at me. "Thanks."

I couldn't help but mirror the action. "So I was kind of hoping you could help me with a secret project tonight."

Tucker dropped the ball. "I'm great with secret projects."

I almost couldn't hold my laugh in, given the fact that I was pretty sure I knew most of the secrets Tucker had "kept" for someone else at some time or another. "Right. Well, this is a secret that I'm hoping can eventually turn into a surprise. But the thing is, I'm not sure yet how long it will take to complete or if I even have all the tools we need."

At the word *tools*, his eyes lit up. "What is it?"

I bent forward, elbows to knees, and dropped my voice. "What do you think about trying to fix that old elevator with me?"

"WHAT? Seriously?" He whooped.

I tapped my mouth with my finger and then pointed up at the ceiling and mouthed, "She can hear that."

"My mom?"

I nodded. "Yep."

His eyes grew large. "She always tells me that she has eyes and ears everywhere. I guess she really does."

"She really does." I unlocked my iPad and pulled up the only YouTube tutorial I could find on a vintage elevator similar to the one in my house. But even with the tack strips on the stairs now, the idea of Val and now Carlee navigating that stairway with grocery bags after a good rain was enough to keep me up at night. "Okay, so here's our issue, Tuck." I fast-forwarded the video and then paused it as the detailed image of our vintage motor surfaced. "We're gonna have to tear this old motor apart and then rebuild it by hand because they don't make them anymore. I've already checked."

He examined the screen and rubbed his chin like a forty-year-old mechanic. "I bet my pop could fix this."

"Your pop? Your mom's dad?"

"Yep. He fixes old stuff like this all the time. He knew all about the radio in it, too. I showed him."

An interesting idea percolated in my mind. "What would you think about us giving him a call together and seeing if he could help us out?"

Tuck's grin was huge. "Should I run up and get my iPad? Mom will let me bring it down if she knows we're using it for a project. But don't worry, I promise not to tell her anything about what it is."

"Sure, go ahead," I said. "Oh, and Tuck? I locked the door to the elevator in your apartment since I had to hand-crank it down the shaft for us to work on it here. Promise me you won't go trying to open that door with a screwdriver."

He laughed. "Promise. I won't."

A few minutes later, Tuck was back with his iPad, calling his pop as soon as he crossed the threshold. I hadn't even had a chance to think through what we would be asking of him yet.

"Hey, Tucky!" a female voice called out.

"Hi, Gram!"

"I was hoping you'd call us tonight," she said. "I loved those pictures of Maple Syrup. She's a real beauty. I hope you're being safe when you're around her. Horses can be dangerous if you don't use proper care."

"Yep, I know. I already researched that with Mom. Oh, hey, Pop!" It wasn't until Tucker flipped the camera on me that I wondered if Val would have any reservations about me meeting her parents this way—without her. I hoped not. "This is my friend Miles. We're working on a secret project together, and we need Pop's help."

"Hi there, Mr. and Mrs. Locklier." I waved, seeing the clear resemblance of Val in her mother's face. They shared the same radiant smile.

"Oooh! Are you Miles as in Landlord Miles?" Val's mom asked in a singsong voice.

"Yes, ma'am."

"Well, now." She studied the screen. "Val failed to mention how young and handsome you are. Are you uh, single, by any chance?"

"Gram!" Tucker slapped himself in the forehead, and I chuckled for lack of response, imagining this same woman taking care of succulents she referred to as her *pretty ladies* while treating them to custom concerts.

"He's Molly's twin, Bev. Of course he's young. They're the same age," Val's dad piped in from somewhere behind his wife. His face was shadowed, but from what I could see, it was clear he was not the extrovert Val's mother was.

"Well, it's not like I spend a lot of time thinking through those details, Dale." She smiled at the camera and touched the ends of her hair. "So, are you? Single?"

How exactly did I answer that? "I'm not married."

By the gleam in her smile, this was the correct answer. "Does Val happen to be around by any chance?"

"Not presently, ma'am, no."

"You can call me Bev."

Tuck had swiveled the camera so his face was now up close and personal. "Mom's upstairs with Carlee."

I cringed inwardly. I probably should have put Tucker on some level of verbal lockdown prior to this call. What I knew about Val's mom had only been mentioned in conversations surrounding finding healthy boundaries.

"Oh? Who's Carlee?"

I quickly took the iPad from Tuck before he could tell his gram the entire Carlee saga. "We're not privy to the agenda upstairs. All we know is that we're having guy time downstairs, right, Tuck? Which is why Tucker had the great idea to call. We're hoping to fix the elevator that goes up to Val's apartment."

Dale moved closer into the frame. "The one Tucker calls his spaceship?"

I glanced at Tucker, and he nodded vigorously.

"It appears that would be the one, yes."

"What do you think it needs?" Dale took the phone from Bev. His skin was more weathered than his wife's, and his knit cap reminded me of the fishermen I used to watch on the popular Discovery Channel series filmed in Alaska. I made a mental note to update my Alaska references soon.

"Well, we're hoping you might be able to answer that for us. Tucker's convinced you can fix anything, and so far, the young man has never led me astray." I ruffled Tuck's hair.

He laughed, right along with his pop. "He's a good boy." He glanced over his shoulder. "I'm headed out to the shop, Bev. Guy time." He was outside a few seconds later, traipsing a path Val must have traveled countless times in her life. The screen went dark for several seconds before he turned on a light, illuminating a toolshed.

Even from my extremely limited viewpoint, it was clear to see that Val's dad was some kind of vintage parts collector. He reached his hand into his flannel shirt pocket and slipped out his glasses. "Now, can you two show me what you're looking at?"

I nodded to Tucker, who flicked on the light in the musty elevator, and then flipped the camera around to show his pop. "We'll do our best."

After an hour or so of shining my flashlight on different components and gears that Dale not only named but had near duplicates of in his shop, he seemed to know exactly what we'd need to fix the elevator "*good as new*." The only issue was, he was going to have to send us the parts I couldn't find online. One thing I'd figured out for sure during the phone call: Dale Locklier shared his daughter's saintly patience and ingenuity.

As Tucker stacked the old gears on my kitchen floor, Dale said, "I'll get those out to you two in the mail tomorrow. Just let me know if there's anything else you need."

"Will do, sir."

I figured that was the end of it. Dale Locklier didn't seem the type of man to hang on the line and shoot the breeze. But right before I was about to sign off, he asked, "How is she?" and something in the pit of my stomach grabbed at his change of tone.

I was no longer speaking to a genius mechanic but to a father worried about his only daughter. I imagined this was the kind of phone call my folks made to Rev about Molly and me after they left—trying to gauge an accurate perspective from someone who was close. Only Val had grown up with the real thing . . . two devoted parents who'd stuck by her in the midst of her most pivotal life seasons.

"She's good, sir. Keeping busy with work and friends and settling into a routine here."

The slow bob of his head reminded me of Rev. "The film mentorship—that's all going okay? She hasn't said too much about it recently." He shrugged. "Takes after me on that, I'm afraid."

I chuckled, encouraged to hear that Val had shared her mentorship news with him. "Her film coach thinks she's as talented as we all believe she is. I think they're a good match for each other."

This time, as Dale put his pipe up to his mouth, he studied me. "What do you do for a living, Miles?"

"I'm an outreach pastor, sir." The title rolled off my tongue like an old habit. I didn't correct the mistake.

He tapped his pipe on his bottom lip. "For a church?"

Funny story . . . *that*. "I actually work at a faith-based family resource center in Spokane."

"So, a church, then."

I smiled. "It's pretty similar to a church, yes."

Again, he nodded in that slow, methodical way that brews wisdom through patience. "Can I trust you to call me if there's ever anything she or Tucker needs?" He stopped then, cleared his throat. "She might be twenty-nine, but she's missed around here. They both are."

I could only imagine how true that was. "You have my word."

"And a pastor's word ought to mean more than most." He almost smiled at that. "Take care of her for me. She's the purest thing to gold I've got."

My throat tightened at his description. "I will, sir." There was no official good-bye, just a deep nod I was certain was far more validating than I could know.

I cleared my throat and set the iPad down.

"I told you," Tucker said. "My pop can figure anything out."

I bent down beside Tuck and his stacked tower of gears. "You were right."

Because in only a matter of minutes, the man across the screen had totally figured me out, too.

· 22 ·

Val

Between the added dinners I'd cooked for four each night and the hours I'd spent prepping a room for Carlee at Grandma Millie's, the week had been more than full. And that hadn't even included the film assignments I'd been turning in to Gwen or the emails I'd been cc'd on sent from Victor Volkin.

VVolkin@VolkinEnterprises.com

GwenChilton@mediaroots.com

Subject: Missing Storyboard

Mrs. Chilton,

Your recruit must have her approved pre-production storyboard submitted within the next thirty-six hours or she will be unable to enter the film competition later next month. Please keep in mind that if she forfeits her place in the competition—either by submitting too late or by not adhering to the guidelines—she will not receive her completion certificate and will be required to send back her equipment asap.

Victor Volkin

Gwen had replied with her usual perkiness before I'd even taken my morning shower.

GwenChilton@mediaroots.com

VVolkin@VolkinEnterprises.com

RE: Missing Storyboard

Mr. Volkin,

Val is drafting a hugely inspiring idea! We will have the storyboard to you well before the cutoff. No worries there. Cheers!

Gwendolyn

I stared blankly at my laptop screen, willing whatever *hugely inspiring idea* Gwen was trying to speak into existence to pop into my head and extend through my fingertips and onto this digital storyboard. *Why am I so stuck?*

As if on cue, Carlee stumbled out from my bedroom, wrapped in the fluffy pink maternity robe she'd been gifted from Miles's friend, Nicky, and plopped down on my sofa in that I-hate-mornings way of most teens her age.

"Morning." I smiled at her. "You sleep well?"

She yawned and spoke through her fingers. "Yeah, until my aunt called and told me I had to watch the video she sent me of a cat fake-breakdancing in a Michael Jackson costume." She rolled her eyes, but I could see the glint of humor she tried to hide. "I don't know why she sends me stuff like that. I don't even like cats."

But I knew why. It was as strategic as it was loving. Carlee's Aunt Lizzy wanted her niece to laugh, to let her guard down a little, and to enjoy some of the simple things in life again. After speaking to her on the phone several days ago while Carlee was out requesting job applications, I'd grown even more confident that Carlee was exactly where she needed to be.

Though Lizzy was only a handful of years older than Carlee, she seemed both levelheaded and reliable, providing many of the fill-in-the-blanks her niece seemed hesitant about sharing. According to Lizzy, Carlee's mom had a proven track record of choosing men over her only daughter, which was the case with stepdad number three. Carlee had managed to hide her pregnancy from everyone in her life until the day her stepfather caught on to the real reason behind her extra-baggy clothing. The fight between them had ended with Carlee packing up her car and her mom doing nothing to stop her.

"I knew something was wrong when I couldn't reach her for almost a week. I finally called my sister and demanded to know what had happened. I was so worried," Lizzy had said. "I've paid Carlee's cell phone bill since the day she turned sixteen so that she'd always have a way to contact me if she needed to. When she finally did return my call that day she met you . . . I dropped to my knees and thanked God for sending an angel to my niece. And I don't even pray."

"I'm not an angel," I'd said gently. "But I do want to help your niece. She needs support right now more than ever."

"My fiancé and I wish we could offer her a place to stay with us, but we live in a studio apartment in downtown San Francisco, and my flight schedule is still all over the place. But I can tell you that with the exception of her last year of high school, she's been an excellent student with no history of trouble. Unfortunately, when she couldn't get the attention she needed at home, she found it in a guy who gave her nothing but empty promises."

An image of Jesse had surfaced in my mind. "If she decides to stay in the area, then I'm hoping she can make some friends here and find a job that will accommodate her throughout her pregnancy."

"Me too. That's part of why we've offered to help Carlee out financially until she gets on her feet—pay her rent and her grocery bills. She told me you've been sleeping on the couch so she could have your room. . . . Again, I don't even have the words to say how grateful I am that you found her when you did. Whatever you've spent on her care, we'd like to reimburse you," Lizzy had offered.

"That's not necessary, really. I'd rather see her grow a savings account for her future." Whatever that looked like.

"Thank you," Lizzy said kindly. "I was hoping to ask you what you thought about the room Carlee mentioned might be available for her to rent across the street from you and your son? Would you mind giving me the contact information for the landlord?"

The idea that Carlee had wanted to stay close by had caused me to exhale a breath I hadn't even known I'd been holding. She might have a hard exterior to break through, but I was convinced her heart was soft. I gave Lizzy all the information she'd asked for.

"Hey, Mom? Has Carlee come out of your room yet? I want to see the funny cat video her aunt sent—*oh*." Tucker slid to a stop at the sight of her on the sofa and smashed his lips together in a look that said *guilty*.

Especially when Carlee hiked an eyebrow at him suspiciously.

"Uh, Tucker?" I asked. "How is it you know about a funny cat video?"

"Umm . . ." His cheeks flamed pink.

"Private conversations are . . ." I started.

"Private for a reason," he finished begrudgingly. "But, Mom, the only reason I listened at her door was because I thought I heard her laugh, and Carlee hardly ever laughs."

My chest pinched at the truth of his words. Carlee rarely laughed, although I had seen a smile when Tucker and Miles had asked her to play Monopoly last night after dinner while I tried to work. Miles had shopped for a variety of game snacks, and Carlee had selected every hot-and-spicy chip option in his bag. He'd winked at me, as if that had been his plan all along.

"What do you need to say to Carlee?"

"Sorry, Carlee," Tucker said dejectedly.

But as soon as she opened her mouth to reply, the distinct sound of footsteps on the stairs rerouted everybody's attention.

"That's Miles!" Tucker called as I swiveled my desk chair toward the door. Tucker rushed to yank it open, and there stood Miles with a carrier containing four to-go cups.

"Ready for Random Coffee Orders with Miles?"

Tucker circled him like a starving vulture.

"What a nice surprise, thank you." I peered up at him, a rush of gratitude mixed with something that felt far too close to the surface in light of our audience.

"Don't worry, Miles," Tucker said. "I haven't told my mom about . . . you know what." My son winked, and I looked between the two of them. Tucker had been quite cryptic about whatever *man project* the two of them had been working on downstairs in the evenings.

"We're really gonna need to work on your game face, Tuck." Miles lifted the first of four drinks from the carrier and handed it to him. "A hot chocolate with extra whipped cream for you." He went back in for another. "And for Carlee . . . here's a decaf white mocha with the regular amount of whip. Hope that's okay? If not, blame Google's most popular coffee drinks list."

"That's really for me?" she asked, looking at the cup he offered her in disbelief.

"Of course," he said. "Though I did have to double-check with my sources on the whole caf, non-caf thing in regards to pregnancy. You do like coffee, right?"

She answered him by cupping the coffee in her hands and breathing in the steam like this was the lifeline she'd been missing all along. Tucker copied her theatrical display, and for the first time, Carlee laughed a real laugh, and I was certain my chest had just been struck by a sunbeam.

"Fine, I'll show you the cat video," Carlee said playfully. "Come over here."

"Oh, yes!" Tucker cheered, and I laughed at the two of them.

"And for you, m'lady," Miles addressed me. "You get to choose from the last two options. Either a salted caramel latte with actual milk from a cow, or an Americano with heavy cream. And yes, there *is* a wrong answer."

It was my turn to laugh. "Those options are opposites."

"Not true." He winked. "They're both coffee."

"Fine," I said, biting back a smile. "I'd like the Americano, please."

With a smug grin, he handed me the coffee. "Good choice. And that completes today's round of Random Coffee Orders with Miles."

After a round of thank-yous, Miles tipped his head to the front door and mouthed. "Can we talk?"

I followed him out, my small porch step shrinking even smaller as I closed the door behind us.

"Good morning," he said in a voice that somehow simultaneously froze and then thawed my insides.

"Good morning to you, too."

He pinched the white string that hung from one of my standard zip-up hoodies, his volume quieting into a tone I'd earmarked from our evening at the fire. "I'd really like to see you again soon."

"I'm pretty sure you're seeing me right now," I said cheekily.

"Please allow me to rephrase: When might you be free to go on a date with your downstairs neighbor?"

While so much of what had happened with Miles felt pinch-me good, this was the part I was far less certain about. The seeing each other in public part. Or rather, the *being seen* together in public part. For Miles, there would be nothing to worry about. But for me, it would be as different as an Americano was from a salted caramel latte. Both coffee, yes, but two totally different caffeine experiences. Hanging out with Miles at the house or at Riverside or at a late-night fire pit where we were the only two people in the world—those had only recently become nothing-to-worry-about situations. But being with Miles in a crowd of unknown people? Judgmental eyes staring at us as I walked across a room with him? I'd seen how Molly had responded when Safety Vest Ed had talked to me at the warehouse. I could only imagine how Miles would have responded given the same scenario, not to mention the level of mortification I would have felt at his protective nature.

Miles knew little about that part of my life. Because that part of my life was limiting. And Miles didn't seem to care much for limitations. He was a goer, a doer, a make-it-happen kind of guy.

"What exactly did you have in mind?" I asked.

"You can leave that part up to me. I just need you to name a night you're free."

Not exactly the answer I was hoping for. I needed a bit more heads-up than that, something I could mentally prepare for in advance. "Saturday?"

His face lit up and then immediately dimmed. "I'm meeting Gavin that evening to confirm the trails and overnights for Dude Camp." He paused, rubbed his lips together. "Actually, on that note, I've been meaning to ask you something about Tucker."

"Sure, what?"

"He mentioned that you haven't given him an answer about Dude Camp yet, and I think he's getting concerned you might say no."

I blew out a breath and glanced down the stairs. "I haven't told him no."

"But you also haven't told him yes. If it's about the money, then—"

"It's not about the money," I said, bringing my gaze back to his.

"Then what is it about? Because he seems to think it has something to do with him not having a real dad to take him."

His words pummeled into my diaphragm, pausing my next breath. "He said that? Tucker . . . told you that?"

Miles nodded slowly. "Yes, and he asked me to talk to you."

An ice-cold sensation walked my spine. Tucker had asked Miles to talk to me?

"Dude Camp is a ministry I feel strongly about—we see a lot of boys who are in need of a father figure or a male mentor at his age. I'm happy to be that for Tuck. It would be an honor for me to take him." He peered down into my face. "Unless there's something else I'm missing."

It wasn't until that very moment that I realized why I'd been so hesitant on giving Tucker an answer. It wasn't the out-of-pocket cost I feared I wouldn't be able to recover from. It was the heart cost—Tucker's heart. It was one thing when Miles was just a kind landlord who'd offered to take my son fishing every once and a while. But things were different now. Messier.

"I'm not sure it's the best thing for him," I said, testing the words like a child sticking their toes into the surf to check the temperature. "Tucker doesn't know how to do anything half-way. He's all-in, running at one-hundred-percent capacity all the time. What do you think will happen if you take him to Dude Camp?"

Miles widened his eyes as if I'd asked him a trick question. "Uh, that he'll love it."

"Exactly. And he'll love you, too." The truth was, Tucker already did. "He gets extremely attached. He's had my dad, and I'm grateful for that relationship, but you're . . ."

"A risk," Miles said, blowing out a breath and running a hand through his hair. "Val, you know I'd never knowingly do anything to hurt him or you."

"But that doesn't change the fact that we don't know what the future holds."

"For us. What the future holds *for us*, you mean." Miles's voice was soft, yet I could feel each syllable he spoke *ping* inside my core. He touched my cheek, pushed the strands that had fallen from my ponytail behind my ear, and for several heartbeats, his gaze roved my face. "All I know is that for these last two years, anything having to do with the future seemed unclear . . . until you and Tucker showed up and turned on a light I didn't even know existed. And all I want now is to keep that light on."

I stared up at him, my throat and chest tight at such an exposing statement. "I'm scared to feel this way about you so quickly."

"You and me both." An easy smile touched his mouth, and something about the honesty of this entire exchange bolstered a change in my response.

"Tucker has always wanted to sleep under the stars on a real camping trip."

Miles's lips parted into a grin. "Then I'd like to make sure he gets his wish."

I nodded and reached for his hand as he took one step and then another down the stairs toward his car.

"Speaking of granting wishes," I teased. "Do you happen to have anything in the way of film project ideas?"

"Unfortunately, no, but I can say that the last time I was in need of some inspiration I was struck on the head by a lightsaber."

I laughed. "So you're saying that maybe if I get whacked on the head at the moms' group tonight, I might get all the answers I need before my deadline?"

With a quick glance up at the window, Miles climbed the steps once again, wrapped me in his arms, and planted a firm kiss on my lips. "And that. That should help, too."

∞∞∞

Tucker had already honked the horn once while he waited in the car for Carlee and me to join him. He was eager to get to Riverside and tell Miles about a package that had come for him sometime this afternoon. I waited outside my bedroom door for Carlee to change into yet another outfit for tonight's group.

I knocked. "We should probably head out, Carlee. I'd like to get there a few minutes early and set up my camera. I'm taking some more pictures for the website."

"I'm not going," a frustrated voice said from behind the door.

"What? Can I come in, please?"

In some otherworldly speed-of-light maneuver, Carlee threw open the door and then dropped back onto the mattress before I even had time to register the action. "I said I'm not going."

By the mess of clothing on the floor, Carlee had tried on every shirt she owned, while the one she currently wore looked more like tinted Saran Wrap over her belly than breathable fabric. I made a note to take her shopping again soon.

I approached with caution. "Is there a reason why you've changed your mind?"

259

She eyed me. "I don't belong there. I'm not a mom. I'm just a girl who got knocked up by a loser with nice hair." She grunted and tossed a lone shirt from the pillow beside her to the floor. "I don't need more people judging me."

Her words resonated in a way I'd never be able to ignore. I'd thought that very sentence more times than I could recall. "I can understand how you feel."

"How? You're like . . . super cute and kind and everybody likes you. Even your own kid. I swear, I don't think I've even seen him roll his eyes at you once. And don't even get me started on how much Miles adores you."

I nearly choked, my face flaming hot. "I've had plenty of reasons to feel judged in my life, Carlee. Believe me."

"Why? Your limp?" She rolled onto her hip, propping her arm beneath her head. "Because I think it makes you look tougher. All the good characters in movies have some kind of scar or something. Maybe that's yours."

I exhaled, trying to get us both back on track as Tucker honked the horn yet again. "I know Nurse Charlotte will want to see you. She texted, remember?" In actuality, she'd texted *and* called more than once this last week.

"She's just doing her job. She doesn't really even know me."

"How can she or anybody get to know you if you choose to stay home?"

Several seconds ticked by as the conviction from that question silenced her. I waited, attempting to exude patience, in hope that she'd change her mind and choose the better option, the one that would bring her the friends and connections she so desperately needed.

Instead, she simply said, "Maybe next time."

As I drove away from the apartment with a heaviness in my chest, I wondered just how many times my parents had felt the same sort of discouragement over my chosen isolation for so many years. It was a question I pondered all the way to Riverside.

After unloading my camera gear from the back of my car while cautioning Tucker about racing through the parking lot, I double-checked that the photo waivers for being on the website were still in the front zipped pocket. I'd be sure to hand those off to Nurse Charlotte before the start of group and ask her to make an announcement. It would be easy for me to slip to the back and take pictures and videos to finish the site.

Only, when I entered Room 112, it didn't look like any of the support groups I'd seen on TV. This room was full of round tables, decorated with flowers and miniature bowls of candy and even a few candles. Clipboards had been placed at a few of them with what appeared to be sign-up sheets for something or other.

"Val," Nurse Charlotte said, her arms extended. "I'm so happy to see you." She pulled me in for a hug. "Is Carlee with you? I'd love to introduce her to a couple ladies tonight. Might have a possible employment match for her."

"Actually . . . Carlee didn't come with me tonight. I'm sorry."

She offered a sympathetic smile and placed a hand on my shoulder. "That's nothing to feel sorry about. The key is to keep inviting her. If you only knew how many invitations I turned down before I finally said yes that first time." Nurse Charlotte's gaze held steady on mine. "According to Pastor Miles, you had no prior relationship to Carlee before the day of the exam when you opened up your home to her. That's a divine appointment if ever I heard of one. Sounds to me like God put you both in the right place at the right time." She touched my shoulder, squeezed. "Your steady influence in this season of her life will hold more power than you can possibly know."

So many thoughts swirled in my head at her confident affirmations, yet the word *influence* lingered like a perfume I couldn't afford to buy. *Molly* was an influencer for products and causes. *Miles* was an influencer of people and ministries. But in no way had I ever resonated with such a term for myself. I wasn't effusive or captivating or even all that persuasive.

"I apologize that I didn't meet you properly during Carlee's exam, but I do try my best to give my patients my full attention.

After all, I've been in their shoes, and I know just how critical those minutes are to build trust when a life is on the line. I wish somebody would have taken the time to really explain all my options to me. I would have made a different decision."

Her words nearly choked the breath from my lungs as I processed what she'd just admitted to a near stranger. Had Nurse Charlotte had an abortion?

The silver-haired, daisy-wearing nurse greeted the ladies who came in the door by name as tables filled up with women of every age. She asked about their children or their jobs or some other significant detail that came from being known. And I wondered what my early years of motherhood would have looked like if I'd belonged to such a welcoming group instead of sticking to the isolating rooms inside my parents' house.

When she rejoined me, I tried to speak, to say something even remotely intelligent, but all that came out was, "You're a great nurse. This facility is lucky to have you."

"Riverside is more than a facility to me." She pointed to the full room of ladies. "It's them. These women." And even though voices chattered all around us, it was only Nurse Charlotte's voice that registered clearly in my ears. "To look at this group, you'd never know the struggles they've overcome. The hurts, the abandonments, the rejections. This is their place. To heal and to help bring healing to others." She smiled. "It's why I became a travel nurse. After my abortion in '88 and subsequent decade of prescription drug abuse and depression, Jesus reached me through a woman who loved me enough to tell me God could use my pain to help others. I'd never heard anything like that before, and frankly, I was too desperate not to believe her. I went back to school in my midforties, leaving my husband with microwavable dinners to feed our teenagers so I could study in the evenings. I became an RN to help educate, equip, and encourage women." Her eyes misted. "You're looking at a room full of one of the most vulnerable and under-recognized people groups in the world."

I scanned the room along with her.

"Single moms," she offered. "And I don't just mean unmarried mothers. I mean those who have raised their babies, aborted their babies, and adopted their babies to waiting families." Her compassionate gaze found me again. "They're often as displaced in our society as they are inside our church walls, and they are some of the most generous and courageous women I know. It's my prayer that God will allow me to meet every single one of them within our city so that I can offer them the kind of hope my sweet friend Donna offered to me over twenty years ago."

Before I could utter a response, Trisha Woodward, the woman I'd met at the welcome desk on my way in, made her way to the stage, and Nurse Charlotte bent low to my ear. "Looks like we're starting," she said. "Better get to our seats."

"Yes." I swallowed. "Thank you." Words that felt completely inadequate, and yet I had no clue what to say to someone who'd just bared her soul to me only minutes into our second meeting.

With a contagious enthusiasm that felt opposite to my current headspace, Trisha introduced herself and briefly explained the evening's agenda. A special panel of moms had been planned tonight—some single, some married, one widowed—all handpicked from within the group to share one vital and unifying component of their journeys. My curiosity was piqued. It was easy to see why Miles believed she was the best administrator for Riverside.

"But before I dismiss you to fill your plates with your favorite snacks, it looks like our special guest has stopped by to make a few announcements."

There was no need for an educated guess at the visitor in question. By the rapt attention of the majority of females in the room, it was hardly a guess at all. I leaned against the back wall, camera still looped around my neck as I watched Miles jog toward the stage, completely unfazed by his captive audience.

"Ladies," Trisha said like a talent show host, "in case you haven't met him yet, this is Pastor Miles McKenzie, the new resident support pastor for Riverside, and I can tell you from firsthand experience that Miles is not only a passionate leader but a true shepherd of people. I've had the opportunity to volunteer with him at Salt and Light Community Church for the last several years, so it's both an honor and a huge answer to prayer to have him join our team."

The room erupted with applause, but not even the sound of clapping hands could drown out the whispers between two beautiful young women sitting at Table 8.

"Um, helloooo. Are pastors even allowed to be that good-looking? Isn't there a commandment against that or something?"

"Ha, I know, right? I went to a class he taught at the church last year, and I was way too distracted by those eyes to take notes. I did sign up for his next class, though."

Laughter. "Is he single?"

"Yep. I totally snooped on him. My aunt told me he hasn't dated in years. Waiting for the right woman, I guess."

"Well, I'd try on that glass slipper any day."

"Me too!"

I bit back a secretive smile as the two women giggled to themselves. They weren't wrong about Miles being attractive, not in the slightest. And as he took the microphone, elaborating further on Trisha's introduction and diving straight into his invitation for the upcoming Saturday volunteer day just a couple weeks away, that attraction multiplied. There was no question that this—Miles speaking on stage, his countenance radiating compassion and grace and authority—was his truest gifting. And for some crazy reason . . . he'd chosen me. Could I really be the woman he'd waited for? The woman meant to wear that coveted glass slipper?

His confident gaze continued to travel the room as he spoke. I'd never understood how some people could be so naturally poised on stage, or in front of a camera, for that matter. I certainly wasn't one of them. But this was his element, no question about it.

". . . which leads me to the next big announcement," Miles said. "Some of you may have heard this already, but Riverside has a shiny new website to share with the community thanks to our new

web designer and talented film entrepreneur." And then his eyes
stopped roaming and his mouth stopped speaking and the smile
he smiled at me plowed straight through the center of my chest.
"Please allow me to introduce Val Locklier." Every head swiveled
to search out the target of his piercing gaze. But instead of handing the microphone back off to Trisha, he waved me forward, as
if the two of us were some sort of planned entertainment special.

I gave the tiniest shake of my head, hoping he could read the
panic emitting from every cell in my body, but once again, he waved
me to the stage. If there was ever a time to wish for a sinkhole to
open up, this was the moment, because I was a thousand-percent
positive I would incinerate the carpet before I even managed three
steps in his direction.

Unfortunately, combustion did not occur as I walked forward,
and I lived long enough for him to grip my hand and pull me onto
the stage beside him. My gaze immediately swung to the back of
the room, landing on the Miles Fan Club sitting at Table 8. Sure
enough, they were whispering to each other again, and it was all
I could do not to assume the worst now that I was their subject
of observation.

". . . for pictures and videos. Is that correct, Val?"

Miles peered down at me as the room fell quiet, waiting for a
response I hadn't even heard the question to.

"What?" I asked in a voice that would barely register on the
most sensitive editing software I owned.

His confidence dipped as concern broke through his gaze.
"Where should they find you afterward—to sign the media waivers for the website?"

"The table," I said, feeling the warmth of his hand hover at my
mid-back. "By the double doors."

"Great. Thank you." The smile he'd stepped on stage with,
the one that could outshine an emergency flashlight, now looked
to be running low on battery. For a man who could make friends
with anyone in any room, he certainly hadn't read this one very
well. The instant Trisha was back on the mic, I exited stage right,

gripping the rail on my way down the stairs as my left hip stiffened to keep up with my pace.

I pushed through the side exit door into the hallway, finding a wall to lean against, to breathe.

"Val?" He was right there, halting to a stop in front of me. "I'm sorry. I didn't realize—"

"Please don't ever do that to me again." Tears I refused to release stung my eyes as Miles stood opposite me, his expression an equal mix of horror and remorse.

"Do what? What happened? Was it stage fright?"

I squeezed my eyes closed, willing my heart rate to steady as his cool fingers found the hot skin of my cheek. Stage fright didn't even begin to cover it, and yet, how could I possibly convey the depth of emotions that had sprung from two decades of stares and jokes and comparisons? "I've told you before, I don't like crowds."

I tried to push his hand away, but he didn't let my fingers go.

"But this wasn't . . . I didn't think . . . Please, Val, just look at me."

Slowly, I shifted my attention away from the faces of the middle school bullies who mimicked my walk and called me a *cripple*. And then away from the face of the man who wanted nothing to do with me or my unborn child. And then, finally, up to Miles.

"I just wanted them to meet you," he explained quietly. "The work you've done for Riverside deserves recognition, too."

"I don't want recognition," I said hoarsely. "I don't need it."

My statement embodied the strange push-pull paradox that expanded and contracted every time I got too close to a breakthrough. To a dream. To a relationship. To a freedom I could hope for but never quite attain. By the look on Miles's face, my reaction was as confusing to him as it was to me at times. How could I want to direct films that mattered to the world and be terrified of the stage? How could I step out and make a difference and refuse to walk in front of a crowd? It didn't make sense. None of it did, and yet the vise grip inside my mind felt as real as the heartbeat in my chest.

My thoughts drifted back to the flirty woman at Table 8 who wanted to try on the glass slipper. I had no doubt she'd fit it better than I ever could. She would certainly walk better in it. But then I thought further back, to another woman, one I'd left in my house after she refused to show up tonight for fear of judgment. I closed my eyes, heaved a sigh. Perhaps I wasn't quite as far from Teenage Val as I wanted to believe.

"That's one of the most beautiful things about you, you know," he said, leaning in closer, his voice low and honey rich. "Your humility. I see it in the way you mother Tuck and in the way you create your art and even in how you interact with and relate to Carlee. I wish you could see yourself the way I do."

Though I wished I could savor the sweetness of his words, cherish them long after this moment had passed, I knew fear was the true main ingredient in what had happened tonight on that stage, not humility. And yet, for some reason, those words were too difficult for me to speak out loud—the admission that even now, even after all these years and all the work and all the positive self-talk, I could still lose this age-old fight. I could still let the fear of judgment win.

I stared into the depth of those hazel eyes and exhaled a slow breath, willing myself to release the insecurities I could never explain to a man as confident as Miles McKenzie.

"I'm sorry," I said, working to reattach the rationality I'd lost during the last five minutes. "I overreacted. I just . . . I don't like surprises that involve stages or crowds, is all." My smile was likely as fake as they came, but I pushed my next words out anyway. "But I'm okay now. I'm good."

His eyebrows dipped into a V. "You sure, because you seemed pretty shaken up when—"

"I'm sure." I nodded with false assurance. "Thank you, though, for checking on me." I hitched a thumb toward the closed door a few steps down. "I should probably get back inside. I don't want to miss any camera-worthy moments."

"Okay." His lopsided grin came easily enough, and with it my guilt buoyed to the surface. I forced it to sink once again. "If you're sure you're good, then I should probably get back to Tucker. I left him in my office with a toolbox. Unsupervised."

I smiled back. "Yes, go. I'll see you later tonight."

"I'm counting on it."

· 23 ·

Val

With my senses reclaimed and refocused, I slipped back into the room to concentrate on the task at hand: to capture the unique dynamics of this moms' group for the website. Five women sat together onstage—arranged youngest to oldest. The early-twenty-something mom, second to the left, snuggled her sleeping infant wrapped in a muslin sling as she finished a story I'd only caught the tail end of. Something about a housing connection that came from another one of the group members who raised her hand at Table 4.

Careful not to be a disturbance, I snapped a few pictures: of the panel on stage, of Trisha facilitating the questions, of the ladies listening intently at their tables while surrounded by other women in variable life stages and seasons. In only a few minutes, I was lost in the visual stories on display in this room. No, not stories, *story*. Because although there were many faces, there only seemed to be one central message strung together here tonight.

As the woman in the middle began to share, I paused my trigger finger and silenced my shutter. She spoke about a sudden job loss in a career she'd held since her teenage son was a baby. Without her salary, she could no longer afford the payments for her mother's long-term care facility for Alzheimer's. It was then a friend of hers discreetly applied for over a dozen deferment options and ended up securing a private grant that covered six months' worth of care so that her mother wouldn't have to change facilities. When she finished speaking, she paused and looked into the crowd as a woman at Table 2 waved her hand and then pressed it to her heart.

By the time the last lady on the panel lifted the microphone to her mouth, I no longer cradled my camera in my hands. It now hung limply around my neck as she shared about losing her husband at the age of thirty-four after ten years of marriage. Struggling with grief and trying to parent two school-age kids while also trying to hold down a job without any close family nearby had thrown her into a deep depression. She explained how there were days she could barely manage to get out of bed until one of her kids' teachers stepped in and offered her practical support in the way of rides, after-school care, and meals from her own support group at The Well. A woman at Table 6 raised her hand.

A familiar drumbeat began to rap hard against my ribs, a distinctive knock I'd answered before. Not the same pulse of fear I'd felt on that stage, but a rhythm I'd come to recognize as something far more significant. A pulse tick that seemed to say *pay attention*.

The same one I'd felt only seconds prior to meeting Carlee for the first time.

"As you've heard and seen tonight," Trisha said, "we aren't just a room of thirty individual mothers representing our own individual needs. We are a connected group called to carry one another's burdens and love our neighbors as ourselves, offering the kind of truth and grace Christ modeled for us in the story of the woman at the well we find in John 4. There's not a single woman here tonight who isn't the byproduct of someone stepping out and taking a risk for her at one time or another—isn't that right?" Several women at tables clapped or responded back. "It's easy to feel so overwhelmed by our own life circumstances that the idea of changing the world seems downright impossible. But our hope with this panel tonight was to demonstrate that sometimes all that it takes is one person being willing to step out in love for the betterment of another to change the trajectory of an entire life."

All that it takes is one.

The knock in my chest picked up speed, volume, intensity.

"So, the big question we'll discuss at our tables tonight is *who* was your one? Who was that person who reached out to you when you needed it most?"

And right then, before I'd even had the chance to process the full weight and impact of that question, an idea was birthed inside the creative storehouses in my mind. An idea that raced freely through the obstacle course of Volkin's film project requirements, completing one easy hurdle after another without so much as a single misstep. Because these real-life hopes and hardships lived inside a tension few could understand unless they'd lived it, too. And that journey, the one of a single mom who stretched out her hand to both give and receive on either side of her own struggle, was a story that deserved to be seen.

Perhaps even a movement that *needed* to be seen.

As the discussion in the room swelled to a dull roar, I took out my phone and began to sort through all the moving parts in my brain—creating a storyboard for *All That It Takes* without the help of the template I'd been using to draft ideas on at home for weeks. My fingers buzzed over the tiny keyboard, adrenaline and passion pumping through me at a rate I didn't even know was possible. I'd worked on countless compilations, edited videos, and created fresh content for Molly's channels. But this was something entirely new.

This was *purpose.*

I didn't bother to consult the time, I simply sent the entire unpolished outline and crudely written premise off to Gwen, praying that she wouldn't make me wait until tomorrow for a reply. But knowing Gwen, she could be riding a camel somewhere in the Sahara without cell service until next weekend. Her schedule wasn't exactly predictable.

I bit my bottom lip and leaned against the wall behind Tables 6, 7, and 8. I tipped my head back and closed my eyes, working to visualize the immediate next steps for my project. First, I'd need at least six willing participants with signed waivers by next week if this idea was approved. I'd also need a proper studio setup to conduct interviews and several visually interesting places to take B-roll in the city. Then there was the minor issue of finding a narrator with a suitable—

Lady Gwen

🌀 THIS is the one! All the other ideas were halfhearted attempts. THIS is where the passion lives inside you. Can't you feel it? It checks all the boxes. Call me in the morning, and we'll start polishing this up together. Don't worry about VV's approval. He'll give it. I'll start jotting down my thoughts on this tonight.

I clutched the phone to my chest, a delirious smile overtaking my face as I tipped my head against the wall and silently thanked God.

"Hey, Val?"

At the feminine voice, I straightened to stare up at Trisha Woodward.

"Hi again," she said. "I just wanted to check in with you and make sure everything was okay? I saw you leave after announcement time, but . . . well, now you seem good." Her tone ended on a funny note as she tilted her head to the side. "You have a really beautiful smile."

I was too irrationally happy to even make an attempt to discount her compliment. "Thank you. Tonight was—this was—" I laughed, and so did she. "I'm sorry. I just had a major breakthrough in something I've been trying to sort out for weeks. I didn't expect to find it here." And yet . . . perhaps I should have. "Do you think I might be able to speak to you and Nurse Charlotte about a project I'm involved with? It's for a mentorship I'm—"

She clasped her hands at her chest. "Wait. Does this happen to be for your big film project? We've been praying for you!"

My brain waves flatlined at her statement. "You've been praying for me?"

"Yes, as a staff—which right now is quite small, as you know. But Miles wrote your prayer request on the whiteboard in the admin office a few days after he started. We pray through the list each morning."

For several heartbeats I struggled to find my voice.

"Oh gosh, I'm sorry, I didn't think that was sensitive information. If so, it's totally on me."

I shook my head. "No, no, it's not. I just hadn't been aware he'd done that." My eyes misted as warmth expanded my chest. "Thank you. For praying for me." Someone she hadn't even met in person until tonight.

"Absolutely. I was actually hoping I could take you to coffee sometime soon? Pastor Miles said you moved here recently from Skagway. I have a sister who lives in Haines." Her smile was as wholehearted as her stage presence.

"Really? Small world." Haines was only about forty minutes from where I'd grown up. "And yes, I'd like that."

"Great, although I hope I don't have to wait till our coffee date to hear more about what you decided on."

I glanced at Nurse Charlotte, who was currently engaged in a conversation with two ladies at Table 3.

Trisha followed my gaze. "Oh, she'll be a while. Trust me. So the project?" she prompted, eyebrows raised.

"Well, okay," I started, feeling a bit odd relaying all this to a new acquaintance, but then again, she was my target audience. "Essentially, I'd like to expand on the concept of the panel you created tonight, sharing the hardship and need of a single mother participant and then highlighting the way it was met by another mother, several times over. My goal will be to focus on the life changes that have taken place in a handful of women after being shown support in all the ways you mentioned earlier: physical, mental, emotional, spiritual. I'll close the loop by showing the reciprocation effect—how those helped have stretched out their own hand to reach the needs of another."

Her jaw went slack. "You came up with all that from tonight's panel?"

"Not entirely on my own, but yes." I had doubted my ability

to hear God's voice before, but this time He'd made it as clear as the billboard I saw on the other side of a river one winter night long ago. "But I'll need some help to pull it off."

Trisha's round eyes brightened. "Of course! You'll need participants." She was already nodding, already calculating something out. "You can leave that part to me and Nurse Charlotte. Leave your media waivers with us, and we'll do some initial networking for you. I'll email you a list of contacts who are interested in sharing their story, and then you can interview them from there. That work?"

"Do you think there's a chance there'll be three pairs of ladies who are willing to share from this group?"

Trisha smiled. "I'd say there's way more than a chance."

· 24 ·

Miles

> **Rev**
>
> Been a while. How's the stillness plan going?
> Praying for you daily.

Naturally, Rev would text me about stillness on the morning I'd been up since five, gathering every cleaning supply known to humankind for today's big workday at the center. With all the calls, emails, and announcements that both Trisha and I had pushed these last couple of weeks, there should be close to fifty volunteers assisting in everything from repainting the exterior trim to landscaping the perimeter of the center.

> **Miles**
>
> Always appreciate your prayers. Good things are happening!

> **Rev**
>
> Hmm . . . that sounds like a deflection if I've ever heard one.

I stuffed the phone into my back pocket and propped the side door of the facility open with a cinder block. Though I believed stillness was a biblical discipline, there was also a case to be made for perseverance and hard work. Besides, so many things had changed for the better since I'd last sat with Rev at the river last month. And exactly none of those things had been on the slow track.

After a year of managing agonizing cutbacks and drowning in the defeat of failed ministries, it was time things moved along at a quicker pace. I smiled as the prettiest of those developments materialized in my mind. Of all the curveballs I'd been thrown, Val was the one I'd reach to catch over and over again. If not for her and Tucker, I couldn't be positive I would have taken Rev's advice and stuck it out here. At least my time at Riverside had provided some much-needed breathing room from Pastor Curtis and his sidekick, Leonard. Apart from our brief interactions between Sunday morning services at Salt and Light, I was on my own during the week.

As I carried some of the supplies inside through the long hallway, I blinked at the darkness, my eyes struggling to adjust. Bumping my elbow along the wall for a light switch, I called out into the empty corridor. No response. It appeared I was the first to arrive. Trisha's oldest son was in a golf tournament until noon, but where were the other volunteers with keys?

Rev

It's a good thing love is patient . . .

I smiled. Somehow, even Rev's attempts at sarcasm were bathed in Scripture. I set everything down on the table adjacent to the refreshment area we'd use for donuts and coffee this morning and then pizza and soda later this afternoon. After one last trip to the car, balancing the bakery boxes and multiple coffee creamers in my arms, I responded to him.

Miles

Sorry, I'm gearing up for a big workday at RFC. Hasn't been a lot of time left for sitting still. My focus has been on trying to build a long-term vision for this place.

Rev

And how is the vision coming?

I studied his question. The truth? I still hadn't quite made heads or tails of this place as far as a cohesive vision went. The flaws in the facility's exterior had been much easier to manage over the tangled web of community classes, childcare offerings, and career services that now filled the online calendar. But I did know one thing for certain: There were more bodies coming through these doors now than in the past three years of patchy leadership combined.

Miles

You want to swing in and see the place for yourself? I'll save you some free pizza and donuts. I know how good you are with a paintbrush.

Rev

At the Oregon coast this weekend with Cynthia, visiting her sister. Would be good to catch up with you soon, though.

My thumb hovered over the text keyboard as I thought about what to say about Val and Tucker. But their significance in my life deserved more than a quick text update. Before I could schedule a dock meet-up, Rev texted again.

Rev

Any news from your father's teams?

I hadn't expected the gut twist that came in response to that one, or the inexplicable desire to ignore his question completely. But even if I did, it wouldn't change the fact that the only communication from my father had been in the form of his newsletters. What did matter was that I'd found contentment outside of my vocation, which meant that for now, I'd stay committed to Riverside. Just like Rev had challenged me to do.

Miles

No news on that front. I'll call you when I leave here later today.

Rev

👍

I checked the time on my phone and unlocked the doors before turning on a playlist suitable for a productive workday. Everything was ready. All we needed now were the people.

∞

By twelve thirty, there were more donuts missing than volunteers who'd come to help.

The highlight of the day so far was when Val dropped Kadin and Tucker off—who were now both officially banned from the donut box—on her way to conduct a second round of initial interviews for her documentary. At least one of us had managed to find a group of devoted volunteers for our respective work projects. Unlike me, though, Val was having to whittle down her enthusiastic list of sign-up volunteers, not entice them with deep-fried foods.

I lifted the clipboard with today's sign-ins off the refreshment table. Sixteen. Sixteen people had shown up out of the fifty-seven RSVPs from personal phone calls, targeted emails, and group announcements we'd made. I tugged at the back of my neck, wondering where I'd gone wrong.

"Hey, Miles? Can Kadin and I do the trash pick-up job?" Tucker asked, pushing in through the front door, Kadin close on his heels.

"Uh, sure. As long as Ray is still out there."

"He is. Where are the pokers?"

"The *pokers*?" I asked.

"Yeah. You know"—he made a stabbing motion in the air—"the ones that stab the trash like the guys in orange vests use on the highway."

I released a laugh that immediately relaxed the tension in my shoulders. "Sorry, dude. I'm afraid this operation is far less funded.

You'll have to bend your knees and use your hands." I flexed my fingers for emphasis.

Their instant frowns prompted another round of comic relief. But it was short-lived, as a tween girl I'd watched grow from infancy strolled through the open door and veered around the boys. Her long blond ponytail and sparkly Converse high tops snagged their attention, causing them to halt their mission.

She waved at me, her pink-bracketed braces glistening under the overhead lights. "Hi, Pastor Miles."

"Hello, Caitlyn." Her name sailed through the air like a question mark. Because Caitlyn wasn't just a kid I knew from Gavin's youth group. Caitlyn was Pastor Curtis's daughter.

"Are there any donuts left? I know it's rude to ask for one before I work, but we just came from my hip-hop class, and I'm *super* starving."

"Oh, sure." I opened the lid to a fresh bakery box, and she chose a cake donut with white icing while I tried to work out the *we* part of her sentence. Who had she come with?

I glanced up at the boys, who hadn't moved an inch from their posts at the lobby door, and tipped my chin for them to come over. "Boys, do you know Caitlyn Archer?"

They both shook their heads, going quiet and leaving me to finish the introductions for them. I asked Caitlyn how long she thought she'd be sticking around—as if that was the only criteria for being paired with a job—but when she opened her mouth to answer, the unmistakable voice of her father came through the door.

Curtis slung an arm around his oldest child, his black jogging pants and Dave Matthew's Band T-shirt not the usual attire he wore around the church office. "Hey there, Miles. Looks like you've had a pretty good turnout so far. It's always tough to get people to give up a weekend day—especially a sunny one like today."

Though his voice gave nothing away, I searched for the double meaning. Sixteen people was the same number of volunteers needed to staff a single Sunday morning shift in the lobby cafe at

Salt and Light. Curtis could blink and make sixteen volunteers appear at his whim.

"No Leonard today?" I asked.

"Not today." By the look on his face, he was struggling to get a read on me, as well. "It's just Cait and me. We thought we'd lend a hand for a couple hours. Feel free to put us to work anywhere you see fit. I brought my toolbox."

Caitlyn ate her donut by picking off bite-size pieces one at a time. "Dad said it's a good opportunity for us to serve people in need."

I opted for a smile, though my mind had quickly filled with the many other service opportunities that had been cancelled under her father's leadership.

I gave Tucker a telling nod, indicating what his next move should be when it came to Caitlyn.

Straightening to his full height, which was still a good three inches shorter than her, Tucker moseyed over and addressed her. "Uh, do you like trash?"

"Do I like . . . *trash*?" she repeated after a confused giggle.

I stepped in and clamped a hand on the boy's bony shoulder. His cool way with the ladies was about as up to speed as my own. "Tucker and Kadin are doing some cleanup around the perimeter. You're welcome to join them if you want to," I clarified. "They can get you an extra pair of gloves. Right, boys?"

"Can I, Dad?" she asked her father.

"Sure. Just don't stray too far from the group."

"Trisha's husband is out there," I said in reply. "The kids will be fine."

After the trio of tweens pushed out the doors, Curtis picked up a donut of his own and strolled through the lobby, peeking his head into the empty admin office behind the glass windows. "Smells the same in there. Like copier paper and old coffee grounds."

"Trisha just ordered some diffusers to help neutralize it." For some reason, this information seemed important to share, as if I was being graded on every update I'd worked to accomplish over the past several weeks.

He stopped his perusal and looked at me. "I'm glad Trisha's still here. Not many remember what this place was like when Otto was in his best health."

Trisha's words from my first day here circled back to me, about Curtis fighting for her to keep her hours when there was so much upheaval happening at S&L. I hadn't understood it then, and I still didn't understand it.

"Otto always had the best stories to share when it came to the community involvement that happened around this place, the neighbors who'd wander in looking for a fresh cup of coffee and a chat, only to later find Otto patching up that hole in their roof by the following week. I swear, he was outside this place more than he was in his office."

Since I'd started, there hadn't been a single neighbor who'd walked through those doors looking for anything other than a class or a sign-up sheet for a specific activity. With the exception of Carlee. And Val had been the one to see her, not me.

Curtis went on. "My sister and I used to joke that Otto's office was like a treasure chest. He used to have this humongous desk where he'd keep these root-beer-flavored candies hidden. We'd stuff our pockets full of them whenever Dad took us by for a visit." He shook his head, laughed. "It's weird the things you remember from when you were a kid. But Otto sure did leave some big shoes to fill." He took a bite of his maple donut and stared down at it in wonderment. After swallowing, he said, "Gosh, I haven't had one of these in a long time. I've seen you and Gavin come back to the office with boxes from Deb's Bakery, but I gotta be honest, I didn't know what all the hype was about." He laughed again. "Consider me officially enlightened."

But it was hard for me to consider him anything but confusing at the moment. What was this stroll down memory lane really about? The two of us had grown up together at Salt and Light; we'd attended the same youth group, went to the same summer camps, and at one point, even had our sights set on the same girl. But we'd never been buddies. Not as young adults, and certainly not now. And I, for one, was not under the delusion that space and time could rewrite history.

He finished the donut and then clapped the crumbs from his hands as if to conclude the reminiscent portion of this peculiar visit. This entire interaction felt off, tilted in a way that left me grappling to find my balance. I wasn't sure what his game was yet. But I knew there would be one if I waited long enough.

"How has the weekly group attendance been?"

Ah, numbers, then. He wanted an oral report to take back to the vision team at S&L. "Well, considering that when I arrived the Riverside website hadn't been updated in two years, it's difficult to calculate an accurate baseline. But we've launched several new groups and have a plan to begin several more by the end of August. I'd say attendance numbers have tripled." A truth, even despite today's minor setback with the volunteers. "The moms' group that meets here on Monday nights has risen steadily."

Pastor Curtis hiked an eyebrow. "Has it? That's great."

"Yes," I said. "Pretty remarkable, considering that the health of any organization is dependent on consistent leadership and follow-through." I paused a beat. "After all, not even the best visionary in the world can rewrite a bad history." A double-edged comment I was ready to expound upon if he was willing to go there with me. But it appeared he was simply going to pretend he hadn't handed me a puzzle with a missing piece. Or perhaps one with a handful of missing pieces. All I knew was that until Curtis was willing to disclose those vital game pieces to me, true growth at Riverside would be impossible to sustain long-term.

And by the way Curtis studied me, he knew it, too.

A silent tug-of-war played out between us. But he didn't pull on his turn. Instead, he looked down at today's sign-up sheet and at the jobs still needing to be checked off the list. "I should probably make my rounds. I'd like to check in with a few volunteers and put my work clothes to good use."

"Sure. Go right ahead." My nod was stiff as he rounded the corner into the first set of rooms. A couple of young moms from ing up the lobby and made room for the pizza delivery order on its way.

But even once the pizza arrived, bringing with it a steady trickle of lunchtime volunteers, Curtis's continued presence at the center unnerved me in a way that sharpened my focus to his every move within the facility and to every person he spoke with. More than once, I invented a reason to stay in earshot, catching his repetitive phrases and questions about where they saw the center going, what hopes they had for its growth, and how it had impacted them up until now. He was conducting surveys inside the neglected ministry he'd handed off to me. But for what purpose?

I needed inside information from someone I could trust.

I propped the shovel I'd been using against the outside wall where I stood near the front lobby doors, tilling the dry soil into something that didn't look so . . . crusty. After ripping off my gloves, I slipped out my phone.

As much as I didn't want to pull Gavin into a mess, I also didn't want to be blindsided the way I'd been so many times in this last year by the same man.

Miles
Hey, have you heard anything around the office recently about Riverside?

Gavin
Nothing since the update at this month's staff meeting, why?

Miles
Curtis showed up for volunteer day today. What update?

Gavin
Really? That's awesome! Was the rest of the turnout good? Nicky was bummed to miss it. Zoey was up all night with the stomach flu. 😟 And I'm still elbow deep in high school summer camp registrations.

Our volunteer list had grown to twenty-four since lunch. But still, that was pebbles in comparison to what the church could bring in for such an event. A fact I was all too aware of with Pastor Curtis on the premises today.

Miles

Decent, yes. Sorry to hear about Zoey. What was the update at the meeting?

Gavin

Yeah, she's lucky her mom's a nurse.

Not much. PC just mentioned that he thought you were the right man for the job. Said he's looking forward to providing reports from Riverside soon.

For the second time today, a text caused my insides to clench. *What reports?*

"Pastor Miles? Pastor Miles? Are you still out here?" I glanced up from my phone to see Trisha jogging through the doors, her forearms splattered with white trim paint.

"I'm right here, Trish. What's up?"

She spun on her loafers. "Oh good! So you must have seen him, then?" Her hand flew to her chest, and she barked out an airy breath. "I got concerned when I saw him head out the lobby doors after I couldn't find you inside."

Had Curtis already left? So much for our check-in-at-the-end-of-the-day exchange. Last I'd heard, he was replacing the old light fixtures with one of the dads from Jedi Knights in the men's restroom. "Yeah, we caught up a while ago. Although, I thought he was still in the bathroom."

Her face looked slightly confused, but she pulled on a warm smile. "Oh, well, good. I just hate when people in need get lost in the shuffle of busyness."

My head swung back to her. "*Wait*—people in need?"

"Yeah." She peered at me, alarm registering in her gaze. "The guy in the blue polo. You spoke to him, right? He was asking to talk to the pastor here—said he'd messed up his marriage and could use some prayer and advice. That's who I was talking about." Whatever confusion she saw on my face had her breaking away and trotting through the parking lot and out to the sidewalk. She rose up on her tiptoes and looked both ways.

Abandoning the shovel, I followed, jogging past her and across the street to search for a man in a blue shirt.

But he was nowhere to be seen now.

Trisha was still shaking her head as we came together again, clearly distraught. "He said when he saw the doors open to this place today on his way to work at the gas station, he took it as a sign. Said he didn't dare darken the doors of an actual church, but he remembered Otto from when he was a boy. I offered him a slice of pizza so I could go look for you. Gosh . . . I should have just called your phone or taken him with me to try and find—"

"You aren't to blame, Trisha. You did everything right." Meanwhile, my own gut churned, my skin growing prickly and hot. I'd been far too caught up in a witch-hunt to see a hurting man walk right past me. Conviction punched me square in the ribs. So much for being a faithful leader.

I touched her shoulder. "Did you happen to get his name?"

"Jed. As in Jedidiah. I remember because I hadn't heard him correctly at first."

"Okay," I said. "Good." Though it wasn't. Not even close.

She sighed. "I'll add his name to the prayer board in my office."

"Yes." I watched the passing cars, wondering if Jed had been on foot or if he'd driven. I'd been too engrossed in my texts to even recall the sound of a car engine. "Please do."

"I'm sorry, Pastor Miles."

I turned to her then, doing my best to silence my own guilt long enough to silence hers. "You have nothing to apologize for. I should have been more available. Forgive me."

She offered a weak smile. "We'll pray he comes back."

Long after Trisha rejoined the rest of the crew inside, pinpricks of shame worked their way through my core and into my limbs.

I'd missed him. I'd missed a hurting man seeking help because I'd been too focused on my own needs. On my own validation.

I threaded my fingers behind my head and blew out a heavy breath, tipping my gaze skyward. Otto wouldn't have missed him. And I knew without a doubt that Val wouldn't have either.

I'd been a front-row witness to such a display only a few weeks ago right here in this same parking lot: Val's pursuit of a stranger in need. Only her pursuit had far less to do with the *need* itself, and far more to do with the person behind it. She'd *seen* Carlee, she'd listened, she'd empathized, she'd validated, and then she'd invited her into her life. Which was exactly how loving our neighbors should be done.

My chest squeezed tight as once again I pondered this woman I'd fallen for in record time, the one who'd spent exactly zero days studying in a seminary or standing behind a pulpit or living abroad on a mission field. The truth was, this same beautiful, unsuspecting woman had somehow become the purist example of servant-hearted leadership in my life.

I may not know the details of whatever game Curtis Archer was playing at, or what that game might mean for my future, but I did know one thing: I couldn't afford to lose sight of the people God had placed right in front of me.

· 25 ·

Val

I was mid-sentence on a Friday coaching call with Gwen, running through next week's filming schedule and the required shots and techniques for the interview portion of *All That It Takes*, when Carlee trudged into my apartment. She froze the instant she saw herself reflected in my laptop screen.

"*Oops*. Sorry," she mouthed, shuffling past my workstation to flop on my couch. Though we'd helped her get situated at Millie's a couple weeks ago, she pretty much still lived here. My apartment had become her daytime house. If she wasn't sleeping or working her new job at the coffee bistro, courtesy of one of Nurse Charlotte's connections, then she was here. On this couch. Usually eating something with a spice level fit for Miles.

At the sound of Carlee's arrival, Tucker shot out of his room. With a Lego masterpiece in one hand, he tapped his index finger to his lips with the other. The two had a silent yet highly distracting miming exchange about needing to stay quiet while I finished up my video call with Gwen.

Despite their antics, I worked to focus on my coach. ". . . So, anyway, I thought when Angela gets to the part of her story about her emergency C-section, I'll do a medium close-up shot to show

287

the intensity of her emotion. She's very expressive. From there I was thinking about an underside shot to get the movement of her hands just before I transition back to a—"

"Just a minute, Val. Would you mind rotating the camera a smidge?"

Confused, I lifted my Sony A7III off the desk and showed it to her, but she shook her head. "No, this one. On the screen." She tapped the camera on her laptop. "I'd like to say hello to your tribe there."

And because she was Lady Gwen, I gave her what she wanted and turned my laptop toward the open living room.

Carlee propped herself up on an elbow and her belly peeked underneath her black Higher Ground Coffee work tee, while Tucker waved with his Lego-free hand.

"Hello there, Val's people. I'm Gwen. And you must be Tucker, and you must be Carlee."

Carlee's surprise was evident. "You told her about me?"

"Well, of course she did, darling. She's required to share the most important details of her life with her film coach. Which means that you, young lady, are quite important to her."

The real story of how Gwen found out about Carlee? She noticed a stack of Carlee's birthing books from the library on my coffee table and asked if there was something I needed to tell her.

But I liked this version much better.

Carlee's lips curled up at the corners. "Val's pretty important, too."

"Oh, don't I know it! I only work with VIPs in my industry." The way she said it beckoned a question I'd managed to suppress since the day I signed her coaching agreement: Would Gwen have chosen me if the pool of talented females had been larger? Or was I simply the only female left?

"Do you think my mom's gonna win?" Tucker asked, coming closer to the screen. "I've been praying she will."

"Well, you keep that up for your mama, young man, because I think she has a strong chance."

When I flipped the screen back around, Gwen was giving him a thumbs-up.

"Okay, now, where were we?" She slipped on her reading glasses again and took out her notebook.

And just like that, the questions of how and why dissipated. Because no matter the reason, I was grateful to be her mentee.

We spent the next thirty minutes reviewing the rough outlines on each of the interviewees I'd selected from the list of names Trisha had compiled for me. After much back-and-forth discussion with Gwen over how best to optimize the visual and storytelling flow of the interviews, we decided on a dual perspective—two women per interview session, one the receiver in the story, the other the giver. Only, the giver would not simply retell the same story but would share the catalyst of her own story. That seemed to be the common denominator in all twenty-four testimonies submitted: one selfless act of love in the midst of suffering and hardship. The visual would be powerful, but the production and management side would prove one of the greatest challenges I'd ever taken on.

As Gwen had said numerous times, this was when the novice became a professional.

"These are stories of the heart, my dear. We don't watch stories with our eyes, we feel stories with our entire being. Every shot you take, every lens you change, every filter you apply, it must come secondary to what is happening here." She planted her palm to her chest. "Don't concern yourself with what's trending. Concern yourself with what's real. Your camera angles should follow the impact of the story—*always*. If it's a lighter moment, have fun! Be artsy! If it's an intensely emotional moment, don't be afraid to get up close, like you mentioned. Put on that fifty mil for a close-up and hold on tight." As if to demonstrate this, she pressed her face closer to the screen, her eyes sparkling bright with the kind of experience one can only earn by living nearly seven decades. "Go over and over the notes you took on your selected individuals, and get each storyboard block in your head. But then, on filming day, let all that go." She made a whooshing sound. "Being present with your talent on that chair is the priority. They will take their cues from you." She ticked off her fingers one by one. "Listen. Feel. Create. Always in that order."

Gooseflesh rose on my forearms as I feverishly jotted down the words in my notebook. *Listen, feel, create.*

When she finished speaking, applause erupted from my living room. Tucker gave her a standing ovation, and Carlee was as captivated as I'd ever seen. I flipped the screen around again so Gwen could see her fan club. She gave a half bow.

"Now, Valerie, you go enjoy your weekend, because next week will start the most intense part of this process . . . well, until the editing stage begins, that is. But we'll face one hurdle at a time. Oh!" She lifted her notepad to show me the last item on her list to scratch off. "I need a sample of your narrator's voice. I still have to get that approved." She rolled her eyes. "I swear, the things I have to pass by Mr. Micromanager are getting quite ridiculous. Rumor has it, some big-time producers are sniffing around the film program, and you better believe Volkin makes sure to wear his best cologne when they do. On our last coaching call, there was a film crew on him—apparently, he's documenting his own success story. Perhaps their influence will prod the chauvinism right out of him."

It wasn't the first time Gwen had hinted at this, but it was definitely the most pointed.

"Oh yes," she said in response to whatever face I was making. "Volkin has never awarded his trophy to a woman. Not once in more than fifteen years. But he's always careful to have just enough female candidates in the finals to push back against criticism." She shook her head. "Too many high-dollar affiliates to cause much of a ruckus. Although this contest round might be interesting."

"Why?"

"One of your competitors dropped out this week for the chance at a paid position with one of Victor's competitors. A young woman—I believe her last name was Adrian."

A bell rang in the back of my mind. "Adrian? No way, really?"

It was Gwen's turn to look confused. "Did you know her?"

"No, but Victor confused us during my interview. He said she was his top pick, that her résumé was one of the most impressive he'd ever seen." Multiple times over. "I can't believe she dropped out."

"I hate to think of the fallout, but men like Volkin don't appreciate being embarrassed." Gwen's sigh was weighty. "Securing the right connections in this industry is far more valuable than money."

Wasn't that why Gwen had joined the ranks this year, too? So she could rebuild her reputation in the industry as a director advocating for equal opportunities?

"Just keep your head down and focus on making your work shine, darling. That's the best thing any creative can do." Her expression shifted into one of maternal pride. "I'm willing to bet there is more heart in this one project than in all eight of the others combined." She gave me a shooing wave with her hand. "Now, you get off this computer and go enjoy your youth! Promise?" She blew a kiss. "We'll talk next week."

And without waiting for a good-bye, she clicked off, yet somehow there were still two sets of eyes on me. I turned slowly, facing the gaping faces from the sofa across the room.

"May I help you?" I teased.

Carlee cradled her phone in her hand. "I'm looking that Volkin guy up."

"Ugh. Please don't," I muttered, already exhausted by the Hollywood-style drama of it all and moving to the recliner—which just happened to be the perfect location in my house to view Miles's car whenever it decided to pull into the driveway. Not that'd I'd been counting down the minutes or anything. But seeing as he'd asked to take me out tonight, the clock had been ticking down rather slowly.

"Found him." Carlee's declaration would have been better suited for the reveal in a True Crimes podcast than the sighting of a middle-aged man on a power trip.

"Oooh, can I see, too?" Tucker dropped himself over the sofa beside Carlee, and like two overprotective mothers, we both jumped to shield her belly from him.

Startled, Tuck rocked away. "Whoa! It's not like I can't see it! It's very . . . round." His shrug made us laugh. But he did have a point. Carlee's belly was definitely getting closer to the final leg of the race. And even now, as I watched her zoom in on a picture of Volkin, I wondered where her mind was this week. She'd finally agreed to meet with Nurse Charlotte a few days prior to starting the job she'd helped her get at Higher Ground Coffee, but there had been no decision regarding the future as of yet. I knew, because her Aunt Lizzy checked in with me regularly to ask if Carlee had attended any of the moms' group meetings or had set a counseling appointment.

My answer to all her questions had simply been *not yet*.

Although it wasn't for lack of praying or inviting.

Carlee tilted her head to examine the picture. "Don't you think he kind of looks like . . ."

"That creepy mean guy from *Beauty and the Beast*?" Tucker asked.

"Yes! Gaston!" she proclaimed, turning her phone to me. "Do you see it too, Val?"

Only I was laughing too hard to even respond.

∞

The instant Miles pulled into the driveway, my phone vibrated.

Miles

May I borrow your son for just a moment, please?

Val

Hello to you, too.

Miles

Trust me, saying hello to you in person will be the highlight of my day.

Val

Good answer. Sending him down now.

Tuck was up and out the door before I even got through the entire sentence. Most days, my time with Miles was shared time. Coffee in the mornings. Dinner in the evenings. Couch chats on the nights when I wasn't working too late and Tucker's ten-year-old detective ears weren't hanging on every spoken word. Though, given his plethora of questions involving the definition and purpose of dating . . . it was obvious he'd caught on to us. But perhaps that was for the best. My live-in roommates—whether daytime or full-time, offered an extra level of accountability to our unique living situation that both Miles and I were grateful for.

Carlee propped and readjusted a pillow under her elbow. A fidget that might as well be a doorbell.

"How was your day in the land of caffeine?" I asked, noting her swollen ankles. "Were you on your feet most of the day again?"

"Have to be when I work the drive-up window. But I make the most tips there. Guess it's a good thing people can't see my fat feet from their windows, huh?"

"I'm glad you're making good tips, but your body needs more rest than usual right now. Your feet and ankles swell because they need a break."

"I feel fine, really. And I'm sure the only reason I'm making good tips is because people feel sorry for me." Carlee rested her hand on top of her belly, a move I'd only seen her do in these last couple of weeks. "Some old dude asked me if I was married."

"What did you say?"

She stared up at the ceiling. "That it was none of his business. I thought my supervisor, Joanne, would get mad at me. But she just patted me on the back and said that was a perfectly fine answer to give."

"I agree. It was."

She released a long, contemplative sigh. "Aunt Lizzy says I shouldn't wait until the last minute to figure out my plans."

I knew which plans she alluded to, although I'd never once heard Carlee say the word *baby*. Much the way Tucker avoided cracks on the sidewalk, Carlee had figured out every possible way to talk about her pregnancy without actually talking about the child growing inside her.

"Whatever I can do to help you process through your options, I hope you know I will. Anytime," I said. "If there are any phone calls I can help with or meetings I can set up, I'm happy to do it."

As I waited for her to speak, my thoughts drifted to Tucker. I thought about how integral my parents had been in helping me raise him. My dad's role had been especially vital in my son's life. More and more as of late I'd begun to make a distinction I hadn't made in nearly a decade of parenting: Though I was a single mom, I'd never been a solo mom. Sure, Tucker didn't have a traditional two-parent family, but he'd always had three consistent adults who'd been invested in his life since before his birth. A blessing I'd only just recently begun to process in light of the many difficult stories I'd heard during my interviews. Many of these young women had next to no support before they were invited into a community of relationships like they'd never experienced before.

She rotated again, fluffed a pillow under her head, and avoided eye contact. "I told Aunt Lizzy you have the most comfortable couch."

I touched her head, marveling at the thick cascade of her dark ponytail. "You're welcome on my couch anytime."

She snuggled down deeper and pretended to fall asleep.

If only life could be that simple.

A strange grinding sound followed by several loud cranks vibrated the floor.

We both jolted to our feet.

"Earthquake?" she asked.

I shook my head, following the sound into the kitchen. "I don't think so."

Carlee trailed close behind me, bumping into my back when I stopped in front of Tucker's spaceship-closet-pantry. The sound seemed to be originating from there.

"Um . . . are you hiding Narnia in there?"

I shook my head and jiggled the door handle. Locked from the inside. Just like it had been for weeks.

But then the sound changed to more of a constant hum that lasted nearly a minute before a hard jolt and the unlocking of a door.

"Hello?" Carlee asked the closed door, as if it were the landing of a UFO and we were about to meet alien life forms.

The door pushed open from the other side to reveal two such aliens. Though neither was green and both were holding giant bouquets of wildflowers.

"Surprise!" Tucker yelled over the top of his bouquet. "This was our secret project! Did you know, Mom? Did you figure out what we've been working on?"

"N-n-no," I stammered, needing an extra second to process what my eyes were seeing as Miles unhooked the knee-high safety gate that ran across the open doorway to the . . . elevator. The now fully functioning elevator.

"Hello," Miles said, stepping out and handing me the bouquet of flowers. His gaze communicated so much more than a casual greeting. "My co-engineer and I figured this apartment could use a functioning elevator, given the camera equipment you keep rolling up the stairs and the special houseguests who stop in for frequent snack visits." He winked at Carlee.

I pressed the flowers to my chest as Tucker gave his bunch to Carlee.

"These are gorgeous. Thank you, Miles." I inhaled the sweet aroma of the lilies before smiling at Carlee, who was currently nose down in her bouquet, obviously fighting back tears.

Tucker clapped her on the back multiple times until Miles gently gripped his shoulder and gave him a single shake of the head, as if to say *not the right move, little man.* The silent exchange between them expanded my heart to twice its size, and suddenly, my own eyes felt damp.

Miles cleared his throat and Tucker straightened, squaring up his shoulders.

"I asked your son for his permission to take you on a special date tonight."

Again, my heart swelled as I looked at Tucker, whose chest was so puffed with pride I worried he would pass out if he waited another second to speak. "And what did you say, Tucker?"

"I asked how many dates it would take for him to become my dad."

Carlee's gasp was the only indication that time was still moving forward.

"Oh, Tuck," I began. "That's . . . that's a much bigger conversation than—"

"I know, Mom," he said casually. "Pop talked to me about it already."

I blinked. And then I blinked again, my voice failing me. "Pop?"

Miles set his arm around Tuck's shoulders, squeezed. "I, uh . . . I had the privilege of meeting your father over FaceTime. He was the mechanic behind our secret project. He sent us the parts we needed straight from his shop—after identifying them over video, that is. Pretty remarkable, actually. The man is . . . well, I'm pretty sure he's some kind of genius, like his daughter."

He'd met my dad. Miles had met my father. On a video chat with my son. The idea circled on a merry-go-round in my mind.

Miles broke free from Tucker and moved toward me, his hands as warm and soft as his voice. "Telling you about the video chat before tonight would have ruined the surprise. I hope I made the right call on that?"

"Did you meet my mom, too?" I asked, still a bit stunned.

Though Miles's face was awash with concern, I felt nothing but affection for him.

"I did, yes. She was lovely. You have her smile." He touched my chin.

"Gram asked if he was *single*."

Carlee laughed, and I closed my eyes in momentary mortification. "Oh, I don't doubt that she did." Only, I wasn't sure how she'd kept their exchange a secret. Or how Tucker had, for that matter.

"They miss you. That's quite clear," Miles said in a tone that made me feel just as hormonal as my pregnant friend. "But they wanted me to tell you how proud of you they are and how much they're looking forward to a long visit after tourist season."

"They told you that?"

"Yes."

I sniffed and smashed my lips together.

"So, uh, you're not upset that I didn't tell you sooner?"

I shook my head. "No, not at all."

The visible relief on his face relaxed me even more. "Good, because I was really hoping you'd still be up for going somewhere special with me tonight." He glanced at his watch. "Is thirty minutes enough time for you?"

I opened my mouth, but Carlee piped up before I could speak. "Um, thirty minutes is hardly enough time for her to put on one of her zip-up hoodie thingies. She's gonna need more time to get date-ready."

"Oh, really? You do?" Miles asked me.

Again, Carlee rolled her eyes and cut in. "That's the most man question you've ever asked. One hour. It's our final offer."

Miles laughed at Carlee and once again looked to me for confirmation.

"You heard her." I shrugged. "That's our final offer."

And before another word could be spoken on the subject, Carlee was handing off our bouquets and whisking me away to where my sad clothing options lived. It didn't take long for Carlee to conclude what I already knew . . . there was nothing in there that screamed *date-ready*! Unless that date was a road trip where only gas stations and drive-thru dinners were involved.

"Um, I think you need to be put on a no-more-hoodies freeze. This is . . ." She swished through the hangers of sweatshirts. "Consider this your intervention. You need wardrobe help."

If it wasn't so true, it would have been funny. Carlee plopped on my bed, narrowing her eyes at me. "Hey, is your fashion friend still in California?"

At the thought of Molly, my chest prickled. She was exactly who I needed right now. "No, she just got back last night."

I slid my phone from my pocket, questioning for all of two seconds if I should give Miles a heads-up to the hurricane that I was about to unleash.

But then again, he'd talked to my parents without giving me a heads-up, so this only seemed fair.

Molly answered on the second ring.

"Hey! How funny, I was just about to text you—"

"Molly." I braced for impact. "By any chance, do you happen to be free right now?"

"Um, I can be. Silas is staying late at The Bridge tonight. Why?" she asked cautiously. "Are you okay?"

"Yes," I said on a laugh. "I'm actually much more than okay. But I do need your help. I'm . . . um . . . I'm about to go on a date, and I don't have anything date-nice to wear. And worse, I don't have much time."

"Val . . ." The hesitant happiness in Molly's voice made me grin all the more, and now Carlee had her ear near the phone, too. "What exactly are you saying? *Who* exactly are you going on a date with?"

Preemptively, I pulled the phone away from our ears and said, "Your brother."

And even with my volume turned down, I was certain Molly's screams could have been heard in Alaska.

· 26 ·

Miles

I never went to my senior prom. But for some reason, this moment—anxiously pacing the length of my living room while Tucker studied me from the couch—had me feeling like a seventeen-year-old kid waiting to go on his first official date. Val wasn't my first date. But I certainly hoped she'd be my last. I hoped for much more than that, actually.

"The jacket's a nice touch," Tucker said, giving my sports coat two thumbs up.

I tugged on the sleeves and straightened the lapels for the twelfth time. "Yeah?"

"Definitely."

"Thanks, Tuck."

The poor kid had taken refuge down here after my sister had shown up with her giant rolling suitcase and commandeered the entire upstairs apartment as "a ladies fitting room." We were out of there in five seconds flat. Even still, Molly had managed to text me a dozen emoji sentences—the majority of which started and ended with party poppers.

Out of habit, I checked my watch again and cracked my front

door to let the breeze through. Luckily, the weather had cooperated with my plans tonight. It had to be at least seventy out still. Not bad for a July evening.

I checked my watch again. The ladies still had six minutes to wrap up whatever magical potions they were applying to a woman who'd captivated me in a zip-up hoodie and lounge pants.

"Miles?"

I stopped my pacing to give Tucker my full attention, as his tone sounded less than Tucker-like. Was that worry? "Yeah, bud?"

"You know how I get to go to Dude Camp with you in August?"

I nodded. I'd turned in his registration form last week.

"It's for three nights, right?"

Tucker knew this answer; we'd spoken about it at length as I'd shown him the map of the hiking trails and each place we'd be camping overnight.

"Yes. A Thursday through a Saturday night. We'll come home Sunday afternoon, remember? Why, what's up?"

He balled his fingers into two fists, a move I'd never seen from him. Tucker wasn't usually the nervous type. If anything, he was the first in line to test the limits. "Will I be able to call my mom— you know, if I need to?"

I sat on the edge of the sofa. "Do you think you might need to?"

He shrugged. "Not sure."

"There won't be much cell coverage where we're going. It's part of the experience."

Slowly, he released a breath. "But what if there's an emergency?"

"Then I'll be there to help you."

"Because that's what you do for people, right? You help them. That's what Kadin says a pastor does—he helps people."

I smiled at the simplicity of his definition. "I'd like to think so."

He sighed. "Okay."

"Is there something specific you're nervous about?" I was prepared to hear a list of possible worst-case scenarios on the trail. Things Kadin or some other kid had told him when he attended youth group last week. Though we always exercised as much precaution as possible on the trails, there were usually a few gashes, sunburns, rashes. Once, several years back, there was a broken arm when a kid slipped off a rock he was jumping from.

"My mom."

"You're nervous you'll be homesick?" That was only natural. He wasn't even eleven yet.

Tucker shook his head no. "I don't want something bad to happen to her while I'm gone."

It was only then I understood. He hadn't been concerned about an emergency for himself; he'd been concerned about Val having an emergency and him not being there. The two had a bond like few mothers and sons I knew. Tucker was more than a child . . . he was a companion. "Ah. I see."

His chin bobbed just enough for me to know how serious he was about this conversation. "Kadin said that when he went to a school camp a few years ago, his mom got hurt. And after that he had to live with Grandma Millie forever."

Only, Millie's daughter didn't get hurt by falling down a flight of stairs, she'd overdosed on oxy. And she'd been in and out of rehab ever since.

"Do you think you should stay home?" I asked.

He looked at me suspiciously. "No."

"Okay, then what do you think you should do? What will help you not be worried about her?"

"I could pray." Not a question; a statement. "That's what you do, right? When you're afraid?"

Truthfully, outside of the parking lot incident between Val and Carlee weeks ago, I couldn't remember the last time I'd been truly afraid. Then again, the day my parents had kissed Molly and me good-bye in our grandma's driveway to take their church-planting organization overseas . . . I'd felt it then. The clutch of uncertainty. The crash of responsibility. The inability to imagine a future apart from the lifeblood of our family—my father. An ongoing struggle even now.

"Yes, I do pray. God is the only one who can trade our fear

for peace. That's one of His promises to us." I knocked his shoe with mine. "But I also think about what is true. And what's true about your mom is that she's strong. Do you know what resilience means?"

He sniffed. "Yes. It was one of my vocabulary words last year."

Of course it was. The kid was way too smart for his age. "Well, that's what your mom is. She's resilient. So the next time you're worried about not being with her, you remember that, okay?"

I expected him to nod or to at least acknowledge my wealth of wisdom in some way or another, but instead, he pointed behind me, to three women located directly outside my cracked-open front door. How I'd missed them walking down the stairs, I had no idea.

But all my senses were functioning at full capacity now.

And nothing could have coaxed my gaze away from Val. Not even the man-sized whistle that escaped Tucker's mouth.

"Whoa, Mom. You're . . . you're like . . . a super pretty lady."

"Thanks, Tuck." Val's cheeks were flushed as her gorgeous amber-brown eyes slid from his to mine, a sweeping motion that could have knocked me off balance if my knees had been locked.

I wasn't sure how much time had passed, but suddenly, I was no longer in a rush to leave. All I wanted was to drink this moment in. To memorize every detail of her in a way I'd be able to recall decades from now. Because this was different from our quick coffee dates in her kitchen before I left for the center. Or our lively chats on the sofa after dinner with Carlee and Tucker beside us. Or even our late-night fire pit talks under a midnight sky.

Tonight was something else entirely.

"You're stunning."

Val pressed her petite fingertips to the place at her left hip where her dress gathered in a cascade of aqua fabrics, glistening like water to her mid-calf. My gaze worked against the tide's pull, drawing up to her slender waist and her exposed shoulders and the high collar encircling her graceful neck before resting on the pink hue of her cheeks and lips. Perhaps I should have paid better attention to the hundreds of fashion videos I'd *liked* on Molly's social media pages over the years, but while I had no terminology for the cut or style or trend Val was wearing now, I knew I'd never seen a dress like this one. Nor had I ever seen a woman like her.

"You look nice, Miles," she said. "Handsome."

But compared to Val, I looked like a gutter rat. Suit coat or not.

Molly clasped her hands under her chin. "You two should go. Val's dress is a rare kind of magic, and it shouldn't be wasted."

I couldn't agree with her more.

I offered Val my arm as Tucker leapt over the couch in time to loop his arms around his mom's waist. He did the same to mine a few seconds later.

"You be good for Carlee and Millie tonight, okay?" Val instructed him.

Carlee set her hand on Tuck's head. "Millie said the boys are asking to watch the original *Jurassic Park* with me tonight. I only agreed because she's making her famous caramel corn recipe, and that will give me something to throw at them if they laugh at me for screaming during that kitchen scene."

"Oooh, that scene is freaky," Molly said. "Even Miles screamed the first time we watched it as kids."

I shook my head. "I don't remember that at all."

Molly rolled her eyes. "You wouldn't."

"Don't worry, I won't get too scared," Tucker said, giving me a knowing look. "I'm strong, like my mom."

I winked at him as Val beamed.

"That you are, Tuck. That you are."

⟨⟨⟩⟩

"Can I open my eyes yet?" she asked for the fourth time since we'd left the car. I'd kept our post-dinner destination a secret from her, which was not Val's preferred method of communication. But since my plan hadn't involved a crowd of strangers or forcing her to stand on a stage . . . I figured I'd be in the clear in just a matter of seconds.

"Not quite yet." Her eyes remained closed as she gripped the hem of her dress in one hand and gripped my arm with the other. Thankful Molly hadn't convinced Val to wear heels, I was careful to keep our pace slow, to be mindful of our every shared step, though I could have easily walked this path blindfolded. My gaze slid to the breeze flirting with Val's hair. It lifted off her nearly bare shoulders, yet somehow, the motion didn't disturb the intricate braids wrapped like a crown at her hairline.

"I hear water," she said, craning her neck to the side.

"What good ears you have."

"You realize that's what the Big Bad Wolf says right before Little Red Riding Hood gets eaten, right?"

"I promise not to eat you." Though whatever tropical blend of fragrance she'd dotted on her jawline was definitely making it difficult not to pull her closer.

"There's a slight step down right . . . here." I tightened my grip on her arm and guided her to the exact spot I'd envisioned revealing my surprise. "Okay. Open them whenever you're ready."

Val blinked three times before she lifted her hands to her mouth. "Oh, Miles." She took in the setting before us—the trees, the lights, the dock, the bench, the dusky sky—but my eyes remained only on her. "You did all this?"

"I had a little help." A few favors had been called in to make tonight possible, but the look on her face was worth every hired teenager looking for a way to pay for the high school summer camp in August.

Her eyes sparkled from the reflection of the white lights they'd strung throughout the trees overhead. There had to be a thousand of them at least. Several flickering lanterns had also been strategically placed along the lower branches by helpers who were far more in tune with how to transform a man's fishing spot into a romantic outdoor space. Gone were Rev's two camping chairs and tackle box, and in their place was a bench seat for two, a cooler tucked inconspicuously beneath it.

When I'd asked Rev if I could use his dock tonight, he had two requirements. One: that I send a picture to him and Cynthia. Two:

that I not leave here without keeping to our decade-old tradition. I assured him both requests would be kept.

She searched my face. "Is this the dock where you've met Rev since you were a teenager?"

"The one and only."

"It's just like I imagined it. So peaceful. And the river is gorgeous."

Not nearly as gorgeous as the date on my arm.

I led her to the bench overlooking the water. The last rays of sunlight reflected off her shimmering dress. A sight I wouldn't soon forget.

Slipping my phone from my pocket, I tapped the playlist Gavin's oldest daughter had curated for me. It connected to the speaker I'd wired earlier to the branch nearest us, commanding an entire Italian symphony to serenade us from above.

Val gasped. "Seriously, Miles? Is this for real?"

"I sure hope so."

I sat beside her, and she reached for my hand.

"I'll never forget how special this night has been." She looked from me to the river flowing under the dock below our feet like a perfectly timed duet with the music overhead. "I never could have planned for this."

But the way she said it, the way her voice constricted, I knew she was no longer speaking about the date itself, but about us. I'd been thinking something similar throughout the majority of our dinner at Antonio's Bistro.

"Can't say I'm too bothered by the fact that all my plans were waylaid right before I re-met you."

Her smile was teasing. "Is that a new vocabulary word—*re-met*?"

"That's hardly the only new vocabulary word I've discovered when it comes to you." For Val's sake, I refrained from speaking it freely as of yet. But my hint was there just the same—like a gentle, exploratory push.

"What kinds of waylaid plans?" she asked, pushing back to reroute our conversation.

Because apparently, my *hint* had treaded too close to Val's boundary lines. They may be invisible to the naked eye, but they popped up from time to time just the same. Asking me to wait. Asking me to tread lightly. Asking me to be a student of hers in a way I'd never had the patience to do with anyone else. But for Val, I would.

I took a deep breath, working to redirect my thoughts to her question. "I'm pretty sure we've talked through all that before, haven't we?" In some ways, that day in the office with Pastor Curtis and Leonard felt like another lifetime. And yet, his hand on my life was still evident. Still pressing down on me even from seven miles away.

She shook her head, her brown eyes reflective and curious. "I don't remember you telling me about any plans you made before going to Riverside."

"I mostly just explored some options, but none of those were meant to be. And that was obviously for the best." I shot her a smile, but she was not deterred.

"Explored options for what?"

"For leaving the church. And the . . . area."

Her hand froze mid-reach for a water bottle inside the cooler I'd opened. "I don't understand. Where and why were you wanting to leave the area? Do you mean to go on another trip?"

I knew I wasn't being clear. And a part of me wanted to keep it that way. This wasn't the *next steps* conversation I'd hoped for us tonight. This conversation had the potential to be quite the opposite. "You remember that day on our driving tour when I told you about being reassigned to Riverside? And how I was trying Rev's perspective of *same calling, new location* on for size?"

She nodded. "Yes, of course."

"I'd written to my dad earlier that week, asking him about opportunities overseas within their church-planting organization—specifically, we discussed the timeframe of potential openings within Central America."

Whatever Val thought I'd planned to say, that was not it. "You wanted to move away . . . permanently?"

"I was in a bad place. Correction: I'd been in a bad place for a while. I was confused about a lot of things, and Mexico has always been this . . ." I tapped a finger to the glass Coke bottle I had grabbed from the cooler. "It's hard to explain, Val. It's like, when I'm there—no matter if I'm inside a church or working on a building project or serving families in need—it's the closest I ever feel to understanding who I was created to be. To understanding God, even. And maybe that's partly because I can better measure the impact of my days spent there. The exhaustion I feel when I leave, the absolute depletion of everything 'Miles' and the fulfill-ment of everything not—it can't be matched." I pondered my next realization with care. "It's in my blood, I think. That feeling. My dad talks about his church-planting organization the same way."

Val's sympathetic eyes drew me in. "Wow. I didn't realize how difficult it must have been for you to leave Mexico that last time."

The Romeros came to mind again. A family I'd watched grow over the years the same way I'd watched Gavin and Nicky's fam-ily grow.

"It was far from the easiest thing I've ever done. But . . . not much about the last two years has been easy. With the exception of renting my upstairs apartment to a beautiful woman and a hilari-ous kid." I smiled at her, willing her to accept my topic transition and move on.

But Val had other plans.

"Because of Pastor Curtis, you mean? Is he part of why you were in such a bad place? Why the last two years haven't been easy for you?"

I struggled to talk about this subject with Val every time it came up. She saw Curtis the way most congregants saw him—as a charismatic teacher of the Word and a gifted communicator. And perhaps those things were still true, but they weren't the whole picture. And unfortunately, the whole picture involved a church family I wanted to respect and honor as much as my own family. I didn't want my personal frustrations to taint her positive per-spective, especially since she'd only recently agreed to upgrade

ALL THAT IT TAKES

her online church experience to attending in person with me on Sunday mornings.

"What matters now is that I'm not in a bad place anymore." I reached out for her again, needing to touch her, needing to warm her always-too-cool hands between my own. "You've changed everything for me, Val. You realize that, don't you?"

"But, Miles." She shook her head. "If we hadn't *re-met* after I moved here, do you think you would have stayed at Riverside? Or do you think you would have moved away?"

I sighed and searched the sky. "Please, Val . . . let's not do this."

"Why not? I don't understand why it's so hard for you to talk about this with me."

Hearing the hint of hurt in her voice, I looked at her again. "Because to me, it doesn't make any sense to talk about something that didn't happen and was obviously never meant to happen. I want to talk about our possibilities, not our could-have-beens." I twisted in my seat to see her face fully. "I've already lived close to three decades without you, Val. So please forgive me if I don't want to think about the ways I could have missed out on you altogether if I hadn't chosen to stay at Riverside."

In the way her eyes crinkled at the corners, I knew my words must have hit their intended mark. "You know, you make it pretty impossible to argue with you when you say things like that."

"Good. 'Cause I don't want to argue with you. I want to make you as happy as you've made me."

"You do." Her eyes misted at that. "Happier, even."

"Not possible."

She pursed her lips. "Can I ask you a future-oriented question?"

I nodded. *Future* was a subject I wouldn't shy away from.

"Do you see yourself at Riverside long-term?"

Somehow, that was not the future-oriented conversation I was anticipating. I took a few extra seconds to sip my Coke. "That depends on how you define long-term," I said. "Do you plan to be involved in The Well long-term?"

Val had grown quite attached to a handful of the women there as of late. And not only the ones she'd met through the documentary she was about to start shooting. By the way she spoke to Carlee about Nurse Charlotte and Trisha, it was obvious her connection to them was more than surface-deep.

"I think Riverside is a really special place with a lot of really special people."

"I agree," I said.

"And I think it's come a long way in a relatively short period of time, but I also think there is a lot more potential there, too."

True, but potential itself wasn't quantifiable. It didn't fill classrooms. It didn't write support checks. It didn't keep the outdated updated. Potential alone couldn't keep a partnership between a church and a family center alive like in the old days of Otto and Pastor Archer Sr. Nor could giving someone the vague job of "creating a renewed vision" without any real guidelines or instructions.

I had no doubt that my days at Riverside were numbered, but I certainly wasn't going to be the guy who closed the doors on another Salt and Light ministry. Curtis Archer would have to be that guy for once.

I looked Val in the eyes and spoke with every ounce of conviction I had. "I plan to stay there as long as Riverside has a heartbeat."

Her eyes filled with tears. "So do I."

After that, our conversation flowed as tranquilly as the river, drifting from one subject to another without hesitation or second-guessing. I laughed multiple times as Val described Tucker's toddler years and his knack for hoarding the chocolate gold coins from her parents' store—how he'd hide them in random places around the house or in his toys or shoes. I would have loved to have known that version of him. Something inside me hurt at the thought of missing it, of missing Val in that season of her life, too. But her stories about the past, about her parents, about her hometown of less than two thousand people always seemed to narrow the void.

Despite her aversion to crowds, she was a natural storyteller.

"Your documentary will win," I said.

Startled by my outburst, she laughed. "You do realize I haven't even shot it yet."

"It will win."

"You sound pretty confident about that." She peered at me playfully, and I wondered if she was going to ask me to put a wager down. I would have. Instead, she asked, "Would you consider being my narrator?"

It was my turn to look startled. "Narrator?"

"There's an intro and outro piece and a few transitional sections between the interviews that require narration. I'll write the scripts—I just need your voice."

I dropped my voice to my lowest register, taking on a John Wayne vibe. "Would you like me to speak like this, little lady?"

She pulled a face. "Definitely not."

"What about this? I could talk about the Red Sox and how much I love clam chowder," I said with a Bostonian flare. "Or I can take it down under to where the crocs and 'roos live." I butchered the Australian accent, and she laughed all the more.

"Your regular voice will do just fine, thanks."

"Does that mean you find my regular voice irresistible?" I waggled my eyebrows, and she rolled her eyes.

"Wow . . . you really are extra confident tonight—"

"Dance with me."

She stopped laughing. "What?"

"Dance with me, Val. Right here. On this dock, under these stars. We even have music."

I stood and held out my hand to her, daring her to say yes.

She narrowed her eyes at me for all of half a second before she reached back. Her free hand graze her hip, which caused her dress to swirl and sparkle under the hanging lights. Molly was right. This dress and the woman who wore it were a rare kind of magic indeed.

She took my hand, and I gripped it tight. If she was willing to trust me in this, then I wouldn't let her slip. I pressed in close, lacing my arms around her back until we were swayed in harmony.

It only took a few seconds for the tension in her shoulders to ease, and when it did, I pulled her in even closer, nothing but the sound of the river and a lone violin to set the rhythm of our steps.

"I made a deal with Rev—in order for us to use his dock for our date tonight."

"Yeah? And what did you agree to?"

"That we'd send him a picture."

She pulled back and glanced up at me. "You should have told me to bring my camera."

"Sorry, I was just a bit distracted by the gorgeous woman on my arm. But that wasn't Rev's only requirement. It was a twofold deal."

"Should I be nervous?"

Gently, I pushed a strand of her hair off her cheek. "Rev and I do this thing—whenever I'm out here with him. He's asked me the same question since I was about eighteen." I looked down at her. "He usually makes me take five minutes to answer it, but I'll go easy on you since it's your first time."

"Now I really am nervous. What's the question?"

My eyes dipped to hers. "What's *not* wrong with your life?"

She gave me the same look I likely gave to Rev that first time. "That's it? I just . . . give you a list of things that aren't wrong?"

"There's no right way to answer it. You just name whatever comes to mind."

We did another full rotation on the dock before she began. "My relationship with my son, my love for my parents, and my trust in their intentions—no matter how misguided at times. Sorry, I guess I shouldn't add disclaimers like that?"

I laughed. "You're fine. Keep going."

"My growing understanding of God, my friendship with Molly, my progress with the documentary and the moms I'm getting to know, my mentorship with Gwen, my time getting to know Carlee." She stopped, as if trying to compose herself.

I bent and pressed my lips to her temple as she continued on.

"Dates on the river. Pretty dresses on loan. Everything about tonight. You."

I took her face in my hands and searched her deep brown eyes. "Now ask me," I said.

She blinked up at me, the boundary line from earlier now nonexistent in her open face. "What's not wrong with your life, Miles?"

I answered her first with a kiss, and then with a statement I was prepared to speak a million times over until the day I could phrase it into a different question entirely.

"Dancing on this dock with the woman I love."

Val stopped swaying to the music, her arresting gaze holding me captive. "That woman—the one you're dancing with? She loves you, too." She pressed her palm to my cheek, and spoke again without the slightest hint of reservation. "You're everything right in my life, Miles McKenzie."

· 27 ·

Val

The next month was life lived on fast-forward—shooting interviews, taking B-roll around the city, slicing audio and adding narration, and, naturally, second-guessing my editing skills as I compared each and every cut with the notes I'd taken from Lady Gwen. All of this while also trying to function as a mom, mentor, friend, and girlfriend. So when Dude Camp arrived on the same weekend as my pre-screening submission deadline, granting me an entire seventy-two hours of dedicated focus, the abrupt shift in tempo nearly gave me whiplash. The only sounds in my apartment on this Saturday afternoon were the low hum of the fridge and the last few clicks of my mouse as I submitted the pre-screening compilation of *All That It Takes* to my coach.

And with over two hours to spare, too.

For nearly five minutes straight, I did little else but stare at the sent folder in my inbox. It didn't feel real. I'd pushed so hard to reach the finish line these last few weeks—we all had. The three pairs of women I'd interviewed had agreed to multiple Saturday shoots, arranging sitters for their children and repeating difficult and impactful stories several times over so I could capture the best take and camera angle. Miles had also been a trooper—recording and re-recording narration after putting in full days at Riverside and then helping with Tucker and meals and trips out of the house when I needed focused quiet.

And then there was Gwen. My cheerleader, my counselor, my critique partner, my coach. I'd always questioned the sincerity of the big award-winners on TV who claimed they couldn't have done whatever they'd so obviously been gifted at without the help of someone in the background. And maybe that was because I had always been the someone-in-the-background prior to this project, but I would never again doubt those tearful acceptance speeches, because I knew fullheartedly that I would not have pushed so hard if not for Gwen.

And I desperately wanted to make her proud. For the first time, I believed this documentary had an actual chance. Not only to place in the top three, but maybe . . . maybe even win. I was beginning to understand what Gwen meant when she said connections were the real prize in this competition. The money would certainly be a great help in starting a new business endeavor, but to have the exposure and potential to continue working on future film projects was the biggest dream of them all.

A notification box at the bottom of my laptop screen popped up: *new email.*

It appeared I wasn't the only one locked to my computer screen today.

To: Val Locklier

From: Gwen Chilton

Looking forward to this! I'll get my popcorn ready and send over any final notes by Monday evening. We're off to Tahoe for the weekend.

Now, go take a nap. You deserve one.

xoxo

Lady Gwen

Tired tears collected on my lower lashes as I typed back a brief reply—I was more than a little excited for her to see this final compilation in its entirety. To date, she'd only viewed a few rough cuts and the storyboard we'd worked on together last month. This would be her last real chance to give feedback before the final cut was submitted for the Volkin Award in thirteen days.

Stiff from the long hours of sitting, I rolled back from my computer and zombie-walked to the couch. Depositing myself on the sofa the way I'd seen Carlee do so often, I sighed and stared up at the ceiling. With the exception of a few light pockets of sleep here and there, I'd been going strong since I'd kissed Miles and Tucker good-bye Thursday afternoon.

I'd have to find some level of energy for the celebration date Carlee had planned for me after her shift at Higher Ground Coffee today. She'd insisted on pedicures and cupcakes, and I had no objections to either.

Blurry eyed, I glanced at my watch. Maybe I should take Gwen's advice and rest for just a bit. I could be ready for a fun night out in under an hour.

But just as I closed my eyes, my phone buzzed on my desk. I considered letting it go to voicemail, but on the off chance Miles had found a patch of coverage, I didn't want to miss catching up with Tucker on his first big trip away.

I ambled to my workstation and flipped the phone over. *Grandma Millie.*

"Hello?"

"Val? This is Millie." Immediately, the breathless hush of her voice spiked my heart rate. "I'm sorry to bother you, but . . . I think something might be wrong. Can you come over?"

My mind flashed through all the possible worst-case scenarios for a woman in her seventies. A heart attack? The onset of a stroke? A fall?

"Of course, I'll come right now." I made quick work of locating my shoes, my keys, my wallet. "Can you tell me your symptoms? Where are you, exactly?" I didn't want to waste time searching the house if she was outside in her garden or with the animals in the barn. I pulled open the door and shifted my legs into a cadence they despised.

"It's not me, honey. It's Carlee."

I nearly slipped down stairs eight, nine, and ten at her proclamation. *Carlee?* That couldn't be right. Carlee was at the coffee shop all day today. Until six. She was going to pick me up for my deadline celebration date at six thirty.

But all that came out of my mouth was, "Carlee?"

"She came home from work around noon today—complaining of a headache. She didn't want to bother you on your last day of deadline, so she said she'd take a bath and then lie down for a while. I gave her some of my Epsom salts and didn't hear a peep from her again. But when I went to check on her just now . . . she seemed . . ." Millie's voice hitched before dropping to a whisper again. "She didn't seem to know where she was, and when I tried to get her to sit up she said she couldn't move."

"All right," I said as calmly as I could, though my mind was speeding ahead. "She could be dehydrated. She's been working so hard lately. Her body likely needs fluids—more than what we can give her." Especially given the near hundred-degree heat wave we'd been experiencing this week.

"Do you think the baby could be in danger?" Millie asked.

"I think we need to get her to a hospital. I'm almost there, Millie, but I need you to hang up with me and call 9-1-1." Pain shot through my hip as I got to the road separating our houses. Nearly halfway across, a tightening cramp forced me into a hop-step, the closest cadence to a run I could manage.

"Okay. I'll call right now. See you soon."

I didn't allow myself to stop moving as I pushed through the front door and up the tall wooden staircase. My nerves pinched and spasmed on my left side, but I fought to make it up the last two steps onto the second floor, where Carlee's bedroom was located. The door was open, and I could hear Millie on the phone.

I limped into the familiar space where I'd helped Carlee unpack her clothes into a dresser we'd found at a secondhand store not too long ago. My gaze locked on Carlee immediately. Her face was ashen—too pale for her naturally bronzed skin—her forehead slick. But even worse, she had little reaction to my presence.

Millie stood near the foot of her bed, phone pressed to her ear. Her worried eyes searched mine for answers I could only guess at. I didn't know all that was going on in the body of my young friend, but I knew she needed medical attention, and soon.

"Carlee." I touched her hand draped over the edge of the mattress, growing more and more unnerved by the cool, clammy feel of it. "Can you look at me, sweetie?"

She blinked, turned her head, struggled to focus.

I turned to Millie. "When can they get here?"

"They're twelve minutes out."

Twelve minutes was an eternity. *But if I can just get her out of bed and down those stairs, we won't have to wait on them. The hospital isn't more than fifteen minutes from here.*

"We're going to get you to the hospital, Carlee. But I need you to help us, okay? Can you do that?"

"Val?" My name was a slur on her tongue. "I don't . . . feel well."

Millie pulled the phone from her ear, asking me questions about her OB-GYN, preexisting conditions, and how many weeks pregnant Carlee was today. I answered every one systematically, reached for Carlee's beloved pink bathrobe behind the door, and made a plan.

"Did you have anything to drink at work today? Any water?" I looped her arm around my neck, trying to encourage her to sit up and use the headboard as a backrest as I worked to rotate her legs to the edge of the bed. But as soon as she leaned into me, my shaky knees buckled under the extra weight, and Carlee slumped back onto the mattress.

I collapsed onto the hardwood.

"Val!" Millie cried, the phone still pressed to her ear. "Are you okay?"

Ignoring the pain humming through my body, I pushed up quickly to check on Carlee. Her face looked about the same, only now she was in a far more awkward position on the mattress. She was also without the cover of her blankets, which were trapped underneath her. I gave several hard tugs to free them, but to no avail.

Though the room was stuffy from the August afternoon heat, she began to shiver. "I'm so c-c-cold."

Leaning against the mattress, I balled my hands into two tight fists. My plan to move her downstairs wasn't going to work. Not even with Millie's assistance. Her back was too fragile, and my balance was too unstable. I couldn't risk getting Carlee off the bed only to lose my footing on the stairs. My lack of strength posed a far bigger threat to Carlee and her baby than waiting on the paramedics.

"What should we do, Val?" Millie asked, the fear in her voice no longer suppressed.

Carlee began to cry. "W-w-what's wrong with m-m-me?"

"You're dehydrated, Carlee," I said, my own panic on the cusp of breaking through. "But help is almost here. They're coming, okay?"

I mouthed for Millie to bring her a glass of water. She hurried to the kitchen.

On fatigued legs, I knelt on the ground beside her bed to stroke Carlee's face and hair, whispering calming words to her as I did. It was all I could do . . . and yet it wasn't nearly enough. Helpless tears gathered in my throat as I tried to soothe away her fears while mine continued to build.

When Millie came back with the water and a straw, we encouraged Carlee to take several slow sips so as not to overwhelm her system. And then we prayed over her trembling body, asking God to protect our friend and her precious baby as we waited for help to arrive.

Relief came with the sound of boots clomping up the stairs.

"Which one of you called in?" The female EMT asked as we moved into the hallway to provide space for them to work. I kept my eye on the tightening cuff on Carlee's arm and the oxygen mask placed over her nose and mouth.

Millie answered her, relaying all that had happened.

"But Val's the one who knows Carlee's history the best. She's the one who takes her to all her appointments."

The EMT turned her attention to me. "And how are you connected to the patient, Val?"

My eyes drifted back to where Carlee moaned and shivered on the bed. "She's family."

Of the many terms I couldn't understand being tossed back and forth between the paramedics in her bedroom, I was certain of this one: Carlee had become family to me.

◇◇◇

Grandma Millie opted to stay back at the house, but she'd asked me to give updates on Carlee and the baby when I had them, which I promised to do as soon as I was settled at the hospital.

Sitting now on the far edge of a waiting room with a couple wearing matching *First-Time Grandpa* and *First-Time Grandma* buttons and holding an *It's a Boy!* balloon, I started a Carlee checklist on my phone, entering all the factual, logical snippets of information I'd gleaned from the nurse. Just the need-to-know details, not any emotionally messy questions or fears.

I replayed the information in my mind once more, working to sort out the facts: Carlee had bypassed the ER at her doctor's request and had since been admitted to a room on the Labor and Delivery Unit. While there, she would be given a full exam and blood workup, as well as IV fluids. And then, as soon as Carlee was stable enough, I would receive a call from a restricted hospital number to verify my information before I'd be allowed to see her.

It was a clear-cut update I not only appreciated but had already passed on to a handful of contacts, including Grandma Millie, Nurse Charlotte, Trisha, Molly, and Carlee's Aunt Lizzy, who hadn't yet responded.

A jarring overhead page asking for an anesthesiologist jolted through my bones, forcing my gaze to fall to the next name on my list. *Miles.*

For the briefest moment, my throat constricted at the thought
of him as I imagined his arms around me, his lips pressed to my
temple, his comforting words spoken in my ear. My finger hovered
over the text box as I glanced at the time on my phone. It was a
quarter after five. He likely wouldn't be back in cell coverage until
tomorrow morning on his way home. Perhaps I should wait. But
then again . . . if the situation was reversed, I would want the news
as soon as possible.

I fought to swallow down the ache, finding it much harder to
text him the same kind of factual update as the others when all
I wanted was to tell him I was scared. And that I wished he was
here with me. And that I loved him.

> Val
>
> I'm at the hospital with Carlee. She isn't feeling
> well—dehydrated, I think. Still waiting on news
> from the doctor. Please stay with Tucker until
> I'm home. I'll text more as soon as I can. I love
> you.

I sent it off, but before I could check his name off my list, a call
came in, buzzing against my palm.

Restricted number.

It was then my entire body started to shake.

"Hello?" I answered.

"Val?" a choppy female voice asked through the crackly receiver.

"Yes, this is Val."

". . . Gwen . . . husband's phone . . . pulling over."

The sound of road noise and static cleared over the next few
seconds as I held the line, trying to piece together why Gwen
would be calling me now when I knew she was headed out for a
weekend in Tahoe.

"Hello, Val? Are you still there?"

"Gwen? Is everything okay?" I asked, the irony of my present
circumstance not lost on me.

"I apologize for the poor reception. My phone stopped working
on the pass. But I didn't want this to wait until Monday."

"Didn't want what to wait?"

Whatever was left in my adrenal glands revived themselves from their hibernating state as soon as I heard her sigh. My nerves rocketed up again. "Part of what makes me a coach—your coach—is honesty. And we've both worked too hard together these last few months to limp over the finish line."

I cringed at the analogy. "Okay."

"I watched your pre-screen, Val. I made Frank wait to get on the road so I could watch it before we left." The seconds slowed as my heart rate increased. "It's not complete."

My mind scrambled to decipher her meaning. "Not complete?" Had I forgotten to scan one of the waivers? I supposed that was possible, although at the moment, I couldn't remember much of anything prior to Millie's phone call. "What did I forget?"

"I've been trying to put my finger on that very thing for the last two hours."

"Gwen, I'm sorry, I'm struggling to follow. I'm actually not at home right—"

"The interviews themselves are solid. Good eye contact, deep reflection, beautiful connection. The editing you've done is both professional and flawless, as are your music choices. But the story . . . the story is lacking impact. The bigger, more purposeful story, anyway. It's missing the *why* that leaves the reader with an answer to a question they never even knew they needed to ask."

Out of the corner of my eye I watched the grandparents with the blue balloon stand and hug and laugh in long-awaited jubilation before being buzzed back through the locked doors on my right to celebrate the birth of their new grandson.

My thoughts drifted back to Carlee. Alone in her room. Still unsure of her plan for the child inside her womb.

I blinked hard to return my thoughts back to Gwen. "So what are you saying, exactly?"

"I'm saying it has great potential—that it's on the cusp of something extraordinary. It's just not there yet."

I breathed out a slow breath to stop the tingle in my nose and walked over to the window to stare out over the bleak parking structure below, trying to think back on where I could have gone wrong. On what I could have missed or done differently.

"Story instinct can be difficult to navigate, and it's rare that any creator gets it right on their first try."

Only this wasn't my first try. This was months of tries. This was late nights and early mornings. It was sacrifice and stiff muscles and long weekends missed with Tucker and Miles and Carlee. It was my best effort and then some. "You don't think it's good enough to submit to the competition."

"I didn't choose to be your mentor to make you good enough for the competition. I chose you because—"

"I was a woman." The sentence leapt off my tongue before I could filter it, as if it had been perched on the edge of my deepest insecurity just looking for a moment to pounce. The long pause on the other end of the line caused my stomach to roil. I hadn't known until now just how much I'd wanted to be wrong. Just how much I'd wanted Gwen to choose me for me.

"I told you from the start that I entered this program to make a statement, Val. I feel it's long past time for a female film director to gain some influence in this male-dominated industry, but you're fooling yourself if you think your gender is the only reason I agreed to mentor you." She took a second before speaking again. "I see glimpses of myself in you, dear one. I have from the start. I hear the same insecurities and self-limiting doubts that once plagued me in my youth when I listen to you. . . . Only, I hope that instead of bowing to the whims and fancies of some power-hungry overlord, you will be brave enough to take a different path. A stronger path. Which is why I'm asking you to reconsider what you have now so that you can be objective to what it still needs."

I paced the length of the window, my muscles tensing with every step. "But we went over every interview before I shot it. You read all the notes on the testimonies I had to choose from early on—we selected these six ladies together." I shook my head. "I followed your steps, I met all the requirements—"

"Art doesn't conform to requirements, darling. It's unpredictable and messy and rarely on schedule, just like life. Just like the women who were brave enough to give away a piece of their soul to an unknown audience for the sake of a worthy message." The unspoken challenge in her voice permeated her pause. "Which makes me curious as to why *you* felt this message was so important to share in the first place. What deeper connection do these mothers' stories have to the storyteller behind the camera?"

Heart pounding, I remained silent.

"If you tell me you chose this project solely based on the commonality you share as a single mother, then I'll believe you. But I think it's more than that. And I think you do, too."

I shook my head as the raspy words squeezed from my throat. "I can't."

"Maybe not today you can't. But when you're ready, I'll be right here waiting for you."

"Ms. Locklier?" I turned to see the receptionist from the front desk walking over in her sky-blue scrubs.

"Gwen . . . I have to go." My voice was little more than a whisper.

But as I pulled the phone away from my ear, I heard, "Don't give up."

My hands shook as I ended the call and made eye contact with the woman in front of me. "Yes? I'm Ms. Locklier."

"I'm sorry to interrupt, but it appears there was a glitch with your phone number in our automated system. The doctor has cleared you to go back and see Carlee now. She'll need to stay overnight for observation and another round of IV fluids, but she's doing much better."

I stood, slipping my phone into my back pocket, and with it, all traces of failed documentaries. "And the baby?"

"According to the ultrasound, he's healthy and strong."

He. Carlee was having a boy.

· 28 ·

Val

On my way to Carlee's room, I passed the button-wearing grandpa from the waiting room. His demeanor encompassed an impossible-to-match elation I knew well. I'd seen it on display for most of my adult life. He gripped a full jug of ice like it was his sole mission on Earth to deliver its contents to the awaiting receiver.

"I guess the ice cravings don't end after birth." He chuckled good-naturedly. "But once a daughter, always a daughter. If there wasn't anything I wouldn't do for her before, there certainly isn't now. Grandchildren are enough to make this old man turn into a human sprinkler."

"Congratulations," I said softly as my thoughts skipped back a decade to when my big, gruff father had cried at the first sight of Tucker, my mom patting his back repetitively saying, *"Can you believe how handsome he is, Dale? He's just perfect. A perfect little bundle of preciousness."*

The man lifted the ice bucket. "Have a nice day."

I smiled back and thanked him, watching him rejoin the room next to Carlee's. Laughter erupted into the hallway as the door swung open and closed behind him.

After using the foam hand sanitizer on the wall outside Carlee's room, I tapped softly on the oversized wooden door and pressed the handle with my elbow to enter. It took my eyes a few seconds to adjust to the dim space and then to make out the form of a girl who'd come to mean a great deal to me in a relatively short time. The way her body was curved toward the window stilled my steps, and I wished I could have captured the sight on film. Because the single ray of sunlight that snuck through the heavy curtains was perfectly stretched across Carlee's chest like a hug. Like hope.

I glanced at the machines and the bags of fluids on her right and moved toward the rocking chair on her left. And even though she looked ten times healthier than the last time I'd seen her, it was impossible to mistake her pinked skin and clear eyes for wholeness. Because at this moment, Carlee didn't look whole. She looked lost.

I took her hand, grateful for the returned warmth. "Hey, there."

Her blink sent a stream of tears gliding over her round cheeks. "My baby's a boy. I saw him on the ultrasound today."

I rubbed my thumb over the back of her hand, taking note of the change in her vocabulary. "And how did he look?"

"Like a tiny little human." Her deep brown gaze found mine. "He was sucking his thumb and doing some crazy high kicks."

I smiled. "A little acrobat?"

She nodded. "The doctor said he looks really healthy, but that I need to drink more water and that I'm not supposed to stand for so long at work now. I'll have to ask my supervisor for a stool when I work the drive-up window."

"I'm sure Joanne will be happy to accommodate you. She's been praying for you today. A lot of people have."

Her eyebrows rose. "Like who?"

"Nurse Charlotte asked the moms' group at Riverside to be praying for you."

"But . . ." She blinked away the tears that coated her eyes again. "None of them even know me."

"But they know God, which means they know how much He loves you and your son."

Carlee slipped her hand from mine and turned her face away. "You wouldn't say that if . . . if you knew."

"I would still say it no matter what. It's true." Without another word, I rounded the bed and lowered the frame to crawl on top of the blankets beside her. Immediately, she curled into me, the way Tucker had done since he was a toddler. Careful not to disturb the drip attached to her arm, I wrapped my arms around her shoulders and tucked her head below my chin. And for the next several minutes, I simply offered Carlee a safe place to break.

When she lifted her head, I handed her some tissues and waited until she was ready to speak again. It wasn't long.

"That day I met you . . . outside the clinic . . . I wasn't there to . . ." She breathed out her nose, her voice trembling. "When I read that flyer in the gas station bathroom, I thought I could get an abortion at Riverside Women's Clinic for cheap. I thought that *talk through alternative options* meant financial options. I only had a hundred dollars left for gas and food, and I'd already spent two nights in my car. I just wanted to start my life over. To forget this ever happened to me and move on." Her voice hitched. "I was too embarrassed to tell Aunt Lizzy that I'd ended up just like my mom always said I would: a pregnant teen who barely graduated high school." She clenched the tissues in her hand. "But then when I met you and Nurse Charlotte that day, I told myself I would give it a few more weeks, that I still had plenty of time to decide what I wanted to do while I saved up money for my own place. I'd looked it up . . . and I knew where I could go to get an abortion further along in my pregnancy." She exhaled a long, weighty breath. "I didn't want to go to the moms' group because I didn't want to feel guilty about the choice I was still contemplating when I knew all the rest of them had chosen to keep their babies." Her gaze flicked away from my face. "Like you did."

Momentarily stunned for words, I pulled her in close, though my thoughts were a thousand miles away. Even now, as my heart rate accelerated and my palms grew damp, I knew the fire in my gut couldn't be extinguished. Not until I was willing to pull my own story up from the ashes.

For Carlee.

My jaw ached as I struggled for words. But as I looked at her, at this precious girl who had been sold the same lie I had at her age, my choice to remain silent no longer felt acceptable.

"I'm so sorry you've been keeping this inside for so long." I hurt for her. I hurt for all the months she'd been afraid to share where she was really at. "But I can promise you, there's not a single woman in that moms' group who hasn't struggled with shame and guilt for some reason or another—most of which have to do with making decisions they think will end their pain." I'd just spent weeks documenting six of them. I rubbed my lips together as the rhythmic tick in my throat became a thud. "It's the same reason why I almost had one, too."

Carlee pulled back, her eyebrows bunched. "An abortion?" And then a dawning. "With Tucker?"

"Yes." The sharp twist of nausea stalled my words temporarily, only this time, I reminded myself of my audience. Not a stranger. A friend, one I cared for deeply.

As I told her about that summer in Alaska, about Jesse, about the pregnancy and then about showing up at his apartment un-invited, I didn't skip ahead to the river and the billboard and the flight back home to my parents. This time I filled in the middle, coloring outside the lines of a story that pained me to think about, much less relive.

"So you got in his truck with him? Even after he told you he didn't want you or the baby?" Carlee asked, her voice still raw from tears.

"I did." And I could still remember the drive, and the way I had to crack the window for fresh air. But between the cigarette smoke emitting from the vents and the sharp odor of crude oil on Jesse's boots, I wasn't sure I could keep the contents of my stomach contained. "He took me to a clinic in downtown Austin and told me his part was done, right before he tossed a hundred dollars in my face and told me not to contact him again. He left me there with my suitcase in the middle of the parking lot."

Carlee studied me, wide-eyed, saying nothing.

"I was in shock, numb at what had just happened. But I went inside the clinic anyway and started filling out the paperwork at the front desk. It felt like the best option. The right option, even. I couldn't be a mom. I was barely a legal adult." I breathed out. "The receptionist said I was lucky because they were just about to close up for the day, and they didn't always have time to take walk-ins. Just like you, I felt like I'd already screwed my life up too much to ever be okay again. But after I got into the gown and laid on that exam table, waiting on the doctor to come in and start the procedure, I couldn't stop trembling. It was uncontrollable. No matter what I tried, I just kept shivering, and something about that made me sit up and tell the nurse I wasn't ready, that I wanted to leave. She tried to assure me that every woman got nervous and that if I could just relax I'd feel better in a minute. But I didn't want to wait another minute to feel better. I wanted out. Without her permission, I gathered up my stuff, left the clinic, and just started walking. Straight into the night, pulling my suitcase behind me, with nowhere to go and no one to call."

Carlee's eyes were huge and unblinking, her head slowly shaking back and forth as I told her about how I'd contemplated ending my life in a river and then about a billboard that eventually led to a one-way ticket back home.

"I don't know much about miracles," she said. "But that sure sounds like one. I mean, Tucker almost died twice in one night. But he didn't."

"Yes, it absolutely was a miracle," I said hoarsely, sincerely.

"It's impossible to imagine Tucker never being born." Carlee blew out a breath. "He has such a big personality." She repositioned herself, sitting up to splay a hand over her third-trimester belly, her gaze falling to it as she rubbed her thumb in an arch. "I'd never thought about when a personality starts for a kid, ya know? But today, when I saw this little guy kicking and sucking his thumb . . . I realized he was so much more than a blob of cells. I mean, what if he grows up to be a little boy like Tucker one day? Maybe he'll love card tricks and horses and Star Wars placemats and nerdy jokes." She looked up at me and chuckled, and I joined her. "That's what I was thinking about when you came in—what kind of life would I want to give a kid like that?"

"That's a really big question."

"Yeah, but it's a simple answer. I want this kid to have what I never had growing up: two loving, committed parents. Aunt Lizzy has always been more of a mom to me than my own mother, and I never even knew my dad." She stared down at her rounded belly. "Do you think you could help me find a family for . . . my son?"

Tears leaked from the corners of my eyes as I placed my hand atop hers. "I'd be honored to, Carlee. Maybe we can even start researching a bit together tonight if you're up for it."

"You're going to stay here with me tonight? At the hospital?" With a jolt, she gripped my arm. "Wait, tonight was—we were supposed to go out and celebrate your deadline with pedicures. Did you send it off to Lady Gwen in time? Is it over?"

My lips trembled as I managed to speak a truth that held so much more meaning than she could realize. "Yeah, it is. It's over."

When a nurse knocked on the door and entered the room, asking to check Carlee's vitals, I took the opportunity to slip out into the hallway and provide a new round of updates. But before I sent off another group text, I sent a private one to my parents that simply said *Thank you for everything you've done for Tucker and me through the years. I love you both very much.*

◇◇◇

I'd just dozed off for the twentieth time, my chin pressed into my sternum, when my phone vibrated the side tray table. I scrambled to reach for it. *Miles.* I swiped left to dim the light and silence the too-loud buzz so as not to wake my sleeping roommate. We'd been up late researching adoption agencies and then talking with

Carlee's aunt, who switched her flight schedule to arrive in Spokane this afternoon to spend a couple of days with Carlee.

I shot Miles back a text.

Val

Hey, sorry I can't answer my phone in here. Carlee is sleeping.

Miles

Just got into signal and got your messages. How is she now?

Val

Doing well. Although they might keep her one more night to make sure all her levels stabilize.

Miles

Okay, as soon as I drop the boys off with Millie, I'll head straight there. Text me a list of whatever you need, and I'll bring it.

His thoughtfulness sent tiny pinpricks throughout my chest.

Val

Actually, Molly dropped off everything we needed last night. She brought us dinner and stayed a bit. What I'd really like is for you to stay with Tucker if possible? I don't want him to worry. We're okay.

Miles

I miss you. Three days has never felt so long.

Val

I feel the same. Where are you right now?

Miles

Standing outside a tiny convenience store while the boys stock up on candy and drinks I know I'll regret buying them in about thirty minutes. At least the coming sugar crash will provide some quiet drive time later. Tucker hasn't stopped talking since Thursday.

Val

😂 I bet he's had the best time with you.

He sent a picture of Tuck standing on top of a giant river rock with Kadin, fishing pole in hand and a ginormous grin on his face. And then a second one came in, this one taken selfie-style of Miles and Tucker together, a campfire and several tents pitched in the background. It was this one that punctured my heart. The awed look in my boy's blue eyes as he beamed into the camera next to the man I loved—*the man we both loved*—catapulted my affections for Miles to new heights.

Miles

Oh hey, were you able to send the pre-screen off to LG before everything happened with Carlee?

My throat pinched tight.

Val

Yes, right before, actually.

Miles

Good! Looking forward to hearing all about it. I'm so proud of you.

I studied his words, unable to think of a suitable reply that could be sent via text. There wasn't one.

Miles

How was sleeping at the hospital?

Val

What's sleep again?

Miles

Was it better or worse than sleeping in a low-slung hammock while middle school boys create sounds I hope I never hear again?

Val

Hmm . . . that's a toss-up. No MS boys here, but I've been sitting in a rocking chair since 10 p.m.

Miles

Yikes. Okay. When will you be home?

Val

Not sure. Carlee's aunt is flying in later today, and I'd like to meet her.

Miles

But you also need sleep. If I had to guess, I doubt you got much prior to your turn-in. I know how late you work. We share a floor/ceiling, remember?

Val

I think I remember that, yes 😄

Miles

Need to get back on the road again. I'm happy to pick you up. Just text me when.

Val

I love you.

Miles

I love you, too.

◇◇◇

If ever there was a time to be grateful for an elevator in one's home, it was tonight. As I pulled into my driveway at half past eight, my limbs felt as if they'd been filled with concrete. In hindsight, I probably should have taken Miles's offer of a ride home. Vending machine snacks, tasteless coffee, and several days' worth of disrupted sleep patterns were not a recipe for safe driving—or for much of anything. But all I could think about when Aunt Lizzy arrived in Carlee's room this evening with flowers and smiles for us both was how much I needed to hug the two special men who lived at this address.

I turned off my headlights just as Miles passed by my upstairs living room window, his figure a silhouette against the illuminated backdrop of the dining room lights. And something about seeing him in my home, and thinking about him making dinner in my kitchen and hanging out with my son when I couldn't, began to steadily unlatch all the emotional boxes I'd been stuffing for the last thirty-six hours.

Only now that I was here, now that I was *home*, I didn't want to stuff anymore.

I didn't want to be strong. I wanted to be held.

I wanted Miles.

Wearing the backpack Molly had dropped off for me last night, I trudged across the thirsty grass to Miles's back patio door, stepping into his kitchen and around camping gear and sleeping bags and into an elevator that had been repaired by the same man who had repaired my wounded heart.

The instant the elevator halted to a stop, Miles was pulling the door open from the other side, his reliably attentive gaze embracing me with such affection I nearly second-guessed the bedraggled state I'd shown up in.

In one uninterrupted movement, I stepped out of the elevator, shed my backpack, and fell into his arms. Tears stacked in my throat. "I missed you."

"I missed you, too." His hold on me tightened as he kissed the top of my head.

"Is Tucker still awake?" I whispered into freshly laundered fabric.

"No, sorry. I tried to keep him up for you, but he was practically falling asleep in his mac and cheese, so I made him go to bed about a half hour ago. All the hiking and road sugar finally caught up to him." He pressed another kiss to my temple and murmured, "I'm so glad you're home."

Home. My home. His home. Our home. It all blended together now, just like the three of us.

"You're exhausted," he said quietly, smoothing my hair with his hand and tilting my head back to look at me.

Silent tears slipped down my cheeks.

"Val. Sweetheart." His expression held such tenderness and concern that it was impossible to stop the flow of emotion now that it had begun. "I knew I should have come to the hospital. You're bone-weary."

I shook my head. "It's . . . more . . . than that."

"Come here." He practically carried me to the sofa, placing a pillow on his lap so I could lay my head down. I hardly had the strength to lift my legs and stretch them out onto the seat cushion beside us. He brushed his hand over my arm in a way that left me fighting for consciousness.

"Millie gave me the play-by-play of what happened at her house yesterday. That had to be scary for you, seeing Carlee like that."

A single nod of my head was all I could muster.

"She called you a sharp-thinking hero. Said you stayed calm the entire time and helped keep Carlee calm, too."

And though I knew his words were meant to be reassuring, comforting even, I felt the opposite of a hero now.

His Miles-sized smile diminished at whatever unfiltered expression he saw on my profile. "What? What is it? Did something else happen with Carlee?"

My weary mind trudged through a fog of exhaustion. "No, Carlee is good. She decided last night that she'll place her son for adoption. Her aunt is there now—so kind and supportive—and Nurse Charlotte is going to give us a few agency referrals. We're going to meet with her tomorrow." I yawned.

"Oh wow . . . *wow*." He blew out a long breath. "It's remarkable—to think about all that's happened in her life since she met you, Val."

"She made up her own mind about adoption." About other things as well, but Carlee's story was hers alone to tell, not mine.

He touched my cheek. "But you've shown her unconditional love for weeks. That's obviously made a big impact on her."

But according to Gwen, *impact* was exactly what my film project was lacking.

Like a Band-Aid needing to be changed, I peeled off the protective covering and exposed my wound. "My film project isn't good enough for the competition."

For three heartbeats Miles said nothing as I watched him downshift into an entirely new world of conversation. "What do you mean, 'not good enough'?"

"Exactly what I just said."

I could hear his measured exhales as if he was waiting until he counted to ten to try again. But it wouldn't have mattered. He could have counted to a thousand and the outcome would remain the same.

"So you submitted it on time to Lady Gwen, and something between then and now has made you question its quality? Why? It's great, Val."

"Not according to Gwen, it's not. And you don't get to say it's great when you haven't actually watched it. You've only seen small splices of it to narrate, not the final compilation." Gwen was the first and quite possibly the last. "She says the story is lacking impact." The ache in my chest spread deep into my lungs.

"Okay . . ." He was treading lightly. "So what does she suggest you do to fix it? You still have what, two weeks left?"

"No." I pushed up on my elbow, my arm shaking from fatigue. "I have twelve days."

"Great," he said. "Plenty of time to problem solve and figure it out."

"No, it's not." I shook my head, waking up under the rush of blood pumping from my heart to my brain. "I think I'm going to withdraw."

He laughed and then sobered quickly when his gaze met mine. "Absolutely not," Miles said, staring at me dead on. "You've worked way too hard to give up at the eleventh hour. You're exhausted, Val. You're not thinking clearly enough to make any important decisions. You need to sleep."

But exhausted or not, something told me her critique of my work wouldn't change with one night of good rest, or even a week.

We'd reached the end of the road. I'd given her all I could give, and it simply wasn't enough. Perhaps I'd been too naive to think otherwise, to think that one seemingly inspired idea could carry an entire production until the end.

Miles studied me, softened his voice. "What else did she tell you, Val?"

One seemingly harmless question that was anything but.

"Val?"

"She said she wants a deeper connection to the testimonies."

"A deeper connection to what?"

"To the storyteller behind the camera." I huffed in frustration. "But I've given that to her already—it's woven all throughout. What she's asking for is elusive."

"I suppose that's one way to look at it." But the dawning in Miles's voice proved he'd come to a different conclusion, one I was certain I didn't want to hear on so little sleep.

With one more glance in my direction, Miles was on his feet, sliding me off the sofa and into his arms once again. "I think that's a wrap for tonight. You need sleep. And quite frankly, after hiking the last three days in the mountains, so do I. Let's resume this conversation when I get home from work tomorrow, okay? There are some things I'd like to discuss with you once we're both well rested."

I settled my head onto his chest as he carried me through the living room and into my bedroom. Through a yawn I said, "Carlee agreed to go to The Well next week."

"That's good."

"It is good," I replied, wondering at his stoic response. "We've been inviting her for weeks."

Gently, he set me on my bed before unlacing my shoes and slipping them off, one by one. He tucked my feet under the covers. "I'm trying to help you slow your mind down. You've had a very full weekend."

And only then did I realize I hadn't stopped my pity party once to ask about his weekend. "You have, too—how was it?"

He smiled as I yawned again. "We'll talk tomorrow."

He pulled the blankets up over me, my body sinking into the mattress. I had a fleeting thought to change into actual pjs, but I abandoned the idea in a matter of seconds as sleep beckoned me close. He pressed a gentle kiss to my lips and then braced his hands on either side of my pillow. "I love you, Val Locklier. Never forget that, okay?"

I nodded.

"You promise?"

"Promise," I said.

He started to pull back, and I reached out and gripped his shirt, tugging him toward me again. "You should probably know I get overly teary when I'm tired."

He chuckled and pressed a kiss to my forehead. And then another one to my cheek. And then another one to my mouth. "And you should probably know I'm interested in more than the well-rested, well-fed, well-hydrated version of you." After one final kiss, he set his hand on the light switch. "Good night, beautiful. I'll stop in and check on Tucker before I leave in the morning so you can sleep longer."

And then the lights went out and all thoughts pertaining to the last thirty-six hours were sent to bed . . . until tomorrow.

· 29 ·

Val

I woke to the familiar symphony of Minecraft in my bed.

Cracking my eyelids open against the sunlight spilling through the slats in my blinds, I smiled at the familiar form gaming beside me. I had no idea how long Tucker had been in here, or when he moved both his pillow and his comforter from his bed to mine, but here he was now. Stationed beside me, iPad in hand.

Playfully, I jutted my arm out from under the covers and swatted at the screen. He yelped and nearly rolled off the opposite side of the mattress. My laugh was raspy from sleep, but his was all the spunk I'd missed since I kissed him good-bye in the driveway.

"You're finally awake!" He threw his body down beside me, bouncing me several inches in the air. Nothing like a soft awakening to ease into the day. "You've been sleeping f-o-r-e-v-e-r."

"What time is it?" I croaked out, blindly patting my nightstand in search of my phone.

Tucker consulted the Star Wars watch Miles had bought him before Dude Camp—a particularly cool gift, since it glowed in the dark and had a compass, according to Tucker. "Nine-o-four. Which means I won."

"You won what?"

"Miles guessed you'd sleep in till ten. But I guessed you'd only sleep till nine. I'm closer, so I win the special prize donut in the box. It's a maple bar the size of my arm *and* it has bacon on it. He brought you your favorites, too. They're on a plate with a note."

"Miles was here this morning?"

"Yeah, he came up before he left for work to check on me. He said I could play Minecraft until you woke up. Oh, and he also said that you can drop me off at Riverside later when you have your meetings."

Flashes of last night reeled through my mind. The weepy hug at the door. The even weepier talk on the sofa. Polished off by a final round of The Tears of Delirium somewhere before I crashed into a dreamless sleep. I cringed and immediately wished I could smash a pillow over my face.

"You're making a really weird face right now, Mom."

I rolled to my side and hooked an arm around his middle, tugged. He didn't budge an inch. "Did you have a great time in the mountains? Tell me your favorite part of the trip."

I'd much rather think about Tucker's last three days than my own. No doubt about it.

His hair scratched against his Minecraft pillow as he nodded. "I had the *best* time. On the first night, Kadin got a bloody nose and it went all over our tent so we had to wash it off in the lake the next morning. It was super gross. Oh, and then another kid—his name was Trevor—got this huge bug bite on his leg and it swelled up like this big. I'm not even exaggerating this time, Mom." He stretched his hands to the size of a grapefruit, which in Tucker speak, was double the true size.

"Oh, really?"

"Yep. But don't worry, his dad was there, and he said that even mosquito bites do that to Trevor. I kinda felt bad for him after that. I told him about how big our mosquitos are in Alaska."

I smiled and ruffled his hair. "I'm glad you had such a great time."

He settled in more now, propping his head on his elbow. "Miles said he'd take me on an even cooler hike in Idaho—to this one waterfall up near Canada. For my birthday."

"Oh, that sounds like a great birthday plan. How are you almost eleven?" I tracked the calendar in my mind, skipping over the ear-marked days I'd mentally highlighted for the Essence of Filmmakers Award Ceremony, and tried to ignore the pit in my stomach it opened up. "Wow, your birthday is six weeks from tomorrow," I said, my voice and heart waking up fully now.

But instead of jumping on the birthday bandwagon and detailing exactly how he wanted to celebrate every hour of his big day the way he usually did, he remained quiet.

I tapped the frown line between his eyebrows. "Is this your way of telling me you want to stay ten forever? Because I'm good with that. You're getting too tall as it is."

He sighed. "I just don't want Miles to miss it."

"He wouldn't miss it. You just told me he wants to take you on a waterfall hike."

Again, Tucker said nothing, but it was the kind of nothing that felt like a significant something. "Tucker," I said slowly, "why would you think Miles might miss your birthday?"

"Um . . . you might be mad at me if I tell you."

I gave him a mom look that said *tell me anyway.*

"It's just, I know what you say about private conversations, how they're *private for a reason.* But I wasn't trying to listen this time, Mom. *Promise.*"

"I believe you," I said, paying careful attention to the stress lines that bracketed his eyes when he spoke. "What happened?"

"Yesterday, on our long trip home, Kadin kept hogging the back seat, and my pillow kept slipping off the window so I couldn't get comfortable. When Miles's phone rang, the music went off in the car and he answered. And then it was their talking that kept me awake."

"*Whose* talking?"

"Miles's dad. He said that if Miles takes the job, then he'll have to move in four weeks, and that means he'd miss my birthday."

Ice traveled my veins, slowing my pulse and my mind simultaneously. I fought to keep my voice steady. "Did you actually hear him offer Miles a job?"

"Yeah. His dad was *really* excited about it, too. Said it was a . . ." Tucker thought for a second. "Dream opportunity. And then he talked a lot about different churches and stuff Miles seemed to like."

The growing knot in my chest twisted and tightened, making my next intake of breath difficult as I worked to keep my smile intact for Tuck's sake. And because there was something more I needed to ask, something I dreaded to ask. "Did you happen to hear where the job would be?"

"Mexico."

His answer circled around me, hovering overhead, as if unable to find a sensible landing place. And try as I might, I couldn't find one, either. Miles had taken the option of Mexico off the table when he'd taken the job at Riverside. He'd told me as much, hadn't he? Was it possible Tucker misunderstood?

"Mexico is really far from here, Mom. I looked at the map in my room last night." Tucker rolled on his back and stared up at the ceiling. "I did the finger measure thing you taught me—from here to Mexico City. Do you know how many miles it is from Spokane?"

"No," I replied softly. "I don't." Though whatever the number, it was too far. Too far to maintain the kind of relationship I'd thought we both wanted.

"Over twenty-five hundred miles. Pop and Gram would be closer to us than Miles would be if he leaves."

I nodded as if this information didn't send an electric shock through my entire nervous system, and then worked to clear the thickness from my throat. I stood from my bed. I needed a shower almost as much as I needed privacy to sort out what this conversation could mean for all of us.

Swiping a vintage baby blue Atari T-shirt from my middle drawer, along with a pair of frayed jeans, I addressed Tucker in what I hoped was a rational-sounding voice. "I'm going to meet with Carlee and her aunt and a couple other ladies from Riverside this afternoon. I'd like you to come with me."

His face crumpled a bit. "But why can't I stay with Miles at the center? He said I could go there—"

"Because, honey, I haven't seen you for three days. I'd like you to stay with me."

"All right." He sighed and picked up his iPad before heading out my bedroom door, only to stop halfway through it. He turned back and searched my eyes. "Mom? If two people say they love each other, then why would one of them want to move away?"

I kept my tears on lockdown as his question tore a hole through my chest. His eyes flicked away, but not before he could mask the sadness I saw there, a sadness that sparked something both instinctual and protective low in my gut.

I touched his chin, drawing his gaze upward. "Sometimes love can be complicated. But not the kind I have for you. That kind of love stays forever."

A slow nod was followed by a heartbreaking admission. "I want you both to stay forever, Mom."

I took him in my arms, wishing I knew the words that would ease his worry . . . wishing I knew the words that could ease my own.

◯◯◯

10:32 A.M.

Miles

> I hope Tucker saved your donuts for you? Also, I'm still waiting to hear who won the bet on your wake-up time . . . ?

I finished smoothing the freshly washed sheets over my mattress, trying not to let my mind wander too far down the road of assumptions or ask one of a million questions I didn't yet have the answers to, like how much longer would this apartment be mine to rent? Or how much longer would my landlord be mine to love?

After straightening the last throw pillow, I closed my bedroom door and worked to close a mental one right along with it. I only had so much emotional capacity to give in a single day, and I'd already promised it to Carlee in a support meeting later this afternoon. She deserved more than my preoccupation with the status of my relationship with Miles. Conversations surrounding adoption were delicate enough without adding another layer of complexity and complication to the mix.

With a shaky exhale, I resolved to deal with the unexpected information from Tucker in the fairest way I knew how: in a face-to-face conversation with Miles. Tonight.

11:17 A.M.

> Miles
>
> You two have a nice morning? I'm sure he's told you a ton of stories. Hear about Kadin's bloody nose yet?

I stared at his text as I brushed my teeth with slow, methodical strokes. Yet even after I rinsed, my mind remained void of simple replies. Perhaps because there was little *simple* about what I was feeling.

I slipped my phone back into my pocket.

12:28 P.M.

> Miles
>
> Is your meeting with Carlee and Charlotte still on? I'm available if you need to drop Tuck off with me here. I have a short meeting at 2, otherwise, I'm open.

12:46 P.M.

> Val
>
> Thank you for the offer, but we need some mom and son time today.

Tucker secured his seatbelt, and another stab of pain jabbed into my ribs as I pondered Miles's casual demeanor over leaving Riverside. As if a job offer overseas with his dad's organization would only affect him?

Another question set to simmer along with the others.

2:33 P.M.

Miles

Haven't heard much from you today. Everything okay? Love you.

3:58 P.M.

Val

I'm walking into the adoption meeting for Carlee. Let's talk this evening.

I silenced my phone as I walked through the coffee shop doors with my son and his iPad. For the next hour, my attention was promised to Carlee, her aunt, Nurse Charlotte, and Trisha. Whatever was to come with Miles would have to wait until we were both home.

5:15 P.M.

Missed call from Miles.

I left the meeting at Higher Ground Coffee Shop and picked up a pizza on the way home for Tucker and Kadin. I hadn't had much of an appetite all day.

5:49 P.M.

Missed call from Miles.

Tucker and Kadin ate their pizza with a pool of ranch on the side as they settled in to watch an action movie in my bedroom. Millie had asked if I wouldn't mind keeping the boys at my place this evening so she could offer Kadin's room to Carlee's aunt. I'd agreed, though I was well aware of the challenge another set of preteen ears might create tonight.

It was just after six when I heard the familiar rumble of the elevator in the wall. Miles rarely took the stairs now—Tucker, either—as the elevator had provided a new level of intimacy between us all. A secret passage between our lives and homes. Yet for how much longer, I couldn't say.

Out of the corner of my eye, I watched the elevator door slide open.

"Hey," Miles said, coming up behind me and placing his hand on my back. He kissed my cheek lightly. "You must have had a busy day? We kept missing each other."

An ache throbbed low in my belly at the familiar kindness in his tone. "Yeah, it was pretty busy," I said, wiping the counter and then moving to the recliner.

He eyed me and then the leftover pizza on the table. He didn't comment on either. "Did your meeting go well?"

I nodded. "Yes."

"Is Tucker home?"

"He's in my bedroom watching a movie with Kadin."

"Cool. I'll go pop in on them real quick and say hello." He headed for the hallway. "It was odd not seeing them today after the long weekend."

An unconvincing smile was all I could offer in reply, my thoughts too plagued by the country-sized secret I'd yet to inquire about.

I could feel his eyes on me as he walked back into the living room.

"You seem . . . ?" He tilted his head and perched on the edge of the sofa, studying me as if he was running through a list of acceptable adjectives. "Preoccupied?"

Preoccupied was what I'd been most of the morning, but I'd had more than eight hours to replay months of shared conversations and sort facts from assumptions, which meant my earlier preoccupation now teetered closer to resignation.

Before I could comment, he tugged at the back of his neck and sighed. "I kinda figured you'd be deep in thought today, after everything you told me last night about Gwen and your film . . . and maybe even a few things I said, as well." His eyes met mine, imploring. "But, Val, you know as much as I do that withdrawing from the contest can't be the solution. You'll regret not finishing the project out to the end. You've worked too hard to—"

"This isn't about Gwen or anything that was said between us last night." I held his gaze. "It's about something I heard today."

He searched my face as if I were speaking in riddles. But the truth was, while Tucker wasn't a great secret keeper and at times could exaggerate stories for humor, he'd never been a liar. Just one of the facts I'd been forced to examine at length.

I glanced over Miles's shoulder to the hallway and the open door to my bedroom. I'd planned to keep this conversation short. I'd planned to keep it quiet. But now that Miles was in front of me, now that I could hear my son's laughter in the background . . . I wasn't so sure I could do that anymore.

"I think it's probably best we have this conversation outside." I stood up from the recliner, and he reached for me. Only I wouldn't give him my hand. I'd given him so much of me already.

And by the stunned look on his face, he was finally starting to understand that this wasn't a pep talk that would end with two clinking bottles of Mexican Coke and a new strategy for tackling my broken film project.

This was about my life. More importantly, this was about my son's life.

"Tucker," I called through the apartment, "I'm going to be outside, okay?"

"'Kay, Mom."

I walked out the front door and down the stairs, keeping my gait as steady as possible while crunching over gravel. Miles followed me to the side of the house.

"Val, what's going on? This isn't like you to—"

Several paces away from the stairs, I rotated to face him, my pulse stable, my mind calm. "Tucker overheard a phone conversation in your car yesterday that confused him. And honestly, it's pretty confusing to me, too."

He stilled. "What conversation?"

"The one between you and your father."

If there had been even the slightest shred of doubt, even the tiniest hint of hope that Tucker had somehow misheard the discussion between the McKenzie men, it was buried the instant Miles's gaze collided with mine. Because his expression now held the same shock I'd felt to my core this morning. Only, I doubted it was for the same reasons.

He scrubbed a hand down his face. "Val, I . . . I promise you, I thought he was asleep. I never would have—" He shook his head, tried again. "Believe me, this is not how I hoped to have this conversation with you."

"So how did you hope to have it—and when?" I asked, still managing to keep my voice low as the knife twisted another rotation. "Because as of nine hours ago, I believed you'd taken the option of going overseas off the table."

He took a deep breath, his gaze fixed on me with such intensity I couldn't look away. "My dad almost never calls me—emails have been our main mode of communication for years given the constant time zone changes. So when he called on the road yesterday, I answered. I couldn't have known what he was going to tell me, seeing as the last time we spoke about the possibility of a job in his organization, he'd said the waitlist was unpredictable at best—anywhere from months to years."

I shook my head, unable to ignore the strong undertow of this revelation. "Wait, you were *actively* waiting on a job with him?"

"I told you I'd turned in an application—"

"No," I said firmly, recalling the conversation he spoke of with vivid clarity. After all, I'd replayed it in my mind multiple times today. "You told me it didn't make sense to talk about options that were obviously not meant to happen."

"But that was before there was an opening for a team lead in Latin America—in *Mexico*." He said the word as if it alone held the answer to every unasked question. "The lead pastor who's been overseeing the thirteen church plants there is retiring early due to some health issues, but my dad says the position's mine to decline."

"In four weeks," I clarified, recalling the timeline Tucker had spoken of this morning. "Is that when they want you to go?"

The spark in Miles's eyes couldn't be missed as he stepped closer. "Yes, but Val, this job is . . . it's more than anything I've ever dreamed I'd do, especially at my age. Not only would I be overseeing the local pastors of those thirteen churches, traveling to each of them on a scheduled rotation, but I'd also be working with them directly on how to build up and branch out when they're ready. It's everything I'm passionate about, only on a much larger scale."

I tried to be numb to the joy in his voice as he described a life void of us, but I didn't have it in me to be so callous. I understood what it was like to dream. And I understood what it was like to sacrifice for that dream. But what I still couldn't understand was how willing he was to let everything and everyone else go for it. "It sounds like a great opportunity for you."

He reared back, shook his head. "What? No. Not just for me. For us."

It was my turn to be confused, as there had been zero references to *us* anywhere in his monologue.

He moved in close. "I want to do this together—the three of us, as a family. I know it's quicker than we've talked about, but this organization has a long history with a great track record. I already know several great families in two of the areas with established churches. Tucker would be instant friends with their sons."

"Miles." I said his name in an attempt to reorient myself and to hopefully reorient him, as well. "We've never even talked about the possibility of—"

He took my hands in his, his voice low and earnest. "I want to marry you, Val. Isn't that what you want, too?"

I broke his hold, and hurt pinched his features.

"Marriage is not one person following the other blindly while they call all the shots."

"Blindly? Val, you've known what I do for a living. I'm an outreach pastor. That's never been a secret between us."

"And what about Riverside? Because last time I checked, that's where your outreach was." Frustration flared as the faces of the women in my documentary populated in my mind, their stories of sacrifice and love for one another impossible to disregard. "You told me once that you were passionate about helping people know God—no matter where they lived or what they had or didn't have. And yet, it's like that passion is absent whenever you talk about Riverside."

"It's pretty difficult to feel passionate about a ministry that's been on life support for years," he said. "It's foolish to think some new vision for getting people through the doors will have any lasting impact on the community. It won't. Riverside is a dying ministry, Val. And it's been dying long before Otto ever took his last breath." His expression shifted into something hard, unmoving. "But even if it wasn't, you can't possibly expect me to work under Curtis Archer for the rest of my life. Not after every ministry I've been responsible for under his leadership has been shut down for one reason or another. Riverside won't be any different." He slapped a hand to his chest, his voice cracking as he spoke. "I'm meant to *lead* like my father, not clean up someone else's mess."

I stared back at him, nearly too shocked for words, and yet I'd never felt so emboldened to speak my mind. "So that's the real reason why you've never been truly committed to Riverside. Your issues with Pastor Curtis."

"No." He shook his head. "It's just the opposite. I've been committed to Riverside *despite* my issues with Curtis. There's a big difference." His volume pitched, but I held my ground.

"Miles, you never even unpacked your desk. That supply box in your office? It's still there, still sitting next to the door as if you've just been waiting for something better to come along." The words constricted in my throat. "And I get it. You crave change and adventure and the constant merry-go-round of meet-and-greets with hurting people you can patch up quickly and send on their way. Anything that distracts you from the monotony of the mundane." Hurt ballooned in my lungs as I struggled for air. "And maybe that's exactly what Tucker and I have been to you from the start. A well-timed distraction you could bide your time with until your next big opportunity came along."

He shot his arms in the air and then immediately gripped the back of his head, his mouth opening and closing twice before he paced and spun. "I'm not even sure who that comment is more insulting to—me, the guy accused of loving you like some kind of selfish coping mechanism, or you, the woman who thinks of herself as a distraction." He kept his distance, as if too unsure of the emotion rolling off him to step any closer. "That's the bigger issue here—your insecurity. Your unwillingness to step out because you're too afraid of being seen, even by me." His voice dropped low, his words punctuated and deliberate. "But I'm not Jesse, Val."

The gut punch at his name nearly doubled me over. "I've never once compared you to him."

"Yes, you have. Me and everybody else you're afraid will reject you." He paused momentarily, searching the skies above. "You're so terrified of being discounted by the world, but the truth is, you discount yourself more than anybody ever could." His gaze landed as hard on me as his words. "It's why you'd rather forfeit your entire film project than do the *one thing* you've known you should do since the moment you met Carlee in that parking lot."

"That's not true—"

"It is true. The story you told me that night at the fire pit—*your story*—it's life changing, Val." He pointed in the direction of Millie's house. "You don't even have to look any farther than the house across the street. Do you really think you would have been open to taking Carlee in without having gone through the experience you went through?" His expressive hands drove his words deeper. "Your story has been at the crux of that entire project, and yet you *refuse* to acknowledge it. You refuse to step out from behind that camera because you're so afraid of being rejected." He stopped then, tilted his head as if to spear the last of his accusations directly into my soul. "So instead, you'd rather do what you've always done: hide behind the talent of everybody else—be it Molly or these women or even Gwen."

I ducked under the conviction he pitched at me and swung back harder, my anger charged and ready. "When will you stop pushing me to be someone I'm not? Because I'm not the front-and-center personality you seem to need me to be so badly, and I don't want to be!" I balled my hands at my sides. "Did you really think I'd jump at the chance to move away with you, without a single thought to the commitments I've made here to Tucker, to Carlee, to Molly, to the women at the center? Not to mention my parents, who are already far enough away from Tucker as it is." My blood heated, then pooled in my chest. "Maybe leaving the people you care about is second nature to you given your childhood, but it isn't for me. My goal in leaving Alaska was to build a home here with my son—not to rip him away from yet another community he's grown attached to." I shook my head. "Or the people he's grown attached to. Not that I expect you to understand that."

I pushed past him for the stairs, gripping the railing for added momentum.

"What's that supposed to mean?" He launched himself up the stairs behind me. "You know I'd do anything for that kid, just like I would do for you."

Except stay. The vicious truth caused a fissure to travel through my heart. "Whatever happened to you being willing to go slow and move at my pace? Whatever happened to you following my lead when it came to Tucker?"

"I have followed your lead—"

"No, Miles. This—" I gestured to the space between us. "You asking us to follow you to Mexico isn't even in the same vicinity as slow." I planted my feet and stared him dead in the eyes. "Nor are all the promises you made to my son."

He fell back a step, his stunned expression teetering on hurt. "That's not fair, Val."

"Are you serious right now?" I gripped the wooden railing so tightly a sliver wedged into my palm. "That little boy inside there believes you're the hero he's been praying for—the one who will take him on waterfall hikes and fishing trips and any number of future adventures you've promised him in these last few months." I swallowed against a surge of emotion I refused to release. "So you don't get to talk to me about what's fair, because after you're gone, I'll be the only one here to pick up the pieces." I started the trek up the stairs once again, only this time Miles didn't follow. And I didn't want him to.

"So that's it? End of discussion?" His weary frustration rang out. "You're just going to walk away from me—no resolution or compromise? You're just . . . done?"

I held the door open just long enough to say, "There's no compromise I'm willing to consider that includes my son."

· 30 ·

Miles

I shot through the side door of Salt and Light's empty gymnasium. Usually the court was where I came to think, to focus. But tonight it was where I came to forget. I shoved my earbuds in, blasted the volume on the latest NF album, and tossed my keys and phone to the scuffed hardwoods.

This wouldn't be a light workout.

My first five serves were sloppy, out of sync, and out of bounds. The returns pathetic. But by the sixth hit-bounce exchange, I found my rhythm: slap, bounce, wall, bounce, sprint, slap. Repeat.

And repeat I did.

Sweat streamed from my scalp in rivulets down my neck and back, but not even the sting of salt in my eyes could have dulled the sting of Val's refusal. She hadn't even considered it—not the idea of marriage. Not the position. Not me. There'd been no negotiations. No compromises. Just her gut punch of a *no*.

"Marriage is not one person following the other blindly while they call all the shots."

I needed to keep moving, needed to exhaust my brain enough to weaken the voice spinning like a top inside my head. *Val's voice.* I sprinted right and smashed the ball to the floor, sending it to the top of the wall. And then again. And again. But with each new hit came a different kind of return, one I couldn't hustle away.

"You've never been truly committed to Riverside."

"You never even unpacked your desk."

"Maybe that's exactly what Tucker and I have been to you from the start. A well-timed distraction."

But the last one left me panting for oxygen.

"That little boy inside there believes you're the hero he's been praying for."

For the first time in over an hour, the ball bounced past me. I bent, hands to knees, lungs hot as embers. Everything was on fire—my body, my soul, my entire world. Only I couldn't extinguish the flames. I was burning from the inside out.

The ball sailed past me on my right, bounced once, and then tapped the center of the wall up ahead. I twisted back to find the source as the driving beat thudded in my ears, keeping a rein on my pulse but not on my thoughts. Those went off tempo the instant Curtis stepped into my unfiltered headspace.

I ripped out my left earbud and spun. The immediate absence of a bass line and kick drum narrowed my focus and my remaining energy.

"Hey." Curtis raised an icy water bottle in the air and tossed it to me. "You look like you could use this." I barely caught it in time.

I unscrewed the cap and downed the entire contents in one long pull.

"Thanks," I muttered, my thirst still unquenched.

He revived the dead ball from the floor, bounced it twice, held. Bounced it twice, held. Bounced it twice. "You know, I think you might be the only one who still uses the old gymnasium. And you're for sure the only one I know who takes the game of wall ball as seriously as you do." He twisted toward me. "In fact, I think the first time we met, you looked a lot like you do right now." He chuckled easily. "Only younger and less sweaty."

I remembered that day well. My parents had left that morning for Indonesia—kissing us good-bye without the promise of a return date. Molly had locked herself in her room. And I'd come here. A lanky, unpopular, parentless teenager on his way to becoming a man. One who wanted to please his heavenly Father almost as much as he wanted to please his earthly one.

"I'm almost finished in here. If you're needing this space, I'll get out of your way." Made sense, seeing as he'd commandeered everything else in my life. Why not this, too? Lungs still seizing, I moved to swipe my towel off the floor.

I could feel his gaze track my movements, the same way I once tracked his—the rebellious pastor's kid who was handed a polished legacy he did nothing to earn and everything to tarnish. While my own father had been off mentoring other young men around the world—shepherding them on how to be faithful husbands, fathers, pastors, and leaders—Curtis was treating his own father like trash, neglecting the one thing I wanted most in the entire world: a dad to be proud of me, to know me.

Not much had changed. I scrubbed the towel down my face and neck.

"Actually, I stopped in because I heard the slap of that rubber ball on the hardwoods and knew it had to be your hand on the other side of it." He nodded to the exit doors. "I've started parking on this end of the building to give me more time to clear my head—especially after my weekly meetings with the elders." He held up the ball he'd confiscated. "Seems like you might be trying to do the same thing. Or that maybe you need to talk?"

If that was his way of trying to relate to me, then he'd have to do a whole lot better than that. Because Curtis and I weren't the same. We'd never be the same. "Nah, I'm good."

"Are you? Because you don't seem *good* to me. You haven't for a while."

So *now* he wanted to be my pastor? After he broke everything in my life? Fat chance. "I said I'm good."

"Our history looks different from the others on my staff, Miles. And I'd like to think we can be frank with each other if there's a problem."

The laugh I released was anything short of amused. "Believe me, that's not what you want me to do." Especially not tonight. I swiped my phone and keys from the floor and started for the back door. I couldn't be held responsible for what I'd say if I had to share another ten seconds alone with him, much less unleash the things I'd held back over the last twenty-two months since he'd transitioned to the lead pastor of Salt and Light.

"But what if it is?" His question knocked me square in the back, halting my feet in front of the exit door. "What if I told you that I'm exhausted from all the political game playing and the verbal tiptoeing that goes on in the office—the constant avoidance of saying to my face what I know is being said behind my back on a regular basis?" Something tight and undefined surfaced in his voice. "I'm surrounded by staff all day long, and yet I can't imagine a more isolating existence than the one I'm living now."

I twisted back to face him. "You're asking me to feel sorry for you?" I'd been on the receiving end of those political games. My life had felt like a pawn this year, moved by his hand over and over again. "Yeah, I'm not the guy for that."

"No." He slammed his eyes closed, his exhale sharp. "I'm asking you to look past my title and speak openly with me the way no one else will."

For what had to be close to a minute, I let his statement hang on the noose of his own making. How many times had I restrained myself from doing the very thing Curtis was asking of me now? It wasn't difficult to drum up every pain point of this last year. He was to blame for them all. Even losing Val.

If he hadn't closed the doors on every ministry I'd poured my soul into, if he hadn't banished me to Riverside when he knew nobody else on his staff would go, I wouldn't have sought out other options. I wouldn't have emailed my father. I wouldn't have known about the once-in-a-lifetime opportunity in Mexico. And most important, I would still have Val and Tucker.

"Fine. If you want honesty, I'll give it to you." What did I even have left to lose? I set my keys and phone back on the gym floor and stared him down. "You've used your father's platform, your father's good name and thirty-year reputation, to build your own kingdom for the sake of your own glory. And now you're reaping the consequences of it—as is everyone underneath your leadership. Your staff, your volunteers, your entire congregation. Your recklessness hurt us all."

To my shock, Curtis didn't rear back. Nor did he seem the least bit surprised by my accusation. Instead, he nodded. "You're right. I did that, all of it. I was arrogant when I first stepped into that pulpit. Immature. It was easy to see all that we lacked when I compared our size to the megachurches that had invested in the very same updates my father refused for decades. I didn't listen to the cautions he gave me about making too many changes too quickly. I made a litany of foolish decisions in those first sixteen months, all of which were under the guise of seeking wise counsel, when really the votes I sought were the votes I knew I could swing."

Unbelieving of whatever self-revelation he may or may not have had, I pushed harder. "You burned through hundreds of thousands of dollars on prideful exploits and flashy technology, all while leaving your staff and their various ministries to suffer. You prioritized numbers and appearances and butts in chairs over shepherding your people. But then when those same lukewarm seat-warmers moved on to the newest flash in the pan and it all went south, you swept your sin and our hurting financials under the most convenient rug, one called 'a difficult economy.'"

He nodded slowly. "Again, yes. That's . . . that's true. It's why Leonard joined the ranks this last year as an executive coach. And it's why there's been weekly accountability meetings between me and the elders every Monday night for the last eight months as we work through a study on biblical stewardship. I made a huge mess, and we've been operating under damage control ever since."

No, it didn't get to be that easy. This new persona of his might work for the elders, but like he'd said, our history was long. Too long for me to trust whatever act he was playing at now. "Why are you telling me all this? We're not friends. We've never been friends." I pitched at him again with a fresh windup of anger. "Don't think I haven't caught on to why you sent me to Riverside. You wanted me to fail. You wanted me to do your dirty work and close it down so that I could be the face people hated around town and not you."

"I've never wanted you to fail." His brow dipped into a deep V. "And I'd rather cut my own salary down to nothing than close those doors."

My grunt of disbelief was enough to make his eyes darken, and for the first time I thought he was finally ready to come at me, to let loose whatever truth he'd been holding back.

"That center means more to me than you can fathom. Caitlyn wouldn't be here if not for the services Riverside provided when Brenna was pregnant with her."

I fell back a step, stunned at his pronouncement. *Caitlyn?* The image of his oldest daughter materialized in my mind.

His jaw flexed and relaxed, flexed and relaxed. "There's not a day that goes by that I don't thank God for Nurse Charlotte and the clinic there." He looked away, blinked. "When I got Brenna pregnant the summer after we graduated high school, we were both so scared. My parents had already bailed me out of so many stupid mistakes by that point, and I was convinced I couldn't go to them again. I couldn't ask for more help. I didn't deserve another ounce of their grace. So I told Brenna I'd help her get an abortion."

The admission ripped through my chest. Brenna had once been a good friend of mine, a sweet girl I'd come to know through a summer program we both served in. Her parents had retired from long-term missions soon after mine had departed. I'd hardly known she and Curtis were dating when rumors of a fall wedding had circulated that summer. I'd always believed it was yet another example of Curtis Archer being handed a gift he didn't deserve. Only the tears reflecting in his eyes now told me he knew far more about the gifts he didn't deserve than I ever could.

"Three days before our scheduled appointment, she begged to go to Riverside first, to meet the nurse she'd heard about from a friend. We argued about it for hours, because I didn't want Otto to find out. He was my dad's best friend. But thankfully, Brenna convinced me." He peered off in the distance. "Our appointment to terminate her pregnancy was at two on a Tuesday afternoon, but Nurse Charlotte got us in at noon that same day to show us an ultrasound of the baby." He cleared his throat, but not before tears escaped the corners of his eyes. "I will never forget that. Two hours and one willing soul are the reasons Caitlyn has a heartbeat today."

Something sharp and unmistakable twisted in my gut. The immediate result of Curtis's testimony brought Carlee and her soon-to-be-adopted son front and center to my mind. Yet hers was hardly the only life-impacting story to be found at Riverside. "I had no idea. About any of that."

Curtis tugged at the back of his neck. "Brenna and I have been careful who we've shared that part of our story with thus far. The elders know, and the college girls she mentors. And a handful of my trusted staff members." He offered me a slight smile, but I was too preoccupied with the familiar clench in my spirit to return it. Too stunned by how the lie of my ego kept me from asking more questions about the future of Riverside earlier on.

"I couldn't tell you the center was at risk of closing when I sent you," he said plainly. "After I repented to the elders last fall, I committed to a twelve-month accountability plan with them. And with Leonard, as well. Part of that commitment is to stick within the parameters we discuss as a vision team. I've agreed not to operate outside of their counsel." He looked at the floor, at the ball he'd set down at his feet. "But Riverside has been a point of tension between us for a while. Frankly, I shouldn't even be discussing this with you now."

The air felt thick with unknowns, more so now than when I'd first busted through those doors. "How long does it have? And what are the metrics the elders are requiring for it to stay open?"

"December. Before the start of the next fiscal year." His voice was strained. "They aren't stuck on numbers as much as fruit, effectiveness. It's why I made sure to come to the workday. I was hoping to glean some insight from the volunteers. Otto tracked all that—he used to keep these ledgers filled with every person he served at Riverside and the community at large. But that was years ago. There's been nothing recent." He studied me. "I didn't have a say over the interns on rotation following Otto's death; they were assigned before my father retired. But after all the financials settled last year, and after the vision team decided to restructure several ministries at S&L, I petitioned the elders to place a permanent pastor on staff there, someone I could trust based on years of steady character and leadership. Someone who'd remained stead-fast during all the years I was a punk kid with something to prove."

The humility in his voice was impossible to misinterpret now. I suddenly couldn't twist or mold it into something of my own making the way I'd done a hundred times this past year. It was clear, sobering. Convicting.

"I sent you there because Riverside deserves a proven, perma-nent leader. Someone with the same rare servant's heart and love for people I always saw as a boy in Otto, and even more so as a man." He clamped his mouth closed, swallowed. "I know Riverside may not be the ministry life you envisioned, Miles. But out of my entire staff, it was your face that consistently came to mind when I sought the Lord for wisdom on who to send. I know it's not glamorous. And I know it doesn't come with many accolades or thrills. But my hope—no, my *prayer*—has been that God would give you an even greater vision and passion for the ministry Otto began over thirty years ago."

Only, I wasn't the righteous man Curtis had believed I was. Because while he'd been on trial, I'd been the first to stand among the scoffers and throw stones. I'd been the first to point out the vileness of his sin all while ignoring the stink of my own. My re-sentment. My jealousy. My pride. And sometime in the midst of waiting for the guillotine to fall, I'd missed both the repentance and restoration of the man standing right in front of me.

The revelation was enough to make me retch.

"Riverside Family Resource Center was never meant to be an island. It was meant to be a bridge, to work in tandem with Salt and Light, just like it did back in the day between my father and Otto. I wanted to believe that, maybe someday, it could be that way again." He slid his gaze back to mine. "But if that's not what God's been speaking to you . . . if it's not what God is calling you to, then maybe my hope is misguided. It wouldn't be the first time I've missed the bigger picture."

Only, it would seem I was the one who had been missing the bigger picture.

"I don't know." The words were a wrung-out kind of truth, the aftermath of a fight battled and lost. But they were true just the same. "I don't know what God is speaking to me."

Yet I did know that instead of being poised to listen, I'd been poised to bolt at my first opportunity. Val hadn't been wrong about that. Nor had Rev.

Curtis put a hand on my shoulder. "Then I'll be praying you hear Him clearly."

⬡⬡⬡

In all the years I'd gone to Rev's dock for one reason or another, I'd never been here alone. I'd never once walked the path under the light of a waxing moon with no other companion than a windbreaker from my trunk and the dried sweat on my back . . . and time.

Suddenly, that was about all I had left: time.

Standing on the dock, facing the hills just beyond the rocky riverbank, everything looked different in shadow. The eerie tree line, the hazy evening sky, the current I could feel swirling underfoot but couldn't see.

My own black soul.

I'd confessed my deepest fears and struggles in this spot hundreds of times, told Rev stories of failures and wins, unpacked the abandonment issues I struggled to hide for years after my parents left for overseas . . . and yet to surrender, to wait, to listen with expectation to the only voice that could illuminate the darkness, was infinitely more difficult.

Trusting that voice, even more so.

I knelt on the damp wooden planks of the old dock, unsure of how to begin. Unsure of how to mute the noise in my head and the doubts in my heart. But maybe that was the thing about finding stillness in God—it required nothing and everything, all at the same time.

· 31 ·

Miles

It was late by the time I returned home. I flicked off my headlights as I crept past the basketball hoop and pulled into my driveway. My lack of foresight had caused enough disruption for one night. The least I could do was keep from waking anyone inside. I peered up at the darkened windows of Val's apartment, but the sudden flash of light to my right captured my full attention.

As did the figure now illuminated on the stairs.

At the sight of her walking down the steps, my chest seized. A strange sensation between hope and dread pumped through me as I exited the car and moved toward her on tired legs. Though I'd last kissed her cheek only a few hours earlier, the events that had taken place since had opened a chasm of unknowns.

I floundered through my mental fatigue, searching for something of worth to say, something that would ease the distance reflected in her eyes. But instead, all I could do was focus on the woman who'd stopped two steps up from the bottom, our eye line equal. Her face had been freshly washed, her hair gathered into a ponytail, her lounge pants tied at her waist as if she'd readied herself for bed hours ago. Yet nothing about her looked rested.

"I was worried," she said softly, "when you didn't come home."

"I went to the gym."

She nodded, the pale curves of her face luminous under the glow of the moon.

"And then I went to the dock. To pray."

In the beats of silence that followed, I fought the urge to reach out my hand. To caress her cheek. To pull her close.

Neither of us moved.

"You should—"

"I don't—"

"Go ahead," I said. "I've said too much tonight as it is."

She glanced down, drawing my eyes to her bare feet, to the way her pants pooled around her ankles. "So have I."

The ever-increasing ache to cradle her, to tell her I wanted nothing more than to undo the past twenty-four hours and toss out any obstacle that came between us, threatened to choke me out. But something about the way the moonlight shimmered in her brown eyes calmed the chaos inside me, as did the resolute expression behind it.

"I don't want you to stay, Miles. Not for me. Or even for Tucker." She shuddered out a breath. "You've made that decision before—you've stayed behind for someone you loved. And you've felt trapped by that decision for more than a decade." She paused, rubbed her lips together, and then, as if reading my mind, she said, "I can't be the only reason you say no to this opportunity. I love you too much to be the anchor weighing you down or holding you back."

"*Val.*" My voice broke on her name. "You've never held me back—not for a single minute." I swallowed. "I love you. I *need* you."

She grasped for the railing at her side, and I understood the need for extra support in an entirely new way. "I know. But loving each other isn't enough to solve this. The answer you need—the answers we both need—they're bigger than what we feel for each other."

I closed my eyes, knowing she was right, knowing this wasn't a simple disagreement that could end in a simple compromise. I'd been wrong to ask Val to walk away from her commitments, to jump into a new life—into a new world—we hadn't even discussed as a real possibility. She'd been right to be angry. She'd been right about a lot of things.

"I wish I could tell you I figured it all out tonight—that God gave me a divine revelation down at the dock when I prayed . . . but I can't." Again, my voice gave way, my throat raw and strained from emotion. "I don't understand the timing of all this yet. I don't understand why God would bring you and Tucker into my life only a few months before this opportunity . . ." I let the sentence trail off into oblivion. The timing of my dad's call wasn't to blame. He'd done exactly what I'd asked of him, given me an out when I wanted it most.

But was that what I still wanted? And more importantly, was that what God wanted for me?

Val stepped down onto the last step and tilted her chin to meet my gaze. "Which is why I think we need to take some time apart. We both need space to figure out what comes next . . . however that looks for each of us. I know it will be difficult, given our living arrangement, but I think it's what we need, Miles. I know it's what I need."

Every cell inside me revolted at her words. Space from Val—*from Tucker*—was the last thing I wanted. Yet as much as it physically pained me to imagine our lives as separate entities on separate paths, another part of me couldn't imagine closing the door on a ministry that seemed tailored to every prayer I'd prayed since I was a boy. But none of that changed the here and now. None of that changed the fact that Val was asking for space to sort out her own plans. Her own callings, apart from mine. She deserved that much and more, no matter how much it would hurt.

"Of course," I said around the painful knot in my chest. "I'll give you whatever space you need."

Tentatively, she reached for my forearm, the cool touch of her fingers warming against my skin as she trailed her hand past my elbow, bicep, and shoulder, and settled it into the pocket beneath my collarbone, directly above my heart.

"I'm sorry." I clasped my hand over hers, my air supply pinched. "I never wanted to hurt you."

"We were both angry." Her eyes glistened with unshed tears. "There are many things I regret about tonight, but in the same way I trust your intention for me, I hope you can trust mine for you."

"And Tucker?" My jaw throbbed. "Do you trust that I . . ." I took an extra second to compose myself, to try to steady my labored breathing. "Do you trust that the very thought of Tucker being harmed by any of this makes me physically ill?" The words rang in my head like an echo. I'd heard something similar earlier this evening in the gym—from Pastor Curtis, as he spoke of his daughter's life. A father's heart for his child. A father's desire to protect and to love.

Tears slipped down Val's cheeks as she gave an affirming nod in reply, and this time I didn't resist the urge to pull her close. With a fierceness I hadn't even known I possessed, I wrapped my arms around her while a dozen pressing questions circled my heart and cried out for answers.

· 32 ·

Val

I scooted the chair farther under the patio umbrella and then slid my sunglasses down over my eyes to block the intense glare from the sky. Silently, I beckoned the clouds to return overhead. Cloudy skies were a rare kind of comfort these days, fitting my mood far more than the incessantly happy sunshine—which, ironically, was all Carlee craved since her stay in the hospital. Since she was still under her doctor's orders to limit physical activity and drink extra fluids, she chose Millie's back patio table to scroll through her recent adoption dossiers on my laptop. All while sipping on a monstrous blue raspberry slushie.

The boys had finished their summer treats long ago and were now off filling water balloons on the far side of the farmhouse. An area I avoided as much as possible, as I could just make out the frame of the basketball hoop across the street. The same basketball hoop Miles had set up soon after we'd moved into his spare apartment. And the one I could still imagine him playing at with Tucker, though that hadn't happened since our conversation in nearly the same location seven days ago.

But if I'd learned anything in the last week, it was that it wasn't hard to imagine Miles anywhere, especially when *anywhere* often consisted of the home we shared approximately twelve hours a day.

Even when I couldn't see Miles, I could still sense him. I could still feel him.

When I cooked in the kitchen, I wondered what he was making for dinner one floor below me. When I ran a load of laundry, I wondered when he'd need use of the hot water. When I worked my freelance jobs till late, I wondered if he could hear the depressed beat of my heart the way he could once hear my joy.

Which was all the more reason to get out of the house this afternoon, even if just to the other side of the street.

Carlee set her foam cup aside and scrolled through the Wardell family's digital dossier, showing me each picture and bio in their file for a second time. She hearted their journal-like entries, and I studied her profile as she read, silently thanking God for her presence in my life.

"I really like this couple. There's just something about them. Something . . . real, I guess. The paragraphs they wrote about each other are really cute. Funny but also sweet. Especially what he wrote about her. Listen to this." She read his words out loud to me, naming his wife's affinity for overthinking as a trait that used to make him nutty but was now something he appreciated—her ability to look at a situation from several angles.

She stopped reading and slowly slid her gaze back to my face. "I bet Miles would say something like that about you, too."

My stomach clenched at the mention of his name, and at the way his face materialized without notice, as if it had been right there all along, waiting to visit my conscious mind the way he often visited my sleep.

I offered her a weak smile in reply. Carlee was doing her best not to pry into the details involving the obvious break in routine between Miles and me, yet just as obvious was her desire to show she cared. About both of us. But seeing as I hadn't felt right about sharing the recent downgrade in my romantic status with Molly— given the confidentiality of her brother's job offer coming from her parents' organization—it didn't seem right to share the specifics with Carlee, either. Those had been difficult enough to try to explain to Tucker, a conversation that had involved both tears and more questions than I knew how to answer.

I pushed the chair away from the patio table, drawing her attention away from the laptop screen. "I should probably go check on the boys."

"All right," she said, lifting her giant slushie cup. "I'd offer to come along . . . but you know, doctor's orders."

Surprised by the light chuckle that escaped me at her blue-tinted smile, I said, "I'm good."

I took several steps toward the front of the house when Carlee called my name. I twisted back, and she shielded her eyes from the sun.

"If I wanted to request a meeting with the Wardells, you'd come with me, right?"

"I'd be honored to, Carlee." An answer that warmed even the coldest regions of my heart and seemed to bolster my strength as I strolled around the farmhouse and stared across the street at an empty house and an empty driveway.

Where is he today? I wondered. And more importantly, where was his heart? Had he accepted the position in Mexico or . . .

Only I couldn't allow myself to consider the *or* in that question. Not when the odds were stacked in favor of him boarding a plane within the month after saying a much more permanent good-bye.

For the hundredth time this week, I debated asking him for an update, asking for the facts my mind and heart craved. Yet by the time I'd made a full loop around Millie's property and spotted the boys playing in the back field, I'd come to the same conclusion as always: It wasn't time yet.

When Carlee came into view, her odd expression slowed my last remaining steps.

"You okay?" I asked

She nodded. "Yeah, I'm fine. I've just been waiting for you to come back." She spun the laptop screen in my direction, and I fully expected her to show me a response from her adoption agency or perhaps even from the Wardell family themselves. I did not, however, expect her to show me the paused title screen of my failed film project. "Can I please watch this?"

I opened my mouth to deny her, to tell her there wasn't much point in watching it now, but the same hope that lit her gaze seemed to still my tongue. And before I could reconsider, I agreed.

The video started without interference or stall. A slow, tranquil pan of the river, showcasing the Madison Bridge and a wide-angle shot of the same cityscape Miles had once mapped out for me on a pizza box lid. The memory caused a flash flood of pain to rise in my core. But that was nothing compared to the way his voice sliced through me the instant his narration began.

Carlee glanced to me. "I didn't know Miles was on here."

Not trusting myself to speak, I simply nodded and continued to watch the polished interviews of the six women I'd seen a hundred times during the production and editing phase and while listening to a script I'd both written and spliced throughout the entire film. Only this time was different. Because this time, I was watching it through the eyes of a young woman whose own experience wasn't too far from the stories I'd filmed.

As the credits rolled at the end, Carlee tapped the spacebar and turned to look at me. I didn't miss the confusion resting heavy on her brow. "Where was your story? The one you told me in the hospital? I kept waiting for it, but you never came on."

"I don't have the same kind of testimony." Something I'd considered at length these past few days. "The women I interviewed all fit into the pattern I was trying to show."

"What pattern?" Carlee asked.

Well, if that wasn't clear to her by now, then perhaps Gwen's critique about the project lacking impact was far more conservative than I realized. "Essentially, in its simplest form, it's a reciprocation effect: One woman in need of support eventually becomes the one who gives support to the next woman in need. And so on."

As if my explanation solved nothing, her brow remained scrunched. "But you do fit the pattern."

"Not in the same way," I said. "I mean, yes, I believe God spoke to me that night using the billboard across the river, and that my parents were gracious to take me back into their home after all I'd done, but—"

"Val, don't you see?" She shook her head, eyes sparkling with tears. "You fit the pattern because you're *my one*. You started the pattern with me."

And right then, right there, as the world went mute around me and as Carlee wiped fresh tears from her cheeks, I saw it clearly for the first time: the deeper connection. Not only to the storyteller behind this camera, but to the Storyteller behind it all.

∞∞∞

It didn't take long to set up a makeshift studio in my apartment. I knew the light placement and the camera placement and every angle, filter, and lens I'd need to match the technical style of the other interviews.

It was everything else that had my insides whirring.

I gripped the pen with shaky hands and began to scrawl out a new script—crossing out entire paragraphs, only to rewrite them again and again.

This narration, both what I'd speak on camera and what I'd weave throughout my last edit, wouldn't hover above the art on screen, detached in some bird's-eye view voice-over like the one I'd asked Miles to read weeks ago. No, these words had been ripped from my memory and carved from my experience.

After I read it over several times, I refocused the lens on the target in the corner. Remote in hand, I crossed the room to the well-lit stool. In all the time I'd spent dabbling in film production, I'd never once been the subject on display.

Until now.

After a deep breath, and a quick prayer, I pressed the record button in my hand and lifted my face to the camera.

371

· 33 ·

Miles

Val had been working later than usual these past few nights. I could hear the telling scrape of her chair every time she got up to stretch her hip or walk through the living room to the opposite side of her apartment. I could only hope that whatever she'd been working on so studiously after Tucker went to bed was connected to her documentary, though I had no way of knowing for sure. All I did know was that these past eleven days had been a rare kind of torment indeed.

But when today's calendar reminder popped up first thing this morning, reminding me of Val's contest deadline set for midnight tonight, I skipped my morning coffee run and instead sat parked at Riverside Family Resource Center, composing a text that had circled my brain for more than a week.

I skimmed the words through one last time, in hopes they would be received as intended: as a confession, with no strings attached.

Miles
Val,

I've debated texting you for days now, but seeing the date on the calendar this morning tipped me over the edge. No matter what you decided about the contest, I'm rooting for you. I will always root for you.

I've replayed the events of that night in my driveway with you at least a hundred times. And I imagine I'll replay them a few hundred more before the week's end. But each time I rewind my memory to our last conversation, I regret not speaking up when I had the chance. So . . . here it is now. I'd apologize for the length of this text, but I suppose you've already figured out that Molly is not the only long-winded McKenzie in our family.

For a lot of years, I wanted to believe that my parents leaving us for the mission field at seventeen didn't have a negative impact on me or my sister. I wanted to believe that their choosing ministry over us was the better sacrifice, the worthier sacrifice. And if I'm honest, no matter how many times Rev challenged my thinking in this, there have been more days than not that I've dismissed his wisdom for my own. But justifying hurt doesn't stop the hurt . . . it only finds excuses not to feel it.

You were right to question my resentment toward Curtis. You were right to question my lack of passion for Riverside. You were right to question my motives for considering the position in Mexico. And ultimately, you were right to push me to see the truth and to take a step back.

This long text message aside, I'll continue to give you space until you're ready to talk, but I needed you to know that I've chosen to break the cycle.

Because of you.

Miles

After a long exhale, I willed myself to exit my car, silently praying for strength to face yet another day without Val and Tucker, and to be present here, at Riverside. The place I'd chosen over the position in Mexico. A decision I was certain I wouldn't have made three months ago.

But three months ago, I hadn't known a life with Val and Tucker. Three months ago, I hadn't understood what I'd only just begun to understand over these last eleven days: that so much of what I'd prayed for, so much of what I'd asked God to do with my life in service to His people, He'd already answered. And despite the many unknown variables I'd face in the future, I trusted He was still answering.

"Good morning, Pastor Miles. You're here early again, I see." Trisha's cheerful greeting was riddled with curiosity, but she was too kind to ask. Still, there were some things that were too hard to hide in an office of two and a half employees. "Are you headed back over to Salt and Light today?"

"Not today, no." It was possible I'd had more meetings with Curtis over the last week and a half than over the last two years combined, but there had been much to discuss after I'd sought his forgiveness. Although there were still many things to sort out logistically, there was little we didn't see eye-to-eye on when we actually took the time to understand each other, starting with how to go about trying to keep this faith-based community center alive past the new year. "I'm actually going to work in my office for a bit."

"Oh, alright." The surprise in her voice was fair, seeing as I usually avoided Otto's office, but today I was on a mission to change that. "Need anything from me?"

"Not unless you know anyone looking for a desk that weighs as much as a school bus?"

She laughed. "No, but if you need Ray to help you move it, he's off at four. I'm sure he'd be happy to lend a hand. Maybe we can list it on some kind of resale site?"

"That's an idea." Although, unless someone was looking for a desk that could double as a Thanksgiving banquet table, I doubted it would have many takers. "I won't turn down the help if Ray's willing. The desk I purchased from Discount Furniture is in my trunk. It's half the size and a quarter of the weight."

"You bought new office furniture?" Her voice took on an ethereal quality. "That's wonderful! It's about time that space gets a youthful facelift."

I smiled at her enthusiasm, though I was far less concerned

about an office facelift than I was about Riverside's continuing presence in our community. It was one of the prayers I was still hoping to gain clarity on soon. But there was still time, still work to be done on every front. Especially when it came to the effectiveness guideline. Curtis and I were equally uncertain of exactly what the elders of Salt and Light would qualify as *enough fruit*.

I began to turn down the hallway toward the office when Trisha called after me.

"Miles? I hope I'm not overstepping here, but when I met Val for coffee earlier this week, she looked about like you do now."

My smile slipped away at the mention of Val's name. "And how's that?"

"Like no amount of caffeine in all the world could perk her up."

The only thing worse than my own pain was knowing that Val was in pain, too. But then the face of a little boy who was nearly eleven flashed in my mind, and I had to recant that sentiment. Tucker had waved at me a handful of times from Kadin's driveway, and once he'd even passed me the basketball to make a shot from the free-throw line he'd chalked out. I'd missed the shot. But I hadn't missed the troubled way he'd studied me afterward, as if he could see the gaping hole in the center of my chest but couldn't tell me how to patch it up.

I'm praying, kid. I'm praying.

"But she's on a good track," Trisha continued. "Letting go of the past is one of the hardest lessons we walk though in life."

A cautious hope flickered inside me. "Has she . . . has she talked to you?"

Trisha smashed her lips together, as if suddenly in regret of saying anything at all.

I held up my palms. "I'm not asking you to share details with me, I'm just . . . I'm relieved to hear she's talking with somebody." Seeing as I hadn't been greeted by the Wrath of Molly yet, I'd deduced early on that Val hadn't shared our distance agreement with my sister. And it was easy to determine why. Our story had become too intertwined. For Val to share any portion of it with

Molly, she'd have to share all of it. And I couldn't imagine a less Val-like thing to do in all the world than break a confidence without seeking permission first.

"She's shared a bit of her story with me, yes. And I've committed to praying with her and for her."

"Thank you," I said. "For being someone she can trust."

Trisha's gaze softened. "She's a special gal."

I couldn't agree with her more.

After making my way to Otto's office—*my office*—I picked up the notorious box of office supplies and moved it away from the door to make space for the behemoth desk to make its exit later today. But first, I'd need to empty Old Goliath out. From what I could tell in the limited number of times I'd been in here, there wasn't much left of Otto in this space. Still, it was uncomfortable, sitting behind a desk owned by the man who'd prayed this facility into existence thirty years ago. I spread my hands over the polished hardwood as if to pay homage, noticing the nicks and pen indentations from notes written long ago. How had he done it? How had he stayed here for thirty years? Had he really been as content as everybody made him out to be?

I opened the first drawer and began rummaging through the contents, sorting my findings into piles the way I'd done when I left my office behind at Salt and Light. Pens, notepads, random paper clips of every size, trash. So far, that was the largest of the piles. There were more gum wrappers and scraps of paper than anything else.

The process quickened as I worked through the middle layer of the desk. The lower I reached, the less full the drawer. With the exception of some worn, emerald-colored hanging files and a massive amount of dust mites, there was nothing left. These had already been emptied. But as I went to close the last drawer on the left, it wouldn't latch. I tried a second time, yet once again, the drawer remained an inch from closing. I pulled it out all the way, removing it from the brass track it rolled on, but I still couldn't see the source of the jam. Sliding off the chair, I got to my knees and peered into the dark abyss. I reached inside. The cool, smooth texture of leather seemed to reach back for me. I secured my grip around the object and pulled it through the opening with ease.

It was a book. No, a journal of some sort. The leather cover was the color of tanned cowhide and wrapped with a single strap that secured the middle. Unwinding it with care, I eased the front cover open, the pages stiff from what was likely years of being trapped behind a heavy drawer. The inscription on the inside caused the oxygen level in the room to thin.

This journal belongs to:
Otto Matteus
Jan 2016 to Jan 2018

Confused, I stood and checked the portrait on the hallway wall, the one marked with his birth and death dates: May 2, 1948 to August 18, 2018.

He'd written in this journal the year he died. Only, as I flipped through it, I realized this wasn't a journal at all. It was a ledger. A list of dates and names—a first initial and a last name, followed by a need and an activity and a next step. I turned several pages, my eyes skimming over the tiny but precise scroll.

3/5/2016: T. Davis, son in hospital. Cleaned garage. Talked about grace. Coffee scheduled. Invited to church.

3/12/2016: S. Whiteman, daughter in Girl Scouts. Car wash at Riverside and pizza. Invite to S&L youth group. Follow-up call next Wednesday.

3/24/2016: N. James, cancer diagnosis. Blanket delivery from The Well. Meals scheduled through chemo. Prayer.

The names went on and on, and I flipped to the halfway point, into late 2017. More of the same. Coffee dates, house repairs, rides for the elderly, checking in with widows, grocery deliveries, setting up after-school care, babysitting for single moms . . . and always a connection point. Always a next step.

And all of it, *all of it,* starting outside these walls.

I slumped back against the desk, my mind buzzing. The Riverside

Family Resource Center that Otto Matteus served wasn't confined to this office or even inside this building. This building was the heartbeat of an outreach that had arms and legs and hands and feet all over this city. And it had started with one man. Only he couldn't have possibly documented it all. Because the legacy he'd started three decades ago was ongoing even now.

Unable to keep Val far from my thoughts, I imagined her once again that day in the clinic with Nurse Charlotte and Carlee. And then I imagined what that day would have been like without Otto's faithfulness to say yes to a vision he knew would never overflow with crowds or popularity. That was never the point. The point was discipleship in its most honest, simplest form.

I didn't know how many hours I sat on the floor reading the ledger and taking notes on my phone, but I must have skipped lunch, because before I knew it, Ray was there to help me move what had to be the only desk in the entire world that could have housed thirty years' worth of service journals.

Otto Matteus had found his outreach within this city.

And for the first time, I believed this city could be my outreach, too.

∞∞∞

It was odd how quickly an afternoon of inspiration could dwindle at the sight of my empty house. There was no Tuck to greet me in the driveway. No Carlee to wave at me from the living room window. And once again, no Val anywhere to be seen.

The only trace that anyone lived in my upstairs apartment was the lingering scent of an early dinner—something garlic heavy and painfully familiar. What I wouldn't trade to be a guest at her table. Whatever remained of my bachelor card, I'd gladly give it up. No questions asked.

Otto's journal in hand, I trudged through my door and tossed the leather-bound book onto the table. It appeared my night would be open for more studying and note-taking.

I went to my fridge, scanning the sorry condiments and to-go containers and debating on yet another bowl of cold cereal, when I heard it. The gear shift from inside my kitchen wall. And then my text alert sounded and something cautious yet hopeful crept through my veins.

Val

> I'm sorry it took me all day to respond to your text . . . I hope I'm not too late. There's a special delivery headed your way.

I kept my eyes trained on the elevator door as I moved toward it, reached for the handle, and then yanked it open.

Empty.

Except, not. My gaze slid down the wood-paneled walls to a tray with a plate of the first meal we'd ever shared together: creamy chicken Alfredo. Plus an ice-cold Mexican Coke.

But those weren't the only items on the tray. I bent to retrieve a small box and place it on my kitchen counter before reaching for the attached card.

I lifted it off the tray and flipped it open.

Miles,

   Thank you for giving me time. These days apart have been excruciatingly long, but I promise they haven't been wasted. I pray you'll come to the same conclusion in approximately 24 minutes and 54 seconds. Thank you for everything you shared in your text.

   If you're still willing to talk . . . I'll be waiting for you by the fire.

Val

Securing the box in hand, I pried the lid open. The contents in question fell into my open palm. A black thumb drive.

I couldn't have located my laptop any faster. Plugging the drive into the USB port to start the download process, I nearly lost my appetite as I waited for the loading bar to complete. But seeing as I hadn't had the privilege of a home-cooked meal in some time, I'd have been a fool to let Val's act of benevolence go to waste. Somehow, the entree was even better this time around than the first.

Pushing the now empty plate aside, I clicked the arrow on the video and gripped the Coke bottle between my hands. The cold grounded my nerves as stunning images of a landscape I knew by heart swept onto the screen, sliding in and out of focus to a perfectly timed soundtrack I'd only heard pieces of during her first round of edits. Pride swelled inside me at the sight. At the true gifting Val possessed to engage the world in such a unique way.

I expected to hear the opening lines of an intro I'd recorded several times over to achieve the correct cadence and inflection. Only the voice I heard wasn't my own; it was Val's.

With sudden urgency, I sat forward on my seat and placed the Coke beside the laptop on the coffee table, needing my hands as unhindered as my attention.

Rolling video of teens, singles, couples, and families flooded the streets I'd traveled hundreds of times as statistics of loneliness, depression, anxiety, isolation, suicide, and addiction faded on and off the screen. Val's sincere and arresting voice wove skillfully throughout the transitions. While I hadn't seen any of her film edits, I had seen her storyboards. And this wasn't anywhere on them.

Val had gone off script. Completely.

"At the heart of every human born on this planet lives the felt need for connection—to a parent, to a peer, to a Creator whose imprint is in every fiber of our beings. And it's this same unyielding, inherent need to connect that has been the nucleus of thousands of studies conducted by high-ranking institutions and universities worldwide for hundreds of years. And while their findings continue to prove what we already know, our ability to discover and maintain these critical connections has only decreased with the knowledge of their importance. As has our tendency to stay isolated within our own existence, to stay crushed under the weight

of our current circumstances and without hope in the midst of trials never meant to be navigated alone."

After a sequence of bustling individuals moving throughout marketplaces and intersections, the camera funneled into a single focus: a woman perched on a shadowed stool, her face illuminated like a candle flickering in a darkened room. Val. *My Val.* The sight of her seized the oxygen from my lungs.

Elbows to knees, I pressed my hands together, lulled by the introspective bow of a violin across strings. But her earnest, gentle presence failed to prepare me for what came next.

"*As a woman who's struggled to accept her physical limitations since the time I was ten, I often sought comfort in isolation. Being on my own never scared me; people did. Their comments, their cruelty, their judgments I couldn't control or change. By my teen years, loneliness was easier for me to cope with than the rejection I feared from the world.*" The music changed to the soft, hollow tension of a sustained violin note. "*But the night I found out I was pregnant, I discovered a new definition of alone. And there was no comfort to be found in it. It was desperate and terrifying, and I felt completely hopeless . . . and without a perfectly timed intervention, it would have cost me my life. And the life of my son.*"

I hadn't wanted to blink, hadn't wanted to miss a single frame of Val sharing a truth she'd kept locked inside herself for more than a decade, including a portion of the story I hadn't yet heard. One that simultaneously ignited my gut with rage and blurred my vision with tears. And yet over and over again, I was nearly carried away by the current of all that I felt for this woman.

Her testimony was expertly timed, the perfect segue into six interlocking testimonies built on the framework she'd laid, sharing how their own individual intervention moments transpired into what would later become the seeds of a movement. Initial connections that transitioned into real relationships that inspired growth and reciprocation.

But just when I'd anticipated the outro, Carlee Sinclair materialized into the frame. And it was that exact moment when I lost the battle waged against my emotions. She shared her rocky family history, her fear over discovering she was pregnant at eighteen, the options she was considering the day she met Val in the parking lot, and the acceptance and support she'd received without question or judgment. Because of the love of one stranger, she'd been given an entire community of women who had made it their mission to lift her up and to love her well.

I was on my feet then, my fingers curled over the back of my sofa at the realization that this was the living, tangible, visible proof of what God had spoken to me through a ledger this afternoon. And what He'd been speaking to me for longer than I'd been open to hearing it.

Val had captured it all—both the vision of what intentional relationship building could look like in the lives of people all across our city, as well as the mature fruit that had been planted and tended to for decades. I simply hadn't known where to look for it. But now that I'd seen it, I prayed I would never be blind to it again.

Or to the woman who'd opened my eyes using the lens of her camera.

· 34 ·

Val

It turned out Tucker had learned more useful outdoor skills at Dude Camp than I originally thought. After my fourth attempt to get the fire going, I finally called him down for some much-needed assistance. My Alaskan pride was hanging on for dear life as I rearranged the wood the way I remembered my dad showing me every summer since I was ten. Thankfully, Tucker was able to coax the wood tepee I'd constructed into catching flame. He and Kadin had also assisted with another part of my plan that involved muscle and youthful exuberance.

Check and check.

But now that the fire was crackling behind me and everything else was in its place, it was an effort to keep myself from fidgeting. Or from watching the clock too closely. If there was one thing I knew, it was the length of my documentary. Down to the second.

I faced Miles's back door, willing myself to breathe. Willing my nerves to calm. Willing his response to be even half of what Gwen's had been when I'd sent it off to her this afternoon in time to submit to the competition upon her approval.

I'd been expecting her feedback to come via video call—which, from the very beginning, had been her favorite way of communicating with me—but instead, she'd sent me a text less than an hour later.

Gwen

Due to the abundance of mascara streaming from my tear ducts, I'm temporarily unavailable for a video chat. But even if I could see you clearly, it's doubtful I'd be able to utter a word to speak.

Darling, you've more than accomplished what I struggled to communicate during our last phone call. This is what I knew was hiding inside you, what I felt even from our first interactions. I'm beyond proud of you. BEYOND. No matter what happens in this competition, please don't doubt your gifting again.

I'm humbled to be your mentor. And I'm honored to be your colleague. I don't have a daughter, but if I did . . . I imagine I would feel for her the way I feel about you tonight.

XOXO

My knee joints liquefied as I heard the back door slide open and I waited for Miles to walk across the patio. Logically I knew it wasn't possible to forget a face in eleven days' time . . . but I was certain I'd never seen Miles look quite like this. The bewilderment of his expression set my own feet in motion, and as we drew closer, I noticed the unmistakable red rim around his eyes.

"Yes," he said softly. "If you're wondering whether you managed to break a dam that hasn't been breached since I was a boy, then the answer is yes." The glint of his eyes reflecting in the firelight beyond seized my breath. "Val, that was . . . I—I'm not even sure I have words for what that did to me, what it's still doing to me even now. To see you on that screen, to hear you tell your . . ." His throat worked for several long seconds, and my own eyes smarted. "It hurts, what I feel for you." He stared down at me. "It's this constant ache that sits right about here." He pointed to a rib over his heart, and I reached out my hand and flattened my palm to his chest as if that was the only invitation I needed to touch him.

"I know the feeling well," I said, my voice thick with truth. With love. "I've missed you, Miles. I've a hundred times more than missed you, actually." His warm hand enveloped mine. "But the time I asked for, the space I asked for, I couldn't have realized then just how much I needed it." I took a deep breath. "The things you said to me that night, the fears you pointed out, they were the same fears God has been asking me to trust Him with long before I ever moved here. You were right to push me on that. Sometimes I need to be pushed." I exhaled slowly. "Which means I want to be open to the possibility of change. Even if that change means praying about living in a different country at some point, or doing something I might not ever have imagined. I know a part of you is in Mexico, and I want to know that part of your heart, Miles. But every time I pray about the timing of this opportunity, it doesn't—"

"Feel right," he said, his eyes shining with a sincerity as thick as the smoke billowing in the air behind us. "I agree, which is why I turned it down. And I have no doubt it was the right decision. God used you to help me see that, Val." He took a few seconds before speaking again, his gaze searching my face. "I value the woman He's made you to be too much to want to change you— your sharp mind, your compassionate spirit, your timely discernment. I'd never want to push you anywhere God wasn't leading you. My hope is to walk beside you in ministry, at a pace that's right for us both."

"I love you," I whispered in response, as if those three words were all it took to banish the remaining distance between us and unlock the next step in our journey.

He pulled me in close, the warmth of his hands at my back igniting every sinew, muscle, and bone in my body. For a wordless moment, we simply held on to each other, as if together we might prevent the ground from shaking or the earth from spinning. Because it was here we were the steadiest. It was here we were the strongest. Our kiss, much like our embrace, was unhurried yet

ALL THAT IT TAKES

intentional, soft yet decisive—a new promise awakening on our lips as we discovered a rhythm all our own.

"I have something to show you," I whispered against his mouth. "By the fire."

"I can't say I'm in much of a rush to conclude this portion of the evening quite yet."

I smiled up at him and took his hand, helping to steer him toward the growing flames.

Only a few steps out, he halted. "Wait . . . you did all this?"

"The boys and I did."

I watched him glance around the fire pit.

He pointed to each new chair represented here. "Tucker, Kadin, Carlee, me, you . . ." He paused.

"Millie," I said. "I know she doesn't venture across the street too often, but I bet we could entice her for a s'more night every once in a while."

His expression was far more contemplative than I anticipated a gift of six brightly colored Adirondack chairs ringing a fire pit deserved. "Further proof of the good you've brought into my life since the day you moved upstairs."

He squeezed my hand, and we moved to sit, selecting the two chairs closest to each other. The green and the purple. As soon as we were situated, Miles said, "I plan to stay at Riverside."

The confident inflection of his tone caused my throat to thicken. "You do?"

"Yes. If the elders approve my new vision proposal, my hope would be to stay indefinitely. Or until God speaks through a burning bush. Whatever comes first."

Smoke swirled around us, but even still, it was impossible to miss the sincerity etched in his face. Something had definitely changed inside him since we last spoke—something significant. "What's involved in the vision proposal?"

His smile stretched wide. "That's what I've been trying to figure out all week with Curtis. But this evening, it became quite obvious." He rubbed his thumb over the back of my hand. "With your permission, I'd like to show the elders *All That It Takes*. I doubt I'll need to say a whole lot after that. Because everything in there, every woman you interviewed as well as the narrative you scripted, it's the exact model we need to be following as an outreach to our city, just on a larger scale. The Well is the perfect example of what an effective ministry outreach should look like, and you captured it all, Val."

I was too stunned to speak.

"What you've done for Carlee. What you're doing even now by creating space for Millie. It's . . ." He took several seconds to think. "You've challenged me, deeply." He kissed the back of my hand. "In the past, with the missions teams I've led, it was always the setup I craved most, the establishment of new leadership, the appointment of teams and volunteers to manage service projects at specific locations for a set amount of time. I loved the fast-paced gratification of it all, and essentially, the distant connection to my parents' legacy." He dropped his eyes to the fire, his gaze pensive and steady. "But I'm realizing now there's also a purpose in growing roots. And I want those roots to be at Riverside. And I hope, in the right timing, with you and Tucker."

I wanted to hold his words like a promise, but they couldn't settle in my heart quite yet. Not until I asked about him and Pastor Curtis. "And what about Curtis? I know you mentioned him just now, but—"

"I was wrong, Val." His head dipped low as his gaze collided with mine, and I suddenly couldn't imagine three more profound words for a man to speak. There was something so achingly beautiful about the words *I was wrong*, perhaps even more so than the words *I love you*. Because a man who could admit wrongdoing, a man who could break through the layers of his own pride, was a man who could love with humility. "I want to tell you about everything—my resentment against Curtis, my realization about my parents, the struggles I've worked through with Rev since I was a teen. And what I'm still working through even now as an adult." He exhaled. "I meant what I said in my text. I'm thankful you pushed me to see the truth."

"I feel the same way about you."

"Good," he continued, his gaze softening on my face. "Because I want to do everything I can to support you in your film ministry."

"My film ministry," I repeated slowly.

He angled his head, questioning. "Why do you sound surprised by that?"

"I guess I never considered it a ministry."

"What else would it be called?" He laughed and pointed back to his house. "Val. Sweetheart. What happened to me in there just now was transformative. And the entire time I watched it, all I kept thinking about was how vital and timely this message is to our world—how it needs to be seen. Can you imagine how many lives might be changed if this resource could be made available to churches and programs and outreach centers nationwide? This is your moment to shine, to show the world the gift God's given you." A sudden look of panic struck him. "Wait, tell me you submitted it to Gwen in time for the competition—"

"Yes, but—"

"Because there's no way that film isn't getting awarded the grand prize. Do you know what kind of production studio you could launch with that kind of funding to back you—"

"Miles." I couldn't help but laugh at his boyish enthusiasm. "Thank you. For believing in me. For wanting this for me." The feeling expanded in my chest like a balloon at maximum capacity. "You can't possibly know how much that means."

"Val, you're making me nervous." He studied me. "You did submit the film to Gwen, right?

"I did." I nodded. "I promise. And Gwen is . . ." Tears stacked in my throat. "She's very pleased with the outcome."

"So what aren't you saying?" The tenderness in his voice caused my chest to warm. "What is it?"

As my lips curved north, tears leaked from my lower lashes onto my cheeks. "I'm not exactly sure, I just . . . when I sent it off to Gwen today, I felt a peace I've never experienced before. Like God was asking me to trust Him with my efforts. And I do, Miles. I really, really do." My teary smile stretched wide. "When I first started this mentorship with Gwen, I thought the only way I could have an impact through filmmaking was by working toward one defining moment, something big enough to define my next steps. I was terrified of feeling like I'd wasted Gwen's time if I failed to place . . . but I don't feel that way anymore." I rubbed my lips together. "I'd much rather my life be defined by a thousand little moments of faithfulness than by one big moment of fame. God's been so faithful to me, Miles. And I know He will continue to be." The faces of seven courageous women came to mind—Carlee's specifically. "I can already see it happening, with Riverside."

"I can see it happening, too." With a gentle tug, Miles pulled me up from my chair and onto his lap. Framing my face in his hands, he touched his forehead to mine. "But for the record, falling in love with you has been, without a doubt, one of the greatest defining moments of God's faithfulness in my life."

For the record, I couldn't agree with him more.

∞

A mere two weeks later, Miles tapped nervously on the dining room table as we sat in my too-quiet apartment waiting for Lady Gwen's call. Today we'd hear which of the top ten finalists would be headed to the premiere, and ultimately, would be awarded the grand prize of fifty thousand dollars and a priceless list of industry-wide connections.

"Do you think you might have misheard the time?" Miles asked, glancing at his watch. "Maybe you should text her. It's nearly forty minutes past."

"She'll call," I said confidently. "Gwen is not the most punctual, but she always has her reasons if she's late."

But just as Miles was about to reply, a familiar melody played from my laptop. Gwen was calling.

"Here we go," I said.

He took my hand as Gwen's familiar face appeared on the screen.

"Hello, darling." She gave an appraising look at Miles. "And hello to you, too. I'm guessing this handsome gentleman is your beau, Valerie? Miles, is it?"

"Yes, Gwen. This is Miles McKenzie."

"Wonderful." She then shifted to focus her attention on Miles directly. "It's more than fitting you're there with her, since you've had a part to play in all this, too."

I swallowed, nodded. "I'm glad he's here, too." I'd want him with me no matter the outcome. Miles squeezed my hand.

Gwen met my eyes. "Valerie." And somehow, this time, when she spoke my name, I discerned the minute difference in her inflection. And I knew.

"It didn't win," I said.

She gave the tiniest shake of her head. "No, darling, I'm sorry. Your film was not selected as this year's grand prize winner of the Volkin Award, but it did place in the top three—which is an enormous feat and one you should be quite proud of given the competition and talent pool represented in the top ten."

Miles slung his arm around my shoulders, and for all of three seconds my stomach swooped low at the news. But just as quickly, a buoy took hold of my heart, comforting me with the same peace I'd felt the day I sent my final project off to Gwen. "Thank you, Gwen. I'm okay, really. I was prepared for this outcome and—"

"But," she said, cutting me off, "the fact that you didn't win the Volkin is not even close to the most important part of this call." With added flair, she cleared her throat. "But we'll get to that in just a moment. First, here is the speech I wrote for you had you won first place. There is nothing in it that hinges on you receiving a trophy, because really, darling, a trophy was never the real goal. Continuing a legacy in transformational storytelling was. And you've more than achieved that." Her eyes crinkled as she smiled. "So here goes."

I could feel Miles's gaze on me as she began to read.

"When I first met Valerie Locklier during a round of video interviews, I knew she was something uniquely special. The kind of special I take note of so that I have something interesting to share at dinner parties with colleagues I generally try to avoid whenever possible." She stopped to look at me again. "This is where I would pause for laughter," she whispered.

"Was my Valerie the most qualified candidate to choose? The most experienced? The most determined or persuasive or courageous? No, no, and again, no. But what Valerie Locklier had, what I could see in her eyes and hear in her voice, was something far rarer: a gentle spirit. A quality that can't be easily faked for long in my field. *Gentleness* is not a momentary act the way kindness can be; it speaks instead of a consistently soft and pliable heart. Someone who would rather listen than hear themselves speak. Someone who observes and empathizes and breathes art like oxygen. She sees the world through a lens of humility and grace and is never too hurried to notice what other people are often too rushed or too busy to observe. And it's this quality that makes her a stupendous storyteller." Tears sparkled in her sea blue eyes. "Stories that can indeed change lives, one person at a time."

Miles beamed and clapped as I took a second to compose myself.

"Thank you, Gwen. That was beautiful."

"More importantly, it is true. Which is exactly why I was fashionably late to this call."

Miles and I shared a knowing look. She went on, undeterred.

"Given my dislike for certain authority figures who run the Volkin Award, I took the liberty of sharing your film with a small handful of trusted colleagues who enjoy coloring outside the lines—several of which have connections to organizations and affiliations that are far better suited for your specific talent, my dear. And like I mentioned previously, the fact that you made it into the top three of this competition only adds to my recommendation of your craft." She paused, glancing between us both. "In short, your career in film has only just begun, and I hope you'll give me the chance to continue working with you on more projects just like this one in the future. Perhaps, even, as a partner. If that's something you're open to considering, of course."

Miles's shocked laughter shook me out of the dreamlike state I was currently floating in.

"Yes . . . yes, of course it is," I said on the tail end of hysteria. "I'm . . . I don't even know what to say right now."

"My favorite kind of reaction." She winked. "I'll work on scheduling some meetings for us, the first of which will involve getting *All That It Takes* distributed to the right audiences. In the meantime, you two should prepare your hearts now, because I think a lot of dreams are about to come true. We'll touch base again soon. Now, you two lovebirds, go and celebrate."

The second the screen went black, Miles turned to me with eyebrows raised and said, "Why do I feel like we've just been christened by a fairy godmother?"

"Because she's Lady Gwen." Which was the only suitable reply.

· 35 ·

Val

FOUR WEEKS LATER

I smoothed the hem of the short black dress I'd picked out at the recommendation of my best friend and focused on the familiar drive ahead of us.

Miles placed his hand over my bare knee and gave a gentle squeeze as he pulled off the interstate and swung a left on Lincoln. "You look extra radiant tonight, if I do say so myself."

"Thank you." I interlocked our fingers. "How are you feeling? Are you nervous?"

"I think you're nervous enough for the both of us."

"It's a big day." I took a breath, thinking of how many people would be gathered together in one special place. "I'm glad my parents could be here for it, too. Thank you for inviting them. I just wish yours could have made it back in time."

Miles squeezed my hand. "They send their love, and I'm sure they'll have reason enough to make a trip back to the States soon." He smiled at me, and I wondered if I'd imagined the extra glint in his eyes as he spoke.

"At least you know your sister will be there," I said, barely

393

holding in a laugh. Molly had offered to help decorate for the grand reopening of Riverside tonight, and while I couldn't be more thrilled to see her and Silas now that they were finally settled back at home, I knew Molly's level of party planning was not necessarily the same as Miles's. "I'm sure she'll honor your requests to keep things . . . mild. Trisha and Carlee volunteered for her decorating crew, too."

"Nice try." He chuckled. "Silas is the only hope I have on capping her extravagance, but I've seen him cave to her charm more than once—which is why I made sure to tell him on their wedding day that there would be no take backs or exchanges, no matter what kind of mischief she gets them into."

"You're terrible." My laugh was full as I swatted at his arm. "She's sweet for wanting to help. You played such a special role in their fundraiser for The Bridge last year, I know she just wants to return the favor."

His lazy grin caused my stomach to swoop. "You did, too. Crazy to think that was where we met for the first time. At a fundraising event, just over one year ago. I still remember the look on your face when Molly asked me to take you and a sleeping Tucker back to her place. I'm pretty sure you were petrified of me."

"No, not petrified, just . . ." I paused in search of a better word.

"Completely uninterested."

"Intimidated," I corrected, turning my head to look at him. "I was a different person back then."

"We both were." He brought my hand to his lips, kissed it.

One year ago. How was that even possible?

My life had changed so much since that day last fall when I flew to Spokane with Tucker to assist Molly on a nearly impossible fundraising deadline at The Bridge. But it was that event that had inspired the start of their branch-off project for Basics First and the job offer that had eventually led me here. And even though the path I was on now had taken an unexpected turn, I remained in awe of each step along the way. They were all important. I could see that now.

Molly had taken her last trip to California nearly two weeks ago, and she was currently on the hunt to employ motivated young women in need of stability and grace. Thankfully, she was more than open to my recommendation of one special girl. I smiled as I thought of the shift manager position she'd extended to Carlee just last week. She'd offered her a flexible start date, as Carlee was due to have her baby in the coming weeks, and we all knew she would need time after the birth to adjust, even after the adoption with the Wardells was finalized. I had no doubt Carlee would thrive in such a position, though, especially in a flourishing community of other young women her age.

"It's hard to believe. So much has happened in both our lives in such a short amount of time." My mind took a quick jog through the film mentorship with Lady Gwen and the projects we were negotiating together now, only to slow at the recent memory of the smiling, joy-filled face of my son. "Did you hear Tucker trying to convince my parents of all the reasons they should move here last night? His arguments were pretty persuasive, too. You'd think he'd grown up here."

"Pretty sure he might have persuaded your dad—he seemed to enjoy himself as Tucker played tour guide today when we were out running errands." Miles followed the road under the bridge and past two grocery stores and several gas stations. "I'm glad Tuck loves this city so much."

"I'm certain it has a lot more to do with who lives in this city," I said confidently.

Miles rubbed his thumb over my palm. "He's definitely played a major role in my change of heart, as well."

I studied him, feeling the rise of emotion in my chest. Tucker couldn't possibly know just how blessed he was to be loved by this man. My son had spent most of the day with my dad and Miles, and though I'd hardly seen him, I had no doubt he'd enjoyed the time with his two favorite men.

Miles veered into the parking lot and pulled into a spot right outside the main doors. He put the gear shift in park and twisted in his seat to level his gaze on me. I looked from him to the facility, where we'd both logged many hours as of late, and in less than three seconds, every thought pertaining to the gathering that would soon be happening inside was replaced by the sight in front of us.

"Oh, Miles . . ." I opened the car door and stepped onto the pavement to see the new signage more clearly.

Riverside Community Outreach
Making lasting connections, one person at a time

"It was delivered today," Miles said, stepping beside me. "Your dad and Tuck helped me hang it this afternoon."

"I love it." My heart soared. "I absolutely love the new name. It's perfect."

He rotated me toward him, capturing both my hands in his. "Your film helped make it possible."

The earnestness in his voice caused my eyes to water. Though I hadn't been present for the official elder board meeting when they'd viewed *All That It Takes* and unanimously approved the renewed vision plan for Riverside Community Outreach, Miles and I had been invited to dinner at the Archers' house later that evening. When I'd stepped into their home and reached out my hand, Pastor Curtis had embraced me instead, unashamed of the tears that streaked his cheeks as he told me how much my testimony had meant to him and Brenna, and just how much Riverside had meant to their family. I was looking forward to seeing them here tonight, along with so many other faces I'd come to know: Gavin and Nicky, Rev and Cynthia, along with several other staff members and church volunteers who had caught the vision for Riverside from the recent announcements made at Salt and Light Community Church.

"Also," Miles said, with brightened eyes, "I found him today. I found Jedidiah."

"Wait—*the Jedidiah*? How? Where?" My laugh was half disbelief, half elation. Miles had been searching for the elusive Jedidiah who'd shown up during volunteer day ever since he brought Otto's journal home. He'd visited at least seven gas stations in the area, asking shift manager after shift manager for an employee with the same name.

He beamed in response. "Believe it or not, your dad actually spotted his name tag first as we were fueling up. Said something like, 'Now there's a name you don't see every day.' I nearly dropped the nozzle. He's working tonight, but we made plans to connect next week."

"I'm so glad." My smile mirrored Miles's.

He offered his elbow and escorted me the long way, through the main parking lot and around the corner to a side door I knew well. I'd met Carlee only steps away from this spot earlier this summer. And then Nurse Charlotte not too long after, followed by Trisha and the rest of the ladies I'd spent every Monday night with at The Well for the last several months. The significance of where this open door had already led to wasn't lost on me.

I stopped at the sight of the red carpet rolled out over the threshold and down the long hallway like a royal procession. A sign read, *Welcome to the Grand Reopening of Riverside Community Outreach.*

I gasped. "Oh, wow . . ."

"Yeah," Miles confirmed, tugging on his neck. "Guess Silas was unsuccessful in holding her back."

"Don't worry, I promise to protect you if Molly hired somebody to jump out of a cake."

"That's reassuring, thank you," he deadpanned while cinching me closer to his side. "Just remember, we're in this together."

I glanced up at him, my gaze as earnest as my voice. "Always."

Miles's next words were drowned out as Tucker and Kadin ran to their posts on either side of the doorframe, one of them in charge of handing out red *Admit One* tickets upon entry, while the other handed us a promotional flyer for Riverside that I'd designed, highlighting upcoming serving opportunities, evening and weekend classes, after-school childcare for working families, and women's health information. Two steps into the room, a buttery aroma of movie-theater popcorn swirled around us. What on earth was that for?

"Val! You're here!" Molly flung her arms around me, then held me out to assess my dress. "And you look *gorgeous*! See? A girl can never go wrong with an LBD."

"LBD?" Miles asked, his eyes darting between us.

"Little black dress," we said in unison.

But my smirk fell away as soon as I faced the room with Miles. Molly made a sweeping *ta-da!* gesture with her arm, and I was hit with such an intense wave of affection for her, I actually swayed on my feet. "Oh, Molly . . . what did you do?"

The same multipurpose room I'd spent so many days inside these last few months—filming and connecting and sharing and praying—had been completely transformed. The entire room now resembled a vintage theater. She'd even managed to make the white pull-down screen on the front stage look like an actual movie screen, draped with curtains tied back with thick gold rope. The chairs on the floor were lined in rows, reserved signs hanging on the backs of the front row. And, naturally, a giant popcorn machine sat to the left of it all.

"We thought your film deserved at least a few showtimes tonight during the grand reopening. And you can't have a film premiere without a theater. Or without popcorn. Or . . ." She pointed to my hand. "Tickets."

I threw my arms around her again. "This is incredible. Thank you."

I twisted toward Miles. "Did you know about this?"

"The film showings? Yes. The fact that my sister recreated a set from Old Hollywood in less than twenty-four hours' time? No. Definitely not." Miles shook his head in disbelief, then pulled his sister in for a bear hug. "You did good, sis. It looks incredible in here. Thank you."

Molly peeked up at him and waved Silas over from across the

room. "To be fair, my hubby and his brother Jake did all the heavy lifting today, and it was our residents at The Bridge who helped us design the stage and sew the red curtains."

When Silas joined us, Molly shifted her affections, wrapping her arms around Silas's middle. He kissed her temple. "I'd like to say I tried to restrain her efforts, but . . ." He laughed. "There was no arguing with her vision for tonight."

She lifted her heels and kissed him fully on the mouth. Silas didn't seem bothered by her public display of affection in the slightest. Even after their lips detached and Molly raced to fix a fallen prop, his eyes tracked her animated conversations around the room. If possible, my admiration for him doubled.

"Thank you," I told him. "What you both did tonight was so generous and kind."

"It's been our pleasure, truly. Seems we share a similar vision with Riverside for reaching our community. We're always looking for ways to partner our residents at The Bridge with local service projects—perhaps we should brainstorm how we might collaborate?" He squeezed my shoulder before clapping Miles on the arm. "We're proud of what you're doing here, brother."

"A service project brainstorm is a fantastic idea. Actually, if you have a minute now, I'd like to introduce you to Pastor Curtis. He's likely in the lobby waiting for guests to arrive. Maybe we can set something up as early as next week."

"Sure thing. I'll just let Molly know on our way out."

Silas tipped his head to me as Miles leaned in to give my cheek a kiss, asking me if I wanted to join him in the lobby or stick around here for a while longer. I chose to stay, at least until I could be certain Nurse Charlotte and Trisha were able to handle the crowds. I didn't want anyone to slip through the door unnoticed. A wild revelation, given that was exactly what I'd spent the majority of my life doing.

Just before the five-minute warning announcement for the first showing was made, I took a moment to stand in the back and take it all in. Tonight would be full of handshakes and smiles and conversing with friends and strangers alike. And for some inexplicable reason, I didn't want to hide from any of it.

Stranger still, I wanted to embrace it.

For the next hour and a half, I stood by the entrance of the multipurpose room, greeting the women and men who came to view the film and offering them refreshments. A handful of people had stayed back after each showing, some to inquire about the film, others asking questions about Riverside's new role in the community. It was a conversation I'd grown comfortable with, as I'd been given many opportunities as of late to share my story since first submitting my film project to Gwen—starting with my son. Using terminology he could understand, I told Tucker the bigger story, the whole story, the night after Miles and I talked about our future around the fire. And then I did the same with my parents and Molly. It hadn't seemed right to offer the world what I'd been unwilling to offer some of the most cherished people in my life.

Wearing an adorable navy maxi dress with big white flowers, Carlee slowly waddled over from the punch bowl, where she'd been stationed on a stool for most of the evening. She nodded toward the credits rolling on the big screen. "My aunt watched it, you know. Last night. I sent her the video link you gave me."

"Oh yeah?" I touched Carlee's arm, knowing she'd also taken a brave step by showing her closest family member her testimony. "What was her response?"

"She said it made her cry—good tears and sad tears. And that she was proud of me for making good friends and for choosing to give my baby what I never had."

I gently set my hand on her belly. "I am, too."

She sighed through a tired smile. "Miles was asking for you in the lobby a while ago—he's been surrounded by people every time I walk by to use the restroom, which is approximately every seven minutes. There's been a lot of peopleing happening in this place tonight."

I laughed. "There certainly has been."

She raised her eyebrows conspiratorially. "Oh, and don't tell him I snitched, but you should probably know that Tucker has had *a lot* of frosted sugar cookies. Like a lot. If he vomits tonight, it's going to be unicorn colored."

I grimaced. "Good to know. Are my parents still out there?" My mom was usually the first to redirect his sugar cravings for healthier options. I reached for my purse and glanced around the room one last time. It was basically empty now, save for Trisha, who was deep in conversation with a couple of young ladies. Not even Molly remained, and she'd been busying herself around this place all evening.

Carlee shrugged. "Couldn't tell ya. I'll walk out there with you, though. I need to use the restroom again. Honestly, that's where I should have been stationed tonight. I probably would have met more women in there than at the punch table."

I laughed and looped my arm through hers. Together we followed the bustle of voices toward the lobby until Carlee broke left for the restroom when I stayed right. She hadn't been wrong about the peopleing. Even though the evening had officially come to an end, people still lingered by the exit doors and in the parking lot—some new, some familiar—all connecting and conversing. All living out the vision Miles and Pastor Curtis had created for the grand reopening of Riverside Community Outreach.

The sight was arresting.

As was the face of the man whose gaze had found me at the same moment mine found his.

Miles held the door open for Rev and Cynthia, who waved their good-byes to me as they headed into the parking lot, then signaled something to Pastor Curtis as he made his way over to me. Tucker followed after him, a frosted sugar cookie clutched in his left hand. My attention snagged on the smear of blue frosting streaked across Tucker's white polo shirt.

"Hey, there," I said, placing my hand on his shoulder. "I haven't seen you for most of the night."

"I've been working at the refreshments table." I glanced up at Miles, whose eyes seemed to say, *Don't look at me—I wasn't the one who put an eleven-year-old in charge of the dessert table.*

I pointed to the cookie in his hand. "You should probably take a break on the sweets, Tuck. You've had a lot of sugar today already, and I think Gram and Pop were planning to take you to an early breakfast tomorrow before they head to the airport." I looked around. "Did they already leave?"

"Yeah, they went home to help Miles set up for—"

Miles slapped his hand over Tuck's mouth, and the two of them exchanged a look that was anything but innocent.

"To set up for . . . what?" I glanced at my watch. It was nearly eight o'clock. What on earth was there to set up for?

"Nothing," Tucker squeaked as Miles peeled his hand away. "Definitely nothing."

I narrowed my eyes. "Definitely nothing sure sounds a lot like a definitely something."

Tucker looked between us, his expression a mix of panic and guilt. He blinked at me. "It's not lying when it's a surprise, Mom. Pop told me that today after we gave our permissions to Miles."

Miles closed his eyes and rubbed a hand down his smiling face, and it was then my heart started to beat a little faster. "We've really got to work on your game face, Tuck."

I said nothing as Tucker stuffed a large piece of frosted cookie in his mouth and then quickly escaped down the hallway and out of sight.

"So, um . . ." Miles stuffed his hands in his pockets as I watched Pastor Curtis walk the last few people from the lobby into the parking lot. "As you may have gathered, I had a nice chat with your dad and your son this afternoon—asked them a few important questions about the future."

"You did?" Was it possible for a heart to gallop out of a chest?

He nodded, his obvious nerves catching me off guard. Miles was a man who could literally talk to anybody at any time without a hint of unease. And yet here he was, seeming to be at a loss for words. "And I was hoping that tonight, before they fly home to Alaska tomorrow, I might have a conversation with you, too.

Around a familiar fire pit. With a handful of familiar people who love us both. But if there's any reason why I should wait—"

"There's not." My vision blurred. "I think that's the best definitely something I could have ever hoped for."

Slowly, he closed the gap between us as his mouth brushed the top of my ear. "Good, because starting a new life with you and Tucker is absolutely the best thing I could have ever hoped for."

The End

Acknowledgments

God: You are the Ultimate Storyteller and Story Redeemer. Thank you for all the stories your hand has faithfully guided, in both my real and fictional worlds.

My hubby, Tim: For the last ten years of my writing career, you've cheered me on through every single deadline and celebrated every single launch day as if it was the first. Your steadfast support and love continue to inspire every fictional hero I write. Thank you for yet another lap around the track with me. I'm so glad you're mine for keeps . . . nineteen years and counting.

Preston, Lincoln, Lucy: Like always, I'm humbled and grateful for your patience and grace during my writing-deadline seasons. I'm so proud to be your mama. Now let's go get some fancy ice cream!

My writing sisters, Tammy Gray and Connilyn Cossette: You are both my not-so-secret weapons as well as true gifts from God. Thank you for the millions of words you've both read and critiqued (on this one manuscript alone—hahaha!). But truly, it's a delight to write with two of my favorite authors (and people) on the planet. Still not quite sure how that happened . . . ☺

Coast to Coast Plotting Society: Christy Barritt, Connilyn Cossette, Amy Matayo, and Tammy Gray. Who would have thought our little plotting group would be celebrating our seventh anniversary this year? Traditionally, I think that means we're all supposed to buy each other some kind of copper or wool remembrance . . . but unfortunately, I'm not skilled in either of those materials. So, this paragraph will have to suffice. I love you. See ya'll at the beach! ☺

Bethany House Publishers: It's an honor to be a part of the BHP family. A special thanks to my editors Raela Schoenherr and Sarah Long. Your expertise, suggestions, and story insights always serve to improve my craft as a writer and as a storyteller. I am so very grateful for you!

Rel Mollet, my trusty author assistant and friend: Thank you for your love and long-standing support of Christian fiction. You are a tremendous blessing to me and to so many others. I pray this year yields much fruit for your faithful efforts of support and selflessness.

My Book Nook and Early Readers Friends: Thank you for all the ways you inspire me to keep writing by sharing your love of reading with the world. A special thanks to Kacy Gourley, Lara Arkin, Renee Deese, and Joanie Schultz for your first-draft feedback.

To our Life Group: Santha Yinger, Jeff and Bobbi Deitz, and Jan and Joanie Schultz. Thank you for the many, many prayers for this book and all the encouraging texts, hugs, and coffee dates. Tim and I are blessed by your community and friendships.

To our home church, Real Life Ministries in Post Falls, Idaho: Thank you for being an incredible example of Kingdom-minded discipleship both locally and globally, and for equipping your leaders to go out and do the same. Your collective heart and love for

God's people is as inspiring as it is challenging, and I'm so very grateful to be a part of this church family.

A special thanks to Jessica Wardell, RN BSN: Thank you for being my sounding board for *all* things medical and for answering all 849,038 clarifying text messages about my fictional people and scenarios (even while you were camping at the lake and trying to cook dinner for your five children)! Your friendship and support are a treasure to me.

To the extraordinary ladies and mentors at Path of Life in Spokane, Washington: Thank you for inviting me to sit at your table that cold February afternoon and for creating a safe place for me to ask my many questions. The Christ-centered services and resources you provide women who are facing unplanned pregnancies was my inspiration behind Nurse Charlotte and the Riverside Women's Care Center, as well as several other key elements in this story. Your boldness and vulnerability to educate, encourage, and equip women in a judgment-free space rendered me speechless multiple times, and I'm forever changed by the testimonies of redemption you shared with me that day. Thank you for being the hands and feet of Christ to our hurting world. May you be blessed beyond measure for your faithfulness.

Nicole Deese's (nicoledeese.com) humorous, heartfelt, and hope-filled novels include a Carol Award winner and RITA Award and INSPY Award finalists. When she's not working on her next contemporary romance, she can usually be found reading one by a window overlooking the inspiring beauty of the Pacific Northwest. She lives in small-town Idaho with her happily-ever-after hubby, her two wildly inventive and entrepreneurial sons, and her princess daughter with the heart of a warrior.

Sign Up for Nicole's Newsletter

Keep up to date with Nicole's latest news on book releases and events by signing up for her email list at nicoledeese.com.

More from Nicole Deese

Molly McKenzie has made social media influencing a lucrative career, but nailing a TV show means proving she's as good in real life as she is online. So, she volunteers with a youth program. Challenged at every turn by the program director, Silas, and the kids' struggles, she's surprised by her growing attachment. Has her perfect life been imperfectly built?

All That Really Matters

You May Also Like . . .

After many matchmaking schemes gone wrong, there's only one goal Lauren is committed to now—the one that will make her a mother. But to satisfy the adoption agency's requirements, she must remain single, which proves to be a problem when Joshua appears. With an impossible decision looming, she will have to choose between the two deepest desires of her heart.

Before I Called You Mine by Nicole Deese
nicoledeese.com

After an abusive relationship derails her plans, Adri Rivera struggles to regain her independence and achieve her dream of becoming an MMA fighter. She gets a second chance, but the man who offers it to her is Max Lyons, her former training partner, whom she left heartbroken years before. As she fights for her future, will she be able to confront her past?

After She Falls by Carmen Schober
carmenschober.com

When pediatric heart surgeon Sebastian Grant meets Leah Montgomery, his fast-spinning world comes to a sudden stop. And when Leah receives surprising news while assembling a family tree, he helps her comb through old hospital records to learn more. But will attaining their deepest desires require more sacrifices than they imagined?

Let It Be Me by Becky Wade
A MISTY RIVER ROMANCE
beckywade.com

◆ BETHANYHOUSE

More from Bethany House

Brielle Adebayo's simple life unravels when she discovers she is a princess in the African kingdom of Ọlọrọ Ilé and must immediately assume her royal position. Brielle comes to love the island's culture and studies the language with her handsome tutor. But when her political rivals force her to make a difficult choice, a wrong decision could change her life.

In Search of a Prince by Toni Shiloh
tonishiloh.com

After her dreams of mission work are dashed, Darcy Malone has no choice but to move in with the little sister of a man she's distrusted for years. Searching for purpose, she jumps at the chance to rescue a group of dogs. But it's Darcy herself who'll encounter a surprising rescue in the form of unexpected love, forgiveness, and the power of letting go.

Love and the Silver Lining by Tammy L. Gray
STATE OF GRACE
tammylgray.com

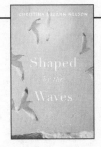

Cassie George has stayed away from her small hometown ever since her unplanned pregnancy. But when she hears that her aunt suffered a stroke and has been hiding a Parkinson's diagnosis, she must return. Greeted by a mysterious package, Cassie will discover that who she thought she was, and who she wants to become, are all about to change.

Shaped by the Waves by Christina Suzann Nelson
christinasuzannnelson.com

⬧ BETHANYHOUSE